I0653293

The Exsanguination of the Second Society:
Scholarly Historical Fiction Relating to
Robeson County, North Carolina's Tuscaroras

Edition II: New Research

Stephanie M. Sellers

2020

©2020 by ATSSDATLLC Publishing

All rights reserved. No part of this work may be reproduced or transmitted in any form or by any means, electronic or mechanical, including photography, recording, or any other information storage and retrieval system, without the written permission of the publisher.

The information in this work has been carefully researched and all efforts have been made to ensure accuracy. Any resemblance of characters is purely coincidental.

Editor: Kathleen Mackinger
Author: Stephanie M. Sellers

ISBN: 978-0-578-70031-1
ATSSDATLLC Publishing
North Carolina

Library of Congress Control Number 2018675307

Dedication

For anyone who has ever lived
or struggles to live now under oppression.

For Donnie Red Hawk McDowell, 2015 University of North Carolina at Pembroke Native American Indian Studies graduate. Donnie's passion for uniting the bands of North Carolina Tuscaroras is proof of the hot Mighty Tuscarora blood written about in early records. He is destined to speak for his People.

For Daryle Emanuel who told me the story of how NC Tuscarora ghosts haunt the highways and forests of Robeson County, and inspired me to write this book before all NC Tuscaroras became "living ghosts."

Chapters

NEW Research identified with *[1], *[2], *[3], etc.

Chapter 1

The Vexing Now

It only takes three generations for a People to lose its language, the corner-stone of ancestry.

Robeson County, North Carolina is home to an underground civil war where sixty-five thousand state recognized Lumbee "Indians" look down on the four thousand local Tuscarora Natives. From Jake's head count, that same threatening ratio was seated in the library's small conference room where he was giving his first presentation.

Jake Wilkes slapped the podium, "It is riot season in Robeson County, just like in the seventies, and we are *still* fighting for our Tuscarora Natives!" The teenager with the bright headband whistled and his enthusiasm drove Lumbees' smiles to screeching smirks against the Tuscarora's pounding applause.

"Our most radical Tuscarora activist ever was Bruce Black. We were best friends and he told me everything. And after talking with all the history professors, and flipping pages of every crusty old book I was turned onto to gather facts and dispel all the," he winced, "*deceptions* we've been fed on the ancestry of our areas' Natives, I must share that we are surrounded, and the Mighty Tuscarora are *still* fighting." Metal chairs squeaked under shifting weight as Jake grinned straight-on, spinning his invisible lasso.

"About five years ago, Bruce told me some things that needed investigating and we'd started, but he, he's not here now and y'all are stuck with me – the white boy," his generous smile was mostly returned, "I really appreciate you coming tonight." Jake's slim muscular build and farmer's tan complimented his hayseed hair and green eyes.

"This is brand new for some, but for others, like our genealogical researchers you're familiar, but some of you have been beat down by the Lumbee council and professors at their university into believing that *all* Indians around here are Iroquoian Cherokee or Cheraw or another Algonquian tribe when they aren't." [1] Jake aimed behind him toward the shimmering screen and when he clicked the projector's remote, a flood of exhales rushed the podium. With a copper bracelet and a gilded crown, the Tuscarora King commanded.

Jake stood taller, "The Mighty Tuscarora ruled the Carolinas and all tribes feared them." When they wanted something, they either traded for it or took it. They were strategists who to this day are planning an uprising," Jake surveyed the tilted heads and lingered on those pressing back against their chairs. "The Tuscarora were the major traders. In 1654, the Tuscarora village, Ocamahawan, included a copper factory comprised of "Europeans," as Captain John Smith's befriended Powhatan friend explained, " a wealthy family of thirty Spaniards with seven negroes in a family totaling thirty Spaniards – who made prolonged trips abroad lived among them." [2] Were those wealthy Spaniards Knights Templars? Were the seven Negroes remnants of discarded sailors? May never know. Whatever, it was a wise move to invest in Europeans. A Tuscarora tribe with guns and powder was met by Jacques Marquette on the Mississippi River twenty years later. The tribe said that they obtained the weapons from Europeans who lived in the east. This tribe also said that these Europeans living among the Tuscarora in the east had rosaries and pictures." [3]

"The Tuscarora saw people who looked different than them and used different tools, people who thought differently, prayed differently, lived differently, and invited them to the tribe. See - it was not the Mighty Tuscs who killed Sir Walter Raleigh's Lost Colony." [4]

Jake's palms flashed as he clicked the projector for the next slide. The bold text read:

The Iroquoian Tuscarora Peoples allowed the colonists to *live* as their coppersmiths.

The Algonquian Powhattan were the murdering rascals who *ended the lives* of most of the colonists.

"Our Lumbee claim Algonquian ancestry and that isn't even logical. The Algonquian were run off by the Iroquoian Tuscarora and what few who were left in the area were taken prisoner or asked the Iroquoian for protection. There wasn't enough Algonquians to start an ant farm, much less a tribe like y'all got today," his arms spread over his audience, "But that's not what the Lumbee Tribe tells you, huh?" His greens glimmered across the rows. "I wanted to bring a population map tonight 'cause it blows the Algonquian theory to dust. The Tuscarora Territory was massive," his palms flashed, "But I don't have permissions in place to share it yet. But it's coming."

"That copper factory began like any small business, with a few employees. Employees are made up of people seeking better living conditions and that's exactly what John White's colonists found living as coppersmiths amongst the Mighty Tuscarora," Jake lingered over their faces, "How many of you been taught this in school?" No one stirred. "College?" Jake huffed, "Think about it. History was written by the conquerors. If we'd been properly educated on the Portuguese, Tuscarora, Powhattan and all the other early leaders, we wouldn't be so burdened by it now." One dimple dug deep as Jake's elbow slid across the podium and his shiny whites beamed down the center aisle. "Y'all sound like cloggers down there."

When Jake sucked in a fresh drawl of brave his shinny blue banner hanging overhead, "North Carolina's Tuscarora Indians and America's First Christians," replicated a guillotine as it popped and rippled when a flying plastic water-bottle lid popped against it and rolled off his head.

"Daggit…" When the brats in the back looked just as surprised. "Na, na," Jake stuttered, "now it's believed by some that the Templars had a fleet of ships at La, la, Rochelle, France, even though there's no proof," his knuckles gleamed at the podium's sides as he made count of how many Lumbee council members were present, and Jake eased back into his role. "They hit the trail runnin' off to the New World on old Viking routes on a pre-Columbian voyage. And like we were just talkin' on Portugal, the Knights Templar did not disband. The knights secretly regrouped and continued protecting the Christians and their holy relics and still do today. Ancient Templars protected St. Helena's finds, bits of the holy cross and the engraving of Christ's name. Hitler vowed to own the spear tip that lanced Christ, believing it held life-giving powers. But is the real precious relic in the blood, the holy blood, *sang real* – the Holy Grail as in the first Christians? Our Tuscaroras, also known as the Croatans, and known as the Hatteras Tuscaroras, knew the state's first Christians biblically and their bloods merged, and I have the research to prove it." [5]

Jake slung his arm backward, targeting the next image and he backed into the projection screen and the giant knight moved as if declaring the caption, "Protect Christian Pilgrims," precisely as Jake proclaimed the ominous creed and some guests awed. The dark-skinned bearded Knight Templar wore a white mantel waisted with a wide red tie embossed with golden threads. It bled from his grasp in one hand and his other held a silver cup as he toasted an ominous hand-hewn cross. "This, this, is why the Indians here today are still fighting," as he jabbed, the silver cup tilted as if liquid would pour from the shimmering screen.

"Christian crusaders?" The dark little lady in the blue pantsuit snapped, "I know I'm in the right room. Are you sure that's written correctly?" she smirked, "Robeson County had 21 murders in 2017. Cumberland had 26 and that county is over double the population of Robeson. [6] I get the daily paper, honey, and I've never read a word on crusaders and knights here *saving* nobody. Uh-uh."

Two rows back a Lumbee sniveled, "Bes a-gaumed up talk. Haint hittin' on Indians er nuttin' like," while others mocked the screen's bright image adding, "Sir," and "Knight" to their names.

"Sir Knight Whopicoddle White Hide," blasted the aged Lum, "Idiot gid hisself kilt don't shuddup," and the growl fumed straight-on, but that hard-bent Jake stretched even taller.

"They changed their name to Knights of Christ. We pass by their lodges every day, Masonic Lodge, the Freemasons, whatever it takes to survive, like our Lumbee." Jake's daring smile pinched, "They changed their name in 1885 and these same people shop for new identities all the time up in Washington. The Lumbee claim that the Tuscarora are a "splinter group" of their tribe when all along, a lot of 'em are

Tuscarora. Did you know that the tribe once tried to claim that they were Tuscarora in an earlier hearing and were denied? [7] If this group of sixty-thousand members, the largest in North Carolina, did not receive funds for economic relief based on enrollment numbers, they wouldn't care one iota that Robeson's Tuscarora are working on their own recognition proposal."

"Ah, hell, you say!" the well-suited man in the mid-section shot up like a silver bullet.

"Now, Sir, I know the truth is a hard knock sometimes, but we need to keep calm. I was warned about how hot this presentation was, and I want everyone to know that this is the same riotous behavior that got those colonists killed," the suited man sat back down, but was wound so tight he'd squeezed all the blood right out of his ears until they sailed white against his blistered face, "Powhattan's priests got the King wound up and slaughtered most of those colonists. Listen: This latest federal recognition deal strikes the history-repeat button here and you'll see it too. I'm gonna explain it: Raleigh's first shipment of Christians were scared off by the Indians and went back to England. Then, in 1586, after Raleigh's second shipment of Christians had been murdered by the Powhattan and the seven colonists; four men, two boys, and a young woman, were seen working as coppersmiths for the Tuscarora, there was a man named John Pory of Jamestown who went and stirred up the crap pot again. Pory proposed that the Algonquin Chowanoke trespass against the Mighty Tuscarora for some western copper mines. [8] Native relations grew hostile again and the reason?"

Jake clapped, "Yep, greed – one of the driving forces that's pushed thousands of Tuscarora to deny their heritage and enlist as members of the socio-economically distressed association of Robeson County, North Carolina – the Lumbees.

Everybody who lives here knows there are not sixty-thousand "Indians" in Robeson County, that the DNA tests required for membership are just for show, and that without the promise of reduced housing and scholarships and the discrimination against non-card holders, that these people would have educated themselves, aspired for better positions in life and left this county. My research shows a handful of Tuscarora-descended names and I've got deeds, maps, and genealogy to back up this desperate group of Mighty Tuscaroras standing up for their heritage and land against the sixty-thousand brainwashed citizens who have worked to keep them oppressed and in a perpetual state of crisis since the Lumbee Act!" His nostrils flared and greens shot, "Yes, the hostiles are hostile, and it is time to break the cycle."

Eyes rolled and knuckles cracked. Jake pressed the projector's remote and a maroon Maltese cross dared to hypnotize. "John White himself wrote that his colonists were to carve a Maltese cross like the Knights Templar's cross should they be in any distress. It was the people's creed. [8] Let me ask you, "Does the Christian influence transcend time, ride some kind of genetic string that is unfathomable to most of us? Who here believes that the Christian influence of their grandparents' is what guides them now?" A scattering of hands flashed and fell. "What about a creed? A Tuscarora creed?"

"The temple those knights built was renamed to the Order of Christ. In 1492, this group from Portugal provided navigators for Christopher Columbus and the Order's cross was sewn on the sails of his ships. We know that Knights have a timeless creed to care for pilgrims. [9] and some say Sir Walter Raleigh had a few Maltese flags on his ship, the Lyon, maned with Portuguese sailors, and that he too was a Templar." His jaw aimed across the back rows. "From what I've shared tonight, does anyone want to tell us what the descendants of America's first Christians and perhaps descendants of knights, are called today?" Jake leaned across the podium and smiled, cheesy-like, from one side of the room to the other like some fool was really gonna raise his hand. "Who want to share what names they believe links Robeson County's Tuscaroras to the Holy Grail?" His boot vibrated against the podium's trim and the sniveler snarled, again, "Hope m' die."

"Look, people changed their names, their social group's names and tried to adapt as the world around them changed, but their blood didn't change. That's my point here. Now, anyone know what pidgin the Lumbee speak? Look, sociolinguistics is a consideration in recognizing any group of people," Jake squinted and pursed his lips like he had an osmosis lead line to tug up an arm. "None of this is taught in school, is it?"

After he'd planted his seedy greens across every single row and didn't get a sprig of reckonin' he doggedly continued, flipping over note cards as he proceeded. The prim lady seated nearby hurriedly marked her notepad, but both she and Jake whoahed real sharp like when the aged Lumbee in overhauls, from deep within the back rows, raised his weathered hand.

His huge shiny palm glimmered as his scarred blackened leather knuckles spread. "Hope m' die, n'er had no White man a-meddlin' on the swamp like dis," his riled voice deepened his atypical tenor into a bona fide bass, "and right in my face, too. Orta notta munk up our chances a-gettin' federal funds, boy. Look at me. I'm Cherokee." His chin lowered and squint glared, "Tell me I haint," he rattled.

"Put a root on 'at boy," a young Lum yelped through his baccar filled mouth. A nasty black line drooled down his chin as he spit into a stained bandana. Shook off what didn't make the cloth onto the carpet and rubbed it in with his work boot.

"Uhm- uhm," the aged Lum's grunt vibrated like it was rattlin' sticky phlegm. His whiskers danced like corn silks on fancy colored Indian corn and his blue eyes sparked like prize kernels heatin' up to 'xplode.

Jake zealously tapped the slide projector's screen and its retraction bar dinged the backside of his head. He politely winced as he worked to still the waving screen, but his hands still shook like he was sifting beans. All the while, the heated Lumbee guest was showing off his hawkbill as the screen lit up with an image of the holy tablet.

The aged Lum flicked the shiny silver blade and scraped out a crusty black line from under his thumb. Perked the blade up in his overhauls' front pocket and with mesmerizing Mediterranean blue eyes glared up at Jake from under a canopy of wily gray curls. "The Lumbee Council'll hear 'bout you a'fore mornin', you see me."

Finally, the cop on duty as umpire shifted from the rear corner halfway up into the room, so everyone could view him straight-on.

Jake fought his contentment, "In 1656, historian William Dugdale wrote that explorer Sir Walter Raleigh visited the area where the section of holy tablet was discovered and was told a story about the Templars hiding treasure there." Jake aimed at the screen's image where an aged map with a yellow cross marked the spot. "Raleigh obsessed over the treasure seeking and even persuaded his wealthy wife, Elizabeth Throckmorton, Maid of Honor to Queen Elizabeth I, to buy land there and hired a crew to dig the ruins of the Templar preceptor. It was rumored nothing was found.

In fact, Raleigh has a whole string of raw deals where he claims to have found nothing. Nothing. Yet he was desired and commissioned. Sent out time after time." Jake spun in a circle. Landed square on his boot heels and cocked a half grin. "No one with any logic would keep spendin' money on a lost cause. Raleigh was a con man, the kind who would sell out to the highest bidder. And there were plenty more like him waiting in line for a chance to find treasures. Treasures like the Knights Templars' collection of Christian relics. The stolen relics." Jake licked his lips and scanned the room, "Like the identity of the Mighty Tuscarora."

"Privateer pioneers like Raleigh are why the philosophers of the Christian crusades, the Knights Templar, created a system of trust. Some say there're groups today using that same system." Jake thrust his palms together, threw them up into the air like he was setting a bird free and lit up their eyes, "You tell, and you die."

They gulped, near about in perfect unison, sat back and stared straight-on.

"Tracing the movement that led to the quest for peace," Jake's water glass slid, but he quickly recovered it, "as well as the quest for the Holy Grail and other Christian relics, leads to," he languished, "leads to you!" The screen beheld a beautiful woman with long dark wavy hair framing her bare brown bosom. "Their language is rich with Portuguese."

Quick as a kid on a wild hare Jake shot a paper wad against the side wall, "Lumbees call the slingshot a juvember or juvemba. The Portuguese use the same word to describe a young kid." He flipped the juvember around and the band flopped. "It's a kid's toy. Juvember is also the name of a Portuguese village." He smiled and some guests responded kindly. "Pocosin, say that around here and first thing that comes to mind is swamp. Pocosin is the name of swamps all around the southeast. In Spanish Portuguese it means "little without dry land" or swamp. And common Robeson County names like Chavis, Chaves, Cheeves and Cumbo are Spanish Portuguese and African. Many people deny any African heritage, but DNA says the same thing as their language does. So, what's the difference?"

Jake backed up to the screen and framed it with his outstretched arms. One arm draped over her head and the other cupped the rest of her. "The Hatteras Tuscarora are documented as living with the Sir Walter Raleigh's Lost Colony. Logically, the whites integrated and adopted native ways that were passed to their children and grandchildren and you," he pointed. "Time passed and people from other cultures blended in and the languages along with it, and now we have Lumbee vernacular. History sets a fine example. Croatoan was first loosely assigned to the Peoples by whites who did not understand their language or accents and wanted to connect them with a location. The island the lost colonists went to was a Tuscarora trading camp named Katearas. Guess what the island is named now?" A young lady called out, "Hatteras!" "That's right, and today we have a group of aboriginals named Hatteras Tuscaroras who are rejuvenating their native language. That is the difference – historical documentation, integrity, and tradition – the aboriginal originals, not a group named by politically motivated whites." [10]

"This is all documented in David Beers Quinn's book, another white Irish boy, like me," Jake's thumb darted at his chin, "only he was a historical *expert*. The logistical sightings prove the descendants of these people, the Tuscarora with their mighty Iroquoian blood, pounds right along with that stubborn English blood in our Robeson County, North Carolina's real

Native Peoples." Shoulders raised and sighs were exaggerated, but the audience waited for Jake to catch his breath.

Jake thrust his palms together, "Our Hatteras Tuscarora are America's first Christians. No other group can claim this honor. Still, you are not afforded the luxuries of your Native American heritage, or the luxuries of a royal Christian heritage. I said this to Bruce one time, and we started to wonder if is it *honorable* to be federally recognized from the United States Government. It is the same government, spawned from the English royals, who took the Tuscarora's land, their language, their culture, their world, as they murdered and enslaved their families," Jake crossed his arms in protest, "Perhaps you have something worth trading for now? Some secret possession?" he leaned toward the balky group, "Bruce and I were close, but he held back on something, and until that secret is exposed, dealt with, or kept secret forever and the Tuscarora forego all their efforts for federal recognition, there will not be room for the Mighty Tuscarora in this century on the government's dollar. It just won't happen," Jake preached as eyes widened and nostrils flared, "The Lumbee Council is sixty-thousand strong and has their people positioned in education and politics to keep the Mighty Tuscarora in their place – in the shadows, the dark abyss of untold history.

The Lumbee recently folded in the Tuscarora as a "splinter group" in a political move to stall recognition efforts and to keep up their enrollment numbers. There is suspicion that administration's Haliwa Saponi rep in the North Carolina

Association of Indian Affairs (NCCIA) is planning a coo on the Tuscarora heritage and is just keeping it out of the hands of the Tuscarora until they get their funds together for applying to the BIA. The NCCIA just voted down the last attempt from a Tuscarora group in 2019. They must," he fisted the podium, "be appeased."

"Let me ask this to anyone of you, what did the colonists have to trade with the Tuscarora to allow them to live among the Tuscarora? The colonists had to have had something of value, something the Tuscarora did not have. Did the colonists have powers? Was it conjuring or what we call prayer? Was it something tangible, like old Christian relics? Would the Tuscarora have been impressed with the colonists' dinner ware and taken them in for a handful of brass dinner plates and a silver cup?" he threw his head back in a boisterous guffaw, "Seriously now, anyone can be trained to beat copper," Jake clicked the remote to the next slide, "There is proof that the Indians looted sailors, and as I've been lecturing, the sailors were mostly Portuguese and they ventured over here long before Raleigh, spying on what this land had to offer, who was here to fight for it, and strategized with others on how to control it and the Indians were watching."

In black and white, the screen bled the truth:

Governor John White wrote: At our returne from the Creeke, some of our Saylors meeting us, told us that they had found where divers chests had bene hidden, and long sithence digged up againe and broken up, and much of the

**good in them spoyled and scattered about, but nothing left,
of such things and the Savages knew any use of, undefaced.**

11

Jake cleared his throat with a chug of water as someone shouted, "Portuguese Christians?" "Holy nothing, we're Indians, you fool," grumbled another as a group of teens began to huddle.

Outnumbered, Jake's repose questioned whether he should continue.

A young freckled boy dressed in a worn thin flannel shirt and holey jeans sprang up, "What kind of gungi dis guy got?" His soprano rose as he reddened, "Bes sense a no man I got ta hear. Malahacked kyarn from wheretell I'm don't cyare.," he plopped back down into the metal chair.

"Called it Grail 'er something," another young boy screeched, and the crowd burst into laughter and chatter sailing a strong undertow of growls.

Hurriedly, the umpire grasped his holster and his big belly flapped up and down over his belt making his holster a game of hide-and-seek until laughter drowned the growls.

"Gungi went out with 'nam," a middle-aged man corrected.

"Youse got a truck to haul my bate a' loot or youse gonna be a cheat and just dole off a pearly piece?" The overhauls man stomped his thick soled boots on the carpet and chunks of smelly stuff popped off. Other Lums remarked that they'd pen out their addresses and to send theirs express mail. Others wanted to know where to find Grail Gungi and who had seeds.

"Holy, Holy Grail!" the baccar-spitter hit his top leg like he was winning a bet. "We's rich! Got da load of relics. Whad e'er dat bes. Mail my piece to da swamp, overnight 'xpress, cuz." A curly orange topknot jerked the back of the baccar-spitter's tee shirt so hard it choked him. With clenched jaws she commanded, "Down."

Jake wrenched his hands, "This isn't about treasure. It's about the origination of a people. This is about our Tuscarora claiming their heritage as America's first Christians and their position as Native Americans in the twenty-first century. You don't need federal recognition to be Mighty Tuscarora. Why would the mightiest Indians want anything from the establishment that robbed them of their entire world?" As clogging and fuming forced forward from the back rows, Jake forced his stuffed notebook from the podium's shelf. "This explains everything. There's grants. You can recreate your heritage on your own terms without the government. Become a village. It's the safest option."

The back rows shuffled as Lums bolted straight-up and Jake was asked exactly how many people he'd told his cockamamie ideas to. "Youse a sharp 'un, but we's already Christian." Fireworks fumed from the curly orange topknot, "We have Lumbee pride!"

Other guests shrunk into their chairs. The ump called for order, and the prim lady up on display next to Jake grew thinner and paler until she faded into the beige wall as nothing except a little pink hole where her thin pink lips sucked in streams of air.

But as Jake spun away from the audience and wildly smiled like an unashamed unconscionable thief, the prim lady, ever so faintly, smiled.

Metal chairs bounced against the royal blue carpet. They rattled. Clanked. Scraped and slid down the beige walls as the Lums in the back rows hauled ass. "Leave peaceably now," the officer ordered as he motioned others to the front of the room. Still, a few Lumbees hurried straight on through the genealogical aristocrats who parted like sliced white bread as the Lums crammed the front desk for copies of Jake's articles and his business cards. Several threats were overhead. Some outright yelled. "Ain't worth killin'!" But the gracious genealogical aristocrats continually tried to calm them, including the dark-skinned blue pant suiter. "Bless your darlin' heart, I know this isn't what you wanted to hear, chile."

The officer braced open the outside double door. "Make sure you have everything. Building's gonna be secured here shortly." They peeled tires, popped over speed bumps and as metal scraped against metal, orange-yellow sparks sparked and their call for attention was declared by an officer's siren as circling blue lights rounded off the evening's presentation.

"Certainly, they're not what Queen Elizabeth had in mind," the prim lady turned up her nose and fanned her damp notepad as she and Jake waited behind the bolted double glass doors. "That is, if you are correct."

"I wasn't done." They exchanged shrugs as Jake moaned at the strewn mess of note cards. Suddenly, with a gleam in his eyes, Jake grasped her shoulder. "You got it. You did. Didn't you? You may be the only one."

After a bat of her eyes, he loosened his grip and she braced as tall as her thin five-foot frame allowed. "You didn't get through all your notes. That's a shame. All that work," her skinny finger traced her matte pink lips, "And the paintings and research, your presentation was so clever and organized." When the screen's bright reflection caught her glasses, she squinted up at the information the riled guests had upstaged:

Excerpt from the 1871 North Carolina Joint Senate and House Committee as they interviewed Robeson County Judge Giles Leitch about 'free persons of color' living within his county:

Senate: Half of the colored population?

Leitch: Yes Sir; half of the colored population of Robeson County were never slaves at all...

Senate: What are they; are they Negroes?

Leitch: Well sir, I desire to tell you the truth as near as I can; but I really do not know what they are; I think they are a mixture of Spanish, Portuguese and Indian...

Senate: You think they are mixed Negroes and Indians?

Leitch: I do not think that in that class of population there is much Negro blood at all; of that half of the colored population that I have attempted to describe all have always been free...They are called 'mulattoes' that is the name they are known by, as contradistinguished from Negroes...I think they are of Indian origin.

Senate: I understand you to say that these seven or eight hundred persons that you

designate as mulattoes are not Negroes but are a mixture of Portuguese and Spanish,

white blood and Indian blood, you think they are not generally Negroes?

Leitch: I do not think the Negro blood predominates.

Senate: the word 'mulatto' means a cross between the white and the Negro?

Leitch: Yes sir.

Senate: You do not mean the word to be understood in that sense when applied to these people?

Leitch: I really do not know how to describe those people. [12]

"They'll come around, eventually," she curiously clutched at her neck, "You realize though, you won't take this podium again. As a member of the library board, I can tell you that we don't want our property vandalized."

"Yeah, I got ya,' but this is just the first try. I still have the surrounding counties," Jake set his jaw like he was bracing for a punch, "Don't know exactly what I'll do next. Got a professor up at Chapel Hill willing to listen, but I don't have time to be tracking up there and back. Don't know if he'd be any real help anyway," he palmed the glass and gazed out, "He's another member of the Lumbee powerhouse."

Jake cocked an eyebrow, "Gotta put my boot down on what'll put the word out best or their blood will be lost forever."

"You could always just tell me."

His Adam's apple bounced as the prim lady marched to the podium. First, she held up his thick notebook, "Black Purse Papers and Beyond: A Study on the Lumbee Subculture" by Jake Wilkes. "This took some grit young man," she pulled out one of Jake's note cards, marched it over and flipped it up in his face. Underlined in thick reverberating lead was, "You tell. You die."

"Yea, they're the ones who cut my brake lines."

Her thin lips spiraled down with her cheeks' wrinkled pockets like an angry bulldog's, "This is Providence," her itty-bitty blue stung, "You must tell."

His passion boiled into a heated roar, "If I had any sense I'd walk away before I went missing." He flatly waved at the remaining guests staring from the other side of the room while the blue pant suiter and her gentleman friend stepped up to the podium and took a business card and the officer unbolted the door and they made their way to their car.

Jake gave his attention back to the prim lady as he traced the deep scar on his cheek to the corner of his mouth.

"You couldn't be dragged away. You grew up with all these people and love them. You're too invested to drop it now," her bony features boldly stabbed, "Besides, I'm the only one here willing to help. I can get your work published, Jake. We can find a way to unite these people, together."

The prim lady's living room was elegant and uncluttered with pastels and layers on layers of sheers over the tall windows. From the first meeting, Jake heated up her house like a simmering coal. She didn't miss a move as Jake sunk into the spring-y divan and propped up his socked feet on her free retirement center's monthly magazine spread open on the maple coffee table.

She resigned to her desk, positioned where her angular profile turned from sharp to mellow as their meetings lingered into the late hours. Stacks of shorthand surrounded the backside of her desk in manila files. Each labeled and dated. Jake bled the story in thirty-minute swells while she slashed the keyboard with shorthand notes, pausing for details, and editing his dictation until her pages were mazes and she stopped him to highlight in pink.

Jake resumed the story of how he'd first learned the secrets of Bruce Black's people and the prim lady's chest heaved as she typed the fight scene, biting her bottom lip until she didn't have a lip at all. "Are you sure you want to be compared to a dog?"

"Yes, that's how it was." Jake sunk further. His arms were so long and her sofa so dainty that his muscular forearms hung off each arm rest. She momentarily admired him then instructed him to close his eyes. "Go back there. Smell the summer grasses and the sour pits of your arms. Can you hear the mosquitoes?" Her voice hypnotized Jake every time.

"Here we go into the thicket where Bruce destroyed your innocence." She typed as he spoke letting her shorthand typos fly by. "Tell me everything you see. The types of trees, water sources, vegetation, any markers, your secrets in the dark woods. Why are these people so important to you, Jake?"

His eyes jerked open. "Miss Lucy, you know why. The same as you, we want them to be happy, and most of all, safe."

"Mmm," she presented a title and he balked. After thirty minutes the collaboration intensified. They debated verbiage, content and structure. After a fair amount of haggling they decided: Introduce the story when the boys were thirteen, because, as they fully agreed, that pubescent period when the brain's neurotransmitters aren't completely formed made for a fair amount of undisciplined and uncensored drama – when hearts are fully open.

Two weeks later, Jake picked up their first efforts. She even included a cover page with her suggested title. "Trying to get us killed?" Jake skimmed the first chapter's pages, "I'll take it to the office. Read it there." When she inquired about security, he informed her that only he and the manager had a key, "Don't worry. Plagiarism is the last thing on her mind these days."

"Actually, it's leaks to the council that concern me." When the prim lady's pointy nose stabbed at the air like an ill-tempered finger, Jake's tender touch melted her, and she returned his pat along with a gentle push toward the door, "Jake, when I agreed to co-write, I didn't imagine my reputation being at risk. This little town, you know people are talking."

"Then you must a' heard by now. Everyone in town knows."

Her eyes awaited like a cast fifty-pound test line suspended over white water as

her gap caught a feisty trout. "You're helping me write a business plan to expand the winery," with that, her gauzily white cheeks perked up like she was still sixty. "I have a lot to learn about you. What other secrets are you keeping from me, Mr. Wilkes?"

"Good-gooboly-goo, Miss Lucy," Jake hurried down her walk, "We have some long nights ahead of us!"

Chapter 2

Cut of His Jib Now [13]

Zoskiroro's Winery employed an all Tuscarora staff, except
for Jake, who was Bruce Black's best friend and had inherited
the business. As the 10:00 a.m. deadline approached, Jake and
the manager, Cassie, grimaced as a goat popped across
employees' car hoods into a truck bed, hopped out and sped like
a rabbit between vehicles. Once cleverly cornered by a
maintenance worker on a three-wheeler and two squealing
ladies between its fence and a tractor trailer, the frisky goat was
scooped up and dropped into the pasture.

"Like ta snub off a front leg so it'd end that mess," Cassie
finished the last of her coffee and shook her curly orange
topknot. With a fisted hip and seriousness about her like a judge
with a gavel she told Jake that if he couldn't see to snubbing,
he'd better come off the hip with some more funds. "You sound
like you own the place," Jake agreed to allocate funds, once
again, on goat fencing and retreated to his office with the
manuscript, "Try sounding like a manager now and then, huh?"
he slammed the door as her orange topknot wagged across the
showroom floor, "hahaha!"

He placed the cover page face down on his desk, flipped it
over and tapped his chin as he fret over the suggested book title.
Flipped it back. Flipped it over again. Spied Cassie's orange
bobbing as she read out another amended list of morning duty to

her store personnel, and flipped it back down, just in case she was going to hand out another pink slip.

When Cassie was out of sight, Jake began reading *Chapter 1, The Vexing Then*, as he sipped the tepid remains from his favorite cup.

"The thicket's stomped clearing held Bruce and Jake in their own trap. The young teens barely moved as the swarm surrounded them. It hummed above in a polite tone as if waiting on an invite and then in a whoosh, droned down welting up their tender flesh as if the mosquitoes truly were sin-eaters suspicious old timers threatened instigators with.

Bruce's warning slapped like sharp cymbals against the mosquitoes' hypnotic hum front row of the fiddling katydids' background chorus in the late summer night. The boys' sour adrenaline fumigated the air as they breathed like bulls sucking in scents of hot cow heat until the air between them became as thick and nasty as death's awaiting dinner bugs.
The teens popped their bare arms and swatted their faces. "Keep your mouth shut, cuz."

When Bruce eased up from his crouch and looked around his crown of dirty blonde ringlets caught the moonlight and glimmered like a willowy dandelion's seed head momentarily marking him as just another sweet young boy while the night wind sang for his seeds to parachute free.

Tree frogs chirped with little baby birds as his old malahacked silver cup tapped. The fluted form hung off a twisted wire wrapped around its thick rim from a Loblolly branch above his humble still. The cup sang its tings and pings against the looped wire like it was being strummed to rally Bruce's turning and burning. The cup would ting, and the baby birds would sing. It was all so pleasant. No one would have ever known from just listening to the sweet chorus the boys had all that ol' kyarn on their hands. The enchantment was so absolutely intoxicating, that for one second, Bruce looked like one of those spirits Indians tell to show up and help-out strangers in need.

But as he fully stood, his ringlets left the light for the moon's shadow. He was not little at all. Bruce Black's thirteen-year-old chest puffed up under his threadbare tee shirt like an ancient bare-chested Chief's out on the edge of the Carolina Coast spying on sailing ships.

The cup's chorus twirled into a tight mesh as the wind suddenly blasted up from over the pond's dam and the baby birds smashed down - stunned into silence.

Bruce checked for the neighbors then scornfully glared down to his side as tender young Jake petrified. Their eyes locked.

Jake just let those mosquitoes feast as Bruce's cold grays threatened, and don't think for one second them totens didn't pay it no mind, 'cause at the same time the boys were 'bout ta go around the choir director's baton poked straight-up and jerked down the entire band from the late summer night's stage. The background music whoahed like a rough riding plow mule;

with a screech from all the bullfrogs, just like they'd been stomped. The katydids did it, too. Then a whippoorwill's alarmed whip followed by several lame tree frog chirps. The baby birds squalled, and the silver cup scraped around the Loblolly's trunk like a guillotine crunch.

It all stopped and got real still and quiet for one solid second, so the last critter's position in the band was amplified, a lone mockingbird's mock of an alpha "arf."

That very instant it became so still and dark, even the mosquitoes left. Like no spirit wanted ta be around for what was gonna happen next, not even a dark toten. Jake's heartbeat pounded, but he didn't dare open his mouth to speak because there was a squealing, reeling voice in his head, absolutely screaming, "Mommy!" Even if he were blind drunk from their homemade hooch he knew not to tell, or let it slip, ever, as his quivering finger pointed to the dripping blade. It all happened so fast. Bruce's top lip rose like a wolf's does before he eats his prey. He held the blade out from his side and shook it. "Bes just like a dog shakes, ha?" Bruce mimicked a dog shaking off its wet coat. His blonde ringlets whipped around his stoic smirk as he bent straight over and used the German Shepherd's cream-colored undercoat right at her butt to wipe off the blade.

The moonlight covered her body as if the Little People had kivered her up with a holy blanket as her dark blood seeped into the bright sandy soil. Jake clamped his eyes shut and caressed her outstretched body like his love alone really could've saved her, and instantly, tears formed. Too weak to move, Miss Scarlet whined as the whites of her eyes flared up at Jake. "Oh, my God," Jake panted. Her chest heaved for one last drawl of breath and that is when her hushed hollow howl totally consumed the boy.

Miss Scarlet died with her mouth hung open. Her pink tongue that had soothed and welcomed Jake so many years hung lifeless and still. Jake quickly grew hot as the moment marked him. His blonde bangs shivered as he trembled, filling up with a passion so powerful right there and then he became a man.

Bruce still scowled directly over him.

Jake cracked his knuckles as his hot glaring greens aimed like poison tipped arrows. Sweat oozed down his back as endorphins rushed down his spine. The sultry summer heat combined with his red-hot fury made his armpits so sticky he had to pull at his pits to loosen the stuck fabric and Jake's thin legs tightened till his bones felt like steel. His skinny frame thickened so much he had to roll his shoulders to keep from ripping his shirt. As Miss Scarlet's ears flopped lifeless like rags on a clothesline Jake became so empowered, he unconsciously gritted his teeth and bared his cusps as he fought the urge to choke his best friend.

Face to face with the threat, Bruce's thick lips parted. "Swanny, I'm had to do it," mutedly, it did nothing to distill his ferocity. He glared, "You gonna stick around and bury that? Don't count on me. I'm berries to pick. Shine to cook. Time's money, cuz."

"I hate you! Just shut up, you stupid Lum."

Bruce's gapped lips closed before slowly and wickedly curling up at the sides as he held the blade out in front of him like a fencing sword.

Jake blew as a snarl twisted his hot face. "She wasn't gonna do anything. She was just warning you." Consumed with the urge to kill, his tight fists pulsed. The hair on the back of his head rose like a dog's sharp hackles and from deep in his chest he heaved a gruesome growl. "You make me sick," his stinky breath reverberated between his clamped jaws. "Why didn't you just shoot her some more hot dogs? You got a pocket of 'em! You just suddenly forget how to shoot that damn juvember? You just get that stupid all of a sudden? Huh? Huh? Did cha?" His nostrils flared as a drizzle of snot rimmed his snarled lips.

Bruce leaned back, "Bes tired of it. Dog was a-gonna mommuck up my source and then I bes, I mean we, bes climbing that hill over at the creek to get my Muscadines. Now buddyrow, can you see us a-toting buckets up and down that hill? Gotta be four miles a' nothin' but ass 'n elbows. Damn, Skippy." Bruce rolled his bottom lip down till it doubled, "It's just a dawg."

Bruce rested his hand on Jake's expanding back and the bullfrogs began to croon again just like a haunt had told 'em to. The katydids fiddled and the Muscadine grapes sparkled like they were just flicked with fairy dust. The damp night air settled down and covered them with heavy swamp scents and the freshness of Long Leaf Pines. "You ain't gotta deal with no crap from nobody. I don't care if some fool's got money or not, or a fool showing you a piece of paper saying her dog's better than my momma's mutt. Nobody's gonna run over me, or you. You always been there for me."

"I can't do this anymore." Jake balanced himself clenching a thick vine and took calculated breaths like he was birthing some big awesome thing he'd just as soon kill when a sweet cool breeze filled his senses and suddenly the night songs came screeching back into his ears while Bruce swatted at the stinging mosquitoes. "Gallanippers gonna gaum me up wid colic. Mess of 'em in these woodses tonight."

"You sure do get on the swamp when we're out like this," Jake's angst amplified between his gritted teeth as he glared up at Bruce, "You sound like your old man."

"Bes what the bate of 'em do, buddyrow; keep the tribe." Mosquito blood was smeared over Bruce's cheek like a battle scar, like he had that day when they were only five, when their backyard opened up to all the sorry in the world.

"Gawd, just talk plain with me," Jake's burning eyes filled. "It's not like you're gonna turn me into a Lum." Bullfrogs croaked rib-dat as Bruce bellowed, "Gotdat, Jack!" and he leaned against Jake's shoulder, "You better not breath it, not to one or I'm put a root on you, and be all the sorry in the world having to do that to you, Jake."

"Yea, nothing comes between good ol' boys and their precious damn shine," Jake cleared his hot face from the grape pickin' gyarb as he held down one nostril and blew out a stream of snot. Then the other. As their standoff over the dead dog subsided a car turned up the hill toward the neighbor's back yard. When they hunkered down deep behind the grape vines, they disturbed the plump Muscadines bobbing near their heads and the air surrounded them with sweetness. Bruce popped one into his mouth and used his chin to direct Jake to do the same. Bruce spat out one seed, then another. Jake bit down. The grape burst wet and cool inside his hot dry mouth, but the connection with Miss Scarlet's blood pulsing from Bruce's faster-than-light gaping hole sent Jake hurling. Jake gagged and grape spewed along with leftover taco salad.

"Baby," Bruce spat as he popped Jake on top of the head. With the car long gone, Bruce directed, "Get home. When your mama smells you munked up wid the colic, and bes all chauld over, tell her you fell out the tree house. Gotdat, Jack!"

In the thick of the vines, with the moonlight behind him Bruce mirrored his sinister old man. "I'm not your cuz. Talk normal ta me. Got that?" Jake spat out the lingering stomach acids as he held his knees.

"You bes right, my friend. You taint got no Lum blood. No warrior in you a'tall, blanko baby," he hovered like a snake aiming to strike, "I'm said it. Tho says a word I'm ta put a root on you. Made dat son a' Dodger's bust his head on a rock right there at school. Fell off that teeter totter and bes sense of a jack rabbit. Say he's gonna be like that straight-on." Arrogance spat off his shoulders like a heavy poison, "I know all 'bout conjuring. 'Member that when youse telling what's up to yer perty white Mommy."

"Shuddup," Jake stripped leaves from a nearby maple to wipe a spew of vomit from his shirt. "She'll want to check me out. I can't tell her I fell. She'll never believe it." As Jake bolted, Bruce grabbed his arm, flung him to the ground, and kicked his shin so hard it sounded like it cracked. But it was only Bruce's worn boot separating from the sole, again. As soon as Jake was sure his leg wasn't broken, he stopped rubbing and rocking and glared up at Bruce like he could kill.

Bruce rolled, "Haw! She'll believe it now when ya' take them britches off." Up like a shot, Jake kicked back and snarled, "Tell your dad you fell out trying to catch me." Right then, the bullfrogs up and croaked all together like a big fat clap. "The Prince got a boo boo?" Jake's shoulder grew wider still.

Bruce's eyes doubled before he doubled over and in one deep guffaw coughed out the pain. "Swanny, you done mommucked up now. Youse fixin' ta gyet crotched up now. Don't cho ever call me that. I'm just a plain ol' Lum!" Bruce's nostrils flared wrongsididas with his thick lips poked out like he was fixin' ta bite. But Jake just shook his burning foot. "I'm done, Bruce. I'm not cookin' anymore. I'm done. I mean it. Do what you want with my share."

Bruce blinked so many times, like he was shifting gears in a runaway truck. "Fine by me. Gets better with age, like women." "What? You have a girl now?"

A lone mockingbird cried out a drawn-out version of his neighbor's call, "Whip-poor-er-will!"

Bruce didn't tote buckets heaped with grapes that night.
Jake didn't either. They toted
shovels from the still site to bury Miss Scarlet. Angry passion
fueled a fast and humongous hole out by the baccar field off the
road a ways, and Miss Scarlet's body sunk into the summer
warmed soil as Jake tossed a handful of stones across her sandy
grave. He prayed aloud that he was sorry and wished he could
take it back and could've done something to have stopped
everything as Bruce kept watch."

Jake slumped deeper into his chair, "I'm the one watch
now, Bruce," he whispered as he discovered Cassie glaring at
him through his office window. He sat up straight and threw the
rest of his cold coffee down the back of his aching throat and
called Miss Lucy, "I have time this evening. Do you?"

Exhausted from a full day at the winery and God's honest-
truth, the mental exhaustion from heaping out all the memories,
Jake took a break from dictating his story to Miss Lucy and
stretched his legs in long three foot spanned steps onto the fall
evening's cool front porch. "It's going to storm tonight," Miss
Lucy warned as Jake kicked the bustling fall leaves from her
doorway. Her quaint old house sat back off the road, lined with
pecan trees, only four miles from the winery. He stretched tall
when suddenly, a fifteen-knot wind gust forced his white dress
shirt free from his waistband. Jake squinted against the cool
blast, but as Mr. Fisk's sweet-sour mash swept in from the wind
his senses were tweaked, and Jake leaned against a column and

stared off into the bare limbed sky. The black limbs thinned out into a deep purple sky with a three-quarter silvery blue moon cresting over a thin maroon waft. Refreshed, he returned to the living room and not finding Miss Lucy there he happily dogged into the kitchen where she was preparing her usual; tea for two and pimento cheese sandwiches.

With two bites left of his sandwich, he lingered over her desk, reading her latest revision as she returned with a plate of butter cookies that she kept out especially for him on the maple coffee table. "You look tired, Jake. Lay down on the divan and get comfortable," Miss Lucy handed him the plate and he laid back and rested the plate on his abdomen. When her fond smile turned zealous, puzzled Jake asked, "What's so funny?" "You look like a dinner table with that shirt untucked and those cookies," her clasped hands folded together under her chin, "tehee, tehee," she snickered back to her desk, rustled pages and handed Jake the pile, "You can read this while I catch up on this stenography. That way I won't have homework," she nearly sang.

When the cover page still had her suggested title, "Lumbees Undone," Jake's tongue curled up over his top lip like a clamp. He propped up his socked feet and continued reading *Chapter 2, Cut of His Jib Then.*

Jake leaned against the free air sign's post at the Wet Whistle One Stop with his cowboy hat over his eyes and a bottle of water in his hand. At fourteen, he was tall and lanky with a mischievous look that made a kid look guilty or look like a whole lot of fun, depending on who was looking. Bruce's dad spun to a stop at the gas tank, jumped out, and ran to the bathroom at the side of the store. Bruce lowered his window and cocked his head over at Jake as the summer heat rose scalding from the concrete until Jake was somewhat forced to fan himself with the brim and Bruce waved for him to come.

Bruce sat lurking in their new truck, the new dirty black truck: Even with their new graveled driveway, dust clung like sin.

Bruce leaned deep into his seat and draped his arm out the open window down the length of the door to show her off. Her long black hair and loud obnoxious laugh were hard to ignore.

Bruce stabbed his chin up in the air like he always did when he was figuring out what to do next as Jake approached and Preacher Black flung open the bathroom door, "Gaumed dat up! Worse 'n stink bugs on soft taters!" Jake popped the top of the hood of their new truck and Preacher Black stomped, "Whoa, mon!" Preacher Black sounded like a stobbed screaming woman as his alligator boot steps quickened. "Geyt! Bes waxing my truck, yurker!" He marched across the steamy hot parking lot stuffed in his black suit with sweat dripping down his red-hot temples like a wrestler on a pay off, but nobody with a lick a sense would've dared laugh, out loud.

Jake nervously waved him off while Bruce begged, "You don't want this slacker kiverin' our truck with paste wax. He'd munk it up," as Preacher Black got closer, he slowed down. Jake wasn't hard to recognize. It's just that every skinny fourteen-year-old boy in Maxton wore boots and cowboy hats. They all pulled time putting up hay for the Thomas,' wore the same soiled jeans day in and day out so they wouldn't wear out their school jeans and hung out at the store to ask for more paying chores.

Preacher Black walked around his truck checking for yurker marks. He said so out loud and then went on to grumble under his breath about suing and having plenty of church people who'd stand up in a court of law and testify against Jake if there was so much as a new pit or wad of gum on the undercarriage knowing full well there wasn't a single soul around from his church. "Swanny, thought I had me a wood toter. You bes lucky today. Don' see no yurker marks no'rs." He pumped the fuel while inspecting his image in the side mirror and adjusted the small Testament in his suit coat's front pocket. He pulled out the hanky, wadded it up and poked it back down to the bottom of the pocket and sat the Testament on top, so it would stand out and anyone could easily identify him as a solid man of The Word.

Robin leaned over Bruce's lap and her long neck stretched till her head was clear out of the window. "Hey, Jake, how's your summer vacation?"

"Hot, but I'm making a little money." Jake threw cool water down his hot throat.

Bruce winked, "Me too," and Robin politely smiled, "What time is it, anyway? I told Mom I'd be back by four. We just got back from the nursing home. We sing for the residents. Preacher Black visited our church and we teamed up. Our congregations are both so little." Robin hadn't taken a breath when she fully leaned over Bruce and asked, "What church do you go to, Jake?"

"It's three-forty-five. We're Presbyterian," after he answered Robin, Jake smirked at Bruce, "Singing hymns? How's that going for ya?" His dimples dug into his sun-kissed cheeks and his green eyes shone like a happy cat's when Robin responded, showing off her glistening whites framed by her full red lips. She grew more beautiful each summer. Jake leaned against the truck. Perspiration dotted his top lip and as Robin shared his wanton moment, whether consciously or not, she licked her lips when Jake waved his cowboy hat over his broadening chest and he flexed his pecs.

Bruce braced his stiffened arm in the window frame like he'd pulled back the trigger on his guns, "Singing in church is like singing anywhere else," Bruce aimed at Robin, "I'm good at it, huh?" When Robin agreed her long black hair bounced against her chest's padded buds.

Jake smiled as he fanned his heated face. "Hey, I know where you can get some good peaches next year."

Bruce scowled at Jake's implication as Robin eagerly leaned up for a better view out the window. "Next year?" she chirped. "We'd like 'em now. Right, Bruce?" Jake's big white teeth were as white as his sun-bleached blonde crew cut.

"Dad's congregation keeps us up in peaches," Bruce cleverly replied.

"I see that." Jake's head rolled like a ball in a poured cement ditch.

Bruce licked his front teeth as he glared up at Jake with his steely grays. "Dad's really into church now. Got religious friends all over town." That's when Jake's head stopped still.

"It's three-forty-five," Robin whined, "I better not be late, Bruce. You know Gili. I mean, Mom," her forehead wrinkled with worry. Everyone knew Gili. She'd made the restaurant notorious. Gili's; don't complain or it'll come back burnt, cussed brown. Jake daringly leaned into the truck. "Do you work at the restaurant?" His full head fit inside forcing Bruce to press back against the seat to keep from being cheek to cheek.

"Dad takes us there a couple of times a year," Jake sucked in her summer scent, "Never seen you working there."

"Well you don't come often enough. I grew up working at Gili's. But I have a lot of demands on my time. I have flute, dance and compete over at the team penning off Highway 42. My horse is double registered. Anyway, I'm not there every night." Robin turned to Bruce and then to his dad who had squeezed in behind the wheel, "Are we ready now?"

"We're always ready to carry out the Lord's work, Robin," as Preacher Black tucked his chin and smirked over at Jake his eyes squinted from the sun, "Wanna come, Jake? Bet you know the words to a few of our hymns." The magnifying sun made his pale gray eyes look like hollow yellow holes. "You Presbyterians got lots of the same songs as us chosen folks."

Robin's wrinkled forehead relaxed as she sighed up at the truck's ceiling and rolled her eyes, "Preacher Black, are we headed somewhere else to sing? I mean, I thought we were just singing at the nursing home? If we're gonna be any later, I'll have to ask Gili," Robin pulled out her cell phone and flipped it open. When the recording requested the caller try again or leave a message Robin flipped it closed. "Busy this time a day. They're all ordering takeout."

"She'll have time for us. Gili'll set us up wid a mou'ful me bringin' her sow cat in," Preacher Black's deep guffaw eased into a sly smile, "I'm smashin' the gas for a bate a' Gili's. Hold on, yunguns."

As Bruce shook his bangs free from his sweaty brow, his blonde ringlets parted to make way for the shame. His eyebrows united and his chin darted about, but there was nowhere for him to hide. Bruce's nose pointed up in the air all around the big blue sky like a bird dog trying to lock sights. Without looking at his dad, Bruce manned up, "Orta notta eat free thyere again this week."

"Shush, boy. She's got in for me, now," Preacher Black patted the Testament held up in his suit coat's pocket.

A car pulled up behind their truck, impatiently honked for a turn at the gas pump and his dad turned the key. Jake threw back the last of his water, "Later, dude." Bruce mouthed bye as Robin stared dead ahead and Sinister Minister wrapped his big open hand across Robin's bare knee and rested it there as he steered away from the gas pump.

Two weeks later, Mrs. Wilkes explained to her son, "Imagine that. An overhead limb breaks the man's neck. Just imagine that." Jake welcomed the little fairies that lowered him into the recliner sewing his gapped mouth shut while his mother handed him the newspaper clipping. "Working in that dangerous environment all his life and struck down by a limb on the path to his truck. It's so odd. The man just turned his life around and the Lord calls him up. It's the craziest thing. Look, *Preacher* Black made front page. That must be inside his little church. It's just the craziest thing ever," she chimed.

Jake sat listlessly, scanning it over and over. When Jake crushed it, his leg vibrated like a muffler on a runner's worn shock until his mother told him to sweep off the steps, where safely outdoors, he promptly cussed, under his breath, "That thing doesn't have a word about Preacher Black being a gambler, one of the meanest, orneriest, most foul Lumbee fools no one with a lick a sense would e'er stow up in a corner without a loaded gun or sharp blade or no will to live on any longer. Nothing about a single one of his stays at the county jail. They keep his favorite breakfast on hand; pig brains – like him!" At the end of the steps he swept the sandy path to the mailbox, "It oughta read that Black was a well-known moonshine-operating possible wife killer and confirmed child abuser," sand swirled until a beige haze separated Jake from his mother at the screened door. "It's not fair! We need to call the paper Mom," but she'd disappeared into the hallway.

Straightaway, the funeral was held. Mr. Wilkes drove around the block searching for an open parking spot. Twice. "It was astounding," Jake's mother had said when they learned that in less than two months Preacher Black had conned nearly three hundred folks into joining his church operating out of the old shoe store right there on Main Street.

"Don't touch anything in here." Mrs. Wilkes instructed as they stood at the entrance of the stale old shoe store turned church. Her jaw literally vibrated as she hissed, "This place is going to be full of scallys, I just know it. We'd better just sign our name and leave." Mr. Wilkes winked at Jake and cleared his throat as he steered his wife inside like she was a little pinto pony.

"Isn't the church where scallys need to be?" Jake's sarcasm met with his mother's furrowed brow.

"Now there's a thought," Mr. Wilkes cocked a half-smile, "You know the Lumbee are thought to be descendants of The Lost Colony." Mrs. Wilkes looked right through him as he continued. "It's legend that Sir Walter Raleigh wanted to form a new society here, a secret one, like the banned Templar Knights, and the Grand Master of the Templar Order, de Molay, who was burned at the stake in thirteen- fourteen by King Philip of France, the same King who pressured the Pope to disband the Order, issued a curse," his dad's exaggerated expression provoked Jake, but Mrs. Wilkes was on the purple side of rage and shook like she had her own little earthquake going on under her meager heels, "Don't fill his head with that mess," she hissed, "Those boys'll beat him if he repeats that and you know it."

Mr. Wilkes held his son's full attention, "The King and the Pope both died within the year. Eyewitnesses say de Molay wasn't even screaming and didn't show any fear. I can see Chavis Black being that way." Mr. Wilkes penned the family name into the registry in the foyer because Mrs. Wilkes' couldn't. Her fists were still clenched. He hummed in reflection of his history lesson, "He was always talking about puttin' a root on someone." He smiled down at Jake, "Good thing you made friends with the family."

The registry book was cream colored with royal blue lettering and royal blue lines. Jake asked for the pen to write "Best Friend" beside his name, but when Mr. Wilkes was about to hand over the pen, he noticed the alternating nude-to-bikini clad busty blonde stretched down the pen's side. It was from the strip joint down in Fayetteville. He slyly held it out and shook it like the ink might be low. The nude lady flashed and flashed as his smile grew and grew. Mr. Wilkes was about to put the pen in his Sunday suit coat when Mrs. Wilkes elbowed her mister and he dropped it, "I said, don't touch anything in here."

As Jake unconsciously quipped, "Good-gooboly-goo," Mr. Wilkes jabbed his side and they all gawked as the humongous shiny white hertz out front, sliding into triple park. The hertz was surrounded with church goers' cars and jar runners' trucks and drunks' clunkers and there wasn't a single solitary police car around. Jake pinched his palms to hurt so he wouldn't laugh out loud. But as his dimples dug in his dad thumped his bony shoulder, hard, and instantly, Jake's smile flipped.

The store church was full of greeters and weepers. From the yellowish brown-skinned and curly headed folks it looked to be mostly Lumbee up where Bruce stood next to his aunt, two old uncles, and loads of kin in every degree. Bruce stood like a full-grown man in his ironed black pants, white shirt and tie. His work boots were either new or stained with black shoe polish to match his pants.

Stoically, Bruce spread his arms open for his dad's store church followers and his dad's old drinkin' pals along with regular family folks and his co-workers from the lumber mill, but Bruce longingly smiled as his favorites appeared.

Cassie and her seven youngins were lined-up red faced and snotted like they'd cried all the way there with their spankin' red faces, some with curly orange heads, some with straight black, and some with blue eyes. Cassie sought out the only Black left, and Bruce took to her hug like a calf to a bottle, holding her so tightly her back ribs showed through her thin pink blouse. "My little pappy sack, youse got a long row now. But youse pure got a bate a' friends who'll be there. Ya know our numbers, Shug." Bruce hugged Pig Pen, Cassie's oldest boy and the rest of her youngins.

When Dan the Man's oversized square frame blocked the light at the front door entrance, Bruce stood up taller. Dan the

Man could've easily snapped Bruce's head off with one hand, same as a government signature killing another attempt at federal recognition for Bruce's people. Dan was the biggest human being ever seen, one of the last giants, and so ugly strangers to town were known to plow into cars while staring. His nose so bulbous and pits so deep roly-polies hibernated in 'em. Their antenna stuck out like whiskers. He had no neck, shoulders wide as the front of a town car's bumper with his head up in the middle like some kind of evil voodoo doll hood ornament made by an unskilled witch. His ears looked like they'd been stretched out, but thick and had so many rises a toy car could run around in there for an hour and never hit the same rise twice. His lips were too big, even for him, and hung all red and drooled shiny like the backside of a mare after foaling.

In the doorway, holding all eyes and the light hostage, he was so extra cross, so extra riled, so extra rabid; his forehead was waded like a blanket over his beady black angry eyes. He was so fearsome that folks sitting clear on the other side of the room shrunk down into their chairs, so as not to bring any attention to themselves. He breathed his nasty breaths like a dying man grasping for air until he plum growled.

For one full gawl dern minute all Bruce or Jake could concentrate on was Dan the Man's brand-new work boots.

Dan the Man boldly smiled at Bruce straight-on and over to Jake when he sported a new tooth too. Gold enamel framed a perfectly white porcelain crown. His giant broken horse-tooth was fixed. The upper one he had broken just a few months before when he got dared to open a tin can of beans down at Old Man Black's likker works. He'd done it for years successfully, but his giant horse tooth had been weakened from years of acidic gastric juices. Dan the Man had always out drunk the others, forcing himself to vomit to make room for more.

Oh, man, and if Dan the Man's new boots and shiny tooth didn't make a donkey out a' that entire shoe store church funeral neither did knowing the place still had four nights of hard work in the back all wrapped up on pallets marked as a defective boot shipment to be returned to the manufacturer. Every single jar runner in the store church was hoping on that last run, but to get that run they'd have to deal with Dan the Man.

The quiet was broke when Dan the Man stomped down the aisle and stopped cold when Bruce locked on him like a hawk on an old farty possum. Dan the Man took off his hat and then with all the gall of an indolent yurker, and with his beady eyes still locked with Bruce's, he eased a nod directly at him to show off his new hair transplant. The long wisps flew over his big old head like fishing line teasing a fat cat down in its bank hole. His hair transplant was just like Preacher Black's. He sported a puffed-up noggin all discolored like flesh does when it fights decomposing in yellow and brown and pink to red with purple dots. Oh, man, did he have guts, big buffalo guts.

Bruce signaled to Jake with his arrogant half a smile, chin up, but not too high, and nose flared. Either Bruce had just fueled osmosis and put a root on Dan the Man or was settin' a dare, a dare so big, so stinkin' crazy, Jake thought he smelled it and his leg quivered in anticipation of the first cue. He rubbed it down hard a couple of times to keep from running up to Bruce right then to plan something extra rotten for nasty old Dan.

Still, the Wilkes family managed the procession line, hugging each of Sinister Minister's relatives as Jake kept a check on Dan the Man. Jake casually adjusted his suit and peered over his shoulder just like in the old timey detective shows. Mrs. Wilkes said polite things about being sorry and it being sudden. While Mr. Wilkes said things about how good it was to see everyone coming to support Bruce.

Bruce's cousin, his mom's sister's son, Mark, explained that they agreed to move in with Bruce and help out. Bruce rolled his eyes, making it look not nearly as agreeable. While slyly, Dan the Man slowly slinked in, almost like he was afraid to walk the procession line. His boots scraped across the tile like a cooter's toenails tapping and scraping and spreading grossed out chill bumps up and down the line. Dan the Man eased his hat back on and retracted from the line. Even his neck sunk in deeper like a nasty ol' cooter when he turned around and headed to the far wall where he pilfered with an orange and yellow funeral wreath.

His big fat clumsy fingers fiddled with the wreath's envelope until he got the card out and he stared at it a long while before a young lady approached and he held it out to her. "For my only real friend all my life," she read aloud. "See you on the other side. Love, The Man," and handed it back to him. His thick pimple pitted chin twitched as she patted his back, "That's lovely, so touching. It has to be the sweetest thing I've ever read on a funeral card." He hung his big fat head so lowly his hat tumbled off. Another lady bent straight over to retrieve his hat, so far over in fact that her lacy black slip showed, but Dan the Man didn't even stare. Didn't gawk. Didn't say a thing out a line, only took the hat as it was handed back and covered his face with it as he hurriedly broke off into the back room where the pallets waited.

Mark said they'd move in the first of the month, when rent came due at the trailer park.

Mark was about six, wiry, curly headed and had those mesmerizing Lumbee blue eyes. Bruce's aunt stood closely to Bruce, "I'm Bruce's Aunt Thelma. Lizzie'll finally rest in Heaven now. She won't have to worry about her youngin' with me. I'm strict and all about higher education. We don't even speak their vernacular. Know what I mean?" Thelma wrapped her arm around Bruce's shoulder, and they all nodded and smiled, except Bruce. His Aunt Thelma looked like all the other Locklears, tawny skinned, with dark brown wavy hair, and high cheekbones.

Both Mr. and Mrs. Wilkes solemnly empathized as Thelma held on to Bruce's rigid frame. Mrs. Wilkes sniffled. "Lizzie must have been her nickname. We went to church together for fifteen years and I never heard her called anything other than Gladys."

Thelma licked her bottom lip, made a quick scan of who was in line and then stepped closer to Mrs. Wilkes. "Gladys

Elizabeth White," she nearly whispered, "an old English name.
It was too stuffy for us on the swamp and Lizzie fit her. She
never met a stranger and treated everyone like they were special.
We sure miss her," Thelma's eyes welled up.

"I know she's happy to have you watching over him now.
We're just through the woods, the yellow house. The boys have
a path cleared. You let us know if you need anything. It's going
to be an adjustment for all of you."

"Thank you," she softened as Mr. Wilkes offered his hand
to Bruce. They shook, but Bruce didn't make eye contact with
him. Instead, all chauld up, Bruce sought Jake. Like a toy
soldier Bruce held out his hand for Jake. But Jake jerked him up
to his chest and used his chin like a clamp over Bruce's
shoulder. After Bruce trembled, just the slightest, Jake let go.

Bruce swallowed, "We're taking his body to the cemetery
off Old Plank Road, the Black's plot. It's private, right after this.
Comin'?" His eyes begged. As Jake affirmatively sighed Bruce
squeezed his shoulder.

The Wilkes stood over Old Man Black's body. His once-
plump jaws folded like sheets down to the satiny white pillow
and his black suit finally fit his deflated frame, like an
impeached politician. Strangely, his face mimicked a painted
Cherokee warrior's. His lips were painted pink and the same
pink was smeared around on his cheeks like the state's coroner
had been bribed to make him look happy. The heavy furrows
across Black's fire damaged forehead and deep grooves around
his eyes, which came from leaning over likker kettles and

stoking fires, stood out like black painted war stripes preparing him for battle. When Jake tried to see how his eyes stayed closed, he was surprised when the left eyelid popped open and threads were exposed. He quickly pointed it out to his dad. "The temperature difference, son. Come on, let's find a seat." The jubious eye drew Jake in for a second look: An eighth of an inch open where spied a dirty white cloud.

Jake popped-in the last butter cookie and glanced over at Miss Lucy, "I swear, this funeral reminds me of the last hearing up in Washington: Blind, crooked and the Tuscarora heritage cover-up," he asked for milk and she remarked that he shouldn't talk with his mouth full. "Yes, ma'am."

Repositioned, Jake returned to the manuscript.

"The uncomfortable metal folding chairs squeaked against the old tile consuming the store church the same way the stink loomed. The big room with its ten-foot ceilings and old plaster walls trapped all the scents from old shoes and new, armpits and cardboard boxes, old dust, pine logger's dust, to the orgy of colognes, and it was baptized with the aroma of an open jar of rotgut. Jake bent over and pulled up his socks to sneak a look over his shoulder.

Dan the Man took up two chairs and his sidekicks, Wart, and Mr. Fisk were there and if it weren't a miracle enough to see those dudes in a church, Scarecrow was there, right behind

Jake. He'd met 'em all through the years and avoided 'em like lipstick lips on Sunday mornings.

With stinging dry eyes Jake studied the lady front and center with short brown hair, big brown eyes and a tight navy suit. She shifted her hips seducing the white podium marked with black scuff marks around its base with one finger, outlining its edges, over and over like the way Bruce held money – with passion. Bruce stumbled as he passed her and took his seat right up front. Her pale skin was over-powdered. Her lip gloss didn't have any color, just wet, and she had boobs as big as cantaloupes.

Mr. and Mrs. Wilkes studied one another while Jake ogled straight-on at the fruit offering. The lady scanned the room, from one side to the other, gradually taking order. She scanned persons as they entered from the foyer, from the side door and then the ones lingering at the racks of soliciting material on missionary work where boots and shoes were still displayed for sale, and when she scanned the ceiling, so did Jake. Aged ceiling tiles, tube lighting along the walls and the one new chandelier held a small black device. He danced his eyebrows and when the lady did too, Jake's eyes grew wider still.

Preacher Black's black coffin was right in front of her. The white podium was the only thing between her and the black coffin. The stand held The Holy Bible. Its golden edges sparkled like a butterfly's wings on a spring day. "Fellow friends, members of the congregation, and relatives of the dear departed, I am Preacher Lilly." Her voice was silky smooth, like a

Southern Belle's from one of those old black and white films where moss hangs from shady trees and everything looks sprawled out and welcoming. Jake swallowed the extra drool pooling in his mouth while Preacher Lilly's cantaloupes shifted. "Our dear brother, Preacher Black, Mr. Chavis Black, has left us to live in Heaven. As any one of us can testify, this man was a saint!"

The Wilkes family checked this news with the others who were also wearing the most perplexed pusses imaginable while other funeral attendees shouted, "Amen!" when all of a sudden, a sly smile radiated from Jake's bashful batting eyes.

Bruce had Preacher Lilly's picture pinned on the inside of his closet behind the hanging flannels and pullovers right in the middle. Fayetteville's infamous Starlight Club was lettered in flaming yellow across her spread-eagle legs with the pole acting as the letter "l." Right after he had acquired the hot "Glossy Flossy" Bruce had told Jake that she had offered to teach him everything he'd ever need to know in life and Jake's eyes had 'bout fell out of his head like they were right then as Preacher Lilly swung her head around and moaned.

"Dear brothers, we're gonna miss this man. This man brought so many of us to the Light. He even turned stone to life. This building was nothing but an old shoe store," she winked, plain as day, at the group of scallys behind Jake. "Now it's a beacon of Light, a holy vessel, a watering hole for the down-troddin' and poor." Poor was so drawled out it had two syllables as her lips pursed up like a hooker's in the movies. "Preacher

Black turned all us 'round from the dark to the Light." She swung her head and moaned again as funeral folks shouted, "Amen."

A man testified that Black gave him money for food. Another squealed, "He lifted me up." One of the scallys behind the Wilkes whispered, "He gave him a bottle."

"Sisters and Brothers, our Bible teaches us that a man in the Lord is a new man! A reborn spirit! Of the flesh of the Lord. Preacher Black gave me new flesh." With her flexed palms, Lilly traced her body from way down at her firm hams and back up to her bouncy lopes, attaining an unconscious rise from Jake's member and most likely every other man. "From his flesh, the Spirit moved him in me, to be new, alive, to feel His power."

Testosterone-driven "amens" sailed in waves through the room, while young Jake grew more hypnotized: Preacher Lilly gently rolled her head around and around as her full mouth hung open. She jerked to a stop before she sashayed down to the front of the coffin and peered down at Black's corpse and began to shamelessly shake and her two blue hams wiggled a quick jig. "Look at him," she spun around with her arms spread back like an abandoned baby doll. "Look at this man of God. Surely there's not one of you who hasn't been touched by his testimony." Folks responded with raised arms, shouts and moans.

A loud squeak demanded all eyes as a metal chair strained against the tile. Abruptly, a woman stood in front of the Wilkes with both arms thrust to the ceiling, "Preacher Black gave me love, pure love," she cried, "He showed me the way. He led me from Hell, Sister." A lady in front of her stood and slapped a tambourine. One poor lady who was moaning pitifully was handed a tambourine from another grieving lady until they were everywhere, and they were all pretty, tightly dressed and had great fruit plates, every single serving.

Mr. and Mrs. Wilkes exchanged glances as the shiny tambourines were played and the row of scallys directly behind the Wilkes clapped in time. Preacher Lilly begged all to stand and sing. Some stood, ready to sing. Others were clearly hypnotized and too enthralled to leave their seats. Preacher Lilly stretched to the ceiling, "Come together, now. Let's praise God for sharing this man with us. Even though it wasn't long enough, it was just enough. Oh, Preacher Black, what are we going ta do now? Who we going to call? Who is going to guide us, comfort us, lift us up and give us the power to go on? I tell all y'all, it'll be Preacher Black's spirit alone. God didn't allow that man to be so low down mean for so long, to change and walk in the Light for no reason at all. No. Our Lord has plans for all of us. His plan for Preacher Black was to live on in us. We carry his spirit in us." She thrust her head around so hard that her short brown hair flew off her head right onto a man in the front row, but she didn't get upset and neither did he. But his fast wife did. She hastily pawed her man's new little brown pet from his caressing hands and slammed it up against the wall where it slid down to the tile floor and landed like a balled-up kitten with its tail on end.

That Preacher Lilly loosened the bobby pins from her long brown hair and cried, "It's all right, Brothers and Sisters. It's a sign. It's a sign from Preacher Black." Her hips thrust back and forth in a quick snap. "He wants us to be ourselves, be free, move in the spirit that moves you." Quick as a pig on a cob she crone down the lid of the coffin and jumped up on top of it. With a gasp, Mrs. Wilkes bit her bottom lip just as many of the funeral folks who were standing, all ready to sing, sat.

Preacher Lilly stretched her arms up over her head until her little blouse untucked from her skirt and the buttons holding in her cantaloupes poked up like little pearl onions, threatening to come a-loose. In one long swoop her long brown hair seduced other women into motion. Tambourine ladies gyrated like long liquid lines from the ceiling to the floor as men clapped. Still fully hypnotized, Jake fit in four claps before his mother slammed down his hands. Jake enjoyed his dad's beet red face while his mother breathed out a freight train into his ear while Preacher Lilly kicked out in anguish. "Is there anyone out there who wants to testify? Get up here and tell it. Tell what our dearly parted Preacher Black did for you. Don't let this moment pass you by." She swung her long brown hair and when she stopped it fell in wild directions all over as the cantaloupes peeked out. "We are only dust in the wind. Be free. Loosen yourselves from this world. Feel His love. Only God's love'll set you free." She formed big circles with her outstretched arms, slipped in her high heels on the slick black coffin and one of the pearl onion buttons bounced free as Jake mouthed, "Only God's love will set me free."

Lilly used her toes to peel off her heels and each landed with a clunk and many a man's wagging tongue. She stood spread on Black's coffin like she was daring someone, anyone to come get her off.

Jake covered his lap as Dan the Man's deep testosterone driven voice broke, "I gotta testify," he cried from a deep abyss threatening the building and all inside, "I feel him. He's here." Jagged and torn, deep and scary, Dan the Man cried. So big, so real that others joined his wails.

"Get up here." Preacher Lilly eased off the coffin. Raised the lid back up and peered in as she directed Dan the Man to also look at the corpse. Her waving outstretched arm drew him nearer and nearer while his quivering bottom lip dripped drool. She kept coaxing, waving and wiping her tears until Dan the Man broke. He took one look and fell to his knees as his head bobbed in and out of the silky death bed in sequence with his fitful cries.

Dan the Man jerked and wailed in fits over his mean old poker playing friend's corpse for what seemed like half an hour, and instead of inviting him to take a seat up front so the funeral could proceed Preacher Lilly rubbed his back. "Mon, my ol' buddyrow you da only real friend I ever knowed. Only one I took kin to. You never laughed at me or put da jokes on me. You took my momma soup," Dan wiped snot with his sleeve,

"I'm a-sorry," he confessed like he was all alone with Old Man Black.

He shook like a quake with vibes so strong the attendees shook.

"Black, you jus made me so mad. Almos' don't believe hit," he inhaled, "Till I see you here. Your head bes a rock. Even a steel-toe boot couldn't kill ya. Member dat? Black!" His wails pierced the bones of every single witness in the store church on out to the passersby on the sidewalk who blocked much of the light as they spied through the entrance glass.

Dan the Man picked up the corpse by both shoulders and Black's heavy head fell backward flush to his back proclaiming his broken neck, while funeral folks gasped and screamed. He cradled the corpse's loose head. "Tain't never had no real money before. You orta notta took hit. Lordy, help me take this back. I didn't mean hit. I'm just awful mad." Dan the Man kissed the corpse on the cheek and gently placed him back down. Then rose like the mighty giant being he was as he held them all hostage."

"Damn," Jake's restless legs flew across Miss Lucy's wooden floor and the cookie crumbs on his chest danced as the reread the last two sentences aloud, "This is great, just like the government holding the natives hostage, making them beg and killing them off and full of empty promises for retribution when all they have is a record of deadbeat bills on file. Lilly tempting everyone – on all sides of government, just like big money does.

I believe this comparison will get them motivated to hire a lawyer for that anthropological evidence they need from East Carolina University, and you know what, Miss Lucy?" his lips clenched, "I think you were there."

"Does it matter?"

"It does."

"Why?"

"Now I know you can keep secrets too."

"I knew Bruce's mother," her confession pleaded for reckoning as Jake closed his eyes and placed her face in the time-swept memory closet where he stored his childhood with Bruce. A few seconds later, he opened his watery eyes, "Thank you," he said, and she told him that the funeral was a memorable event for her and everyone else in town.

After he returned from the bathroom, Miss Lucy looked up at him from behind her desk, "Jake, I'm just one of many who knew her and, and just keep in mind that we were friends and that she was one smart cookie and so is your Bruce." He momentarily studied her face before easing back down into the spring-y divan and yawned. Miss Lucy told him that he only had a few more paragraphs and to go home and get some rest, but he couldn't stop. He moved the cookie plate over with a foot and propped up to finish reading.

"With eyes so wide open they looked like they'd pop out a' the sockets, Dan the Man's giant fist punched a hole straight-up in the store church ceiling right next to the new chandelier and he fished for the electrical wires dangling near the overhead light. When he couldn't reach them, he cried out like a squealing baby.

"He's gonna hang himself," whispered Scarecrow, and Wart repeated it to Mr. Fisk.

"You girls come put yer hands on him! Conjure up his life breaths!" Dan's booming demands matched heartbeats as that Preacher Lilly continued to disdainfully glare with her hands on her hips as Dan the Man commanded her, "Come here!"

Mrs. Wilkes whispered that it was time to leave, but Mr. Wilkes shook his head because young Bruce had risen from his seat. Even with a stiffened back and his muscular build the closer Bruce got to that giant nasty the more he looked like an elf.

The chairs behind the Wilkes squeaked as the scallys, Mr. Fisk, Wart and Scarecrow leaned into a huddle. While up front, that Preacher Lilly positioned herself smack dab between the giant angry ugly and young Bruce.

With her back to the frightened attendees Preacher Lilly whispered to the angry ugly as he bent down into her face. He looked away from her and out into the crowd as Bruce stoically approached the coffin and looked in. He growled like bear, pushed Preacher Lilly aside, and tore into Dan the Man like a raving maniac. Bruce swung and kicked at Dan, but Dan held Bruce's face in his palm, keeping his punching fists and kicking feet from reaching. Preacher Lilly said something else, something stern, but the words weren't clear over Bruce's heinous growl.

Whatever it was, it made Dan crazy, "Tyake me, Lord! I's jus a low down drunk. Tyake me! Tyake me!" He cried in fits as the room echoed his giant wails and Bruce wildly climbed up Dan's outstretched arm and folks cheered, "Go, Bruce! Get him!" "Pull his eyes out!" "Climb up there and bite off his nose!"

The chairs behind the Wilkes screeched and squalled and crashed against the hard tile floor as the scallys rushed up front. Mr. Fisk and Wart fumbled with their baggy pants' pockets and pulled out what looked to be wooden clubs as long-limbed Scarecrow lurched to Dan. "I'm a-gonna whopicoddle his ass!"

Mrs. Wilkes then shouted for mister to call the police, but he insistently pointed out a man in a worn corduroy blazer with an empty holster. Their heads snapped back to Dan and Bruce as Mr. Fisk and Scarecrow peeled Bruce, now frenzied mad like a raccoon took fresh from the wild, from Dan the Man's arm. Bruce punched at the bate of them and got in a couple of good whacks before he calmed to a slow foaming mad.

Jake leapt around his dad's legs and ran to his best friend. Scarecrow hovered over Bruce and held his jean jacket around Bruce's face, like a shield. But when Jake begged, "Let's get out of here. Come on," Bruce pushed Scarecrow aside. Scarecrow quickly shined his silver badge at the boys and jutted his chin at the man with the corduroy blazer who had a sweet forty-five pointed directly at Dan the Man.

With Bruce still under his arm, the boys hurried on numb legs down the cracked tile aisle when Lilly's pearl onion button shone up from the rank floor like a cornucopia symbol of pure raw lust. Jake scooped it up without missing a step as the chandelier bulbs burst: Crack-crackle-pop, one after the other and the boys looked back toward the black coffin's happenstance as if the Little People purposely busted those bulbs over Dan the Man's suffering head. Glass penetrated his weakened flesh and blood spilled in streaks down his face like black reflected prison bars in the dim light.

Dan the Man was on his knees. Scarecrow dangled handcuffs over Dan's head. Wart and Mr. Fisk stood to the side or rather wobbled at Dan's side, flabbergasted with seemingly sober eyes, as they nervously worked to lift the giant man's hands up into the handcuffs for Detective Scarecrow, and low and behold, that Preacher Lilly also had handcuffs and hers were enormous.

She held them down in Dan the Man's face as he sulked like a cow sucking in a deep breath before a long drawn out bellow, the forlorn cry of the beast's suffering. Then those two perky navy-blue hams wiggled up in the air as Lilly bent straight over to clamp the restraints around Dan the Man's thick ankles.

Simultaneously, both Jake and Bruce hollered, "Good-googoboly-goo!"

Everyone else in the shoe store church looked on catatonic; too flabbergasted not to look, still too scared to move, and real excited they didn't have to pay a dime for the best show in that little town for at least two generations. Dan the Man was ne'r 'bout hogtied belly down perpendicular to Black's black coffin with the tall law and all the church people hollering, "Amen!"

Miss Lucy asked Jake if they should edit out some of the funeral scene and Jake said, "Nothing about Lilly though. She's juicy."

"R-right," her sarcasm was second to her agreeing tone. "We need to think about your research, Jake. Save room for that. I have a general outline prepared and I think it's best if you make a copy of your research and leave it with me. I believe there is nothing the council would not do to stop this publication."

"I know," Jake said, "I had a fair amount of obstacles just getting the research."

"So, when can I expect that?"

"How's tomorrow?"

"What time?"

"I can bring it around lunch."

"That works," Miss Lucy said, "I haven't seen anyone on this road at lunch." Concern loaded Jake brows, and she elaborated, "There've been strange vehicles on my road this past month, around the time you arrive."

"That's not good."

Chapter 3

The Game of "Dare" Now

Two nights later, Jake eased the prim lady's divan back onto its lion claw feet, "That should keep the spring secure," as Miss Lucy blushingly suggested he purchase a belt, "Aiming to, Miss Lucy."

Headlights illuminated the layered sheers and he rushed to the window as he instructed her to stand aside. The truck slowly passed her house and minutes later hushed-rushed rubber over asphalt announced it had left the area.

"That's one quiet truck," Jake analyzed from the window, "either black, brown or dark blue."

"Know who it could be?"

"About a hundred yards from here to the road. My guess is there's a silencer on that muffler. Keep your eyes out when you're in town and I'll check around too."

"I don't know what to look for," she spat.

"We'll look it up on the computer before I leave."

"Really, I don't go many places. I go to the library and food store and church and home," she pinched the tip of her chin, "We can call the parts stores and ask if there's been a newly purchased device."

"Yeah, that's an idea. If someone just started spying on us, it might work, and I got a hunch that truck was old."

"On what basis?"

"The headlights were dim, chrome on the sides and a square frame."

Miss Lucy gleamed, "You are phenomenal, such a smart man. I'm so fortunate to have you as my friend. I am positive you will learn who is spying on us and will be speaking to the Bureau of Indian Affairs for the Robeson Tuscarora and help your friends attain the recognition they have prayed for all these years." Jake's solemnness piqued her, "What's wrong? You look like you suddenly lost your best friend," she teased, and he hung his head, "There's some truth in that," he grunted.

"Miss Lucy, I have wondered what you would think of me when you realized the truth," he adjusted his jaw, "I believe the Tuscarora are better off without the government's help. They need to focus on education. History is not the government's agenda. They are a money monopolizing outfit that doesn't really care about their heritage and culture being preserved. Our Tuscarora need to request recognition and attain some retribution funds and land, but as far as getting set up like the Lumbees, I think that's all wrong. If they go after welfare programs, they will just be another welfare group. That is not who the Mighty Tuscarora were."

"Exactly what do you suggest they do?" her nose flared, "They are among the most economically distressed groups in North Carolina."

"They need another "copper factory," his jaw jut affirmed, "and I am not suggesting casinos. Lord, this county doesn't need to invite any more criminals in. They need manufacturing, textile, like hemp. The college is working on buying land right now for hemp."

"Are you serious? Our university is getting into cannabis?" disgust hung from her lips.

"Yep. I read it in The Pine Needle. The University of North Carolina at Pembroke is working on grants to attain equipment and land for a large-scale industrial hemp program that will integrate with their new Bachelor of Science degree." [14]

"That's perfect," her soprano sang as she organized her desktop, "Our Hemp Gatherers have a real chance at reestablishing their heritage."

"They have a chance at reestablishing themselves as major traders," he corrected behind her desk, "Bruce wanted this, believe me," his voice deepened, and she told him that he probably did as she rested her hand over a copy of Chapter 1.

Miss Lucy handed him Chapter 3, The Game of "Dare" as she revealed, "I make back-up copies of everything," and she asked, "Had any calls?"

"Is it all over my face?" He flashed a shiny white. "I almost drove over here to tell you,
but it was a Wednesday. Thought you'd be at church." When she posed like a gopher on lookout, Jake divulged, "There's a Lumbee out there thinks I'll hand over a reward for information. Threw out some large sums, five-hundred thousand, seven-hundred-fifty, all round and fat like he'd get that out of me. Said he knows a place in Maxton that's protected, boys might be protecting thousands of pounds of what I'm looking for, the

little shit. Wanted to know what it's worth to have the evidence now versus later." Miss Lucy didn't flinch, but when Jake picked up the stack like he's set on reading she tapped her hard-soled slipper on the desk leg and like a hawk, set sites and aimed her bright blues. "What?" Jake's squished lips parted, "You could be in with him for all I know."

"As a history major with a minor in religion, my concern is in the honor of recording history as it occurs. As a senior citizen living alone, I worry about my safety and learning about a stranger's intent on blackmail is dangerous news, but I realized that chapters ago. What else is there to do with my time?" she huffed. "As the co-author of your novel, I subsequently intend to document the outcome."

"You're doing a fine job, too. Like how you put it together. So, what do you predict'll happen?"

"The Lumbees will have to face facts that they are like all other Americans and blend in. They will abandon their vernacular. The Lumbee Council will most likely face charges and disband and welfare will fill the gaps as a socialistic government does to prevent their entire community from becoming a burden."

"You're so invested."

"Well of course I am. My lineage affords me honor as second nature."

"Oh," Jake marched to the window as headlights mark the sheers again, "Tell me one thing." "You're in a mood, Jake."

She motioned for him to sit as he aimed for the divan, "Why do you think the council will take the fall?"

"BANG! Ka-boom!"

Jake flattened against the wall as Miss Lucy rushed under her desk. When the rubber rushed past, Jake slapped his chest, "It's definitely an old truck."

She laughed as she rose from under the desk, "We're getting paranoid."

Jake plopped down on the divan, "Have you told anyone about the story?"

"Not a soul," she whispered.

"Me either. My girlfriend thinks I'm helping one of my employees with a bathroom remodel. She knows I'm not expanding the winery. Had to tell her something."

She jabbed him with her little blue eyes like they were prickly pin tips. "One of your employees? Did you give her a name?"

"Yea, I told her it was Dodger," his top lip curled, "So what?"

"No woman is going to let that go unchecked. Uh-huh. You disappearing on Friday nights, half the time you end up here on Sunday afternoons. I don't care if she is working. A woman keeps tabs on her man."

"You're right," his long arm swung toward the sheers across the room. "That was probably one of her bus boys. They don't make nothing at Gili's, minimum wage. She gives 'em a twenty just to go check on her horse."

"There you go. Now stop worrying, pony boy."

"Pony boy?" he laughed, as he scanned over the first page and she straightened her desktop. "Really, do you think the council knows about us?" She slid her crossed legs out in front of her and admired an old English countryside oil painting. The fox hunters behind the old pitted glass proudly announced a kill as a child pours refreshment into small silver cups lined up on a linen covered table under an outcrop of leafy trees. "Would it make a difference? Would you quit?" Her itty-bitty blues bit, "Just walk away?"

"No. Like I said before, there's too much at risk."

Her pale heart-shaped face tilted, "For history's sake, or for your friends, the Lumbees and Tuscaroras, or do you really believe someone out there has ancient Christian relics?"

Jake shifted down into the worn divan as he propped his socked feet onto the magazine she kept on the coffee table and cocked his jaw at her, "I believe there is physical proof out there that links the Tuscarora to the first Christians and that it can dramatically change their future." Miss Lucy shivered and wrapped her sweater up around her neck.

He read over their progress as she dove into translating shorthand into prose. This time, Lucy Henrietta has shortened her name to H. Prickenrath on the cover page. "Like your new writing name, Miss Lucy. Elusive." She looked over her shoulder at Jake, "You can still call me Miss Lucy." "Yes, ma'am."

"*Chapter 3, The Game of "Dare Then"*

"Jake's new sports car gleamed showroom shiny inside the garage as Jake hid outside behind a porch post while Bruce drove by for the third time looking for it or the old family clunker, Crash. From his hidey hole, Jake admired the hot pinstripe on Bruce's ride. His rims were all right too, shined it up good. When Bruce slowed down on the fourth attempt, Jake stepped off the front porch. Bruce pulled up into the drive and turned down onto the sandy area where Jake usually parked. Bruce leaned against what once was Old Man Black's Jesus truck, waiting for Jake waving his ball cap. "Come here, you." The truck shone like new. Bruce was all cleaned up, even wearing jeans without holes.

"Whew!" Jake whistled, "Buddyrow must have a date."

The scent of aftershave and mint gum tumbled from Bruce's shaking head. "Where's Crash?" Bruce strained to get a view into the back yard. "Why'd you hide up there anyway? You stink-bomb, you were laughing when I came by. Huh?" When he bit the tip of his tongue and smiled his bright whites shone too.

"You betcha. Laughing good. Not often I get one over on you."

"That's right. Take it in, boy."

"Got my car inside. Knew when you came by the first time you were looking for me."

"You finally sell Crash?"

"We're restoring it."

"Crash? It's junk. Your dad bought that thing when you were born."

"Makes it a classic."

"Do what you want," Bruce threw up his hand. "I think you've lost your mind."

Jake rounded out his right cheek with his tongue.

"Liar, you had me," Bruce squints. "Really, where is it?"

"It's in the shop, nothing big, just hoses and lube, stuff to keep it going."

"You really think it'll be worth something one day?"

"I don't know. Dad holds on to it just in case. He worries I won't be able to make the payments on my new car. Least I'd have something to get around in."

"He ought'a be making the payments," Bruce's resentment deepened his tenor Lumbee.

"Dad's business is slow. Advertising is one of the first things to get cut. My vet's only keeping me on because I'm the one people ask for to hold their babies. He's let two others go. One of those was part time, after school, like me."

"It's tough everywhere. Thelma's lucky to be with the State. Says she missed being laid off based on seniority by one year. She says it's fate, the move here, the new job. She's engaged to him now."

"The round guy who pulls out his ear hairs and looks at 'em? Oh, man, and you're gonna have to live with him." Jake slapped his thigh and Bruce swelled up and stood tall as if he was about to make an official announcement for a political campaign. "No. I haven't told her yet, but she's gotta move. I got a buyer for the home place. I'm going to college, Jake, and buying a new spread."

Jake worked down the hairs on the back of his neck with one hand and patted Bruce's shoulder with the other, "Gawd, that's great. That's the best thing I ever heard. What are you taking?"

"Business, two-year degree at the community college. Going to have a legal operation."

Jake peered into the back of his truck and quickly guesstimated the number of empty sugar bags in the nearly clear trash bags. "Legal likker?"

Bruce popped Jake's shoulder. "Yep. No more smugglin' hog corn. Cassie's boys'll be in uniform drivin' big rigs - You see me. I'm going to have a winery, a fine place, with wood floors, cheese tasting and classy music."

"When did you decide all this?"

"When I was thirteen."

The momentary silence ended when Jake lightly popped the truck's hood, "Remember your dad's face first time I ever did that?" "I saved you," from a dank reflection pool, Bruce replied and began to speak again but a mockingbird zoomed astonishingly close and missed squirting their heads. Still, they both checked their heads and Jake looked Bruce firmly in the eyes, "I want to be there for you, Bruce. Whatever you need. I'm there."

"That's my Buddyrow," Bruce heaved as his grays locked. They stared at one another as the neighbor lady across the road pulled her mail from the box at the end of her drive. "I hate you moved when Dad died. It was a long year for me, Jake." Tiny blonde curls rounded over his scalp making his eerie gray eyes stand out against his handsome tan. "I spent all my time making wine, turning those Muskies. Thought I'd turn into an alcoholic, be a thirteen-year-old drunk. Carry on that Lum tradition, too."

"Sorry. Dad had me busy here, getting the yard done. We built a storage building." Jake pointed it out. "They kept me busy that year. What was it, maybe three times at best?"

"At best. Thelma did it, too. We took out all the furniture, cleaned it. Washed walls and painted. Put up new curtains. Thelma runs a tight shift, a real tough lady."

"To deal with you, she'd have to be." Jake cocked his head. "She did something right. You're going to college."

"Thelma's a tough one. Says she's got radars on my scheming. Reckon she knows I turn but won't mention it on account of I don't ask for any money long as I got some. Don't think she really knows how much, or she'd be needing this and wantin' that. And she'll slack off on the cleaning chores, but pushes me on school, manners, stuff you've been doing all along, momma's boy." They chuckled. "College'll make a big difference for the Black name." They agreed. "You still going?"

Jake studied the tops of his shoes. "Yea and no."

"What's that? Part time?"

"My plans minimized from veterinarian to vet tech. You going to the Lumberton campus?"

"Yeah," Bruce studied his friend's face.

"Me too. That'll be good. We haven't been in the same school district since the move."

"Robin's going, too." Bruce piped.

Jake's greens dug into the news. "You still keep in touch?"

"Ran into her in Pembroke. I was paying the light bill. She thinks about me," Bruce beamed.

"Dah, everyone remembers you."

"No. I mean thinks about me as maybe we'll date in college. She's taking restaurant management."

Jake huffed. "That's a waste of money. Robin'll always have a job. She'll own Gili's."

Bruce leaned back against his truck and looked up into the bright sky. "Liable ta give it up and work with me."

"I wouldn't wait on that," Jake scowled. "I'm going to ask her out."

"Naw, you need to find your own girl."

"I've been friends with her longer than you. You just showed up in her life with the church."

"I'm set on her now."

"Get unset."

The boys seethed and the heat between them intensified and dispelled only when a truck whizzed by and backfired. "What was that?" Bruce blew and Jake smirked, "It's a work in progress from what Dad and I can tell. Not long ago it was a car with half a roof and the backseat was full of bloodhounds like they tried to convert it into a hunting truck." "Must've got rid a' the dogs," Bruce surmised. "Yeah," Jake tongued his bottom lip and asked, "So who are you dating these days?"

"No time," Bruce was fast with a reply, "I was steady three months this year with one. I messed up. Don't call your girlfriend's co-workers to check up on her."

"No girl is going to cheat on you. Your body's a rock, Bruce. Look at you. Weight-lifting?"

"Lift a lot of product."

"How much?"

"Moving forty to sixty gallons a month. January and February are nil. You know that. I hold enough back to keep a supply."

"Dang, Bruce. That's a lot of money."

"Can't spend it on anything that shows. Got an undercover who won't take a bite - Yankee from hell."

Jake bit his lip, "Better be careful. Jail is no place for a perty boy."

"Jail? It'd be prison. With the sums I'm bringing in I could do two to five or more," Bruce quipped, "I keep it coy."

"I hope so," Jake's chin bobbed, "That Scarecrow sure got Dan the Man. I'll never forget that. Lord was watching over us, Bruce. As many times as we met up with Scarecrow, Wart and Fisk, and they didn't get us; wasn't dumb luck."

"Wart and Fisk are cooks. Scarecrow's the only one on duty. He's alone now. But he's got a dog. Don't think he ever brushes it. Looks like it's got mange. It's a sniffer."

"Drug dog?"

"You're really out of the loop. Yea, drugs, guns, likker. They train 'em to find illegal tacos, too."

"I haven't seen Scarecrow in a couple of years. I was at the ball field off First Street. Now that I think about it, there was a dog. It stayed right behind him. He never touched it, through the whole game. Couldn't decide if it was a stray or not." Jake checked the sugar bags in the back of Bruce's truck again. "Scarecrow knows your cooking. Why hasn't he come after you?"

"Money."

Jake briskly rubbed his palms together, "Are you going to quit when you start the winery?"

"I plan to quit this year. As soon as I sell the house. But I need your help."

Jake's Adam's apple made a loop as his throat tightened as Bruce stretched out his arm alongside the rim of the truck bed until he could reach Jake's elbow and tapped it, "Jake, The Company's got to be moved. Needs to be done carefully. Gotta do it at night and gotta move it clear out of town. My plan is to do it all at once, in one night, the night I know that damn Yankee is out of town."

"How will you know that?"

"Leather likes the girls. But the girls love me. He goes to Surf, that nice one in Southern

Pines, and so do I."

"I don't know," Jake turned away.

"Listen at me. The Company's in jeopardy. Scarecrow said their fixin' ta put helicopters on watch and got a grant for drones. Too much money going around. Think one of the runners got busted and's keeping it hushed. Worked out a deal for walkin' shoes. That's okay. Can't say I wouldn't do the same if I were him. I checked it out. It's true. County got that helicopter deal and is workin' details. The Company's been there too long. And my name was on top of the list." His jaw dropped as he waited for Jake. "Old Man kept a few on pay off, but Crow's my one and only and he's killing me. Goes up every year. Tells me that he has to pay off others and that by paying him I keep my name out of the loop. But either he's lying or I'm just too big for this little town and it's pissin' off the punk cops they got in D&A." Bruce licked his dry lips, exhaled and gritted his teeth.

"You're asking me to step into a wad, here, Buddyrow. I can't make college tuition. How am I gonna make bail?" Jake crossed his arms. "This is too big. Too much can go wrong."

"Jake, I don't have anyone else I can trust," Bruce burned red. "I don't have anyone." The hot rushed words were hard for him and came out that way.

Jake's eye nervously twitched, "What time frame are you looking at?"

Fervently, Bruce leaned in, "A couple of weeks."

The lady across the street tossed pinecones from her drive, turned and faced them, then scouted out more near the roadside.

"What night, exactly?" Jake softly asked.

"Won't know till I get the call," Bruce cupped his hand up over his mouth. "Then I call you. You'll have to be ready. Think up a reason now to leave in the middle of the night before I ever call. Something your parents won't question you on or you'll give us up." Bruce licked his lips and cocked his expectant grays as his eyebrows danced. The look was thirteen. The look was excited. It was a look of invitation to live to tell the tale and it was contagious as hell.

"I'll say," When Jake spoke too loudly Bruce motioned for him to tone it down, "I'll say there's an emergency at the vets. No. That won't work. They'd call when I was gone too long. I can tell them I have to help a friend deliver puppies. I can give 'em a name of someone I don't really hang with so they can't check."

"I'll pay you, too." From his front jean pocket Bruce pulled out a roll thick enough to plug a judge's sentence and set-up the judge's mistress in an oceanfront condo.

"Put it back before she sees. She watches me all the time," Jake demanded like the neighbor lady might read lips and it made him appear like he had a case of lockjaw coming on. "She'll tell everyone she sees that I'm selling drugs if she gets sight of that roll."

When Bruce waved, the neighbor lady smiled and waved back, "She's harmless. We oughta go help her out. Looks like her yard needs raking," he took a step forward, "Come on, let's do it."

"Really, she doesn't like me."

"Too bad. All ladies like me, especially the gray hairs." Bruce flicked the edges of the bills like he was counting them with his fingertip then tossed it to Jake and he examined the roll of Franklins. It was at least twenty k. Jake slowly handed it back, "Impressive. You know how to take care of a dollar."

"Just like women. Pet 'em till they purr, and you will, too," as Bruce's laughter caught the attention of the neighbor lady, she grinned at the handsome young men and Jake popped the truck bed. "You charm 'em, all right. Looks like that one wants to call you Sonny Boy."

Bruce's boyish cheeks bounced up, "True enough." Bruce juggled the roll from one hand to the other, occasionally toying with Jake that he was going to toss it to him. "Had dinner?"

"Nope."

"Let's go get a pizza." Bruce pushed the roll deep into his pocket.

"Sounds like a plan."

"You gonna tell them you're with me?"

"Yea. Well, I'll write a note. My phone's out of minutes. On the bargain plan," Jake jogged to the house and scribbled out a quick note that he was with Bruce, then just as quickly wadded it up and threw it in the trash. Took it out of the trash and hid it in his pocket. Finally, he wrote that he was with a friend and not to wait for him for dinner. Jake hurried to his room as he peeled off his tee shirt and pulled out a fresh one – navy with a double collar in white. He checked himself in the mirror and ran his fingers through his blonde layers and jogged back to Bruce waiting in the truck. Jake lunged in and fastened his seat belt. "My renegade is going legit. Man, this is something to celebrate."

Bruce adjusted his seat belt over his full taut chest, backed out of the drive and checked out Jake, "You were in there primpin', huh?"

"Just changed my shirt."

"Let's go to that hole-in-the-wall place in Maxton."

"Hadn't been there in years."

"I have," Bruce's smile dug deep, and the truck rolled, "Like watching that old man whiz the dough around on his finger. It's cool."

"Yea, it is. I remember him. There's paintings on the ceiling, right?"

"Yep, and on the walls. Owners are good people. They knew Mom."

On the highway, Bruce kept his truck in the fast lane, passing the slugs. One hand on the wheel, another on the door's arm rest. "You sure keep the truck clean," Jake tested the ashtray.

"Take care of what I've got."

"I've seen the inside of this truck when I wouldn't let a flea live in it. Must be Thelma's boot camp." Jake slapped the top of his thighs in cadence, "Left, clean, left, clean, left," and laughed, but Bruce stared ahead, "I was drinking more product than test tasting. I don't know. Drinking made me lazy. I could tell a difference right away and Thelma had a lot to do with it. She put the fear in me. She's my legal guardian and can make my life living hell. She cares though. It's the way I remember Mom."

"That's all right, Bruce. I'm glad. And Mark?"

"Mark's a good kid, the little brother I never had. We fight some, but no big stuff. He's like you, been college-bound all along. Got him an account started."

"You're all right. Isn't it funny how things happen? You needed a mom and got one. I moved away, closest thing you had to a brother. And you got a new brother."

Bruce smiled at him. "Thought about that, too. Thelma and Mark are my real family. Guess that's why it's gettin' to me that they're going to have to move. I dread it. Thelma's been my mom, but she's stronger than Mom was. She left her husband after the first slap. Won't take junk from no one."

"Like you."

"Yep, and I did some serious buckin' and kickin' when Thelma first started in. But she didn't take any of my junk. Tried to run away once and she carried my things to the end of the drive."

"Dang, that is tough love. What happened?"

"Two trucks passed and neither stopped to pick me up. Knew both drivers, too. Got dark and those coyotes seemed to get closer and closer, know what I mean?" They laughed and Bruce looked up to the iridescent sky. "Man up there knows. Certain of it. Had to carry it all back in, by myself. Then I had to write her an apology."

"And you did it?"

"I did it. Got up the next morning and stared at that paper like I could set it to fire. Took all afternoon to write that one paragraph. I was burnt slam up, wanted to go in the kitchen and, and hit her or something. But she opened up the oven and her broccoli casserole got the better of me."

"Saved by the broccoli, who'd a seen that coming?" Jake laughed.

"She and Momma are two of kind," Bruce swallowed. "I owe her. Know of any nice places for her and Mark?"

"No. What about her fiancé? Won't he move them in with him?"

"That's their future plan. Don't know when. They haven't set a date. She won't move in with him till they're married."

"Tell her you got a buyer. Then they'll set a date."

"Thought about that, but she'll be hurt."

Suddenly, Jake's cross face filled the cab. "You never have a problem with manipulating me," and immediately Bruce's chin aimed up at the sky. His jaw tightened as he stared straight ahead then took a deep breath and delivered his calculated answer. "What was I going to do, beg? I can't ask anyone else but you."

"Why?"

"You're the only real friend I've got," he eyeballed Jake, "Satisfied?"

"Yea, ditto."

"We only get one of those in life." Bruce passed another car. He went from the fast lane to the slug lane and back again. When the needle hit seventy-five Bruce smugly said, "When I get my new place you could live there. We could set you up with a trailer."

"Really?"

"Yea, you could be on dog patrol."

"That won't work. I want to raise dogs, heal animals, all kinds."

"Then you're right. It won't work. I don't want no dogs peeing on my vines, digging up my property or running off with my property." Bruce's hateful words filled the void between them. "Business is business and I'm not gonna let some filthy dogs interfere with my profit."

Jake cooled his hot hand out the window in the cool early evening air. "Police dogs come through the vet's office for their exams all the time. Sit for some. Gonna raise German Shepherds. The officers say I'm a natural dog trainer."

"That's a laugh."

"No, it isn't. Bet I could even train that mangy dog of Scarecrow's to like grooming."

"You want to raise shepherds because of Miss Scarlet."

"That's part of it. She was a smart dog."

"If she was so friggin' smart why didn't she save me?"

Jake wildly blinked, "Dog knew she'd be killed. I don't know. Your dad probably hit her at some point. He hit everything." He sat so still he looked like he'd been turned to stone.

"He didn't hit Mom's dog," Bruce nearly squeaked.

"She's always carrying it around, petting it or talking to it. Could the dog even walk?"

Bruce threw his head back and snickered, "Momma said Muffin knew words. She had that baby trained. Knew the difference between a wet dish cloth and dry. Put the wet ones in the laundry basket. She even taught it to wipe its feet on a rug before it came inside."

"I remember that."

"Dad sort a liked her. It didn't act like a dog."

"He never hit Muffin?"

"Don't think so. Once in a while he'd give her scraps. He'd do it to make up to Mom, for being mean." Bruce swallowed as they passed the restaurant's worn billboard.

"You say the pizza people knew your mom?"

"Mom worked here when she was young and after she and Dad married, they'd come
up and they'd always give 'em a deal. Mom said they'd make up a special or say they had a fake call in. Mom would jump in and help. She liked it. Mom liked people. I must get it from her."

"Right," Jake drawled it out into two long sarcastic syllables. "When did you become a people person? You get some cordiality lessons?"

"Naw," he laughed, "I can read people. I get along with anyone, long as they don't misrepresent themselves."

"What stations you got programmed on your radio?" Bruce pressed the button and fiddles and a dulcimer tinged and pinged while Jake tapped the handrest. When the instruments ceased and a torn-up gal singing a sad ballad began Jake popped his thigh. "All we need now is a drink of Muscadine."

"Like this, huh?"

"It's all right. Listen to a lot of country. Like the eighty sounds, too."

"I want to fill the store with this." Bruce changed the station and a Celtic ballad strummed. "Met a dulcimer player at a wine tasting in Southern Pines." Jake interrupted, "You go to wine tastings? That's so friggin' bizarre coming from you. Gotta admit I never thought you'd be the one."

"Be the one to what?"

"Make it big."

"That's what I thought. That's what everybody thinks," Bruce huffed. "Well, everybody is gonna be real surprised." His tongue flicked across his full lips. "I'm buying a piece down by the railroad in Pembroke. I want you to be a part of it, Jake," his grays softened.

"How? I want to work with animals."

"But I trust you not to cheat me."

"You'll come across someone who wants to work wine, someone you can trust."

Bruce sat rigid, "You can train dogs on the side."

"I could. But I wanna be a veterinarian."

"Then be one."

"I told you, there's not enough money. The economy sucks. Advertising's getting cut all
over. And we have too much to qualify for a grant."

"What about a loan?"

"If the economy turns around that'll be a choice. Right now, I can barely afford gas to drive to school. It's so bad Dad told me to work this first year I'm out and go to the community college next year."

"Like you said before, it's funny how things happen. You're going to college with me, Jake. I'll pay you enough to help move the company to cover your first year."

"You'd do that?"

"Don't you get it?" Bruce barked, "You're my brother," his eyes burned, "Indian or not," he wiped his nose with his forearm as the evening's orange sky blended into the pine's sparkling treetops and faded into a darkened purple as night called and the methodic rhythm of the tires rolled down the highway mimicking the music of ocean waves.

"Help me think of a name for the winery," Bruce broke. "It's the only thing I haven't figured it out yet."

"Okay. How about naming it GotDat Winery? Or Pow Wow Winery, uh, Chief Black's Winery!"

"That's close to what I've been thinking. Zoskiroro's," Bruce diplomatically offered, as Jake made dunce faces which unbeknownst to him, were reflected in the pizzeria window as the truck parked front-center. The pizza dough twirled on the old man's finger like a muted dinner bell as Jake blurted, "Zoskiroro. Zosky's Winery, Zoskroo's, Funky Zoro's," until Bruce told him to quit, "Zoskiroro was another name for Tuscarora. The chief of Zoskiroro was ZackuSarah, one of the baddest chiefs known," Bruce explained as he stepped into the parking lot, "Lederer ran up with him in 1670 and was so terrified he handed over his weapons immediately." $_{15}$ "Bad dude," Jake exaggeratedly mimed a terrified man handing over his weapons to "Bruce The Chief," but when Bruce wouldn't play along, Jake pretended to throw his pistols, one at a time, over his shoulder – one from each hip, his belly gun, his ankle-biter, and one strapped to his back and Bruce played along by kicking gravel over them as if he'd buried the stash, and they entered with delight and saliva-filled mouths as the browned crusts and piping hot pepperoni scents rushed over them. "Welcome, laddie!" Cheered the familiar old man as he twirled the dough from one finger over his bald head to his sprawled-out fingertips on the other hand.

The fresh-faced waitress sported a ponytail, white apron over her black outfit and carried a fresh basket of hot buttery breadsticks. Bruce and Jake agreed on an all meat pizza with extra cheese and two large sweet teas. "You have such fine hands to do such hard work," Jake absorbed her pepperoni and lemon dish detergent scent, "Someone must be taking good care of you."

"Good try," her ponytail bounced, "Anything else? Side salads?"

Jake answered, "Not this time," while Bruce dismissed her with a flick of his chin and Jake checked out the paintings, "See that one, next to the door?" It was a black velvet, ten-by-fourteen with the classical poker playing dogs. "Remind you of anyone?"

"Could be - Dad's the boxer," Bruce centered the salt and parmesan cheese as they broke out in toothy grins. Black velvets, all paint by numbers and a few freehand paintings were mounted everywhere. They covered the walls and the ceiling. Families with children fidgeting with silverware, couples consumed with one another, and loud old people filled the pizzeria's wooden tables. "Where are you moving The Company to?" Jake blurted.

Bruce's nose widened as the waitress served their large sweet teas in the thick red mottled plastic glasses, the good ones that hold the cold in the glass, not in your hand. After the waitress walked away, Bruce leaned across the table and whispered, "Out of town."

"Oh, got it," Jake looked around the restaurant to see if he recognized anyone. When he was confident he continued, "Is it far from me?"

Bruce rolled his eyes and pursed his lips in the hush gesture, "Out of town," they leaned across the table until their noses could have touched, "five miles from you. Before you get to the tracks, coming from 71, take a left. There's no visible road, just a grass path right now. But just wait." Bruce sipped his sweet tea, smiled, and quietly said, "It's like buying back my history."

"How's it your history?"

"My people come from there," He leaned across the table again and beamed. "We're the ones who established the Tuscarora of Robeson County."

"How do you figure that?"

"My granddad. His told him. It's tribal." Bruce's chest rose. "All real Tuscs know."

"Know what? I've lived in Maxton all my life. I never heard anything about Tuscs settling the county. There's the Brooks Reservation [16] but we just know there's Indians there."

"You're not a Tusc," Bruce looked around and leaned in closer, "Our history isn't taught at school. It's told from the elders. My real people were Dials and Locklears."

"Wait - Are you telling me that Chavis Black is not your real dad?"

"Yes, it's a fluke that I even know. Mom told me just a few days before she died. That's when I started questioning this Lumbee heritage stuff and got hooked up at the university. Without the research, I wouldn't know. The real Tuscarora history just isn't taught in school. Period," he stared at his knuckles, "Sometimes I think she was getting ready to leave him," Bruce's head hung lower, "and I was fed a sack of lies all my life."

"I'm sorry. That's something you'll carry to your grave, huh?"

They locked eyes when the waitress dropped the metal tray and pizza crusts scattered across the tile. They both stretched out to see if the pizza was ready on the pick-up counter, and the waitress called out, "False alarm, not yours. Yours is going in now." Flames licked at the shiny steel pan and the fire's woody scent lofted over.

"Dad's people, the Blacks, were given a hundred-acre allotment by his owner after emancipation. He married a Tuscarora and in the deal got a passel of free labor. They lived like Indians do, in units and apparently, she insisted that her family live on the land with them. We'd still have that hundred if Dad hadn't bet it off. But we got the pond and twenty of it. Better than nothing."

"I don't smell any liquor. I don't smell any wine," Jake sniffed at the air, "I smell a storyteller." He pointed at Bruce and when he wouldn't take the bait, changed his tone, "Tuscarora don't want to be associated with the Lost Colony, do they?"

"I shouldn't even tell you," Bruce swallowed and scanned the other diners and when no one was looking their way, leaned up closer until nearby conversations invaded their space.

They took long sips of tea and simultaneously stared at the spinning dough behind the counter until the television in the upper right corner fuzzed. When a man scooted his chair back and his heavy boots boomed across the tile to turn the channel the people seated nearby said they didn't want to listen to that sport's announcer. The lady with them said she was going to change it as soon as that man left.

"They don't even know we're here," Jake stared down Bruce, "Tell me. I really want to know this stuff."

Bruce sported a winning smile, "I know. I know you do. What's it worth to you?"

"Oh, man, you always do that. Okay, how about I help you move?"

"You already said you'd help me move."

"I agreed to help you move The Company," Jake quipped, "I didn't agree to help you move from the house." With his hand shaped like a gun, Bruce surrendered, laying his gun on the table, "You got me."

Like a six-year-old kid, Jake confiscated the pretend gun. "So, tell me already," as he greedily sipped his tea and spilled it and the waitress ran over and quickly wiped it up with a thick white towel as she informed them that their pizza was in the oven and wouldn't be much longer. When she walked away, Bruce leaned to Jake, looking over his shoulder as she approached the counter and hummed over her healthy hams and Jake's green eyes glazed over like hot honey.

They sat stretching out across the table like they were sharing secrets, "The Lost Colony and Tuscarora Peoples blended. In schools around here, it's all about Croatoan being carved on a tree and pushing the Algonquian agenda for Lumbee enrollment. Teachers don't go deeper, to the truth. Croatoan Island is Hatteras Island and is Hatteras the region, a huge tract of land, originally named Katearas by Tuscs. It's marked in a 1585 map that Katearas is the same. [17] Names were spelled out phonetically. Like Hatteras was taken from the Tuscarora word for their trading camps, Katearas, so the elders say and it's only logical to deduce that this variation occurred as educated people encroached the native areas. The research goes on about how the Tuscarora left the coastal areas due to violence and chose to live in the swamps as farmers."

Jake picked up his glass and handed it out for an invitation to toast, "You're off the swamp, Buddyrow. Sound like a freakin' lawyer or something."

"Sorry, just read all the time and sometimes regurgitate it. Trust me, I'm still on the swamp, Buddyrow, when I need to be."

"So, why do we hear Croatoans and Lumbee were with the colony people?" Jake rubbed his belly, "I'm starving, you?" "Yeah, it's worth the wait, remember? Eat another breadstick. I already had two." Jake pushed the breadstick halfway in and wiped off the liquid butter with the back of his hand as Bruce leaned across the table again, "Public schools teach government indoctrination. Textbooks and instructors are required to teach under regulated plans, and they do not have an Indian scribe from each of the Six Nations hired for any plans or books. What we got in school was from the white perspective because they won America," the vein in Bruce's forehead grew more pronounced. "The Lumbees are sixty-thousand strong and those people don't want to hear about Tuscaroras. This generation believes they are Cherokee or Cheraw. It wasn't a month ago, I spoke with an attorney who dabbles in history as a member of some lost colonist club who really believes that there is only a slim chance that colonists mixed with Tuscarora and he thinks it's because of the river boundary and due to them being so bloodthirsty. I got a map I need to show him one day. [18] The Tuscarora were all over these Sandhills and I know just by looking around here tonight, with the dark-skinned family sporting their red-head baby, that we mixed. Look at all the curls," Bruce leaned back and waved for the waitress and she motioned that their pizza was being cut.

It's about blood and I got a string of charts with Tuscarora families here in Robeson County going back to 1778 that no government official can debunk." [19]

"I still feel like you're not telling me everything. You have a history of that," Jake drank an entire glass of sweet tea and waved for a refill. "If only this were beer. Maybe that'd loosen your lips." Bruce was all smiles as he rocked backward in his straight back chair when his cell phone rang. He checked the number and answered, "Go to one." He listened.

"Then hit 211 this time and take your time. Call me when you're tucked in," and folded it back down into his jean's pocket.

"Always on duty."

"Not hard to guess what that was about."

Bruce cleared his throat. "Tuscaroras are everywhere. You see, not all the Tusc prisoners stayed in Maxton."

"Prisoners?"

"Jake, my people've handed down this story for generations. We all know. Zoskiroros took the colonists as slaves and had children with them and some of them married freed Blacks."

"That's not how I learned it."

"Who wrote the history books? I told you this already."

"I guess it was researchers, institutions, businesses."

Bruce's gapped mouth clenched, "The conquerors who ended up owning every freakin' thing. Caucasians wrote what we're supposed to accept. Think about it: Schools don't want any riots. Too many Lums around to teach the truth. Schools teach what's politically correct and go on about how Lums're recognized by the state and sooner or later hope to get on like the Cherokees. But the real trigger is the Cherokees want all the funds for themselves and we Tuscarora want restitution. Besides, some of our Lums are really Tusc."

"Do you have any proof?"

"What kind of proof are you wantin'?"

"Something in writing or an artifact with some kind of certification. One of those reports where someone traced their roots back to the English."

"Yea, that's it," Bruce motioned for Jake to get closer, "Or get some DNA from White's descendants and trace it back to me," he whispered, "I overheard that one when Dad was calling her out on a bad night."

"That's large, cuz. Youse a nugget a history- Lost Colony mystery solved. Piss me off and I'll hold you for ransom," Jake guffawed, but when Bruce scowled, Jake sat up tall, "Contact someone over in England and ask. There's gotta be research on them and there's gotta be at least one who'd be willing to help." They resumed normal positions and Jake rested his chin on his propped hand, "Okay, that's a long shot. What about the internet? Get on the Lost Colony site. Post your theory and,"

Bruce interrupted. "It's not a theory. I know who I am." The Lumbee families sitting at nearby tables turned in acknowledgement.

"I believe you, Bruce. It's not me you have to convince." Jake surveyed the restaurant's colorful tables as the ponytailed waitress brought their piping hot heavy meat pizza. The sweltering heat brought out her womanly scents permeating Bruce and Jake as she placed the hot pizza on the center of their table. She smelled of freshly sliced bell peppers, musky young woman sweat, and bacon. Lots of strong bacon scents like she must have helped chop it and wiped it across her apron like a love-spell.

The red-cheeked waitress served Bruce, then Jake and quietly darted off to the table in the back with the loud toddler in the highchair happily slinging stringy cheese smothered in pizza sauce in all directions. A long string of red cheese landed on the black velvet poker playing dogs striking the bulldog with a haunting gash across the skull. After the waitress carefully pulled it off and wiped the painting free of sauce with her thick white towel the young men turned their attention to devouring their pizza.

With a slice aimed at his chin, Bruce leaned across the table. "You're right about one thing; Lums don't want it known about English blood. They want federal recognition. In the 1800's they were close, and again in the 1960's with Kennedy. But no one else wants them getting federal funds, especially the big tribes." He pointed at Jake with his slice. "The Lumbees are right off highway ninety-five and drug trafficking there is already horrific. Fed's won't recognize the Lumbee because they think they only want to open big gambling rigs. Majority do. But the wise ones know the Tribe'd be a regular Sodom and Gomorrah. They've stuck a no-gambling policy on their website now." He smiled and crammed down the pizza slice.

"I'm so proud of you. You've really done a lot of research and I love listening to all this history fresh from the mule's mouth," he showed his teeth like a mule doing the flehmen response, and Bruce held his napkin over his stuffed mouth. "I remember this trip we took right before Momma died. It was real secret-like and everyone was touching my head. I don't know. Maybe it was a dream." Bruce folded over the next slice in his hand, opened his mouth like it was a big oven and pushed it in as he placed another slice on his plate.

"You mean they were popping your noggin for mommucking like you always did? You were so rowdy."

"Naw, naw," Bruce's chewed extra fast as he held up his finger, "Don't try to talk on the swamp if you can't do it right. It was a ceremony. We'd gone to that play, *Strike at the Wind,* and I can still see Momma's face every time I hear those lines in my head, "My great great great great great grandmother was Virginia Dare." [20] At the meeting, seems like they gave Momma something or passed it around and Momma held it a long time. Anyway, I do remember what they said about The Society. No one outside the walls could know; hush-hush the whole time."

"Could know what?"

Bruce flashed a quick smile then leaned across the table. "This real old guy, bent over. He was white headed, had Momma sitting in a chair out in the middle and I had to sit on somebody's lap and I really didn't want to and the old guy said she was a queen." Bruce picked up the red glass hexagon decanter and held it up to the light and then over his head like a crown, "Uaah," Jake's greens adorned the ruby crown before Bruce shook out the parmesan cheese covering his steamy slice. "I love this pizza. This whole place, makes me think of Mom." He shook out more cheese until the next slice was snowed. Took a sip of tea and looked around the room and strained toward the party room, but it was closed. "Proof would be real nice. Maybe God'll give me that next."

"Yeah, real nice or a great way to get killed off."

Chapter 4

Between the Lines Now

Miss Lucy held the door open, "I wasn't excepting anyone," while her faded flannel and blue jeans held faint traces of soil. "I've been pulling weeds, getting ready for spring. Tried crowding them out with radishes last summer, but the weeds won." Her fingertips pat at her forehead down to her neck as if she was damping off sweat beads. "If weeds were dollars, I'd be rich," she laughed but Jake didn't budge, "Someone poisoned my dogs," Jake's eyes were lined in red, "Onacona didn't make it."

"Your girlfriend's dog?"

"Fiancé," Jake quivered, "vet still has two."

"When do you think it happened?"

"Had to be last night."

"Oh, Jake, I'm so sorry."

"I was worried about you."

She asked if he needed something to drink as her gaped face drew in heaps of warm air. He pulled off his boots and placed them on the rubber mat beside the front door she had placed especially for him and took a seat on the divan. When she returned with two tall glasses of sweet tea with lemon he was bent over with his head in his hands. She placed their drinks on the magazine and ran her hand over his back. "I'm so sorry, Jake. This will pass."

"No. We've got to stop."

"Oh, no," her outburst surprised him, "we've come so far."

"It's just the beginning. Scarecrow told me."

"You talk to this man?"

"He's a friend, yeah. Said there's rumors. Like they've been rumored to make accidents happen in the past." He looked up at her like a baby bird from its nest. "It's no secret. The more enrollees in the Lumbee Tribe the more money they get and that's the only reason they hold onto the Tuscarora as a splinter tribe and then say they can't give them assistance until properly enrolled Lumbees are served. It's a 21st century tribal war!"

"Rumors about this have been around a long time."

"You've heard 'em?"

"In passing."

"What does that mean?"

"I didn't have anything relevant to add to the conversation. I walked away."

"So, you agree."

"No." She rolled her head. "The council is an educated group of business leaders. They wouldn't dirty their hands with criminal tricks."

Jake sprung up, "You'll be next."

"No one wants me," She palmed the stacks of papers on her desktop and turns around to

face him. "I'm invisible, the old librarian."

When Jake jerked a crumbled paper from his front jeans pocket and pushed it at her she flattened it out and anger filled her pale frame. Red crayon spelled out the jagged note:

"Done mommucked up. Let it be or thoust be next."

"Ridiculous," she spat, but as the sheers waved the freshly mown grass sounded off alarms and she stood frozen. "I never open the windows. Not with my allergies." When she struggled and the tight wooden frame wouldn't budge, Jake told her to move over and asked who mowed her grass and she said that it was a young man from her church and that she was certain he was not responsible.

"You're coming home with me," his command pleaded like his heavy greens, and with the newest revision safely in her arms they roared down the blacktop. "I've gotta make a phone call before we get on the highway," he said and she grasped the Jesus bar as he left a message for Scarecrow meet them, "I'm not sure what to do here. Hoping you can help me out," he pushed his phone back into his jean's pocket.

Scarecrow and Lilly rushed to meet Jake and Miss Lucy on the highway and made contact in less than five minutes and decided it would be best to follow them back to Miss Lucy's house.

"Don't worry," Scarecrow's short deep words kept them glued, "They'll be back, and we'll be ready," he assured her. They gathered her clothes and toiletries, five pairs of shoes, her computer and shut off the water. "You'll be fine at Jake's. The Crowsons always have someone around to keep an eye on things," Miss Lilly reassured her. With Miss Lucy's key in his pocket, Scarecrow strode into the kitchen, "Do you have flour and peanut butter?"

"Yes," Miss Lucy hurriedly pulled it from her pantry and in moments her doorknobs were set, and doorways prepared. "Mmm, no recorders or wires, just food staples? Seems like your concern is rather relaxed." Scarecrow backed out of the living room threshold and waved for everyone to go outside as he floured the front door's entryway."

"Old timers knew what they were doing, Sugar," Lilly directed Miss Lucy to Jake's truck and Miss Lucy pulled out her car keys and informed them that she must take her car. "I have to get to work."

"What do you think, Hon?" Lilly asked Scarecrow.

"We'll follow you there. Jake leads."

Jake's little house on the Crowson's farm was lit up inside and out. "Is someone here?" Miss Lucy asked as they carried her essentials. "Naw, I uh, I turned on the lights when I went to get you," he opened the door, and she asked, "To get me?" and he laughed, "You know what I mean, to warn you." The historic 1800's thick wood paneling and fireplace mantel was maple and the ceiling was hand-hewn tongue-and-groove white oak. The country dust and bristly German Shepherd hairs flaked across the heart pine floor as they trafficked through to the guest room decorated in steel blue with country curtains. Jake pointed to the bathroom and his bedroom and to the door with the heavy-duty lock and told her that it was part of a historical tour and they didn't use it unless it was an emergency. "I've heard about the Underground Railroad tours here and never took the time and now I'm going to live in it. How crazy life is sometimes!" She clasped her hands over her stomach while she nervously giggled, "I haven't had supper, Jake. Do you have anything to make sandwiches?" Lilly offered to help as Jake handed Scarecrow a beer. Miss Lucy sliced the roast beef very thinly and used two lettuce leaves and Lilly found pickles and chips and they set the table.

"So, uh," Scarecrow swallowed, "what *are* you two doing every night?"

"We are working on a pamphlet for the library on Robeson's unique vernacular," Miss Lucy's busy little hands flew, "I have a clipping from The Fayetteville Observer, 2017," she rushed to the living room table where she'd placed her files and produced the clipping to read it aloud as Scarecrow leaned back in his chair.

"The late Adolph Dial, a Lumbee Indian who headed up the Department of American Indian Studies at University of North Carolina at Pembroke and served in the N.C. House of Representatives, was convinced that the lost colonists were the ancestors of the Lumbees. He believed that he himself was a descendant of Virginia Dare. Dial was 73 when he died in 1995."

Miss Lucy cleared her throat, "Dial said, "The oral tradition is clear that Virginia Dare's family survived and that the Dials in Robeson County are her descendants," he told the Chicago

Tribune in a story published Aug. 18, 1987. "Even today, if you pronounce Dare with the accent people speak here, it sounds very much like Dial. ... Not only that, there are at least 41 names of the lost colonists that are still among our people here in Robeson County — names like Brooks, Berry and Jones." [21] "Elizabethan era influence is still heard

today. A young man was in the library a few weeks ago and said that he was "gaumed up" in the reference section and wanted help. Gaum is the Elizabethan term for mess."

"That's our language – a mess," Lilly laughed, "Thoust bes a kyarn cooter get snatched up by Scarecrow!" she piled on the Southern drawl and he grabbed her wrists in a make-

"Kids, listen to Miss Lucy," Jake schooled them, and she apologized, "Well, they might be tired of me."

"No, we're not," Lilly's sincerity sang.

"Oral history was the tradition of early people everywhere. Why it's discounted for Indians is the selfish conspiracy of the government to deny appropriations," Miss Lucy's finger dashed, "Take Locklear. It's unique to this region. In 1790, it was spelled, "Lockaleer," on the census, and the oral history is that it means waterfall. In the book, "Indians of North Carolina," she pulled the book from her satchel, "Locklaha is referred to as a Cherokee word and that's acceptable because the Iroquoian language was spoken by both Tuscarora and Cherokee. There were several dialects, and they used a lot of the same words." The book sported bright sticky tabs with her penned references that created a bouquet of colors as she spread it open on the table. "I'm not saying this is absolute, but I am saying that oral history needs more credibility. It is only commons sense when you see "Locklear" in these different spellings, considering the accents, that it is quite plausible. Walk into any business in Prospect and listen to someone pronounce it: Lock-a-leer."

Scarecrow sat up and said, "Elders say we used word pictures, metaphors, like "it's a nose-cutting morning" for it's cold.[22] Locklaha being waterfall is the "blood that stayed" after the Tuscarora War when the Hancock group of Tuscs went to New York near the waterfall. This name doesn't show up until that period. Elders always said it's the name of the ones who stayed."

"It must be," Robin agreed, as Miss Lucy turned the page, "This section was written by Angus W. McLean in the early 1900's. There's a lot of incorrect data out there simply because research techniques were not as streamlined and a lawyer seeking election as governor is the least of credible in gathering Indian data." Her cheeks perked up, "Let me show you why: After McLean's alliance with the Robeson Indians led to changing their name from Croatan to Cherokee Indians of Robeson County, he became a senator and governor of North Carolina. It was Jim Crow's south and these Indians had been pushed to the bottom of the social ladder. They were called "Cro," in a derogatory manner and were ready to do anything to climb that social ladder and McLean knew it and used their weakness to get votes to support his interests.

He wrote this to further his interests and in doing so, helped to erase the Tuscarora legacy in this state. The Lowry gang was in every paper across the country and they wrote that he was Tuscarora. You know McLean read that. He grew up hearing it just like I grew up hearing about Vietnam. He did record some facts and my notes are all there. I've researched his research and it's clear: The Cherokee and Tuscarora both spoke Iroquoian languages, so any heritage claimed by language alone is not efficient." [23a]

Scarecrow guffawed, "Your new roomie is loaded, huh? She may have fired off to the wrong side and didn't realize it."

"Actually, you are the first I've recited this to and Jake is helping me with his history of the language because he grew up playing with children who spoke the vernacular and has employees who still do," Miss Lucy flipped the pages.

"She knows her stuff," Jake gleamed as Miss Lucy tapped at the page, "Read this." They took turns reading the page and Lilly looked up at her, "I don't see the problem."

"The problem is that it is wrong, all wrong. That James Lowry was saying his people were Cherokee to satisfy the writer, Governor McLean, who cleverly writes that Lowry's ancestors signed the 1806 Jay Treaty as Cherokees, the one allowing access to travel and trade from here to Canada which then was then Great Britain. McLean writes that Lowry said the Locklears were originally named "Braveboy," and mentions a 1790 census, but research today shows that this James Lowry, born in 1833, is the descendant of William L. Locklear, born in

1778, and he was Tuscarorian. Lowry wanted to be identified as the Cherokee, plain and simple, because the Tuscarora were known as the hostiles in Robeson County. Read that page." [23b]

"She's got it down now," Scarecrow nodded, "Up to now, it's all been word of mouth you might say."

Miss Lucy fished out a notebook and turned to a genealogy chart, "There's James Lowry, date of birth is 1833. The date of the McLean's publication is 1915. That makes it true that Lowry was indeed 82, but this testimony," her fingertip pressed white against the chart, "is from the Duke Professor, Dr. Peter Wood, who is an authority on the Tuscarora – let me clarify, he is an expert witness. Dr. Wood gave this to me to use for the greater good and," her eyes met Jake's and she joked at herself with a resounding clap and her head tilted back, "I get too carried away. I just love language. I've collected sociolinguistic evidence from natives and our Chapel Hill experts. I'll get the vernacular pamphlet in print soon enough." [23c]

"McLean coached those Indians for votes, huh?" Scarecrow smirked and Jake sighed, "Like Hamilton McMillan coached for his votes and has a following of sixty-thousand all the way into the 21st century. One day, those real Indians are going to get rid of McMillan's statue."

Lilly slapped her thigh, "Won't change a thing, will it?"

"You know McLean was buying votes when he wrote this, not only from uninformed citizens, but from congress too because soon after, he served in the treasury department," her rigid frame proclaimed. "No telling what he promised that man to coerce him into saying he's Cherokee."

"But if you go to the Bureau of Indian Affairs with this," Lilly pondered, "they'll wonder how you can claim political bias when Adolf Dial was also in government. He was a North Carolina House Representative."

"Yes," Miss Lucy agreed, "but Dial was a history professor and was requested to join the house as a Native American Indian. He created the American Indian Studies program at the university. His legacy lives on today in the Lumbee Bank and shopping centers and buildings dedicated in his name. He was a giver, not a taker." [24]

"I get it," Lilly interrupted, "Dial invested in us. McLean profited from us."

"Yes, and more than that, McLean wrote the Tuscarora out of history. He has a record of less than honorable mention," Miss Lucy shrugged, "They both grew up on farms, were educated, but somewhere McLean lost his raising. He wouldn't even vote against child labor laws. What kind of man does that?" [25]

A silent chord played as they each dealt with the history and when Jake pondered aloud how to present those facts in a court of law, Scarecrow and Lilly replied, "With a lawyer." Rounds of relieving laughter hugged the guests "good-bye," with promises of morning phone calls and getting together again – soon.

After Scarecrow's truck had left the drive, Jake complimented Miss Lucy on her quick-thinking and asked, "How much research is in your file?"

"I'm not done. You are welcome to read it, Jake, but you need to read the draft of Chapter 4 before you do anything else. If I'm going to be stuck away from home, I'll need to keep busy writing to keep from worrying myself to death." She handed him the draft and he told her goodnight as he propped up on bed pillows.

Miss Lucy called out, "Jake?"

"Yes?"

"All this unexpectedness, the rushing and fright, reminds me of when the Tuscarora surprised the colonists in the seventeen-hundreds and were ostracized. We never know really, when our time is going to be called. Thank you for being my friend, Jake."

"We're fine. Get to sleep, lady."

When the cover page still read, "Lumbees Undone," Jake Wilkes, Co Author, H. Prickenrath," Jake hollered out, "We need to talk about this title in the morning," and she exaggeratedly yawned like a bird being squeezed.

"Keep that up and the buzzards will be after us too."

Childlike laughter ran the halls and Miss Lucy sighed in relief as Jake reviewed her work.

"*Chapter 4, Between the Lines Then*: On a Thursday night at ten-forty-five, the phone rang. Jake's sleepy eyes sprang open as he sat up and his dad walked down the hall. He opened the door and handed Jake the phone. "I don't know who it is. She sounds hysterical," Mr. Wilkes grumbled.

Jake swung his legs over the bed, "Hello?" as Bruce's phony feminine sang, "Time," in a girlish squeaky voice Jake crammed his tongue to the back of his throat to keep from laughing and waved at his dad to leave. When he finally closed the door, Jake said, "I'll be right there."

Mr. Wilkes was standing in front of the kitchen sink when Jake appeared fully dressed.

"My number got out as someone to call to help with deliveries. Gotta go." Jake sat the phone back on its charger. "Pups could be in trouble."

"Where?" Mr. Wilkes stepped toward the counter nearer to Jake. "Are they paying you for this?"

"They'll give me a little something," Jake swallowed, "I'll be back."

Mr. Wilkes' wedding band twanged the top of the counter like a snare as he gruffly whispered, "What time should I expect you?" Without a flinch, Jake punched his time-card, "By daylight." Mr. Wilkes sipped his grape juice, "Be careful."

Pulling the door behind him, Jake called out, "I know what I'm doing. Don't worry," as he flicked on the floodlights, patted the trunk, slid in and pulled out of the drive. "Come on, Crash," he begged the big old four-door.

Bruce was twenty minutes away so with the window down and the radio up Jake peeled off on his mission of mercy. "The puppies I deliver tonight are gonna be big dogs one day- the business that puts Maxton on the map. Good-gooboly-goo." He sang with every song that blared out of the radio as he rushed, but not more than five miles over the speed limit, to the dirt road.

The badly washed and pitted dirt road took seven minutes to safely travel down to the dead end where The Company was hidden. But the seven minutes stalled into what felt like thirty sweltering minutes in the hot ass car. With no wind, the heat sweltered up like a barbeque pit. There were washes, some two feet wide and a drop off in a curve that looked like there was nowhere else to go, but off a cliff's edge. Jake put Crash into park and jumped out and shook his damp tee shirt off and tried to move the boulders.

Bruce and Jake had made them, thanks to masonry class during their freshman year when they learned how to make sculptural forms with vermiculite and cement. Jake had taken the class when Bruce suggested that they'd have fun. Making the boulders was the last thing Jake helped with before finally cutting ties with the The Company altogether.

Jake struggled to pick up the big cumbersome boulder blocking the path. It had absorbed some water through the years. But it didn't weigh near what a normal three-foot circumferential boulder weighed. Jake rolled the others till he made room to the grass-lined path for Crash. He jumped back in and turned off the headlights. The moist grass reflected the partly cloudy sky's three-quarter moon's light, making the sand grass shine silver. Jake sat up in the seat straining to see the sandy path then jerked to a stop as he realized he forgot to put the boulders back in place. He popped back out, leaving the car door open and walked back about ten feet. He scanned the area, feeling like he was being watched, and didn't see a thing except dark timberline.

As faint footsteps harkened, he jerked around to look and then hurried down the sandy grass path. He lifted a boulder and cautiously turned back around to place it into position. He checked again for the faint footsteps. He placed another and checked again. He repeated the steps until done. A soft wind swayed, and treetops swooshed as he hurried back to Crash. He jumped in and slammed the door when something cold pressed against his neck. He clasped his neck then ne'r 'bout sat on the dash as he checked the back seat. A giant dog stared straight on.

Jake leapt from Crash. Flung open the back door. Pointed for the giant dog to get out and was surprised when it did. It had the outline of a German Shepherd. As the dog disappeared into the dark timberline Jake nervously laughed as he wiped sweat from his forehead. "Okay," he sighed as he closed the door, started Crash and eased down the dark tree-lined path confident the fright of the night had come and gone.

As he squirreled down the worn narrow path the chrome on Bruce's truck sparkled. He pulled in behind, the only place to park, and walked around the bend to The Company. Lanterns were spaced along on the ground to line the foot path like there was some kind of shindig about to commence. Twenty feet from the stills, a ping pierced like a cymbal and Bruce's shadow became clearer. Bruce had most of the stills dissembled and stopped stacking the stainless steel and copper to wave. Still, metal clunked and clinked as frogs croaked and the wind swept the timberline like a hush-a-bye song over the soft pat of water against the rocks.

Jake carefully made his way over The Company's loose parts. Stainless steel buckets and copper were strewn everywhere, both squirrelly and jointed. He alternately checked for clear stepping and for Bruce as he cautiously managed the hazardous path with its grabby thorn bushes and what looked like moccasin tails hangin' from overhead limbs. Just as Jake was about to shout out good-gooboly-goo, a figure in the lantern's light filled the hideout. Fire lit up in Jake's eyes like they had their own lantern wicks. "Behind you!"

But instead of scrambling for cover Bruce laughed, along with the figure. Slowly, the figure behind Bruce grew familiar. Then a dog appeared from the black timberline and jogged straight up to Jake. It sat and whined like it really was Miss Scarlet's ghost. As he bent over to pet it Bruce warned, "Leave that dog alone and get busy. That dog's got work to do," Bruce grunted out a German command and the dog disappeared back into the black as Jake stepped closer and closer.

"What do you want me to do first, Bruce?" Jake examined the figure.

Bruce's smirk hadn't changed a bit. "That's Scarecrow."

"Hey, there," Jake called out.

"Call me Russ. Wan'na hold the light up for me while I loosen this nut?" Scarecrow wore a goofy grin and sweat beads that dotted like glitter, resembling one of those long carp out of the river that'd learned to walk on land and when he talked his mouth exaggeratedly opened real wide gasping for air and closed back again. His boots set at the end of his frame sort a' splay-footed like fins.

"Sure," Jake replied, but as he stood face to face with Bruce he whispered, "Thought I was the only one you could trust." Bruce shrugged and sucked down a bottle of water as Jake turned and left. Jake carried one of the lanterns that had lined the path and Bruce directed him to use a flashlight instead. "Good thinking, but I left mine in Crash. Didn't think I'd need it with all these lanterns," Jake replied as he neared Scarecrow and held the lantern up high to get a closer look. He was older than Jake estimated, maybe fifty, and his tall skinny frame pushed out a flabby knapsack of a belly.

"Surprised to see me?" Scarecrow asked as he strained over a tight three-quarter stainless-steel nut and the veins in his long spidery fingers wickedly pulsed.

"Your dog surprised me. Got in my backseat when I was moving the boulders."

Bruce coughed out a guffaw. "Hey, bet the Little People made the dog do it. Sneaky spirits."

"Sneaky shepherds, good watchdogs, but mine doesn't have any bite." Scarecrow cocked.

"Oh," Jake mused.

"You driving Crash?" One eyebrow lifted up halfway up across Scarecrow's forehead.

"Yeah," Jake's response lingered like a question.

"Bring the dolly?"

"It's in the trunk," Jake glanced over at Bruce.

When Scarecrow finally loosened the nut, he smacked loudly and it startled Jake.

"Nerves on end, huh? Don't worry. We're in the clear tonight. Why don't you go get the dolly? Okay?"

"All right to take the lantern?"

"Yea, but let's not give any teeny boppers lookin' for a place to park a reason to be suspicious. Keep it at ground level."

"Right." On his way down the dark grass path the dog whined, and just as he was about to pet its head Bruce warned, "Leave that dog alone."

"Chill out." Jake's harsh reply barked against the pond's lush night songs playing through the dark timberline as the dog followed him to Crash. The moon slit through the sky like an eyeball through a tiny keyhole with little light to spare as the deep green grass hushed against Jake's heavy steps. The dog's sharp whine shrilled up Jake's spine like a toten trying to get under his skin. He lifted out the dolly and closed the trunk while the dog continued to whine. He stroked its neck and the dog's sharp canines sliced his wrist. When he jerked back cussing Scarecrow whistled and the dog jogged away.

Jake reopened the trunk and pulled out a cloth from Crash's toolbox and as he did, spied the flathead screwdriver and shoved it into his boot, between his sock and the leather, just in case. He slipped his tee shirt back on and wrapped the red mechanic's cloth around his wrist, securing a knot against the hot damp sting. He grabbed his flashlight from the glove box and wedged it in his waistband at the back of his jeans. The dolly had been squeaky, dusty, and unused in his dad's storage building. So, Jake had given it a dose of lubricating oil, so it rolled like a new one, fast and furiously over the sandy grass path. Jake knocked the first copper vat he approached with his class ring and it chimed over all the other night sounds.

"Enough a' that," Bruce scowled.

"Right, Sarge," Jake sarcastically sang through his rushed breaths, "The Little People might tell the neighbors," as his dimples dug into his cheeks. Bruce's grays shot a bullet straight at Jake's forehead like a thump against his skull and it made Jake reconsider his tomfoolery. "Aren't you taking a risk, moving all this and don't really own it yet?"

"I own it." Scarecrow dropped the stainless-steel buckets into a wooden crate.

"Bruce has it going on. Everything's going his way now, even the law," Jake laughed and Bruce dashed off the fact that Russ owned it on the deed, but they had a private agreement of their own and that he was making payments, in cash.

Bruce continued organizing parts as Jake rolled the dolly up to the nearest vat and eased it on. "You got something to cover these with?"

"Got a pull-out cover affixed to the truck last week." Bruce didn't stop working. "Got the best price from a dealer in Apex. Had Cassie run it up there for me."

Jake steadied the vat. "Scarecrow, you got a tie down of some kind?" Jake struggled to keep the awkward turnip shaped copper boiler from sliding off the dolly.

"Call me Russ, if you don't mind." With long rushed steps, he brought over a handful of elastic straps from his toolbox. "You think it'd be cooler out at night."

"If wishing made it so, Russ." Jake pulled open the neck of his tee shirt and blew a cool whistle down his damp pecs, "Y'all got the flake stands hid somewhere?"

"Just drums. Hauled 'em off already. Kept the pipe works though," Bruce clarified. "We want you to haul the pipes and caps. Don't want all this together."

Scarecrow made firm eye contact with Jake, "Anything could happen."

Jake speedily fastened the straps. Rolled the dolly to the back of the truck as Bruce followed and aimed the flashlight when he unfastened the straps. "You'll follow me. Stay a car or two behind. I'll slow down for you to catch up when we get close to the tracks. If we get separated just remember that the road looks like this one, but there's steel posts with a new gate.

And if you can't find it do not drive around looking and back up in somebody's driveway. Come back here."

"Got it." They lifted the vat up into the truck bed and Jake jumped up and scooted it toward the front. He checked out Scarecrow who was kneeling down dissembling pipe. When Jake jumped down Bruce whispered, "If anything goes wrong tonight, I want you to look after Thelma." He held out his hand with a thick roll of bills.

"Like what? You think Scarecrow's going to pull something, double-cross you?" Bruce held his shoulder. "Just coverin' the bases." When Bruce signaled by cupping his package and darted his eyes. Jake pushed the roll down into his underwear. Then he stretched around the side of the truck. Scarecrow was still on his knees. "Does he help you cook and run too? I thought he just took hush money?"

"You think right." Bruce held onto the side of the truck like he was fixin' to hurl. "I've picked him up and brought him here to help. Runs jars when I'm in a bind. And he's in my pocket every month, but tonight, he showed up on his own." Footsteps gained up behind them, but it was just the dog. Bruce pulled at his sticky wet tee shirt. They made certain Scarecrow was still back there working, then Bruce explained, "We agreed to be partners when I start college. He'll distribute. I'll cook. And he gets half."

"Why?"

"He insisted. Made the deal right before you hit that vat."

"Damn," Jake winced.

"I'm startin' ta hate that Lum fool." Bruce rubbed over his hawkbill. "He's too much like my granddad's regulators. Had the balls to tell me he came by to check on his investment. Fool says he didn't have a clue I was moving tonight and expects me to take his jubious karyn just like that." Bruce's knife was still in its sheath. "I swanny. I laughed at first, sure he was just pulling my chain."

"Where's his car?"

"By Thomas's hayfield. You know the spot. We ran through there a few times when we
thought we were being scouted out instead of going straight up the trail to the back yard."

Jake fisted his hips while he spanned the distance between the fake boulders and Crash and then between The Company and the light behind the trees where the hayfield began. "He's probably been watching for years."

"Too late now," Bruce seethed. "Glad I got dad's first still hid over at my new place. His daddy made it. A turnip. Hammered. All copper. Got the cap, worm and the same thumper he used. Used to seal it up each firing with biscuit dough and clay to keep it from seeping. Fed the pilings to the hogs." Bruce wiped his jaw. "I'm tellin' you, if my old man had a caught Crow watching bes a mommucked up UC."

Suddenly, a roaring roll from the dark waters ran up their spines, and like a toten done snatched their throats, in unison they hotly whispered, "A dead UC." Again, the gator hissed, and the water rolled. Jake's eyebrows met with worry. "Gator was comin' up on the bank, wasn't it? How fast do they get around?"

"Cam down. Don't worry. I keep 'em fed." Bruce covered the surrounding ground with the flashlight. "Alice doesn't like undercover meat anyway, just chicken."

"Alice is a stupid name for a prehistoric carnivore."

"Alice the alligator, get it?" Bruce's grays danced. "I was just a kid." When he pointed to The Company, they headed back.

"Was Alice down here when we were cooking?"

"Alice's been taking care of thumper tails and any mash that got scalded. Had to beat 'er back when we cooked nanners. Kept the smells down, too. Well, cooking smells down. Been here since I was five."

"And you just forgot to mention that? Huh? Like you do every other most important detail."

"I did tell you."

"You did? Well, we sure were dumb little pricks, then. That thing could a' had us for lunch. Gawd, we were dumb."

Bruce smiled, "We were industrious entrepreneurs."

"Whatever. I really don't think I would've forgotten or blocked out Miss Alice." Jake whined as their pace quickened. Bruce did a good job counter-acting their long departure by jerking his zipper like it was stuck. He even had Jake hold a lantern on it right next to Scarecrow.

Scarecrow stood up and hollered, "Spit on it." And all three laughed.

Jake slapped his leg. "Glad it's not my zipper. I'm so nervous my spit dried up. I swear if a helicopter flew over us right now, I'd faint. I pure tee know it."

"I wouldn't bet against it." Bruce miraculously got his zipper up and whistled out a relief.

"Want a drink?" He motioned like he was going to give Jake a drink of shine from a copper worm's money piece.

"Better not. Underage. The law could be anywhere." Jake joked.

Russ struggled to pull a pipe fitting from a long curly copper coil, and they rushed over to help him. Jake grasped it with both hands while Bruce held out his hand to catch the fitting before it fell into the grass. The homemade copper band landed in Bruce's hand and he dogmatically handed it to Jake. "Make sure all these fittings are boxed up together."

He pointed to some boxes on the edge of the lantern walkway.

"Always a planner."

As Scarecrow stretched out from his tedious task of dissembling the tight-fitting pipes the lantern light highlighted his lumpy mid-section down to a small pile of pieces at his feet.

"Scarecr, I mean Russ, don't step forward. You got a pile I need to get squared away before it's lost in the grass."

"Thanks, kid. I didn't plan on working tonight." He said so incredibly distinctly, like he
was so tired he had to think to speak.

"Too many characters to play, huh?"

"When I'm not Scarecrow I'm the Wizard." Russ pointed up at the sky.

"I believe it." Jake situated the box off to the side so he wouldn't block the lantern's

light. He scanned the immediate area then back to front and center and froze at the sight of the plastic bag hanging out of Scarecrow's shirt.

"Brrring!" Like a shot, Jake sat straight up, and his pillow fell to the floor. His bedside phone rang twice while he managed Miss Lucy's pages, trying to keep his reading spot. "Hello?"

"Jake," Robin softly cooed, "did Onacona suffer? I mean, I know she did. But for a long time? Tell me the truth."

"You don't want to know."

Her grieving squeal sent Jake into a crunched-up hump.

"Gili wants to know too. You know how she is. She's already talked to someone. If her person finds the one who poisoned Onacona first there won't be any legal proceedings. Do you know what I'm telling you? Jake, she can't stand it when I'm hurting."

Silence held the line as their breathing patterns proclaimed their intent. "Come over. Spend the night," Jake kissed at the phone. "Gili said no already," Robin warned, "I can't make love to you dead."

"That's not funny."

"I don't want a husband who doesn't understand me, Jake."

"Look, there's a lot going on, Robin. Stuff going on that you are better off not knowing. I need to protect you and if that means you are going to step back for a while that may be the safest way to go."

"I don't like this. What our relationship has become. It's too scary. This just isn't normal. Dogs don't get poisoned for no reason at all. And it certainly isn't part of a normal relationship."

"Are you scared or rationalizing a break-up?"

"Not a break-up."

"Sounds like it."

"I'm not. I'm just scared."

"My cowgirl, my romping stomping cow chasing cowgirl can't be scared. Pull up the sheets and yer boots, baby. I'll bring you a gun tomorrow."

"I have a gun."

"You do?"

"A shotgun and a twenty-two. And I have a carry concealed license."

"Then what are you afraid of?"

"I'm afraid for you. Jake, they came to your place. Onacona was in your home. I'm afraid of losing you to this maniac or thugs. It could be gang related. One of those Lumbee gangs getting revenge and thought Onacona was one of the detectives' dogs. I still don't understand how Bruce talked us into robbery."

"Repossession of personal property."

"Sure. Whatever. Just tell me what kind of person poisons innocent dogs?"

Jake's finger held his place on the manuscript as he pushed his tongue up against the roof of his mouth before finally assuring Robin that everyone was safe. "I've got a UC on this now and he came over tonight and everything is going to be okay, Robin." After they exchanged sweet good-nights and hung up the phone, he laid still to make sure he hadn't disturbed Miss Lucy sleeping in the far bedroom as he repositioned himself on the propped pillows to read the remainder of *Chapter 4, Between the Lines*.

"Jake wiped down the hairs on the back of his neck and pushed his tongue up against the roof of his mouth before aiming the flashlight in Bruce's eyes and then at Scarecrow. His cue worked. But Jake was so friggin' nervous he yelled, "What's the bag for?"

Scarecrow twisted his hand up under his shirt. Pulled out the bag and shook it. "Didn't know if you'd have any gungi growing out here or not."

"Man, I ought'a knock you out. I been scared to death you been setting me up, showing up here. Gawd, Russ, just ask somebody next time." Bruce cussed and returned his knife to its sheath as Russ smiled and asked, "Well, do you?"

Bruce laughed so hard he went into a fit. He was bent at the hip while he held his thighs and squealed and hissed like a funny monkey. His contagious relief sent Jake and Russ into rolling waves of laughter, and the dog whined. Bruce sat down and slapped at the earth as Jake held his bulge and stepped away to relieve himself at the path's edge.

Bruce called out, "Don't pee on my plants. Russ is gonna smoke 'em. He loves some Paw Paw and Thistleweed." Russ told them to calm down, that it wasn't that funny. When they finally did, he captured their funny faces in the lantern light. "Do you have any gungi?"

"Mon, stop it," Bruce snorted, and the laughing fit resumed. Jake yelled, "I feel like I'm in a time warp, man."

"Yes, we have no bananas or gungi." Bruce managed through his snorts. "That stuff's illegal." He rolled across the grass till he hit a pine tree. "Shit."

"The law, the law's coming." Jake teased as he steadied a box of still equipment on the dolly.

Russ clanged two pipes together and yelled, "Hide the law. Here comes the liquor. If we had a dancer, this would be a reunion."

"I really could take a drink." Jake checked out the chances.

Bruce winced a negative on the drink, and then stood up and brushed off to make eye contact with Scarecrow. "What if I did? You wantin' ta sell it or smoke it?"

"Sell, of course."

"A lot of money in weed, but a lot of trouble, too. You get pot heads around, then addicts want your numbers. I like my old guys, the backyard boys, those that just wanna sip." Bruce patted his knife. "Shiners don't want trouble and potheads are nothing but trouble."

"Don't see too much difference myself." Russ tried to take lead. "Bout the same sentence for selling either. Except THC messes with hormones and'll give a man titties and temper. Likker gets tempers, too, but the fat goes all around. Overall, though, neither one is as good a high as a long-legged woman in a real short dress. Whew!"

Jake quickly filled another box with parts, "Shine is safer," and he stacked it on top of the other.

"I concur." Russ clanged his pipes again. "Shine is a gentleman's best choice when it comes to a high. But if you ever wanna deal in big money gungi is the way to do it. Stay away from crack, pills and anything imported. Time is harder on those. Grow your own and hire out the work. It's not that difficult with so many illegals around. They're hungry, mean and cheap, better'n any watch dog."

Bruce tossed an armful of clanging pipes to the center of the path. "Have you given any thought about where we stand when I go legit? I'll pay you to do security."

Startled, Russ stood like a man called out to a street fight. "Yea, I could do security, part time. Watch the back of my eyelids for three or four hundred a week."

"Security guards get about ten to twelve an hour. You must be planning on retiring to put in that many hours."

"I bring a lot to the table."

Bruce stood back. "Look, I'm buying your land. I'm paying a fair price. You got cash down. And I got a signed note saying you agree to sell it to me at that price soon as my house sells. Wantin' to back up?"

Jake did. He backed up against a tree and looked for a clear path.

"Hey, settle now. I'm just kiddin' around and I'm tickled with the land deal," Scarecrow said.

Bruce went back to dissembling and so did Scarecrow while Jake rolled the heavy boxes to Crash. When he finally reached Crash, he exhaled a deep, "Oh, Jesus." The trunk was open. After he scanned around, he pulled the screwdriver pressed tightly against his shin out of his boot and kept it on top of the hood as he jerked the flashlight out of his waistband and turned it on.

Tree frogs chanted squirrely tunes from the nearby timberline like they were mocking his fraidy-cat motions as Jake dropped the flashlight in the thick grass. It sunk in quick and went black in the grass. He fished for it with his boot while "fraidy-cat" mocked him like a chorus louder and louder until Jake scooped up the flashlight and scanned.

He grabbed the screwdriver from the top of the car and crept back to the open trunk with the flashlight steadily aimed. When he reached the gapping trunk his shiny keys dangled from the trunk's lock right at his forehead. Relieved, he wiggled them out and poked himself, chanting, "Fraidy-cat," and his prize trinket caught his eye. Attached with heavy duty fishing line,

Preacher Lilly's pearl onion button glimmered in the moonlight from his keychain. He packed the keys down deep in his pocket, the screwdriver back into his boot, and squeezed the boxes into the floorboard before hurrying back.

The dolly whizzed without weight and as Jake took a moment to thank God, he noticed something else. All the stars were twinkling onto the dew-covered grass and they seemed to move little sparkling eyes. At The Company tension and time grew. It festered and lingered. The sultry summer heat pulled every drop of moisture from their pores. Every turn of the wrench, every pull on the pipes, and all the sounds around them, filled every inch of space until they were crowded with anxiety and hyper awareness of the threat of light. Every single sigh was reckoned with on account of Alice's similar hiss, and to top it all off the frogs were so loud it was maddening.

Their communication became nods, shrugs, points and gestures until they lumbered into their vehicles and started the engines when each of them recharged for the next step in the night move. When Jake pulled up close to the deceiving ditch on the gravel road, he prayed Crash didn't tip over and in. His car was full, packed to the dashboard, side windows, rear headrests and the trunk would hardly close. Jake had to sit on the trunk to force the latch knowing the copper caps would be bent but could easily be hammered back into shape. The worm coils and parrot pipes packed in the seats were draped with sheets, Bruce's pink sheets. When asked about the pink all he had said was, "Washed 'em with a red sweatshirt. Won't do that again." With Crash being factory original sky blue, all washed out and pale, Bruce and Scarecrow razzed Jake about his ride being a pastel blue baby crib with soft pink lining. Bruce said, "Baby want a bottle?" as he held up a jar and Jake replied, "Yes, Sir, soon as this is over."

Bruce's new truck bed cover concealed the five copper vats. Scarecrow rode with Bruce.

Since there was no room inside the truck, the dog stayed behind. Scarecrow said the dog would go to his car, not to worry about Napoleon. Bruce planned to drive Scarecrow back to his car later. Jake cringed as they separated, and Bruce's big truck barely scraped past. Jake eased Crash back to the center of the gravel road, put Crash in park, popped out, and jogged back to replace the boulders. He became alarmed when he realized he forgot the flashlight halfway to the boulders and turned around, running.

He covered the ground with the flashlight, then the boulders, and shoved it into his back pocket. Once he was confident that there were no moccasins and Alice was not around, he worked in record time to replace the boulders, then sprinted into Crash and barreled down the haphazard road. The pipes and pieces clanged like a wrecked band as he practically went airborne over the ruts and deep washes. The old shocks creaked and twanged but held up and made Jake proud.

By the time he reached the intersection Bruce's truck was out of sight. There was little traffic; two cars, one coming, one going. Jake left The Company's road with a swirling dust trail.

Crash spun out onto the highway as Jake quickly pressed the top of his head to relieve his stinging tension while the gas pedal took his thrusts. Jake's anxiety peaked not being able to touch base. Bruce was going to buy more minutes for Jake's phone in case of any mayhem but had decided phones could become something more along the lines of evidence than convenience if mayhem got the better hand. When Jake finally spied Bruce's tail-lights, he slowed down from seventy-five.

When Bruce saw Jake in the rearview mirror he also slowed down, and Jake got up to three car lengths behind.

The pink sheets covered the goods and summer's red-hot heat covered Jake. His damp tee shirt stuck to the plastic seat and to his skin. Jake pinched the money wad and was sure it was soaked and staining his whites. He tugged till it didn't touch his stuff, but as soon as he released it the wad bunched up again. He rolled down the window down about an inch and stole a cool breath, but when the sheets shifted, he rolled it back up. He reached down beside his lap to get a water bottle but couldn't feel it. He strained as he checked for it in the floorboard. Felt around on the seat again, with no luck. His dry throat scraped against the back of his tongue as he swallowed a dab of saliva.

As The Company's convoy passed a convenience store Jake nearly waved for them to pull in. He was absolutely parched and so hot he felt like he had a fever. But he didn't dare take the risk. They were nearly done. When the bright store lights shone into Crash, he made a quick check for the water again. A movement on the floorboard reflected light. He reached for it as his eyes darted from the road to the floorboard. But it wasn't a shiny plastic water bottle. It was a shiny water moccasin.

Jake bolted straight up and made himself skinnier as he tightened up and for some foolish reason, held his breath till he saw stars, and the pressure of the pitiful little excuse for a weapon in his boot did nothing but scratch his calf like a snake bite. He screamed like a little girl as he darted from left to right searching for a place to pull over, then back at the floorboard to see if it was still there.

Both easements were just grass. No telling how deep or dank the drop-off. He was out of options as the moccasin's tail disappeared under the passenger's side. Jake veered onto the shoulder of the road, jumped out and slammed the door as zooming lights blinded him straight on.

The headlights weren't really an issue. He knew headlights would pass. It was the blue squirrelly one. Jake's mind worked faster than a nerd's calculator in honor's math. He removed the red cloth from his dog bite, so as not to draw attention, and thankfully, in the moonlight it was no more than a scratch. But his mouth was so dry that his tongue was sharp enough to peel a pineapple when he swallowed. He cautiously inspected his haul: The sheets were secure, and he repeatedly whispered, "Don't ask. Don't tell."

Then boisterously, Jake called out, "Hello, Officer, a moccasin got in my car. Know any
good snake charmers?" Dubiously, he remembered to politely smile.

The hefty Sherriff's Deputy politely smiled back. "Mon, that's a new one." He adjusted his belt, or rather pulled it out from under his dunlap and held onto the top of his club like a cave dwelling Neanderthal hugging a drumstick as he licked his lips. His thick tongue reached and stretched but could not remove the breading and cole slaw crumbs from his prickly double chin.

Jake nervously laughed. "There's a guy in Chatham County that does pest removal. Bet

he handles snakes, too. I petted a dead beaver in the bed of his truck once. I don't know if there's anyone around here, a snake charmer that is, not a beaver, Sir. Hey, what about the park's wildlife rescue? Don't' they have a group of activists or advocates or something like that? Seems like I read in the paper when they protested draining the pond on account of fish fatalities. They said the fish had feelings. Wasn't that Chatham County?"

He shifted the club around in his belt's holster while he shifted gears from friendly to drill sergeant. "State your name." He chewed up the remains of something and swallowed.

"Jake Wilkes."

The officer stepped closer and a foot away stretched his neck out to see through Crash's windows. Then rolled his eyes at Jake and checked him out from head to toe, "Ever think of painting this ride? Might wanna go with maroon to match the interior." His tongue punched his cheek like his joke punched Jake. "Can't believe your dad lets you out in this thing. Looks like something a fairy'd drive." When he laughed his belly lunged up over his belt and back down. "Tell him to trade out with Humphry's Tire and Body Shop. They could use some business. His wife's hung up again. Number four. And you might wanna check on tires, too." He grunted as he walked around the entire vehicle with the flashlight outstretched, "Swanny, I wouldn't let my dog out in this."

A slow-moving truck came up behind them as Jake's armpits flooded with a stink that'd piss off a skunk as Bruce passed. Jake licked the sweat from his lip as he prayed all mayhem had been completely doled out for the evening as the officer leaned so far over Crash's driver's side window, he lost his balance. In his struggle to keep balanced he ended up tap dancing across the pavement like an awkward ostrich with his club stuck out like tail feathers from behind. "Sure there's a snake, boy?"

"It's a moccasin, Sir."

"What else you got up in here?"

Jake's pecs tightened and his dry tongue up and grew two big devil horns that scraped across the roof of his mouth as he swallowed and reckoned on a good enough lie while the officer busily zoomed his flashlight over the pink sheets. Abstract forms, shadows and lines begged for definition. The copper worm coils were outstretched in the floorboard with the other pieces on top. From where Jake stood the front section suddenly formed an abstract sculpture of a giant officer with a rifle in one hand and in the back seat, the outline of a jury box appeared with twelve finials pokin' up like real heads.

Without further ado, Jake offered his lie, "Propane equipment, a lot of copper, some advertising client of Dad's. I got the short end of the stick and look at me now. Helping in the middle of the night moving this big job they're trying to finish up before a new work week starts over."

"Pink sheets?"

"Don't want thieves seeing it."

"Washed red with 'em, didn't cha?"

"Yeah," Jake tried to look ashamed.

The Officer poked his flashlight at Jake like a teacher's pointer. "Thief take anything copper. Honest man ain't got a chance." And with that, took his phone out of the snapped black cover and identified his whereabouts and asked for his buddy, Roe, "Got anyone from the station which can remove a live moccasin tonight from a working man's vehicle?" He winked at Jake as he held the phone away from his ear. The laughter boomed and the officer rolled his eyes.

"Jerks," he told Jake. Someone yelled that he should use his whistle. Someone else said to call Fisk and Jakes eyes popped wide open, and they widened even more. "Fisk lives off Old Plank Road. Bes ten minutes away, but don't know what level bes in. Got his number? Call back." The officer put his phone back in its cover. "Well, we got a feller, a snake procurer, who can do it, Jake. Dispatch'll call right back. Don't worry. Be back on the job in no time."

"Thank you, officer." Jake kicked the small stones out in front of him on the side of the highway into the grass just like a child innocently does when he's out playing in the wide open outdoors all carefree and without a lick to worry on. The dark timberline lined both sides of the road some forty feet back with a chorus of critters, known and not. He listened intently for a bird, a holy sign, and when he didn't hear one attempted to whistle, to perhaps bribe one into the area. But his mouth was so dry his lips threatened to crack when he puckered up, so he just listened to the frogs calling for mates, and one croaked, "Jailbird."

As the hefty officer headed back to his patrol car, he called out for Jake to come sit, too. But Jake informed him that he was just fine out there. From behind the wheel, the officer unwrapped a snack cake and pushed half of it into his mouth as Jake took a seat on Crash's hood. Jake sat there for only a few short minutes, peering constantly through the glass for the moccasin, and finally jumped off the hood.

The officer chewed down his snack cake and made his eyebrows dance as he held onto the steering wheel with his elbows raised up stooging around like he was going to race as Jake approached. "Do you have an extra water, Sir? I sure could use it."

"Sure, son." He quickly opened his cooler on the seat and gave Jake a water bottle and he drank it in one long continuous gulp. "You just saved my life. Thanks, Officer."

"Anytime. Keep a-plenty. Ne'er know what'll happen in a night. Don't want to be left high and dry." The Officer winked. "Get it? High and dry?" He laughed and choked up cake and when he spit it out the window, he barely missing spewing it on Jake.

Jake paced from the grass on the side of the road to the gravel and back. He finally locked his weary legs and folded his arms and in a kinetic exercise tightened and relaxed his aching muscles while he prayed with all his energy that Fisk the feller was out cold, and they'd have to call Chatham County's snake procurer. The hefty officer maneuvered out of his patrol car and marched over to Jake in the grass. "Your lucky night. Mr. Fisk bes on his way. One of his friends bes driving him. Need to warn ya, kid, Fisk drinks. Well, he's a drunk. Know your dad wouldn't appreciate a drunk being called to help, so, let's not breath it. Deal?"

Jake stood up straight and tall as a heap of grief rushed up into the air. "Good idea, Sir. Wouldn't want Dad to skip this year's free advertising for the Sherriff Department's Benefit up at the Pit and Pie Palace."

"Naw, we need all the sponsors we can get. It takes a lot to keep a town safe ya know. We've even got undercovers and trained dogs now." He rubbed his belly. "Pit and Pie's my favorite."

"Naw? Mine too." Jake fought the grin till he had to look away like he heard something in the distance.

"That's just a frog. We've picked him up before. Fisk, that is. He's like a regular, in and out in a couple of days. He cooks a lot. Good meatloaf and hashbrowns. Never burns nuthin'. Serves me extra. Good ol' Lum. Bad luck tho. Fisk grew up in Lumberton with a litter of little sisters. They went to selling themselves and got famous around there and Fisk took off. He was a teacher at one time. Oh, he's a character now. A few scraps. Mostly drunk or petty theft. Been known to hold up his poker buds with poison snakes. He pure tee ain't afraid a' snakes. Some say he eats 'em." The Officer contorted his jaw as frogs off in the timberline grew louder and louder in their competition to mate. Then one of 'em won and croaked this real long drawn out croak like it was doing orgasms and the officer made a most unexpected uncouth comment along the lines of it being a good night for lovers.

"Heard they taste like chicken," Jake laughed, and the officer winked, "Women or frogs?"

"Frogs."

"Hain't wasting my time cleaning frogs. Not enough meat to keep up a man's strength. Slimey, too. I won't bother with frogs." The Sherriff's Deputy clapped his hands. "Shut up," he hollered at the timberline, "Stop it. Go courtin' somewhere else you stupid toads." He looked over at Jake real annoyed like and said, "Can't hear myself think with all that."

Jake played fool and closed his gapped trap.

But both jumped as if a lightning bolt struck fire to their boot soles when a bumping-thumping hissing grabbed a hold of the highway stage. They stared dead-on at Crash from where they stood, frozen, checking Crash from the distance for snake leaks when it thumped again. Its nose wickedly bumped up against the front windshield, wide as a soda can.

The officer aimed his flashlight as he grasped his pistol. The light zoomed across the windshield as the big thick moccasin coiled and curled onto the dashboard and it popped the glass. His long-forked tongue flickered while his light brown belly stretched up stiff as it glided against the incline of the glass.

"Damn." It burst out of Jake as the moccasin's mouth opened against the windshield.

The moccasin's mouth was pink and white and sharp and fangy, and he was trying his darndest to bite a hole in that glass, so much so that his mouth flattened out against it as he arched up and pressed down till it popped closed, over and over again, flashing its fearsome fangs. It tried and tried to bite a hole in that glass. Then it coiled up and slapped its tail as it gapped its lethal threat when a car pulled up. No. It was a truck. No. It was a car with the trunk cut out and a truck bed welded on. The ramshackle vehicle backfired as it came to a jerky stop and the officer's jaw twisted in a gross configuration. "I hate snakes," He said as he ferociously waved.

Mr. Fisk and Wart tried to get out. Their heads wobbled out from the doors first, then arms, trying to balance their heads. One leg, then the other followed. Jake cocked his head at the officer, and he squinted as he bit the tip of his tongue. The pair wobbled up to Crash with a sack and a shovel. "I'm doing this free tonight, my good officer." Mr. Fisk announced with a tuck of his chin like a gentleman would do if he was meeting special folks. He pointed at the officer while Wart held out the heavy cotton sack. Two cords hung from its hand stitched top. Wart opened it up and looked inside.

"Knew we could count on ya, Fisk." The officer's fat cheeks bounced. "You got one in there already, Wart?"

"Look 'n see." Wart drooled from his snaggletooth gap.

Mr. Fisk angrily pulled Wart's sleeve, "Swanny, you toss one a' awers in thar?"

Wart looked into the sack again and his hat fell off. He tried to pick it up but couldn't.

Even his fingers were likkered up. The officer laughed through his nose, then collected himself and pointed, "Bes up here, Fisk, in the front windshield." But Fisk was too busy watching Wart. "Fisk, Fisk, the snake is on the dashboard. He's biting at the glass." Wart moved real-sudden like and the sack wagged, and he dropped it. Wart jumped on the sack and stomped it good then picked it up and shook it again and looked in. Satisfied, he fetched his hat and squished it over his greasy gray curls.

Mr. Fisk kept the shovel over his shoulder and fashioned his free fingers into a snake snout and snapped at the air. "Fisk, Fisk, Fisk, knows where snake bes. I smell him. I taste him. Fisk knows where all kinds a snakes is." Fisk scowled at Jake and gestured a snake bite then wove and wobbled around to the front of Crash. His shoulders were up so high he had no neck, but his humped back still humped and his wire rimmed glasses hung off the end of his red tipped nose, so close to the nub, they threatened to fall. Fisk flung open Crash's front door making the old hinges gnarl as the door bounced and the snake coiled onto the dashboard ready for a strike.

He held the shovel out in front of the coiled moccasin like he was going to train it to walk the plank. "Come on, Buddyrow. Oh, yese a bigun." Fisk hollered to Wart, "Get up here with that sack. I taint carrying him all da way back thar. Why he might jump off dis shovel here and squirm up dat boy's leg."

When Fisk voraciously aimed at Jake, his big thick lips formed a big black hole and it was clear he had only a few molars left. "Gid up in here, Wart." Panic stricken; Wart hurried with the sack. "Bes all de sorry in de world dat snake gid up yer pants." His motions were so exaggerated his hat fell off again, but this time he didn't stop to try to pick it up. Wart ran with the sack held out in front of him like he was already totin' a live wriggling moccasin.

A laugh welled up in Jake till he plum jittered as the officer pat Jake's shoulder and they enjoyed the fiasco. The officer leaned hard against Jake's shoulder as his rolls lunged up and down in sequence with his heaves, so much so that Jake had to brace his legs to keep from falling. Jake struggled to hold in his own laughter so he could concentrate. "I can't believe this," Jake said, and the officer commented, "Crazy as politics get I reckon – snake charmers working for the law," he hissed as his shoulders rose and fell in delight. "These two are definitely FBI agents," Jake pointed as the action grew dangerously intense.

The snake straightened out like a stick inspecting the shovel, but Fisk didn't cut the snake into a gazillion tiny pieces. He scooped it up like it was a delicate little creature right off Crash's dash. The giant shiny viper weighed so much Fisk groaned for help as he backed up out of Crash's door. It stretched out its big ass head at Fisk and wrapped its tail around the handle, one lick at a time, all the way down to Fisk's bare hand while Wart did his best to talk it into the sack.

The officer released Jake's shoulder to secure his unsecured pistol. "That's a poisonous snake now, boys. Not a kitten. Got that, Fisk? Don't cuddle up and try to kiss 'er now."

The officer kissed at the air as the viper's tongue tasted.

Jake stepped back. "That thing's ten feet long."

"Least," the officer gasped, "and you were in there with hit. You got angels wid cha, boy. That moccasin's mouth'd cover yer entire hand."

Fisk slowly twirled the snake covered shovel over Wart's open sack. The moccasin's head slimed over Fisk's shovel-bearing fist as he shook harder and harder when the moccasin refused, Fisk heaved up and blew a rotten stinkin' stroke of stench right into that viper's snout and it dove inside the sack unwinding its tail from the handle as it raced inside.

When Wart looked into the sack with his face so close he could've counted its scales Fisk hollered, "Bes in dar. Close da sack, Wart. Tie 'er up." In three licks Wart knotted the cords and held out the heavy sack as high as he could, which was close to three feet off the ground before his balance was tossed. Fisk proudly thumped the side of the sack and the moccasin pummeled around in thick waves like a cat daddy does when it rolls a bream. "Swanny, thoust eat like a King for a week on this 'un." He glared at Wart. "I get the choppers first." Wart just shrugged as Mr. Fisk continued his victory speech. "All we need bes a few hot ellicks to wash 'er down."

With that, Fisk stabbed the shovel into a crack on the roadside's worn pavement with a victory ping that rattled everyone's nerves as he shot Jake and the officer his best snaggle-toothed grin. "No moccasins running loose on yer highway. No, Sir, Sirs. Maxton bes all cleaned up, officer." He spit when he laughed, "No, Sir. No moonshiners, gun runners or nuthin' illegal like dat with our fine officer on duty." Fisk nodded bye and rushed back to his truck, car, car, truck, whatever, pulling on Wart's arm as he hurried.

The officer called out to Jake to drive safely and not to stop anywhere and then added, "Don't drink n' drive, son. And don't tell your daddy 'bout these two. Promise?"

"I won't. No sir. You can count on that. Thanks again," Jake called out to the officer who hurried after Mr. Fisk and Wart. Jake thanked his little good luck charm with a kiss as he jumped into Crash and right away noticed the gleaming copper beside him. The sheet was peeled back just enough to see the two-inch diameter pipe. A rush of fear and that damn thrill to live to tell the tale filled his blood with vinegar again, and the moccasin's sharp musky scent stabbed his nose till it twisted his guts. He guided the front tires onto the highway, locked in with stink and good deeds gone dirty in what had to be one hundred and twenty degrees and a water bottle bumped his foot. He pulled it up and drank the warm water in one long continuous gulp and checked on the action in the rear-view mirror just in time to witness the officer directing the snake charmers to his patrol car.

The officer pointed his pistol at the pavement directing the moccasin sack to the ground, but good-gooboly-goo, with one swift jerk Wart emptied the sack into the back seat of the patrol car, propelling the moccasin inside. The officer screamed as Wart and Fisk darted back to their truck, car, and Jake laughed out loud as he peeled Crash out onto the black highway sort of singing, sort of shouting, "I'm not supposed to tell anyone what I'm doing tonight. I'm not supposed to tell anyone what I'm doing tonight. I swear. I swanny, even, not to tell anyone what I'm doing tonight," as he finally cranked down the window and prayed, "Lord."

A part-black Tuscarora holds a stone ax with carving on it on the front
porch of his home in Bertie County, NC's Indian Woods in the 1960's. Photo
from the F. Roy Johnson Collection. Digital. NC State Archives, Raleigh,
NC. Call no. PC 367. Mars ID 877.

A part-white Tuscarora holds a war club. Taken during 1960's in Bertie County, NC's Indian Woods. Photo from the F. Roy Johnson Collection. Digital. NC State Archives, Raleigh, NC. Call no. PC 367. Mars ID 877.

Chapter 5

The Good-Old-Boys Club Sucks Now

Miss Lucy found eggs and canned biscuits in the refrigerator and had breakfast on the table at 6:30. As Jake sat in front of his scrambled eggs across from his roomie, he said, "Bes a gaumed up mess. Sorry I got you into this."

"No," her gentle smile warmed the cool kitchen, "I haven't felt this alive since, since, a long time." They returned kind expressions and drank a pot of coffee as Jake read through her clippings and stopped when a headline revealed that in 1973 several thousand pounds of stolen Bureau of Indian Affairs reports had been found in Maxton, NC.

"Appalachian State's website has a chronological list of events on the Robeson Peoples, but fails to include pertinent details, so I found the newspaper clipping from a library database and made a copy." "And this?" Jake slipped a stack of stapled papers from under the couch cushion, "Sorry, but I couldn't resist." "I had a feeling you'd take the bait," she sipped her cold coffee staring out the window at her little car and Jake turned to page 3, "We are proceeding on the theory that people who exercise authority should be held accountable for what happened." [26] That is the meat of the Indian problem right there in one sentence." When Jake's twisted repose led to a couple of fast tears, he wiped them dry. "Bruce was," Miss Lucy stalled, "he was not a part of that."

"His people though, they got him into this. It just rubs me wrong, the same thing - the conspiracy against Tuscarora by the Lumbee. There's a interview out there with Dr. Malinda Lowry - wrote the book pushing the Siouan theory, and she says she's close friends with Nancy Strickland at the university's museum. [27] Henry Berry Lowrey is their hero, even have a film on him, but nothing about him being a Mighty Tuscarora. I swear, there is some kind of cover-up going on." He sniffed, "They're so outnumbered."

Her shoulders rose and fell as she contemplated sitting at the table again, "The tables have turned on the Mighty

Tuscarora but like the Bible says there is nothing new under the sun and I believe it. Like poor Israel. Did you read the seizure report in full?" "Yes, and I woke up thinking about that fat satchel full of files – called me like donuts about four o'clock." "You stinker, like Christmas, isn't it? Learning something new and what a fiasco, Lord," she giggled.

"It must a' been like that in the seventies," Jake mused, "Indians fit in with all the other extremists and had reached their boiling point. But I never heard of the Trail of Broken Treaties."

"Well, your age and this county account for that. It's operated on Lumbee ideology," she spouted, and he agreed. "They'd started out in the Arlington Cemetery on a Friday the 13th," she tskd, "The Indians made 20 demands on the federal government after breaking into the Bureau of Indian Affairs and caused 250 thousand in damages and stole 700 thousand dollars-worth of art and artifacts, on top of walking out of the building, in and out for 6 consecutive days, carrying over 7 thousand pounds of reports and no one stopped them, not even the U.S. Marshalls." [28]

"I read that, and administrators formally declined written requests for them to testify on what happened. [29] That's mighty curious, don't you think?"

"Indeed, that and the fact that they paid these protestors 66 thousand to get home and no one faced charges until someone tried to return a few boxes. [30] Curious indeed," she rose and pulled another file from her satchel. "This is the chronological list I mentioned on the Lumbee history. The TBT as it was called, is not on the list. It's next to impossible to locate a newspaper clipping covering this or the aftermath – the burning of businesses or Old Main at the university. I studied this and seems like there's still some three-thousand BIA files out there. They might have the exact treaties needed for reparations to begin and I hope they do and that we find them before the Lumbee." [31] "Especially considering those Lumbee have infiltrated the NCCIA, the federal government and every business and office, including education and controls what history will be told in the future – just like their conquerors did."

"The Tuscarora will be forgotten."

"Not if we do this right, Miss Lucy." They shared determined expressions when Jake broke, "We need to know what made the Indian activists reach that boiling point and get motivated again."

"Well, you can only push a person so far before they explode and, personally, I think their buttons were on fire after Collier, the Commissioner of Indian Affairs, who really demonstrated good intentions, helped get the 1934 Indian Reorganization Act passed. [32] The act was nothing more than an economic plan to reduce the federal government's burden of appropriations for wrongs against Indians – a pure sham, nothing but," she stared out the window as individual cloud-puffs swept over the field marking shadows that could have easily been interpreted as tee-pees.

"I learned about the act in school, ya know, it was a federal program, so it was taught. What I don't understand is how these activists stayed for 6 days without an insider's help." Jake got comfortable on the couch and added that the winery would be fine without him.

"Politics are always involved in things like this when the entire Indian population was named Croatoans, and renamed again by McLean, and again when that McMillan conspired a way to secure his future by dispelling the Tuscarora heritage by naming them Lumbees, [33] and then in..." Jake interrupted, "That weasel's statue needs to be used for ammo."

"See," she squirmed, "you aren't even one of them and you're quite affected. Imagine how these people felt. The Maynor vs Morton case was denied. The Original 22 Tuscarora who were officially recognized as ½ or more Indian under the IRA of 1934, were excluded from benefits, such as grants, under the Lumbee Act. Their entire identity was deemed null and void. Another paper genocide tactic. Some of the poorest of the poor were denied. The very settlers of this region, the very blood of their kin turned against them. [34] I'm telling you: They were hot!"

"How can the government do that?" Jake sat up, "I mean that's what the Lumbee Tribe is, a government system."

"Yes, they've become a child of the federal government, Jake, and don't you know that's the exact question those activists asked, "how?" There had to be an inside leak for the activists to know who was safe to talk to. Their "released" investigation reads that the FBI did not find efficient evidence to say that their public relations director had been involved – one Mr. Tom Oxendine. In the end, the BIA Solicitor's Opinions, as documented in the reports stolen from the BIA reveal that they did not have the right to remove previous rights, like the Original 22's, and that is exactly why the reporters were arrested. Had they been able to write positive remarks on the government agency, believe me, they would have been rewarded in some way – advanced positions in journalism or given awards even for their participation in transporting some of those boxes back to Washington." [35]

Jake walked towards Miss Lucy with his head cocked and a confused expression. His green eyes devoured her tiny frame until her chin ever-so-slightly quivered. "You know a lot about their history to have just begun researching, Miss Lucy," his stale coffee breath bounced off her forehead and he apologized. "I need to get to work. If you want to explain anything to me, you can call me at the office."

"I'll think about that," her radar blues followed him out the door as he clenched the draft of Chapter 5 under his arm.

Without a word, Jake hustled to his office and closed the door, booted his pc, sent a memo to Cassie to handle any issues, unless it entailed a pink slip, and searched: 1972 BIA Occupancy, clicked on one, a second, and read the third, hosted on Muckrock, a journalism website featuring FBI data.

Forty-five minutes later, he checked his notes: California AIM activist, Bill Sargant, shows up in Pembroke, NC to establish AIM branch. Tom Oxendine with BIA as Public Relations officer has contradictory statements on communications with the ringleader, "Hank" Henry Adams. Adams traveled to Pembroke where most of the stolen BIA documents were stored. Columnist Jack Anderson offered to buy several boxes of the docs for 200k, reported an UC officer. Anderson, Less Whitten and Anita Collins and Adams were arrested after Adams had told Oxendine he was returning some of the docs. Oxendine had conflicting statements concerning his communications with the activist. The boxes contained reservation data, including mineral and water, land appeals, letters and many Solicitors' opinion reports, including the 1912 Report of Com. Of Indian Affairs. Item Number j. contains 20 points, on Restoration of Constitutional Treaty, and Item Number d. is 30-page report, "Trail of Broken Treaties – Chronology of Events." [36]

"Fu-uck," Jack flopped down into his chair, "Oxendine was a Pembroke man." [37] with his eyes closed, he cussed, "Mafia. Swamp land mafia," and growled through his teeth. He scrolled through the list of stolen docs again and was nearly frothing as squashed his notes, rolled them into a fast ball and threw it at his office window. Cassie walked past and shook her head, "Mon, thoust bes gaumed up this morning. Ellick time?" she held up her bright gold coffee cup and his emblazoned face aimed down at his desk and declared, "This is my winery and my office and I can get fuckin' mad if I want to," not in a roar, but not quietly either, "Leave me alone."

Jake pulled the pillow from his bottom drawer and placed it on top of his desk, pried off his shoes, rested his heels on the pillow and began reading the draft: "*Chapter 5, The Good-Old-Boys Club Sucked Then.*

Steel posts and a new gate easily identified Bruce's new place just off the railroad tracks on the back road behind Maxton's one-man post office. Jake slowed to a mere crawl at the entrance as his heart thumped against his sternum and Crash putted over the flattened grass path. The cooler night air purged through the passenger's side window as the radio announcer's deep sultry voice shared the time, two-twenty-two, with a cheatin', drinkin', don't-come-back-no-more-love song.

Bruce's truck was parked by a newly built shed and most everything else was obliterated by a powerful spotlight. As the light x-rayed the sheets covering the copper-pipes Jake held one boot on the brake, the other on the gas. The closer the light came, the more intense until a figure filled the driver's side window.

"Sorry 'bout that," Bruce turned off the spotlight, "Just verifying it's you."

"Shit," Jake turned off the engine, "Where'd you get that? Military torture kit or what?"

"Raleigh, an outdoor sports store. Keep it in the toolbox. Come on. Get out. It's gettin'

Late," Bruce called for Scarecrow as Jake stretched out, leaned against Crash and took deep breaths of the crisp clean night air, but Bruce and Scarecrow demanded Jake tell them what in the hell happened.

Instead, Jake gathered an armful of pipe, "Am I the only one working now?" He bent over and eased the pile down next to Bruce, then face-to-face sternly stated, "I'm not supposed to tell anyone what I'm doing tonight. Remember?"

Bruce threatened to tie Jake to a tree as he aimed at the swamp. "I'm gonna let the moccasins poison you and the skeeters suck out whatever life is left."

Jake grabbed a hold of Crash's hood, slapping, spitting and hackling, "Good-gooboly-goo!" Bruce smiled at his hysterics, "Why'd you get stopped? That's all we wanna know." Intoxicated with delirium, Jake propped up on the hood, locking his arms out straight so he wouldn't fall over. Scarecrow called him a goof and it gave him the giggles again it spread to Bruce as he fought to seriously tell him to shut up, "We're too tired for this. Tell us already."

"A water moccasin got in Crash. It went under the passenger's seat."

"Holy Moly," Bruce declared while Scarecrow gawked, hardly breathing at all.

"A cop saw me. He called dispatch and they sent out Mr. Fisk n' Wart," Jake's story rushed out. "Did you know they're the county's snake trappers?" Bruce rolled his hand around and around, urging Jake to tell the tale so Jake did, emptying the entire snake sack as they took turns popping the hood and busting a lung.

"That made my night," Bruce said. "Perfect. Perfect ending to a nerve killing night. I swear it couldn't get any more perfect than that."

"Yea. That one'll get around quick." Scarecrow rubbed over Jake's head like a grandpa does a little one. "Glad it wasn't Alice."

"Geez, me too."

They finally finished unloading and covered The Company's parts with a thick camo tarp, securing it to the ground with large steel stakes at the edge of the swamp in a thicket so thick they had had to carry parts up over their heads with flashlights gripped between their teeth. In some places they were on their hands and knees to scoot the parts along in front of them. The dirty work disguised them as wild boars gaumed up in black swamp dirt and its dank decay with briar scratches spurtin' fresh blood each time they swat off the feasting gallanippers.

Bruce insisted they toast their grand deed with his most potent Muscadine wine. He attached a pulley to a concealed heavy-duty metal ring. Threw a rope over a limb and pulled up a four by four patch of ground to reveal his bounty. The clever earthen cellar held countless jars. Jake took the narrow earthen steps down and began counting rows.

"Damn, Skippy. Regular fox den, huh? How far back does it go?"

"Fourteen feet. Had the old man's last two pallets down here, but his lids were no count. Swamp land ain't like the clay.

Moisture eats the pallets and those cheap lids. Stainless lids on mine."

"You sell his?"

"Never. It's in a pit over at The Company. Off the timberline overlooking the water. Up high about ten feet from the top of the hill. Clay there's like brick." Bruce aimed his light at a row with plastic wrap askew. "Bring up a jar and we can celebrate proper."

"In a couple of years," Bruce held up his plastic cup to theirs, "we will do this again with my Zoskiroro's Dewberry Wine. Thanks, you two. And even though I am so looking forward to going legit and putting this town back on the map I have to admit I'm gonna miss this.

And I sure regret I didn't get the chance ta mommuck up that damn Yankee."

"Think of it this way; you've increased your chances of living long enough to have kids to tell your stories to one day," Scarecrow toasted and poured the burning potion down his throat and held out his cup for more.

They each relished the burn while they slowly allowed their stinging highs to loosen the last knots in their tight tongues as they continued the toast of living to tell the tale and beamed like they were heroes. They relived the night with their, "When he did this," and "When you did that," and slapped their thighs and one another's backs and got all toothy and drunk with both endorphins and likker. Round after round, until Bruce's jar was empty, and they stood shoulder to shoulder like comrades after war.

"I love you, man," Bruce told Jake. "You're the brother I never had."

"You too, Buddyrow," Jake marched off behind the shed to relieve his bladder letting go of some powerful gas pains, petting the German Shepherd along the way. It wagged its tail and disappeared while Scarecrow covered their newly made trail using a hardwood limb to scratch it all up. Crow put on gloves and scattered pinecones, straw and his special nasty mixture of wild critter scat. Bruce inverted his empty jar on the freshly pruned scrub oak and thanked the guys repeatedly then asked Jake if he needed to take a nap or wanted to stay the night in the shed. "There's a couple of sleeping bags for occasions like this. Slept out under the stars till a cooter came up. Didn't wanna risk my nose again. It's cozy and no law'll be looking for ya in there."

"No. I'll be fine. I'll go real slow."

"Well I'm gonna follow you home and then I'll take Scarecrow to his ride, just to be safe."

"That'll work."

Bruce told Jake to tell his parents, "The puppies were packed tight, had to wait over an hour for the runt."

"I'm no runt. You're the runt. Runts are always the trouble-makers."

"At least it's airish now," Scarecrow blew down his damp tee shirt. "Lost five pounds tonight."

With jelly legs and a humbled head, Jake fell into Crash and switched on the engine, "Sweet Jesus, keep me around to watch over Mamma." The headlights shone on Bruce and Scarecrow as they climbed into Bruce's truck. With eyes burning for sleep Jake opened them wide and yawned as he fished for another water bottle. He downed most of it and splashed the rest over his face. When he finally got Crash turned around, he took a deep breath of sweet swampy summer night air, full of pine and Bermuda grass. He stuck his arm out to wave it in the cool air and pure joy covered him. He was singing when the gunshot pounded, "Boom!"

Instantly, Jake was sobered. From the rear-view mirror, hope was dashed. Bruce's truck was surrounded, and Bruce was flattened into the grass while the German Shepherd held Scarecrow spread eagle by the upper thigh. "That damn Yankee!"

Camouflage and aimed rifles filled the mirror. "Good God, get me out of this!" Jake peeled out from the slick grassy entrance with squealing tires and went airborne over rut traps. Almost at the end of the haphazard road he met Old Bucky. But he didn't slow down. Oh, hell no, Jake calculated impact with the legendary eighteen-pointer. Swerved to miss the thick ass buck and missed his fluffy white flag by inches as he managed Crash over the rutted road at ninety. His head twirled to check traffic as he slowed at the stop sign. Crash lurched onto the highway. Thirteen miles later, at the Pembroke intersection he checked the rear view again."

"Gawd, just like yesterday," Jake skimmed through the chapter's remaining pages and told himself that he'd finish reading later. Still in a mood, and Zoskiroro's being quiet, Jake ordered take-out from the deli and had it delivered, telling the teen delivery driver to knock on his office door before entering, and he did. After consuming the meatball sub, he set the timer on his phone for three o'clock and took a nap with the pillow on his desk. The alarm went off only minutes before his office phone rang and he stretched back to life and handled business until it five o'clock and he left for home.

Miss Lucy was already at his house when he arrived and everything looked normal outside, so he didn't bother to knock. "You didn't call me today," Jake's dull tone mocked Miss Lucy's efforts at preparing a fried steak and gravy supper, and she let him know as her arms gestured toward the table. "Let's eat first."

"I can't eat. You don't know how torn up I am. I'm doing my best to be polite, Lord knows I gave the staff a bad turn today and I need to go in tomorrow with my head together," he stepped up to the table and held the back of the chair, "I want you to tell me who you are in this story, this research, everything. The deeper we go back, the more I feel like you've walked right beside me."

She sat down and longingly gazed over her shoulder, "I once loved a man who was like you, Jake, involved, and you struck me as someone like him and I jumped at the chance to relive those feelings. That's it, I swear."

"Was he from here? Indian? White?"

"Half, like the rest of Robeson County."

"You're not half."

"What makes you so sure?"

Jake studied her closer; tall planks under her projectile blue eyes, her strong nose, and as he delved into the magnificence of her rolled and set hairdo, her red curls faded into black and gray roots. Miss Lucy grimaced, "It's time for a touch-up. I've kept it red to stay employed - as a young single woman, just the way it was back then. My mother was an orphan child and sent me away with a slip of paper," Miss Lucy opened the locket on her bracelet and the glass encased slip, oxidized tan to brown at the edges. It read, "Stargazer Locklear." "Her roots have continually eluded me, and this work with you now, it inspires me to have a, a glimmer of hope that I might come across someone who says her name or looks at me and somehow knows. You aren't the only one in this world with a quandary, Jake."

"I hope you do find Stargazer's roots and that they'll be as black and gray as yours," he laughed and she swat at him from across the table, "You stinker, I just love that about you."

After supper, she offered manila files labeled in chronological order, "I worked on this all day," she proudly spread held a file out to him, "This might help you understand the driving force of the BIA occupancy. It covers the "self-determination movement" begun in the thirties, officially in the forties and the "self-determination movement without termination" that came after Nixon. [38] Indians across America clashed with the government's waddle over how they should be able to govern themselves, the rights to their lands, and what funds were due. For the life of me, I can't see why there isn't an ongoing protest."

"I'll never get through all of these. What is it, a couple a dozen?" He eyed the satchel like a dog eyeing an abandoned sandwich.

"Thirty-nine files," she sniffed, "I'm exhausted. If you don't mind, I'm going to take my laptop and watch a movie in my room." At the threshold, "Hey, has Scarecrow called with any updates? I'd love to know if someone walked across my floors when I wasn't home."

"No. No news is good news. I'll reach out to him tomorrow."

"Thank you, and what about the dogs?"

"They're going to be okay. Vet said it looked like antifreeze and another poison mixed in. Mean stuff."

"Mean indeed. I'm glad. I mean, you know what I mean – I'm tired. I'm going to relax tonight."

"Sure, I'll be in here, reading my eyes out on Kotlowski's 2003 academic view on Nixon and the BIA. You enjoy your movie. I might be in here in the morning. Don't be surprised," he called out and she told him to enjoy it because she was already working on a list of new research, "Uh, thank you," he wearily replied. The material's intense contagiousness led to notetaking and as Jake stretched his back and flipped the page, a sentence jabbed: This article argues that grass-roots protests shaped federal Indian policy by first placing and then keeping Native American concerns on the national agenda." [39] Dogmatically, he reached for his cell in his jeans' pocket, but sunk back into the cushions. "Sure wish I could call you, Buddyrow." The buttery manilla files layered like a baker's thinly sliced pastries invited him to indulge and by 2 a.m., he had penned a chronological list of events while her files resembled the remains of a kindergartner's birthday party.

"Ahh-no," her hushed anger moved Jake to reposition on the couch and when he nearly fell off, was awakened. Miss Lucy pressed the automatic coffee timer and asked, "You want eggs?"

"Sure," he rolled off the couch onto the floor and yawned, "I never realized research was so painful. My whole body hurts."

"Coffee will be ready in a minute," her curt tone awakened Jake to the realization of his strewn mess and he said, "I'm going to get everything back in order before I leave," and rushed to get ready for the day, "I've got so much to cover, to do at work today." His door closed and she stood over the coffee table and started organizing her files. By the time he came out, they were tucked into her satchel again. "I said I'd do that," he apologized, "I don't have time for breakfast today," he explained as he poured coffee into his thermos. "The window comes through my window every morning and tells me the weather," his cheerful tone delighted her. "Today will be cold and windy. Bundle up," he rushed out the front door and she fished out a bound report from her satchel and finished her coffee in the quiet country house with her copy of "Tuscarora Roots" by Dr. Peter Wood which had arrived the day prior.

The University of North Carolina at Pembroke was only twenty miles from his rental at the Crowson's farm, but he made it in fifteen. He parked in the visitors' parking behind the CSX railroad tracks directly in front of Old Main, the historic building that was the sight of the original "Indian" school. With his 26x camera, he took several shots of the tall dark Hamilton McMillan statue and read his politically charged plaque.

Old Main's columns suggest stature to a higher calling and the foyer is also remarkable with inviting views inside the Museum of Southeast American Indian through the sophisticated glass panel doors. Jake was welcomed by a young man behind a welcome desk and he offered a guide. "Perfect, but I need a streamlined version." "No problem at all." He began with a painted wall where local Lumbees had come to jot down their feelings about being Lumbee. The word "proud" was repeated and so was "family."

A log cabin in the far-right corner served as a colonial view of Indian life. It was no different than a white colonist's cabin. Jake was led behind the cabin to view seven walls with photos of Lumbees. Some were labeled with names, and other events. Some were not labeled at all. "Who is this?" Jake asked of the bare-chested dark-skinned man in regalia and the host told him that it was a man who attended most of the pow wows and a New York journalist had interviewed him. "Lumbee?" Jake asked and the host replied, "Yes, everyone here is Lumbee." "But this one is the only one carrying on traditions?" Jake asked and the host's back arched like a striking cat and replied, "We have a craft corner up front where anyone is welcome to make an Indian craft. We, I'm Lumbee, help school children make corn husk dolls and we watch videos and teach them Lumbee history."

"Now aren't they the ones who are trying to get recognition as Cheraw?" When the host listed several tribal affiliations and said that it was complicated, Jake squished his eyes like he was terribly confused, "What about the Tuscarora?" "They are separate from the Lumbee and there are reports of them acting out in violence against the Lumbee and the college. This museum is supported by the Lumbee Tribe and the college."

"I see, so the name "Southeast" is just a name?" Jake asked and the host said that he might want to make an appointment with the director because he did not know how the museum's name was chosen.

A glass-encased pinwheel quilt was in the far-left corner near the Henry Berry Lowry exhibit with the rotten tree the museum was passing off as an antique Indian canoe. "We just acquired this quilt. It is a real treasure. The pinecone patchwork is the Lumbee symbol," said the host and Jake read the plaque and scratched his ear, "I guess the design is in the public domain or something then because this design was made by a Tuscarora."

The whites in the host's dark eyes shined like he'd been handed a firecracker and spouted, "The Lumbee are state recognized Indians and our North Carolina Tuscarora have not been and the maker of this quilt, Polly Braveboy, was an Indian and the community changed its name after the river in the 1950's after the Civil War when they were getting separate schools and this college was built on that name."

"That's fine, but this is a Tuscarora's work. I'll show you," Jake held out his cell phone with a photo of the Descendant's Chart. The first name was William L. Locklear-40 (1778). Jake pointed to Polly's name and with a tight jaw, the host ask, "Where did you get this?"

Jake grinned and slipped his phone back into his jeans. "A professor from Duke studies these Indians around here. I took a photo of this chart to show my friend."

"Is your friend a Lumbee too?"

"Oh, I'm not Lum. I'm a mutt from Ireland and England and who knows where else."

"I mean is your friend a Lumbee?"

"No, he's a Tusc." Jake took three steps and made it back to the front where another Henry Berry Lowry exhibit was and asked, "Is this a film on the Tuscarora legend?"

"It's a film about when the Ku Klux Clan tried to run off the Indians or kill them and instead, they ran them off." The host asked Jake if he had time to watch it and he said, "Not this morning. You've watched it probably a hundred times, huh?"

"Oh, yes. He is our hero."

"Do you remember if the actor mentions that Lowry was Tuscarora?"

"It doesn't."

"So, everyone thinks Lowry was a Lumbee?"

"It's not recorded what Lowry was, so we don't know for sure, but his descendants are Lumbee."

"Now, I have a copy of that professor's research, the one from Duke, and it has several corrections this museum needs, primarily, the name Tuscarora."

"I'm sure our director would like to see that." The host handed Jake a card and asked him if there was anything else he'd like to see and Jake said, "Yeah, there is – a photo of Leola Locklear with a plaque stating that she testified in 1991 to the U.S. Congress that she was Tuscarora," and the host chuckled as he flopped down into his chair behind the desk. "That's not going to happen here," he could barely talk for laughing and Jake said, "Bes gaumed up, Buddyrow," and he bolted out the glass doors.

A well-placed directory read that the upstairs includes several departments, including the Native American Indian Studies Program. Upstairs, Jake found a professor of NAI history sitting in his office and politely knocked on the threshold, "Got a minute?" "Come in," he waved to the cushioned chairs in front of his desk and asked, "How can I be of assistance?"

"I just want to ask a couple of quick questions about the Native American Indian program."

"Sure, I'm happy to give you a fast run-through," the professor let his phone ring while reading the caller's I.D. and said, "I need to make this quick," he checked his watch and added, "Class in ten minutes."

"Thank you," Jake tugged a book from inside his jacket and opened it to the page marked with the colorful tab, "This is a chapter where the author interviewed several Lumbees, some from the university and this Dr. Stanley Knick over the Indian history department said that the Lumbee had no identifying language, and is quoted in here, see," he pointed, "it reads like Knick believed the Lumbee interacted with the Lost Colonists. [40] Is that what the Indian program here teaches?"

"Yes, that's right," he pulled a book from his shelf and flipped through the front matter. "This is a newer publication, just a couple of years ago, from Dr. Lowery, a Harvard Professor and Proud Lumbee. She was invited here by the Lumbee council to speak on our indigeneity."

"Oh, she's a regular on campus then? Like an adjunct?"

"No, more like a feature speaker. We host events around her." The professor silently read a few lines from Lowery's book and his whites sparkled, "Siouan Indians of the Lumber River," he smiled at Jake, "That was our name in the 1930's before European influence and it suggests origins, including our language." [41]

"Siouan is Algonquian?"

"Right."

Jake stood to read the passage, "There's no footnote to refer to this source."

"It doesn't matter. She's a professor."

Jake read the next line, and mused, "Tuscarora, which is one of the tribes to which we trace our ancestry, has been used off and on by community members since the nineteenth century. "Lumbee Tribe of Cheraw Indians" came into use in the 1990's and references tribal member's ancestry and one of the federal government's many opinions about the primary historic tribe from which we descend." [42] So, every tribe around has a different name for a different time period depending on the political needs to change a name. Then people who question origins are called out for not being inclusive. Isn't inclusiveness a communist tactic?

"Are you a student?"

"No, I'm just gathering research. Thinking about writing a book."

"Thank you for stopping in. If you have any questions," the professor handed him a card, "use my email. I respond within a couple of days."

"Thank you so much."

"What did you say your name was?"

"Just call me Jake," he answered over his shoulder as he performed a perfect pirouette to avoid bumping into an elderly man in overalls outside the office. He quickly apologized as he waltzed down the stairs and vanished out the front door.

With one hand on the wheel, he called Robin and chimed, "It looks like we have a Lumbee professor who knows the Tuscarora history. Lowery wrote two years ago that the Tuscarora identity has been in a continuum cycle, whereas the other identities were either politically charged or manipulated histories written in books to appease the federal government or cultural misconceptions."

"This is good news, right?" When her chopped words were indicative of rush hour at Gili's, Jake asked if she could set him a plate of lasagna and he'd be there in less than five and she told him, "I'm putting the order in now, baby." She panted, "Hey, you need to be careful up there. Those professors are all Lumbee. Did you tell him that you were helping the Tuscarora?"

"No, no," Jake breathed into the phone, "I made it out that I was more interested in political discrimination, which is becoming clearer as the reality here. When I said inclusiveness was a commie thing, he suddenly had to leave."

"I guess so," she huffed, "You're a smart jerk sometimes."

"Sometimes, baby," he kissed into the phone and said, "I'm almost there. I can smell you already."

"Ohhh, you animal," she purred as she ended the call.

Gili's parking lot was a mix of new cars with fine wax jobs and so full that he had to park in the grass. He squeezed in between two late nineties two-doors and locked his truck as the infamous car-truck sputtered into the grass parking lot. He casually entered Gili's at the front door instead of the back through the kitchen and Robin met him within seconds with a sweet kiss on the cheek. The usual crowd nodded as she led him to a seat in the back near the kitchen and she bent over and whispered, "I only have a fifteen minutes for break today," and he did not whisper, "Mom is working my girl too hard," and a steel cymbal rang from the kitchen verifying Gili did not care about his opinion. "I'll be right back with your lunch," she rushed through the swinging doors and he pulled out his book and spread it open on the red tablecloth.

Mr. Fisk and Wart were escorted by the waitress who always wore her long black hair in two braids over her brandy wine muffins. Today she was wearing a new pair of white pants with her deep gold uniform shirt and had cleaned her white sneakers, and her customers had cleaned up too. Both were wearing clean overalls and light blue shirts with collars and were carrying reasonably new coats. The pair worked so hard not to look directly at Jake that it was obvious, so Jake stood up and walked over to them as soon as they were tucked behind their booth just three tables up.

"Hum-m-m-m," lowly growled from one of the men as Jake spoke, "Good to see you in town." When neither had anything to say Jake leaned over in as if they might have developed hearing issues and Wart's condition became clearer. He had been to the dentist and was so numb that drool spilled onto his chin and off to his hand where it rested on the table. "Nenis," he mumbled, and Jake winced, "how are you going to eat?"

Their waitress had overheard and said, "Just point to what you want, and I'll handle it. Sweet tea? Right?" she handed them menus and they motioned that sweet tea was fine and she quickly inquired, "Ice or not? I know cold is an issue after the dentist," and Mr. Fisk signaled, "no ice," with a baseball umpires' "strike" motion. They both pointed to the artichoke risotto and as she strode to the back with their order Jake told them, "Glad you two are doing well. Catch you next time when you can talk," and they each gave a nod.

Robin sat Jake's piping hot lasagna in front of him and when the steam rose and warmed his ears, instead of reaching for his fork, he reached for Robin's folded hands on top of the table where she sat gazing at him. "Mom says that if you get the Tuscarora federal recognition you might be worth marrying one day," she flicked her long loose black hair over her shoulder and chuckled, "Well you tell your mother that I'm worth something now," and a steel pot clanged as Mr. Fisk motioned for his waitress.

In a few minutes, their waitress returned with their orders in take-out boxes and they whizzed out the front giving her a five dollar tip which she waved like a fan under her little chin and Robin asked, "Do you think I should wear braids?"

"Mmm," he studied her face and lingered at her peaches and his dimples dug, "If you have one of those little Indian maid dresses, I'd let you spend the night. Try you out," and her full lips parted, "In fact," he squeezed her hands tighter so she couldn't jump away, "I'd marry a girl like that," and Gili flung open those swinging doors sporting a steel ladle. "We're not marrying you! We don't even keep costumes."

An argument arose outside the window of Jake's booth, diverting his attention from Robin. Mr. Fisk yelled something about "report" as they hurried to their car-truck.

"I never said costume. I said dress." Jake released his grip on Robin's hands and the two gave their attention to Gili.

"You made it "costume" with the way you said it. I know what you mean," Gili's five-foot frame seemed much larger when Jake was sitting down, and she was puffed up. "Now, settle down, you know I don't mean anything other than joking around."

"How do we know that?" The ladle jeered off her hip like a gun. "You a white boy chasing an Indian girl and sounds like you are trying to bribe her to stay with you. You really think you can get the government to sign on with the Tuscarora?"

"Yes, me, someone has to try. I'm getting research together and doing what I can, Gili."

"Humph." Gili pushed through the doors and yelled, "Get that man some coffee. I think he's drunk!" She laughed and he closed his eyes and when he opened them Robin was grinning. She leaned in closely and whispered, "I think there's gum under the table," and perplexed, he felt underneath and found wide duct tape leading to a baby monitor. "Can I get a take-out box? I'm running behind," Jake said, and she hurried back with the box and slid his lasagna inside. "Walk me to the car?" he whispered, and she nodded, "Yes."

Fall weather in North Carolina is unpredictable, so the afternoon warmth was a welcome respite from the cold windy morning. Robin leaned against Jake's truck as he placed his take-out inside, and he leaned over her with his hands on the rooftop and his lips on hers. "I haven't been to the office yet," he kissed her neck and she told him to stop or they would be throwing that lasagna on the floorboard and he'd throw her on the seat. "We can do that," he smiled as the afternoon sun heated his back and she ran her fingertips up and down his spine until he stood back and said, "Oh, God, I have to tell you." "What?"

"Aboriginal history is a requirement for federal recognition and Miss Lucy talked with a professor at Duke and he sent her a book with the genealogy and the references and everything we need. He's got thirty years of experience in history and won all kinds of awards. I think this is it."

"Do you have the book with you?"

"No, I, uh read through it last night. It was in a stack of papers she'd brought in."

"Jake?"

"She wouldn't care. Really wouldn't. She even said she wants me to read all her research."

"Okay. So, what next?"

"I'm going to talk to Cassie and,"

"Cassie? She's so one-sided."

"She's a smart lady, Robin, and she knows all about the history too and lives with them. I'm an outsider."

"Not for long," her black eyes stirred deep within him until he hurriedly kissed her, "You're going to say "yes," and your mother will too." They kissed good-bye and he watched her stride back into the restaurant as he lowered the window to cool down as he sped to Zoskiroro's.

There were seven vehicles in Zoskiroro's parking lot as customers left with shopping bags and Jake parked at the side entrance. With the coast clear, he checked his package and certain the afternoon heat had cooled, scooped up his take-out box from the floorboard and made his way inside. He stopped in the break room for water and extra napkins and Cassie spotted him as he opened his office door. "Got ten minutes boss?" she stalked after him inside even though he said that he wanted to eat first, and she quietly told him that he could listen and eat at the same time.

"Okay."

Cassie closed the door behind her and shut the blinds and when Jake appeared disgruntled, she said, "They'll interrupt me over something they should be able to figure out on their own."

Jake opened the box and having not eaten since six o'clock the night before forked a hunk of lasagna, "Maybe you haven't trained them properly," and shoved his mouth full and had another forkful ready as Cassie began explaining her take on the Tuscarora getting federal recognition. She spent six minutes on history then handed him a scrap of paper and he balked, "This is not going to help. I'm not getting those people involved."

Cassie shrugged and rose from her chair and opened his blinds. With the showroom's brilliant sunshine behind her her curly orangey topknot sparkled with blinding diamonds.

Jake tossed the box into the trash can and missed, got up and put it in and rubbed his hands together. "I fully agree on your historic claims, Cassie. I do. I believe the majority of Lumbee are descendants of the Tuscarora. The Cheraw population had been decimated by smallpox and those who survived either left or were absorbed by the Mighty Tuscs, the same Indians who absorbed the colonists. Being Indian in the 1700's was dangerous. Being a "murdering" Tuscarora was deadly. Of course, there were Peoples who pretended Cheraw origins. In 2003, the Lumbee Council claimed to be Cheraw and Bruce said that was partly true because the Tuscarora had absorbed them. Back then they also claimed to be Cheraw just so the whites would do business with them. Heck, everyone had learned that money was the game by then and Tuscarora were the major traders. Just makes sense." When Cassie hadn't blinked, Jake excitedly added, "It's in the professor's book I read last night. After the 1700's period of stealing their land and selling their people into slavery and the Tuscarora War, there was this man named Mooney who called himself an anthropologist and screwed up the Iroquoian history because he was biased toward the Siouan. Got the same shit going on now with Lumbee professors. For hundreds of years now, people have been quoting this man's work and that's half the problem."

Cassie closed her eyes and grunted, and when Jake reached out to hold her hand, she turned her back to him as Jake pleaded, "The history problem needs to be fixed first before we can fully address recognition. The petition packet demands verification material and I think this professor's work. He's got thirty years in it, Cassie. It's all documented. They had no choice but to go to the pines. He's got references to the deeds and a governor admitting they were swindled out of their lands. This is proof of who they are." [42]

Cassie scowled over her shoulder, "Tuscs have always known who we are," and slammed the door.

Chapter 6

The Cycle of Mayhem Now

The scent of bakery goods and fried chicken lofted through the open kitchen window where Miss Lucy waved at Jake as he returned home. Jake was lifted inside and sat at the table with a magical smile. "Getting you here is the best decision I've made all year," he smacked over his plate of mashed potatoes and gravy, green beans and fried chicken thighs and said, "Will you marry me?"

"Well, of course I will," she placed her napkin in her lap and asked, "Do you believe in God?"

"Yeah."

"That's important with couples – to be equally yoked. Bow your head." She recited a short common prayer and added, "May our marriage be short and sweet as the fools' lives who've entered my home."

"What now?"

"Russ visited me at the library today to report that someone had entered my home today. In the middle of the day," her blues stung. "Couldn't see anything out of place, so we drove out there and I couldn't either. He wants me to stay here until we get to the bottom of this."

"Did he bring the law with him?" When Miss Lucy was taken aback, Jake said, "He's an independent detective. He did a little time, very little. Won't give me the details, but he traded information and swears it wasn't anything to do with Bruce that night."

"I did not realize that," she stabbed at the beans, "He certainly puts himself out there like he's an officer."

"Yeah, and I commend him for being professional and all and trust him to help but he's not with the county or state or anything."

"I see," she swallowed her three beans and asked, "Are you paying him out of your own pocket to help me?"

"I'm writing it off on the winery. Don't worry about it, really."

"You haven't been there long. Are you making profit already?"

"Yes, ma'am," his greens enlivened, "Robeson County's been put on the map. Zoskiroro's is a tourist destination. You should visit."

"Yes, I should," her chin tucked, and she added, "I'm going to need a drink if this goes on much longer. I'm going gray," her head bounced back as she rolled off some tension.

"So, what did he find out? What happened?" Jake asked and she explained that two sets of footprints were there when he went to check on the place at three o'clock. "Russ believes it was my neighbors, the winos." Jake's jaw dropped alligator wide, "Fisk and Wart – I saw them today. They may have overheard me talking to Robin about the research and what we're doing."

"You told Robin about the book?"

"I told her about the book Dr. Wood sent, the report and how it will help the recognition efforts."

"Oh," she relaxed, "Well, nothing was damaged and he sent me back to the library and he parked in the old chicken house, the cement structure where the tractor used to be and said that he was going to hide-out there and wait and see if they returned."

"I hope he finds what those idiots are looking for before they do."

"Idiots? They know I'm assisting the Tuscarora and have ties in Washington. I wouldn't call them idiots."

"You what now?"

"I forgot to mention that," she meekly revised, "I have friends who work at the library, the archives, so attaining materials is not a major obstacle."

"I understand that, but how do you figure they know?"

"I'm just assuming. Guess I shouldn't."

They enjoyed the fried chicken thighs and mashed potatoes and Jake wiped his mouth and asked, "Are you as paranoid as I am, or did you hear something outside?"

"I heard something."

"Shit," he motioned for her to stay put as he looked out the kitchen window and Scarecrow jumped up from under the windowsill and motioned for him to stay put as his hands signaled for him to keep talking.

"Miss Lucy, you know what would make this the best meal of the year?"

"That would be," she looked around the kitchen and Jake held up a cellophane wrapped treat, "homemade apple pie," she burst, and they paused as the rear deck creaked.

"Yes, ma'am," and I have everything we need right here. I'm going to make it with you so I will know how when I surprise my Robin-bride with a ring inside."

"Propose, with a pie?" her palms rose before her and she was at the counter nervously washing their dishes in two seconds flat. "Now, you need to put it in something, or you'll have a snaggle-toothed bride if she bites down on it." "I've already got that planned," he held out the two clamshells resting on the windowsill and she said, "Perfect!" "We found these at Holden Beach. She found one and I found the other." "Why they're a perfect set." Jake opened the pantry and from the back pulled out a box of crackers and under the one stack was a jewelry box. "I bought this a few months ago."

"You'd better give it to her soon."

Jake peeled apples and Miss Lucy cut butter into flour and told him, "Keep your water in the freezer a few minutes and add it after you have everything ready to roll the dough." She sprinkled flour across the counter and finished up the last of the dinner dishes and told him to find the brown sugar. "You need a good mix of cinnamon and sugar to brine those slices with," she asked for his knife and cut a few slices, "Not hunks, thin wafer slices," and Jake said, "I hope I can do this again in August."

"That's when you plan the proposal?"

"She has a break from classes and usually takes a week off from Gili's. I'm planning a trip and I'm gonna have a picnic lunch for the ride."

"Oh, that is so sweet," Miss Lucy beamed as Jake daydreamed and cut his finger. "Shit," he ran his finger under the facet and outside the kitchen window a German Shepherd stalked after a figure into the woods that line one side of the driveway opposite the field.

With a paper towel wrapped around his finger, he told Miss Lucy, "Looks like Scarecrow left with his dog. Must be in the clear now."

"Must be? I won't sleep until you're sure and even then, it will be hard."

"Okay," he slipped on his jacket and went to his room and returned with a .38 pistol and a ballcap fitted with lithium lights on the bill. "I'll be right back. I've got a key so lock yourself in."

"You be careful," her stern warning followed Jake into the cold dark night. It was so still and quiet only rustling maple leaves and the crunch of his boots against the gravel disturbed the silence. When he had finished walking around the front of the house, he turned on the cap's lights and daringly walked behind the barn. He walked halfway and stood perfectly still. No cows were up, and the chickens were in a chicken tractor in the side pasture. He walked down to the rear corner and stole a peek down the side and when it was clear, walked back to the front double-doors and went inside. He slowly pulled on the feed room door when "Jake! Jake!" shrieked through the silence and he *flew* back to the house with his pistol in both hands out in front of him.

Nothing was out front, so he went around back, and the back door was jutted open with a crowbar pried into the jam. "Fuck!" Jake ran to the side of the house. Window good. Ran down to the basement. Lock secure. Ran to the edge of the woods and fast-fleeing steps faded into the black forest.

Jake did his best to calm Miss Lucy and when that wasn't enough, he instructed, "Don't remove the safety until you plan to kill somebody," and handed her his .38 and she didn't balk. "I'm going back to the barn and get some boards," he told her, "If I'm not back in a few minutes call the sheriff's department." "I will." She told him that the number was in her cell phone. "Good," he kissed her cheek and she smiled, "We'll be okay. I think it's your winos. They must be after your research." "You think so? Then they must work for the Lumbees," her eyes grew wide, "We're outnumbered here, Jake."

"I'll think of something," he sighed and lurched off the steps toward the barn.

He returned minutes later and pulled out the crowbar, screwed down boards strapping the back door tight and hid the research satchel while the apple pie finished baking. They retired for bed and each tossed and turned until almost midnight, finally dozing off after prayers.

Morning was quick with coffee and apple pie for breakfast. Jake followed Miss Lucy to the library, and they took over the administration department's copiers and made duplicates of everything and put one set inside her filing cabinet. "The board and I are the only ones who have a key," she told Jake for the third time and this time he asked, "Are any board members Lumbee?" Her shoulders dropped when she answered, "All but one," and they removed the duplicates.

They paced around the copy room as Miss Lucy called out various places and suggested her bank, which was secure, but the drawers were too small. "I know who," Jake's wildcat expression declared it was the last person she'd expect, "Cassie," he said, and she replied, "I had a feeling. Yes, I did," she quipped as Jake's jaw jutted out proud, "No one would dare mess with Cassie's place and she's always got someone around too. I have the perfect little safe to put it in. I'll keep the key though." "Ohh, that's perfect," she absolutely purred.

Jake carried her satchel and the duplicates to his truck while she followed with a copy of the Chapter 6 draft. "Now remember not to let her have this, Jake," her blues were firm, but Jake said, "She's going to know. She probably already does. My face is an open book, Lucy. I go into work and close myself off and she knows I'm doing something and that it's Tuscarora work because we've discussed what the People need to do next. She wants me to write the U.K. for a letter of recommendation to the BIA and I told her that it would be best to do history first."

"Now, she has an idea there, Jake. The U.K. is a strong ally for the federal government, and you know they don't want to offend. The U.K. is partially to blame, well, mostly, for the genocide of the People, and why don't you let me take care of that?"

"Gladly, but Cassie wants to read it first."

"Jake, uh, she's a tough cookie, smart, I'm sure, but is she really qualified to proofread a letter?"

"Trust me," his towering frame's shadow pointed into a spear against his truck when the wind caught his willowy blonde hair and she patted him on the forearm and asked, "Should you follow me home tonight?"

"No, I'm going to take care of your winos myself today," his voice had deepened, and she beamed, "See you tonight, Jake."

Jake phoned Cassie from Zoskiroro's parking lot and asked her to come out to his truck and she said that if he had something heavy that she'd send one of her boys. "No, this is between us, just us," he explained and with her long strides they were eye-to-eye in less than a minute. Jake explained that the research was paramount to the Tuscarora hearing they were preparing for and that his librarian friend needed a safe place other than the library because most of the board members were Lumbee. He held out about half of the stack of duplicates and the other half sat in the seat.

Cassie thumbed through some pages on the top, "How long is she staying with you?" and stealthily, Jake pulled some from the stack she was holding. "These are the only ones we need you to keep."

The top document had the letterhead of the Department of Interior, United States Indian Service and was dated March 2, 1912.

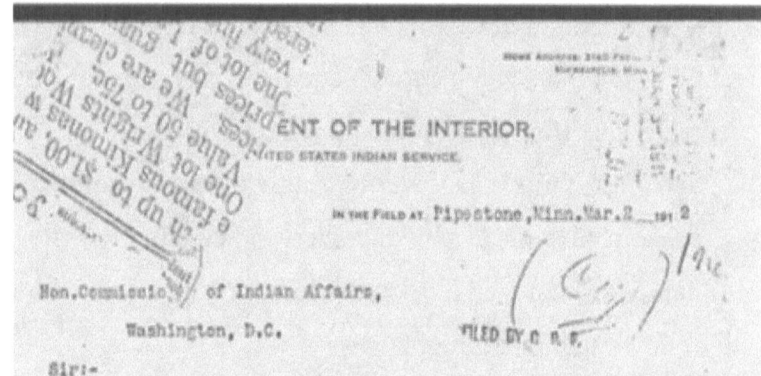

ENT OF THE INTERIOR.
UNITED STATES INDIAN SERVICE.

IN THE FIELD AT Pipestone,Minn.Mar.2__191 2

Hon.Commissioner of Indian Affairs,

    Washington, D.C.

                             FILED BY C A E

Sir:-

    I have the honor to report a short visit among the Croatan Indians,living in the vicinity of Pembroke,N.C. While at the Cherokee school I learned that an effort had been made by these people to secure the passage of an Act in the North Carolina Legislature,allowing them to take the name of Cherokees,and to become a part of the incorporated band of Eastern Cherokees. I also learned that an effort was about to be made to secure federal aid for the establishment of a government boarding school for them,and in order to familiarize myself with the situation visited Robeson county in which they reside.

    The Croatan Indians,as these people are called,number about 10000 people,about 7000 of whom reside in Robeson county.

    There has been considerable doubt in the past as to the ancestry of these Indians,who seem to stand alone as Indians in this section of the country. However,historians of recent date have now practicallyagreed that they are a mixture of white and Indian,the white blood being that from the colonists of the Lost Colony of the Roanoke,and the Indian from remnants of the once powerfull tribes that inhabited the region south of Virginia.

La...on ..n early historian who visited this section of ...orth
Carolina in 1709 states that the Hatteras Indians,who then lived
on Roanoke Island,told him that their ancestors were white people,
that they could"talk from a book",or read as he did,and that they
were proud of the fact,and showed ever readiness to do the most
kindly acts for him.

Lawson classed them as being a mixture of English and
Hatorask Indian,and a people of more than ordinary ability.
In conversation with one of the old men of the tribe,who spoke
excellent English and was very intelligent,he stated to me that
his"grandfeythers" had told him that their people were part
Tuscarora,and that when the Tuscaroras were driven north from
the Carolinas,many friendly families of them fled to white
settlements,where they were protected and took up their homes,
and that later on friendly Indians from other tribes joined them
and all moved to the region of the Lumber river where they have
lived for the past two hundred years.

.. That the Indian blood is from more than one tribe is
plainly seen by one familiar with Indian characteristics,for in
the schools and at other gatherings one meets with positively
different types of Indians.

.. It is also a fact that since the first discovery of these
people they have had no Indian language nor Indian customs,and
are not able to communicate with other Indians except through the
medium of the English language.

In the use of this language they still hold to some of the
Old English forms,such as "mon" for man, "feyther" for father,
"wit" for know, etc. It is said that an Old English expression

The whites of her eyes forewarned, "What the bloody fuck!
This government's known all along we're Tuscarora and they let
these political assholes rename us, over and over again. What
the bloody fuck. Look at that. Hatteras, "Hatorosk" Tuscarora.
They've known all along. That's why the Lumbees friggin hate

us. We need to sue them and the Lumbee council. You know they knew this too and they've been collecting HUD on our headcount and not giving us shit. We're not their fucking splinter group. We're their brothers and sisters. We're always told, "We serve enrolled Lumbee first." I bes crotched up wid you on this, Buddyrow." The aged pages under the government documents caught her eye and trembled along with her jaw jut out like a bulldog's.

CREATIVE ARTS

Our Hatteras Tuscarora people are very creative and very dextrious with their hands. For recreation they enjoy basket weaving, making quilts, crocheting, ceramics and macramae.

EXECUTIVE BOARD MEMBERS

Vernon Locklear .... Chairman

Leola Locklear .... Vice Chairman

Emma Jean Locklear .... Secretary

Lamon Locklear .... Treasurer

Dale Maynor .... Field Director

COUNCIL BOARD MEMBERS

Benny Locklear – Chief	Lena Bullard
Lewis Barton	Jerry Ray Deese
Mary C. Hunt	D. L. Locklear
Willie James Locklear	Daniel Locklear
Nathaniel Locklear	Ruth Helen Locklear
Inez Deese	Don Barton

THE HATTERAS TUSCARORA INDIANS

H T I

SYMBOL

MOTTO

"LET US
PUT OUR
MINDS TOGETHER
TO
SEE
WHAT KIND OF LIFE WE CAN
MAKE FOR OUR CHILDREN"

PARENTS – CHILDREN – COMMUNITY

HISTORY

Robeson County, located in the Southeast section of North Carolina is the home of approximately twenty five hundred Hatteras Tuscarora Tribal Members.

Our history relates back to 1641; our ancestors were located around Lumber River (better known as Drowning Creek). The Hatteras Tuscarora Tribe has had a burning desire for many decades, to be recognized by the Federal Government.

From 1835 the tribe has been organized and has been struggling for equal representation. The Henry Berry Lowry War which lasted ten years from 1864-1874 brought some improvement for Hatteras Tuscaroras in improving human rights, making available educational opportunities and improving living standards. In deed Henry Berry Lowry was a Hatteras Tuscarora and his spirit will continue to live on in future generations.

LOCATION AND PROBLEM AREAS

Many of our tribal members have settled along the banks of the beautiful but treacherous Lumber River, which flows through our county. Fishing, hunting and trapping along Lumber River is a means for food, income and enjoyment for our people.

Indian schools were intergrated in 1966, causing the termination of Indian schools. Many of our Indian youth had trouble adjusting to intergration and did not complete their high school education. Farming was the most prevelant employment until 1960. However, due to the increased importance of manufacturing, by 1970, Robeson County experienced a dramatic change from Agri-business to agri-industrial business proliferation. The industrial revolution has had harmful effects on the life style of the Hatteras Tuscarora people, causing family dislocations, loss of small farms to large cooperate entities, and forcing both family members to find employment.

Much like other minority groups we live in a rural, economically disadvantaged area and our people have developed a poor self image. A feeling of not being able to rise to standards of living enjoyed by other races, especially in education and employment opportunities.

ORGANIZATION

The tribal government consists of seven executive board members and the council board members consist of twelve members. Our meetings are held once a week.

OBJECTIVES

The objectives of the organization is to address the needs of the Hatteras Tuscarora Tribe in the area of health, education and to continue to pursue Federal Recognition. It will provide technical assistance and professional services to private and public agencies national, state and local seeking to eradicate the problems of poverty. It will also assist the community in social and economic development. The Hatteras Tuscarora Tribe will strive to cooperate its efforts with other service agencies to help improve and expand existing services in the Eastern Carolinas.

"This is Leola's work and it's been where all this time? In some fool's attic? This is us. This is Robeson County, North Carolina, and it's been stolen from us." Her stale coffee breath fumed like steam from the espresso machine and Jake clenched. "The big fish eat the little fish," Jake's refrain fed her fire as she flipped pages and she aimed at the satchel, "What about those?"

"That's my shit."

The gingham satchel's straps were bright yellow except at the middle where they were dark yellow.

Cassie tucked her brilliant blues under her coy smile and asked, "What are you trying to hide?"

"That's my shit, Cassie. I'm working with a developer. Thinking about expanding."

"Liar."

"I own this place, free and clear and you were chosen to be the manager, but it isn't in writing anywhere that I have to keep you on."

"I'm going to read these."

"That's fine."

"I mean, I'll read all of these - you see me," she threatened, and Jake's stoic reaction relit her fire as she blew, "I'm takin' a early lunch." She marched off toward her car and Jake called out, "Take as long as you need."

As soon as her car hit the highway, Jake called Miss Lucy, "This whole thing is worse than I thought. I can't trust Cassie anymore. She knows you're staying with me and I haven't told a soul. Have you?"

"No, Russ told me not to," she panted, "I've been busy this morning and ran across a travel snippet on Hawaii. Ever been?"

"Naw, what the, what are thinking of doing?"

"We could go there, on separate flights, and finish the book. I'll go on the guise of a vacation, the first in five years and you go on your honeymoon."

"Great idea, bad timing though. Robin doesn't get more than a week break in August."

"What if we went at Christmas?"

"That's just a month away?"

"Think you can remember how to bake that apple pie?"

"Lucy, you're getting me into more things. I swear."

Two cars pulled into Zoskiroro's and five ladies huddled together and entered the showroom while Jake and Miss Lucy decided on where to hide the duplicates. "I had to give Cassie some or she would have caught on that I caught on that she was getting information on us from someone other than me."

"Well did you screen what you gave her? This could be a mess."

"It's already a mess. I only gave her the file with previous hearings and all those denials."

"Well if she's as clever a cookie as you say, she's going to question your and I guess mine as well, research abilities. How much do you share with her on this recognition effort?"

"I mentioned Dr. Wood's name and said that he'd sent his report. I seriously doubt she'll reach out to him, but it can't hurt if she does. At this point, I'm not clear on what her motive is anymore, but I do believe she wants the best for the Tuscs."

"That's what matters," she asked if he wanted to bring Robin for dinner over the weekend and he agreed, "But I'm not ready to bake that pie."

She guffawed and said, "See you tonight."

"Tonight." Jake threw his jacket over the stacks of duplicates and it covered the satchel in the floorboard as well and he carried his copy of the Chapter 6 draft into his office and locked the door and closed the blinds.

"Chapter 6, The Cycle of Mayhem Then," Jake read the title and laughed, "What goes around comes around, from the frickin' 1700's to twenty years ago and damn, right up to now and tomorrow isn't promised either. Lucy's got a way with words," he leaned back in his comfy office chair with his socked feet on the pillow atop his desktop to enjoy the pages:

"Driving Crash?"

"Crash is gone. Block cracked."

"Didn't update me. Doesn't matter. Drive a tractor if you have to," Bruce vibrated with
excitement.

"Do I need to bring you any clothes, your boots? Or are you gonna start a orange jumpsuit trend?"

"No orange. A decent shirt would be all right. I've got jeans."

"At nine?"

"That's what boss man says."

"Good boss man. Sending you home early, too. Can't beat that. Call if there're any
changes."

"There won't be. Thanks, Jake. I can always count on you."

"Sure. Glad to do it, Bruce. See you tomorrow, Buddyrow."

The ride over to Beacon Prison in Richmond County took two hours, but it felt like only a few minutes. Jake sang the entire trip, sporadically shouting," Good-gooboly-goo," but Jake's happy expression was soon overcome as the reality of prison socked him in the nose. The heavy smells of prison;

disinfectant, stale and sour humans, pungent food odors and strong stale piss hit the pit of Jake's stomach as he was instructed to wait near the entrance by the cracked-open window where the stale funk slowly seeped.

Fast footsteps beat back the nausea as Jake smiled at his dear friend hurrying with an open smile. Bruce's steps quickened when Jake's dimples appeared over the guard' shoulder, and the guard stepped aside. "We all like Bruce. Guys call him The Prince, us too. Got a smart head on his shoulders."

"That he does." Jake clapped with a smile so white and shiny it could've fooled a dying man into thinking he'd seen the holy light, "Buddyrow!"

"Brickhouse," Bruce drawled it out. At three feet away, light flooded his face. He was carrying six haggard years under his eyes. The black half-moons under his eyes aged him. The old jeans he wore in six years before hung on his lean hips. The tennis shoes were plain white, newish, from the state. The guard mechanically handed him the bundle of clothes Jake had brought and Bruce didn't miss a step as he pulled off his thin assigned tee shirt and slipped on the new one.

The guard reached out for Bruce's hand and shook it as he handed him a suit on a hanger and a sealed envelope with the standard mediocre allotment and release statement. They each said good-bye and the guard opened the glass steel bar reinforced door and Bruce stepped out into freedom under the hot Carolina summer sky.

His eyes adjusted and wandered over Jake's scared face as he reached out and gave him a manly hug. Jake had become a strong example of healthy living and was every bit the sexy country boy. Bruce was not. Bruce's full hand softly patted Jake's scarred cheek. "On you, it's just a beauty mark."

Jake absorbed Bruce's knowledge of the scar along with his friend's pale gaunt reflection.

"It was in all the papers." Bruce explained as they stood toe to toe.

"Yea. Half the time, don't remember it's there." He blinked through the lie as he held Bruce's shoulders. "You need to get some rest and some meat on your bones." When Bruce didn't respond, Jake asked, "How much do you know?" "Cells are like echo chambers; fools talk all night." Bruce tried not to stare at the scar. From the corner of Jake's generous mouth to his cheekbone and back around it formed a hoof print. "Is it quiet at the farm?"

"Yea, real quiet. You're gonna love it. Night is nothin' but crickets and frogs. In the summer we get the whole band and in the winter you can hear snow falling. Cows and ponies all the racket you're gonna get at the Crowson's."

"Sounds perfect. You sure the Crowsons don't mind?"

"Don't mind? They were excited to be helping you. In fifteen days, we added a new bedroom. Buddyrow, when word got out, we had to turn helpers away. Mark, Edge, Scarecrow, Dodger, all your jar runners showed up."

A smile spread over Bruce.

"Let's go. We'll talk in the truck."

"Truck? What about your neon green thing?" Bruce squeezed his shoulder then turned around and looked back. Dark finial forms lined the cinder block building's fenced exercise pad. Projected from deep shouts they chanted, "Brickhouse. Brickhouse." Outstretched waving arms pushed Bruce's chest like they'd touched him and propelled him backwards a step.

"You okay?"

"Yea. Drive me across the river, cuz." Bruce threw up his hand and spun toward the
road. "So, where's the green thing?"

"I needed a truck. Green thing's gone."

"Good. Truck looks great on ya." He laid the suit over the middle of the seat. Then pulled his seat belt over his chest and the rigid folded statement in his new tee shirt's pocket crinkled. Bruce stared at the figures and fingered its coma's position as Jake fastened his seat belt and switched on the engine. Bruce asked, "Is this a joke?"

"Stock you wanted skyrocketed. Got lucky, that and a smart money market manager. You're rich, Bruce."

"Bruce Black is rich." His arm swung up over the back of his head and he clutched it like it may tumble off. "I'm rich. Six hundred k, Robin'll want me now."

Jake stiffened all over as he backed out of the parking lot and eased onto the highway while Bruce stared at the bank statement. When he slapped the dash, he laughed and it startled Jake, but Jake laughed along with him and then turned on the radio. Old Country Classics twang out the last of a you done done me wrong love song and up started the next, a how to leave your man song, like they were specifically chosen to poke Jake in the neck. And the poke slowly burned as Bruce sang along with each cheatin' song.

When Jake swallowed the angst his Adam's apple bobbed like a little hand puppet flying up and down his stiffened neck, grabbing his words and holding 'em down while he tried to come up with something good rather than the plain truth. His big green eyes blinked over and over as he struggled to concentrate on keeping the truck between the lines and was relieved by the slight flow of oncoming traffic.

That only lasted ten miles. A twangy tune on taking someone else's man blared out like a Bob White's call from a strutting suitor. It rattled Jake's nerves till he had to loosen his jaw with a faux yawn.

"When's the last time you saw her?" Bruce leaned up.

Jake stared straight ahead. "Robin and I have been dating three months now. We're going to South Carolina in a couple of weeks to look at a horse. Gonna make a mini vacation out of it since Charleston'll be close by."

Charleston South Carolina is where couples go to step back in time and allow the architectural ambiance of the eighteen hundreds seduce them along with the natural esthetics like the moss wavin' in the trees and shady lanes with that fragrant wisteria lofting down into their lust hungry snouts. "We're practically engaged."

Bruce hastily folded the statement and shoved it back into his tee shirt pocket while his feet jittered, and he sucked in a red-hot drawl. Bruce changed the station, going from rock to rap to political talk and settled on modern country. Radio filled the truck with a ridiculous watermelon ruckus as Jake and Bruce swelled up with testosterone headiness. They were like toads that had been kissed by a princess and liked it, a lot, but with neither having full and proper mating rights, the truck cab was not nearly big enough for both bloated toads.

"You just forgot to mention that? Oh, that's right. It wasn't on the list of topics."

"I knew it'd be like this."

"Shoot straight with me, on everything."

Jake's eyebrows rose. "I shouldn't have waited. But I didn't lie to you." Jake's stern

response bordered on angry.

"Look. People change. I know that."

Dogmatically, Jake's ears heated. "Damn it, Bruce, it wasn't planned. We just fell for each other. She was over there with Exilee at the farm all the time and you know how she is. I couldn't ignore her." Jake checked his response and blew when Bruce stiffened, but Jake's chest broadened. "Robin and I are serious."

Just like that, Bruce was thirteen and stood in the dark with that blade catching the moonlight under his twisted grin.

They rode on about five miles in nothing but radio racket when Bruce finally spoke.

"Aunt Thelma and her husband still doing okay I guess?"
Jake stared at the road ahead.

"They're fine. I see 'em out in their yard. I helped with the move. She gave me your old cap guns and some other stuff. She even boxed up your stuffed bear, the ratty one without eyes and your books, even your first tool set. Guess what else was in there?"

"You looked through it?"

"Hey, I saw that teddy bear's ear sticking out and had to see what else was in there. Okay?"

"Yea, so what else?"

"Your Glossy Flossy poster from the closet."

"I'll want that back." Bruce's sly smile highlighted his cheekbones.

"I know."

"Thanks. Where'd you put the rest? I know she wouldn't throw out Momma's things. I had her boxes in the storage building and some under my bed."

"I put 'em up. There's safe and dry. Don't worry."

"Did you go through her stuff, too?"

"What's wrong with you?"

Bruce gazed out the window and slowly leaned back, hypnotizing himself with the humming highway. Seconds turned to minutes as miles turned to medicine until Jake swerved to miss a squirrel. Bruce plucked the statement from his pocket, "This is from the home place, a third with interest alone, plus the stocks I wanted and market accounts?"

"Yep, just like you wanted."

"What about the cash?"

"Safety deposit box. We can go now if you want."

"Now's perfect. I missed the smell of money. I love its stinkin' old paper, nasty fingers all over it. I love money."

"I know you do." Jake bobbed like an excited kid.

"How much did you pay yourself?"

"Damn it. We went through this on the phone. Played it out like I was selling puppies in
that conversation. Remember?"

"Course I do. But it's only human nature. Have that much cash at your fingertips and not borrow some, it's not natural. How much?" Bruce smiled. "One, two thousand?"

Jake pressed hard against his seat's headrest. "I told you. I didn't. Knew you'd need it more than me. Never took a single bill."

Bruce's smile faded into a queasy frown. "The whole wad is in there?"

"Hey, you wanna roll down the windows? I bet you missed the smell of fresh air, too."

"Sorry. A hundred years of fresh air and honest faces that'd be good, real fuckin' good. Sorry. But yeah, real good." Bruce held his arm straight out the window letting it hover through the streaming rush. "It's gonna be an adjustment, Buddyrow. Hope I can do this quick and get on with my life. Got a lot of work to do."

"You'll have help." Jake patted Bruce's shoulder and Bruce's eyes welled up. "I'm beginning to see that."

"You've always been there for me," Jake softly reminded him, and Bruce let the tears fall. "I bes mommucked up. Hope you can stick with this silly chauld. I don't usually get so tore up." He wiped his cheeks and sucked in the fresh air. "I missed a lot in there, Buddyrow. Missed pickin' on you."

"Good. I did, too." Jake inhaled one of those deep breaths drawn before a shout. "This is a wild and jubious world, Buddyrow. Welcome back."

Radio's mindless bliss and wind gushing in from the open window purged the truck cab as they reached the edge of Maxton near Bruce's land for his new company. Jake stopped at the railroad track instead of just easing over, but Bruce signaled to just go on down the road like he could wait. They turned onto the back road that lead to Jake's bank. Jake told Bruce to open the console and get the key. "There ya go. Already signed the box over to you. Ask for Mrs. Parker. She has the papers. Just sign your name and show 'em your I.D."

"The statement says it's with Federal Credit. What are we doing here?" Bruce held out the key and read the engraved number.

"This is my bank. I just put the cash here 'cause I was here. We can go switch names on the investment account after this. Okay?"

"Why isn't here, too?"

"Investor over at Federal Credit knows his stuff better than the eye candy here. Look, Buddyrow." Jake pointed at the hot doll opening the door for the wheelchair bound gentleman. "Ah, I'd let her open my door. Hey, pretend like you're touched, and she'll hold your arm when she walks ya into the vault."

"Idiot."

"Hey, wait a sec. I've been holding on to this." Jake grabbed the token from the cup holder and jutted it out the window at Bruce and he licked his thick red lips. Wiggled it like a cigar and slid the perty pen with the flashing nude into his shirt pocket. "Sounds like a side trip, Buddyrow-silky thongs and dirty songs." He whistled and shivered. "Man, we can stroke on by this weekend."

"Ladies are waiting in line for you. On poles. All slick and shiny. Screamin' for Brucey."   Jake back whistled the saliva like he'd been at a pig-pickin' barbeque contest where all the juices linger in the air and you can lick your arm and taste the sauces.

As Bruce returned with a beefy smile and a fat envelope sticking out of his front jean pocket, Jake turned down the radio and yelled out the window, "Hope you're up for a party. Got a few friends coming tonight."

"Whose friends?" Bruce pushed the envelope down into his pocket. "You doing this at the farm? The Crowsons'll call the law." Bruce plopped down on the seat and gave Jake his full attention.

"Not that kind of party. Some of my friends, and Thelma, Mark and her husband, of course, and Exilee and Ken, no jar runners invited, just in case."

"Believe me, they'll come if they get wind of it; a party and their old boss with rumors of a fine winery going up?"

"You're right, but," Jake whined.

"I know what you're thinkin,' Mr. Fisk and Wart."

"Why would I be worried about them? What would they want with you?"

"Oh, they don't want a thing," Bruce's grays darkened. "I do. I want my money."

"What are you gettin' at?"

"The night we moved The Company and the law called for our good buddies to get that moccasin out a' Crash, I figure that's when those pallets of Dad's shine that got missing. Idiots probably been watching me since Old Man Black sucked his last molecule. God knows how many times I was out there diggin' and hiding dirt piles under leaves and pine beds and felt like I was being watched. I was. I carried every jar down there on a separate day and they're the only ones stupid enough to dare Old Man Black's kid. Don't cha reckon?"

"I'll give ya that."

"Will ya? Look, Mr. Fisk and Wart took a big risk running from that fat daddy. Think about it. Fisk threw that poisonous snake in an officer's vehicle, was DUI and running from arrest. Serious stuff for two drunks who stay over so much at the county hotel they cook for fat daddy and his brothers, huh? I could see that in the winter when it's too cold to turn and they're out of cash. But it was cookin' season and he took his chances that night when he figured we'd all be busy, including Scarecrow." Jake cussed. "Are you sure?"

"Fisk got a look at that copper tubing, didn't he?"

"It was sort of uncovered when I got back in. It's likely. Yea, he probably did."

"Well, I got the word they "bought" a second still a month after. A big honkin' copper vat, big as a baccar barn. Had Crow go check my hidey hole and pure as goanna on a hawg's ass it was gone. Didn't even put my cedar slabs back. Shitheads."

"Can't be. No way that'd ever get through town unnoticed." Jake scratched over his head and down to his neck.

"Twelve by fourteen sheets on a flatbed covered with a tarp."

For the first time in a long time Jake grinned like he did when they were kids – yurkers who taint got no business with shine, and shouted, "Good-gooboly-goo!"

Bruce guffawed, "That's what she said!" followed by a deep gruff hasp and slapped his thigh. "If they can't get my money up, I'm confiscating that vat."

"I know you will!" Jake was all teeth.

"You mean, we will."

"Oh, shit."

Traffic was slight on the two -lane country highway. Its forests, fields and homesteads lined the road like rich oil paintings and Bruce studied each one. Jake commented, "Nothing like the country, huh? Freedom and sunshine."

"Damn skippy." Bruce inhaled a passing farm's odoriferous cow manure, its earthy plowed scents and exhaled a little sigh of content. "Beautiful. My farm'll smell like fruits of the Gods and goat."

"Goat, huh?"

"For the cheese and eyes. They're cute little boogers."

"Their cute enough, I guess. You'll have to keep 'em off cars. They climb. You'll spend a fortune on fencing alone."

"It won't hurt too much." Bruce patted his shirt pocket.

"That's right, moneybags. You got it all covered."

"That's right." Then Bruce rubbed his palms while his tongue poked his cheek. Jake passed a vintage setting; a three-story white plantation set back with a row of granddaddy oaks on a rich black section of earth with a pond all of ten acres. "Know what I missed? Those naps under that granddaddy oak after fishin' out on the back ponderosa."

"The ponderosa," Bruce sighed. "Long spell since I called it that. But you won't miss it now that I'm back. Liketa get a stringer a' pumpkin seeds and fry 'em in cracker crumbs. Um-mm. If the cooters and Alice haint et 'em up."

"New owners won't care?"

"I only sold the house and the road frontage, five acres. That back section was in my family before I was a spark. It's like it's in the Trail of Tears, man. Got stories tied to it that are tribal and sacred. Need ta preserve it no matter what. Section was deeded over to my people after the Tuscarora War, when my great, great, great, great, great, claimed to be Cheraw just so the whites would sign the deeds legal."

"How do you know that? Mom tell you?"

"Read it. Did my time with my head in a book. Kept out of trouble. You know, I run my mouth and won't back down, so a book was the best place to put my face."

"Gawd, I know that's right."

"All I had to do was ask for a book and in a week or so, it'd show up. We didn't call ourselves Tuscarora because of a slew of events over a period of three years or so. By 1714, the Tuscs had a reputation as murderers among the whites everywhere and they passed a law not to do business with us. That's why so many fled to New York and the rest of us lived in the swamps here where we could live in peace. Let me go back: Now, the Monacans, the aborigines of Eastern Carolina and by the time whites showed we branched off here and called ourselves Tuscarora and had 15 towns, more than any other tribe in 1710. What ruined it was that we took revenge on the settlers and murdered eighty of their babies and one-hundred and twelve adults in 1711. That's why Mom said we called ourselves anything but Tuscarora when the whites were around and that's why it was so easy for those fucking politicians to talk us into changing our name to Croatoan and then Lumbee, the stupidest shit I ever heard of – Lumbee." [43a]

"Yeah!" Jake cheered him on, "They stole your history right out from under you," and Bruce's big eyes dug down into slits and darted like a rabid beast's as his chest puffed up and he seethed, "They did steal it. The whites stole it and tried to exterminate us and now our brothers have changed at least half our people's names to get rid of the rest of us."

"It's not fair. They get away with everything. I mean, the whites have killed scores of Indian families. Wounded Knee - drunk soldiers shot down women and children, scalped some of 'em, threw them in a pit, $_{44}$ and you didn't hear about any of them changing their names, so Indians wouldn't be afraid of them."

"Whites have changed names before. Immigrants from Europe took the names of people in America that would fit in well; tried to blend in. Same type thing, only a different situation: Immigrants weren't known as murdering Indians and when I say what they did was something awful and word got around, people probably couldn't look at us without being afraid."

"Like what, scalping?"

"Worse. First, it was a sneak attack, in the morning, like they usually did, and nothing like war the whites knew when they let someone know they were coming to kill. Naw, they were sneaky. The Natives enslaved by the whites got word on the war and when the free Natives showed up asking for food, the whites were not alarmed but the Natives inside their houses already knew what was coming and helped them. When the Tuscs called out war whoops, the butchering began. The white's leaders, namely the surveyor Lawson who'd staked out our land to give to the whites, was tortured. They stuck his body all over with lighter splinters, fine as boar bristles, and set him on fire alive. They went off torching houses and flushing out families and killed them, no matter what age or sex. After they got into some liquor, it got nasty. Let me hold your cell phone and I'll pull up the university's digital copy of this letter I found. Hellish, man. You can read it later. You'll see why the Tuscs went with calling themselves other names. From that day forward, the whites had declared revenge and it's still going on." [43b]

A LETTER FROM MAJOR CHRISTOPHER GALE.
[From Nicholls' Literary Illustrations—Reprinted from Hawks's History of North Carolina.]

Charleston S. C.
November 2 1711.

My Dear:—

I cannot omit, by all opportunities, to inform my second self that you have still living in a brother the most faithful friend that ever was, though perhaps by as signal a hand of Providence as this age can demonstrate.

I will not trouble you with repetitions, but refer you to the after-written memorial which I laid before the government, and shall only acquaint you how far I had been concerned in the bloody tragedy, if kind Providence had not prevented.

About ten days before the fatal day, I was at the baron's, and had agreed with him and Mr. Lawson on a progress to the Indian towns; but before we were prepared to go, a message came from home, to inform me that my wife and brother lay dangerously sick; which I may call a happy sickness to me, for on the news I immediately repaired home, and thereby avoided the fate which I shall hereafter inform you.

The baron, with Mr. Lawson and their attendants, proceeding on their journey, were, on the 22d of September (as you will see by the memorial) both barbarously murdered; the mat, on which the baron used to lie on such like voyages, being since found all daubed with blood, so as we suppose

-------------------- page 826 --------------------

him to have been quickly dispatched. But the fate of Mr. Lawson (if our Indian information be true) was much more tragical, for we are informed that they stuck him full of fine small splinters of torchwood, like hogs' bristles, and so set them gradually on fire. This, I doubt not, had been my fate if Providence had not prevented; but I hope God Almighty has designed me for an instrument in the revenging such innocent Christian blood.

On Sunday, October 21, I arrived here in the quality of an agent, and in order to procure the assistance of the government to destroy our enemies, which I doubt not in a little time to effect. The family I left in garrison at Bath town, my wife and brother pretty well recovered; but what has happened since, I know not. Two days after I left the town, at daybreak (which is the Indians' usual time of attack), above 100 guns were heard, which must have been an attack made by the Indians upon some of our garrisons, which are in all eleven in number; but cannot hear the success of it, though a small vessel came from the out part of our government there the other day, by which I have the following news: that on my coming away, Captain Brice detached from our out-garrisons fifty men, and in the woods met with a body of Indians, who fought them three days, and forced them at last to retire into their garrison. The Indians lost in this engagement fifteen men, and we took two, one of whom was killed by one of our men. During this engagement, another body of the Indians, being advised that the garrison was weakened by this detachment, came and attacked the garrison, and at the same time a number of Indian prisoners of a certain nation, which we did not know, whether they were friends or enemies, rose in the garrison, but were soon cut to pieces, as also those on the outside repelled. In the garrison were killed nine Indian men, and soon after thirty-nine women and children sent off for slaves. This is the condition we at present labor under. I shall not trouble you with a particular relation of all their butcheries, but shall relate to you some of them, by which you may suppose the rest. The family of one Mr. Nevill was treated after this manner: the old gentleman himself, after being shot, was laid on the house-floor, with a clean pillow under his head, his wife's head-clothes put upon his head, his stockings turned over his shoes, and his body covered all over with new linen. His wife was set upon her knees, and her hands lifted up as if she was at prayers, leaning against a chair in the chimney corner, and her coats turned up over her head. A son of his was laid out in the yard, with a pillow laid under his head and a bunch of rosemary laid to his nose. A negro had his right hand cut off and left dead. The master

-------------------- page 827 --------------------

of the next house was shot and his body laid flat upon his wife's grave. Women were laid on their house-floors and great stakes run up through their bodies. Others big with child, the infants were ripped out and hung upon trees. In short, their manner of butchery has been so various and unaccountable, that it would be beyond credit to relate them. This blow was so hotly followed by the hellish crew, that we could not bury our dead; so that they were left for prey to the dogs, and wolves, and vultures, whilst our care was to strengthen our garrison to secure the living.
The ship by which this comes is ready to sail, so cannot enlarge; only desire my duty may be presented to my father and mother, my sincere love to yourself and brothers, and service to all friends, hoping for a speedy answer to my last by Madam Hyde, is what offers from
Your sincerely affectionate brother,
CHRISTOPHER GALE.

FROM CHARLES TOWN, CAROLINA.

The Memorial of Christopher Gale from the Government of North Carolina, to the Honorable Robert Gibs, Governor and Commander-in-chief, and to the Honorable Council and General Assembly.

To lay before your honor the prospect or representation of as promising a country as was ever watered with the dew of heaven, would take up more time than the present exigency of the affair I am now set upon would give me leave; but much more time, and a hand more skilful, would be requisite to give you a view of the calamities and miseries of so fine a country laid waste and desolate by the most barbarous enemies: I mean the Corees and Tuscarora Indians.

Although I shall not use much eloquence to implore your aid and assistance in revenging such injuries, causes of that nature when truly stated being their own best orator; yet, I presume, I have all the advantages that may be of making a true representation of that affair to your honors, being an inhabitant of Beaufort precinct, where a great part of this hellish tragedy was acted. I shall, therefore, inform your honors, that on Saturday the 22d of September last, was perpetrated the grossest piece of villainy that perhaps was ever heard of in English America. One hundred and thirty people massacred at the head of the Nuse, and on the south side of Pamptaco rivers, in the space of two hours; butchered after the most barbarous manner that can be expressed, and their

-------------------- page 828 --------------------

dead bodies used with all the scorn and indignity imaginable; their houses plundered of considerable riches (being generally traders), then burned, and their growing and hopeful crops destroyed. What spectacle can strike a man with more horror and stir up more to revenge, than to see so much barbarity practised in so little a time and so unexpectedly? And what makes it the more surprising, that nefarious villainy was committed by such Indians as were esteemed as members of the several families where the mischiefs were done, and that with smiles in their countenances, when their intent was to destroy. I must inform your honors that the governors of North Carolina are not in a condition to take a full (I might say any) satisfaction on the enemy, nor to prevent their further progress, by reason their neighboriug Indians are not to be relied on for any assistance, but rather to be feared they would be prejudicial in any expeditions; if not joined with the enemy as we have good reason to judge by their behavior both before and since the act was committed: therefore a strict and jealous eye is necessarily kept over them by the government, and our whole country drawn into garrisons to prevent mischief that way, which very much hinders the getting men into a body to pursue the enemy, who are at present between two and three hundred effective men, and above one thousand women and children; and I believe your honors will be of opinion, that it is altogether impracticable to attempt such a body of men, flushed with their first success, without Indians who are acquainted with their manner of fighting. Wherefore, on behalf of the government of North Carolina, by which I am employed, I earnestly entreat your honors to permit and encourage so many of your tributary Indians as you think proper, to fall upon those Indians our enemies, whose families are since fled down to the seaboard between Weatuck and Cape Fare rivers, whilst their men are still ravaging and destroying all before them, within sight of our garrisons; that by your assistance exemplary justice may be done to such barbarous villains as have laid waste and desolate such a flourishing part of the lords proprietors' country, and which, without your speedy relief, will be wholly deserted. If any Indians are found innocent of that massacre and will assist in the destruction of those inhuman wretches, care will be taken to distinguish those from the rest; but I very much fear that upon strict inquiry, it would be found that the whole nation of the Tuscaroras (though some of them may not yet be actors) was knowing and consenting to what was done; and that the success of those already in motion, if not put a stop to, will at last induce the rest to join with them in carrying on these bloody designs. Beside the daily expectation of a considerable number of Senekoes [Senecas],

-------------------- page 829 --------------------

which we are certainly informed are coming to cohabit with the Tuscaroras, our enemies, this winter, and become one nation, which in time may affect our neighboring governments as well as us. I firmly persuade myself that

so much prejudice as the lords proprietors will receive by that fatal blow, the barbarous murder of so many of our fellow-subjects, among which number is the Honorable Baron de Graffenried, a landgrave of Carolina, and a member of the council, Mr. Lawson the surveyor-general, with divers others of note, will excite your honors' compassion toward such a country and hasten your assistance and relief.
I am, with all respect,
Your honors' most obedient, humble servant,
CHRISTOPHER GALE [43c]

"Hell, the Tuscs knew the English were taking over their county and were dead set on stopping them. That King of England had already doled out our lands to his Lords and their heirs – our land! Don't take my word for it, you pull up this link docsouth.unc.edu/csr/index.php/document/csr01-0441 tonight and check Christopher Gale's full letter. Read the diary letter and that letter to Robert Johnson. Burns me up. Think they didn't plan to change the name of our Peoples? Think again. They thought if they erased our Tuscarora name that they'd never have to settle in court with us. Because we wouldn't exist! And here we are. They had traitor tribes telling everything and killing our Peoples and so we had no choice but to go to the swamps and hide – from all of 'em. And they kept after us until we had no choice but to keep raging war too after the war and damn it, I'm glad they did. If only it'd worked. But we were outnumbered, they made up their own laws to get what they wanted, and we didn't know their language well enough to know what we were signing. They perty much bullshit us out of our own country. [45] If we'd had support of all the tribes, there'd be a different world here and it wouldn't be named America – you see me!"

Bruce returned Jake's cell phone, "Might not get it read tonight, but you're right."

"I know I am," Bruce's hands spread tapped the headliner, ferociously, "You know what else burns me up? Those royal shits were mad at Colonel Barnwell when he didn't exterminate us "savages" when he had the chance. He's got a fort named after him and what do you see at our site, Indian Woods? You see freakin' condos. [46] That's some shit now. I'd like to see a park set up at my place and call it Indian Woods and let the whites come and see a presentation of what it was really like when the whites came and stole our country. That would be incredible payback, but not big enough. What I want ta see is complete appropriation. I want a tax on every firearm sold to go directly into a non-government Native Peoples' appropriation fund with a requirement for all members to choose a traditional name to satisfy my Peoples' spirits."

"You really thought this through. Incredible, man, but I still think you oughta turn it into a park or something. Wouldn't that be a come-back?"

"From Old Man Black's piece a' ground with gator dogs and toten haunts? Never
happen, and booby traps still hanging, and who knows what else, yea, that'd be a miracle."

Jake pushed back against the seat and his green eyes glistened like an angel just perched on his shoulder. He shivered and turned away the air conditioning vent. "Never say never. Anything can happen."

Bruce searched Jake's face and the scar pit against his stomach like a punch. "You're right. But that's way on down the road. I'm set on getting my business off the ground. That is, right after you and I catch up. Can't tell ya enough how happy I am right now that you're okay and we're headed off to start over together. It means everything. I've thought about this for six miserable years, Buddyrow."

Jakes turned off the radio. "You're gonna love the farm. It's awesome. My life is nothing like it used to be. I get up every morning to do something different. I see what I've done. David's gradually retiring, so I do most of it. His son Ken does some, too. Most of the time it's just me out there, the ponies and cows. I've got three rows of tomatoes, two hundred plants, green beans and twenty-five acres of corn about to tassel. Some of that's for feed, and okra."

"Feeding the county?"

"Wholesale and retail and put up a lot. Can and freeze."

"You ever whoop okra?"

"Missed that. Say whoop?"

"Whoop the leaves off before it buds, and it'll produce double the pods."

"Whoop it? Like hit the plants?"

"Take a baccar stick and knock off the leaves. Do your plants have buds yet?"

"Nope."

"Good. I'll do it for you."

"Better work or David's gonna be real sore. He'd eat okra for breakfast if Miss Sarah'd cook it. It turns more per pound than tomatoes."

"Trust me, Jakey boy," Bruce drummed the dash. "Hey, did you get the dewberries?"

"Got 'em planted, too. Was hoping to make that a surprise, but you know me. Exilee and I pick early in the mornings. Miss Sarah freezes 'em. Got a freezer full, 'nugh to make a batch. Then we start on the farm. We're all rootin' for you, Bruce." Jake smiled over at Bruce and discovered his hardcore business buddy all red faced. Bruce coughed out the lump in his throat. "I'm going to pay you for those plants, Jake."

"David bought 'em for you. They're a gift."

"Mr. Crowson? He doesn't even know me. Why would he invest in my winery? What does he want?"

"Nothing. Not all people are like that. Crowsons are good old Baptists."

"Baptists helping turn?"

"They don't see it that way. Believe me. They do not condone drinking. They're just trying to do what God would have them do."

"One God comes to many people." Bruce announced his faith like an old best friend.

"Do they know about me? What I was doing?"

"It doesn't matter. You're my best friend. That's good enough for them."

"From our phone visits, I thought I was replaced with Crowson's daughter-in-law. You talk about her all the time, in every phone call, and to tell you the truth, I'm jealous. She took my place and I want it back."

"Exilee struggled all her life, being mixed, in the South and without a mother and with a mean ass dad. She's had a rough one. Makes me think that we were put together because you were gone, and she needed someone like me, and I missed you. Ya know what I mean?"

Bruce smiled at him and directed his attention back to the road.

"She believes we live a cumulative life from our ancestor's lives and the more mixed we are the richer our lives. Says she's Tuscarora High, because the blood comes from all of them. You know, the mix with the English settlers, she says they're her blood, and even her white dad's German blood and the black blood and Irish. She called living their experiences retroactive psychohistory."

Bruce cleared his throat. "That's something man, to hear you talking like that."

"Like what?"

"Like a Native. You have a big spirit. Exilee can call it what she wants. We'd say she has an old spirit." Bruce's mouth tightened as his face plumped up red. "I love you, Jake. You're my brother. Don't ever forget that. No matter what happens." He quickly turned away and looked out the open window.

"I love you too, brother. Hey, that's why we spent our childhood turning Muscadines."

Jake's shiny smile filled the dark gaps between them.

"I want you to be a partner, a real one with a monthly deposit."

"That'd be great. But I don't have time, the farm, sometimes pony rides and the dogs. I

spend two to four hours a day working dogs for police training. That's where I make money."

"You're joshin' me, right? I have a fat wad ready to share with you and set you up for

easy street and you're gonna tell me no?"

"What about the dogs? I wanna work with dogs."

"We'll see what happens down the road. You'll want on once I get the store front up

and music and wine flowing. You'll change your mind."

"I don't know, Bruce."

Clearly annoyed, Bruce's nostrils flared. "I can't protect you from everything, like that scar, but I believe you'd be safest under my business. You just know too much, Jake."

"Whoever it was that attacked me was not after what I knew."

"That's not the way I heard it."

"It was just a thief. I was putting your things in storage with some of my parent's and grandparent's storage building and they just appeared out of nowhere. I saw them go inside when I was on the ground and go through stuff but didn't see anything missing."

"You moved it again, right? You said it's all in the barn now, right?"

"Yeah. There's always someone around at the farm."

"Good," Bruce asked if Jake was going to get cosmetic surgery and he told him that he was cute enough, and Bruce said, "I wish I could get cosmetic surgery to remove the scars Old Man Black put on me."

"I'll never forgive him, Bruce. He scarred us. And your mom. And who knows."

They took turns changing the radio like they couldn't get the music to block out the memories:

Five-year-old Jake had walked the wood's narrow path between their houses like he'd always done, but only different that day because he didn't have a grown up to watch over him. His parents had decided he was responsible enough to go on his own. He had gone over to play but stopped cold. Blood trickled from Bruce's cuts, like ticks burst when you stomp 'em, fast little splatters. Blood was smeared across Bruce's hands from trying to protect his bare legs and back. Blood colored his blonde curls and cheeks like an ice-cream cone drizzled with strawberry swirl and then thrown out a vehicle's window, abandoned, alongside a dusty dirt road.

Between thrashings and cussings, Bruce had kept watch on Jake who hid just inside the timberline. Miss Scarlet, the neighbor's German Shepherd, had sprung up growling from the clearing on the other side of the timberline and made her way to Jake in silence like a grunt on the front line ready to defend and protect when Old Man Black's terrifying voice warned of more impending blows, so Jake pulled her up close.

Bruce began to methodically rest his arms down at his sides as everything seemed to move in slow motion. Even Old Man Black, vicious, still wild drunk from the night before, streaking Bruce with the switch and name calling so sorry in the world nothing could ever take it back, moved across time like drips from a leaky faucet. "Youse a Lum. Youse a Lum. Youse never gonna be more than a loggin' likker Lum! Say it, boy! Say it!" When Bruce refused, "You Momma's boy, you fairy tale prince, you slimy little shit! Say it! Youse a Lum!" With Old Man Black's characteristic gentle Lumbee voice long-gone from a lifetime of chain smoking, the wickedness crashed over the child.

He had pulled Bruce's arm up over his head, jerking him off the ground as the switch cut through the air in jet fast cuts at Bruce's fair legs, and Jake covered his mouth so he wouldn't scream while Bruce gasped for breath.

Jake had been on the verge of running home for help when Bruce's dad finally flung the switch to the ground. Old Man Black lit a cigarette and blew a hot suck of smoke right into Bruce's little face, but Bruce didn't flinch. Old Man Black jumped in his rattletrap pick-up, slammed the door and with full headiness ordered, "Gyet that grass mowed for dark or you'll know all de sorry in the world cross da rest a yer hide." His yellow teeth filled his face like a nasty cheap circus clown's entering the Gates of Hell as his truck spit out a dash of hot oil.

Sweet young Jake had hushed Miss Scarlet's whining with kind words as she tucked her muzzle under his arm and she faithfully waited. He stroked her smooth ears and when the truck was out of sight Jake went to Bruce, but Miss Scarlet didn't. Poor Miss Scarlet, Jake had warned her, "Go home," and Bruce had hated her ever since.

Little Bruce's white underwear was peed yellow and dirty brown from where the wobbly legged five-year-old had fallen to the ground, unable to balance with his jeans shackled at his ankles, but what stood out most of all was the bright blood trickled lines. His quiet tears had dried instantly when Jake touched his shoulder. Jake had to zip him up. Had to work the metal button into the hole while Bruce's hands hung at his sides. Bruce was quivering, shaking. Streaked from tears, red from blood, white in shock. His gray eyes locked. Bruce just stood still, practically lifeless, in a catatonic state for the longest time while Jake had spoken kindly and softly, like a Christian does for ailing kin.

Jake had told him that they were going to be okay now. Told him that he could come spend the night and his mom would make beef stroganoff and they'd eat cookies in bed. But Bruce only blinked. A few minutes later Bruce walked over to the garden hose and wet his jeans down, gritting his teeth to bear the pain. When Jake pointed to Bruce's head he held the hose over, and the weight of the water flattened his curls into long strands.

Jake mowed while Bruce wandered through the timberline until he discovered a jar of pure medicine as the moon's clock threatened and his mother's blood stained the kitchen. He got drunk and sick and stayed sick for three days, long enough for the cuts to scab over good.

At his mother's funeral, Bruce had been rigid against the hugs and polite words of his mother's church people. His mother would have normally been at women's circle meeting that day his dad had come home mean and mad after losing big on card night. But she didn't have a clean dress and didn't have any offering. The power'd been cut off for weeks. Bruce said not one of those church ladies had been by to see her. Several years later when Jake had said, "No one gets that hurt from falling off a step stool," Bruce looked like he could've stomped a feral bull into hamburger, but he never said a word.

In the truck cab, Bruce still looked like he could stomp a feral bull into hamburger, so Jake licked his dry lips before mutedly asking, "Do you think about her?"

Nearly alarmed, Bruce darted his chin about the truck's cab for a way out, steadily blinking.

"Your mom shouldn't a died that way. She was the most-gentle person ever. It was so wrong."

"I don't talk about it."

"It's eatin' you up. You need to get it out."

"Can't change anything about it. Leave it alone." Bruce's leg jittered. He noticed and stopped. "It's not like your deal. You've got a scar you'll have to look at every day for the rest of your life."

"It's like a flag."

"How's that?" Bruce rolled his eyes.

"Umm, a signal like a victory over evil."

"One God knows and sees all. I believe that's why I was incarcerated. I would have killed the bastard that got you Jake, bad."

Fully aghast, "Hey, what about Dan? Is it true Dan the Man is at the mental hospital? He really went crazy?"

"That's what they called it. Went to talking to himself, then yelling and trying to save food for his invisible friend."

"Really, an invisible friend, like a little mouse or maybe one of his cats, like a ghost cat, huh? He had way too many cats on his place, mean ones. Probably just all those years of drinkin.' It accumulates. Or maybe it's the Little People."

"Naw. Little People do good. A toten got him."

"A toten got him," Jake softly mulled it over. "How do you know? I mean, Bruce, I really believe your people's stories. They're like your Bible."

"Not stories. It's just the way it is. You touch something with a jubious link, something that don't belong to you or someone leaving and their spirit jumps in, that's toten work. Sure as I'm in this truck taking in all this gorgeous land and talking to my best friend in the world, I am certain it was my old man who took up inside that murderer's head."

"Could be."

"Could be -nothing! My old man hated me. He'd a been after me every minute making the rest of my days headiness, pure stinking mean. He put a root on Dan with his own spirit."

"You really think your own dad would've done that to you?"

"What? Don't you remember anything?" Bruce scowled. "He was jealous momma loved me and did for me. He wouldn't even let her read to me. Said I didn't need school smarts. He was gonna raise me to be a real Lum and make my way in the world like him, a shiner. I had to play dumb whenever I had words to say or he'd slap me or Mom or both of us. Called us wannabe brickhousers. Said we'd never leave the swamp."

Jake slowed down. "He was a son-of-a-bitch all right. I hope he does spend eternity in Dan's head."

"He got in there at the funeral." Bruce stoically stated. "When he lifted him up out of the coffin and his head went back and everyone fainted. That's when he got in there. I know it 'cause I could feel my old man's spirit like a rabid black dog gnawing on my bones up to that very second. He made me pure ache all over from the moment he died out there cutting logs. He was on me every single day up until the funeral. He barely let me sleep. And there's no way I believe Dan would ever confess to anything. He made him do it. Got in his head to make him confess and stayed. I know it." He seethed.

"Did you see his ghost?"

"Why?"

"You seem convinced, so sure."

"I saw something. Momma said I was born with the veil. Seen all kinds of haints in my childhood. Try to block things now."

"Damn, that's cool."

"Not so much." Bruce tapped his fingers and fidgeted with his seatbelt. "You know he took Dad's money roll and that that money roll first belonged to Dan?"

"No way?"

"Those two stole it from each other. They were a pair."

"A pair, all right."

"Dad would a' stole it back. I know. Wonder how long that went on?"

"The stealing from each other?" Bruce calculated. "Long as I can remember. But they'd still play poker. Recon it was their kind of bingo?"

"The stealing?"

"Yea."

"They liked it, or they wouldn't 've kept playing. Only them, the ugliest puss and the meanest Lum."

"Oh, man, even with the new tooth and hair, yea. You know, I figured Dan must've got his hands on that roll, but never figured on him murdering his only real friend. 'Cause he didn't have anyone. I mean Dan had no one. Zilch. He looked up to Black. Everyone else was too afraid." Jake's eyes peeled back. "I remember the first time I saw him. It was that bad summer. Just a few weeks afterward and we were coming back from fishing at the small pond and had three bream. Remember?"

"Yea, he was just waking up. Bet he'd been sleeping there all night. Probably heard every word we'd said. Bet he didn't mess with us 'cause he knew who my daddy was."

Bruce snapped his fingers, "I bet he's wished a thousand times he was still napping on that pine straw bed 'cause he's paying now. They say his eyes roll around in his head 'till all the nurses can see is white and he screams bloody murder till they have to sedate him. His shirt stays wet from slobbering all over himself."

"That's gross. Who tells you about him?"

"We stick together out in the pines. One word, you name it, we'll do what it takes to make things right. Nurses from Beacon's mental unit treat some of the birds at Beacon Prison. Lot of 'em are Lum."

"You have three families then," Jake smiled, "the Lums and mine and the Tuscarora." As Bruce's teeth shone his pronounced cheekbones puffed up so high you could pitch pennies off the edges, so Jake went on. "I bet if you hadn't been in prison you would have hunted him down and cut him to pieces. Left him for the buzzards."

"Got dat Jack," Bruce's slapped the dash as Jake slowed the truck onto the dirt road where the Crowson's property began and Bruce belted out, "Good-gooboly-goo," as the tires crunched against the gritty gravel road. Yellow ribbons streamed from the wooden fence line and cars filled the Crowson's drive. "They put up a lot of ribbon for you, Buddyrow. Ready to party?"

Bruce solemnly surveyed the Crowson's pristine spread and when a million little butterflies tickled his head, ran his hands over his head. "Mon, I bes nervous wid dis. I's crotched up like," he panted.

"Hey, it's okay," Jake said as he explained that everyone was probably in the house cooking and that they'd go over when Bruce was ready. "We told people to be here at six, and so, I'm sure that's just the cooks in there. If your people come, it won't be until later. You ever notice how you go back talking "on the pines" when you're upset?"

"I know. It's natural. We've had everything taken from us and talkin' our talk is all we've got left to identify us, but," Bruce grinned, "I managed to get an Iroquoian book on customs and plan on rejuvenating my people's language."

"And you'll do it, too. I'm sure – you see me!" Jake chuckled.

Calves were jumping and butting heads and ponies neighed and ran to the barn as Jake pointed out David Crowson's house, the main one, and then his. "Biscuits and gravy Sunday mornings over at the big house. Then Robin and I go to church, same one as Miss Sarah and David. We both believe in raising children in church. It doesn't matter what kind, and I'm okay that she wants to keep up with her Tuscarora beliefs. They're a lot alike."

Bruce rolled his eyes. "Already talking children?"

"Dating is a step in finding a life mate, and you know Robin. She likes things her way and has some strong opinions. Better we get it all out front." Jake's diplomatic response left Bruce with a cold expression.

"Well, since you're being up front about it all. Know that I'm ready to handle her if you can't."

"I pick my battles and I know how to compromise, but she loves me. She's told me so."

"When did she say that? When you gave her the dog?" Bruce craftily dodged the subject as he scanned over the farm, "I love it. This place is all the fine in the world, Jake. The way the housen face off, it's like an old plantation."

"It is." Jake pointed through the row of barns and sheds on out to the field, "MacGregor's Crest is over there. We put up a post and beam over it. Used rough cut lumber, wide floorboards and have big lit up shadowboxes with Underground Railroad information hanging on the walls. There's a heavy glass panel over the opening in the ground so you can watch as the other tourists leave the underground passage out in the field. The tours begin in the basement of our house."

"Say that again."

"The tours begin in the basement."

"How does that work while you're living there?"

"There're two doors to the basement. The inside door near the laundry room is kept locked. We don't think anyone would do something stupid. But you never know. The other is the outside door. The basement had sliding glass doors that went to the patio. Exilee made the patio years ago. Now it has primitive looking wood doors. Painted the cement floor to look like the clay in the passage. There's a picture map for children and one for adults and there's some life-size cutouts of people dressed in vintage eighteen hundred's clothing."

As soon as Jake pulled in under the unattached carport Bruce hurried around to the front yard and absorbed the view. The Crowson's house was a larger version of Jake's place and was surrounded with vintage everything.

Jake unlocked his front door and held it open for Bruce. "Welcome home, Buddyrow."

"Cuz." Bruce entered like a child discovering a candy store. "I love your place. It even smells country. Smell. Smell the walls." Bruce was close to hyperventilating as he toured around sniffing everything like a hound dog. "Country vittles and a granny's dusting powders, tonic and dog." If Bruce had had a tail, it would've wagged.

"Onacona lives in here, too, when I'm here. When I've got one in training it has a time period for indoor behavior and discipline training. You can keep your door closed."

"Hey, I'm not complaining. I love it. Even dog smells don't bother me." Bruce wiped his palms over the furniture, outlined the lamp and went over the top of the kitchen table with his open hands. "It's amazing what you miss. The little things, the sounds of the birds outside. Love the open windows. The wind, smells of normal life, not two thousand people crammed into one cement hole." Bruce opened the refrigerator and looked inside. He opened the stove, the cabinets under the sink, the cabinets over the coffee pot. "I haven't seen a normal kitchen in years. I might be in here a while, do all the cooking till the new wears off. That okay?"

"Good with me. Do anything you want." Jake's orders poked Bruce like a hit in the chest. Bruce held onto the back of the kitchen chair and tried to hold back the raw emotions as his face twisted. "Anything I want. Sorry," he added when Jake reflected his angst. "It's just so good here, so good to be out. Free," his throat squeezed the words, "I couldn't even sit without permission."

"You can be yourself with me, Bruce. I know who you are." Jake's soft words pushed out everything else till it was just the two men.

"Who?" Bruce's face was so distorted. "Who am I? The son of a con, a Lum who got caught selling shine? I'm a loser. An ex-con, a man who served time, that's all people see." He took the statement out of his pocket and shook the crap out of it up at ceiling. "Even with money that's all they'll see. The Mighty Tuscarora is dead in me."

"Just sleeping, Bruce. I know you'll get your fight back. I just know you'll find a way and your friends will be back rallying for you and love you for helping get their repatriation."

"I don't have any friends. Just you. Everyone else just worked for me. Only people ever near me are the ones waiting for me to hand them something," He ripped paper towel from the roll next to the sink and blew his nose in the colonial colored kitchen. It was brown and orange except for the yellow curtains that hung tied-back with strawberry print ribbon above the kitchen sink. The worn throw pillows on the couch were orange, but a warm orange, the kind that comes from years of use. There was one picture on the wall. It had a black frame.

But the picture was brown, too, a tired early eighteen hundred's sketch of cowboys taking saddles off their horses in front of a barn with a nearby two-story clapboard house. A young child played in the dirt yard with a stick as an attentive chicken cocked his head at him. Holstein cows were in a side lot. Through the kitchen window a woman wearing pants and oversized shirt with long locks escaping a haggard bun told of the drudgery as her hand swept over her brow. The scene held Bruce like he was trying to plant himself there, in that time.

When Jake couldn't stop looking at him Bruce told him to take a picture and Jake laughed. "You have no idea how tickled I am. This party tonight is all for you, my friend who educated himself in prison. The smartest man I have ever known is my best friend." When Bruce's uneasiness wore over his forehead like a burden, Jake continued his reaffirmation,

"Your dad didn't have your determination. He didn't have nothing on you, and now you're going to have it all and I believe that's God's reward because you're going legit. You're going to be rich and famous. Remember, you're going to put Maxton back on the map. That's who you are, Bruce Black. You are bringing the Tuscarora a leader with the knowledge to get federal recognition and you are providing jobs. These people will forever be indebted to you."

Bruce inhaled the picturesque scene, "Thanks, but that's only how you see me."

Jake lowered his head as Bruce neared. "What do you have to drink?"

"Sweet tea. The water's good, too. Well water from right out there." Jake showed him the well house through the open kitchen window. "I keep a jug in the fridge."

Bruce opened the cabinet above the sink and commented on his glass collection. Chose a blue glass and poured the cool water from the fridge and savored it. "Pure. No after taste." He poured another and enjoyed the cool water with his eyes closed then held the glass to his chest. "Ahh. It's amazing what you miss. I feel silly. You want some?"

"Sure. Pour me a glass." After the cool water Jake excused himself to the bathroom.

"Hey, can I take a whiz off the back steps?"

"Just make sure no one's around."

Bruce searched for a good spot through the screened back door and then gleefully stepped off the back porch. There was no one below the elevated steps at the entrance to the Underground Railroad, so he went down the thirteen steps to the grass. He bent over and ran his hands over the blades then briskly rubbed it. Pulled up a handful and sucked in the crisp earthy scent. He briskly approached the old pine trees, a pristine bunch, some so old their tops were twisted with curly limbs and gnarls. Pulled down a limb and sucked in its sweet pine tar perfume and rans his hands over the trunk's rough bark and flaked off a chunk. Crumbled it and marched through the thick sand grass. Over a thick blanket of pine straw and maneuvered through the scattered thorn bushes and willowy mimosas flocked in fluffy pink. He leaned his head back and inhaled the fresh hot summer pine thicket's disturbed floras and with full sunshine in his face he unzipped near a significant prickly pear outcrop.

The indigenous cactus was one that local Indians knew as edible, medicinal, as a base for likker, and used its leaves' pectin as a binder in plaster. Prickly pear cactus was a symbol of transformation and strength to Native Americans. The outcrops' yellow flowers and red fruit also attracted bees and the yellow jackets which busily hummed near Bruce's knees.

Bruce zipped back up immediately, when less than fifty feet away through the old growth Longleaf Pines, Robin's hair shone like black silk, glimmering as it swayed in cadence with her song and horse's rhythm. Still as a fox on a quail, Bruce went unnoticed, until Jake let the screen door slam. Robin reined in her horse and smiled.

Bruce appeared trapped in the blooming prickly pears. She urged her mount forward as Bruce pulled up a bloom and offered it. "It's yellow," softly, but testosterone driven, his symbolic gesture reddened her cheeks as Jake stepped off the back porch.

"Like a ribbon," Robin backed up her mount a couple of feet away and Bruce emerged from the prickly outcrop. "Should I hold it between my teeth?" He dared her as he tapped his front teeth together, "There aren't any big oaks along here."

Jake's lengthy steps depicted a soldier on ploy. "Did you say oaks? There's some small ones." Jake pointed, but neither Bruce nor Robin looked.

Bruce folded the slick yellow bloom down into his palm and turned to Jake. "Is it okay if I take a shower, Buddyrow? I'm all hot and sticky now."

With his hand gripping Robin's calf, Jake caught his breath. "Ya don't have to ask. This is your home long as you need it. You're free to come and go as you please."

"Thanks," Bruce humbly replied. "Good to see you, Robin."

"You, too. See ya later. Mrs. Crowson and Exilee've been cooking all day." Robin's head was tilted so far, her long hair tickled her mount's side and as the gelding vigorously twitched her deeply cut tee shirt deepened her valley and her mountains quaked.

"Sure, I'll pleasure it, ma'am," Bruce abandoned the couple with a quick wave as he hurried back. Once there, he unfolded his other palm and held up the slick yellow bloom over his hot face sucking in his dreams.

Zoskiroro's lights blinked and Jake sat upright and stretched. He opened the blinds in his office and when it was reasonably quiet, phoned the front desk and told his point-of-sale clerk that he'd be leaving early. Fifteen minutes later, he passed Miss Lucy's home and parked in Mr. Fisk and Wart's drive and honked the horn. "Miss Lucy got her research and now I'm gonna get mine," he whispered as he searched for their notorious car-truck and instead pulled up next to parts. Junk metal, engines and tattered tarps tossed over things held down with buckets of black water filled the side yard next to the old barn that was gently puffing smoke from its stack.

With one leg out the truck door, a sow rose from a mudhole near the shanty's screened porch and Jake sat back down and honked again. "Fisk!" he yelled as the sow approached. Bristly brown hairs poked out from her mud-encrusted thick skin like a 300-pound porcupine's. Her ears were up and flopped eagerly towards the truck and as she smacked her yellow tusks flashed. The sow rubbed her backside on his front bumper, grunting up his frame and squealing back down. "Pig-fucked," he smirked, "sums up every dealing I've had with these two."

Jake tossed an empty soda can at the barn and yelled again, "Fisk, I know you're in there. Come here!" He waited a few minutes and turned the ignition, draping his arm over the seat and was prepared to abandon his mission when something shiny dangling from a scrub oak caught his eye. The sow had followed her new lover and was rubbing again as he stopped to get a closer look and Jake rolled down his window to consider getting out when she opened her mouth at him, "No treats in here, girly," he reached down to rub her head and she turned her backside to him. "All I need is to get bred by a sow. Haven't done that yet," he halfway chuckled and looked back at the shiny and drove to the gas station as fast as he could.

He bought a three pack of crème-filled cakes, two bags of popcorn, and a sweet tea. He sped toward Miss Lucy's and when all was clear as he drank the tea and tossed the waxed paper cup in the floorboard. Fisk's car-truck was still gone, so Jake pulled up as closely as possible to the barn near the scrub oak and left the engine running as he spied the sow. She was back in her mudhole near the shanty, a good fifty yards away, and spotted her lover immediately jogging toward the bumper. Jake tossed the cakes and out she came barreling. He ripped open a popcorn bag and flung it out front of the truck where the sow greedily gobbled - snorting and smacking, as he ripped open the second bag and carried it with him out the passenger's side. Smack. Slurp. Smack. Five feet from the scrub oak, the shiny cup dangled. Squeal! Squeal! Snort!

Chapter 7

Pirate's Blood Now

Ken Crowson was at the front gate bent over with his toolbox open on the tailgate of his pickup when Jake reached the sandy drive home. "Just great," Jake sighed as Ken stood up and smiled with an outstretched arm fixing to lean into the passenger's side when a wind gust soured his greeting. "What the hell've you been doing? You okay?"

"Fell in some mud. It's nothing," Ken's deep refrain held down his chin, "What's up? School closed?"

"Took a few days off before the Christmas crazies. Where's there any mud around here? It hasn't rained in weeks, not more than a sprinkle," Ken winced over the sulfuric stench, "That's p-ig." He pinched his nose.

Jake closed his eyes, "I was running an errand and meet up with sow and her boyfriends. Did you know male pigs pee on one another when they greet each other?"

"Yes, I did," Ken's curiosity kept pulling him to the open window even though it made him cough. "Where'd you go?"

"Fisk's place," he shivered as the cool wind brushed over his wet clothes and Ken guffawed and coughed and slapped at the side of Jake's truck, "You were asking for it. What were you doing there, by gawd?"

Jake's truck came to a quick start, "I gotta get out of these clothes, later, Ken," and he looked back in the rear view as Ken hollered, "Souiee! Sook! Sook! Sook!" and Jake shot him the finger.

Jake stripped down to his underwear in the grass out back and left his soiled clothes there while he showered. Afterward, he turned on the television and the four o'clock update chimed, "Showers tonight and possible thunderstorms," and he playfully sang, "This is the way we wash our clothes, wash our clothes, huh-huh, huh-huh!" He dusted the furniture and replaced two dim lightbulbs with new ones and vacuumed. He wore his favorite tee shirt and sweatpants and sprayed linen-scented air freshener throughout and made a pitcher of sweet tea.

Miss Lucy arrived at five-fifteen lugging her satchel and a bag of take-out. "You're home early," she beamed. "I have a surprise. The church had a spaghetti dinner, raising funds for a cancer patient in our congregation, and I brought home two plates. No time wasted on cooking tonight."

"Wasted, huh? Your meals are divine, but if you want spaghetti, that's what we'll have."

"That's not all. For dessert I have a letter requesting recommendation for the U.K. I also have the names of several soft allies and a judge, here in Raleigh, and a lawyer willing to work pro bono," Jake's delight spread as his whites brightened the small colonial home, "and a television channel who wants to work with us on educating the local Indians on the true history of the Tuscarora." Jake squeezed her and when she squealed, he burst into laughter. "You're never going to believe what I got into today. But you gotta tell me how you did all this in one day, lady. Geez. I thought I was on top of things today."

"The church people, Jake, I told them we needed to do something to help our local Tuscarora Indians because as a splinter group they couldn't get the benefits promised by the Lumbee Tribe. We hadn't discussed this situation and were eager to help, especially after our Tuscarora members spoke up about their problems getting HUD benefits and forms of assistance that Lumbees take for granted." Her pointy finger stabbed up and down, "Reverend Jacob straightened us out. He said our congregation was beyond our doors and we need to see what we can do for those suffering under the oppression and it was past time they put their heads together on this." She told him to set the table and she'd toast the garlic bread, "It got cold in the car," and she pushed the Styrofoam boxes onto the counter and he said, "I can heat this up and set the table, honey bunny. Shoot, with all you did today makes me look like all I did was waller around," as he snorted into a burst of laughter.

"Glad I made you so happy tonight," she bounced into her room and took off her coat and shoes and slipped on her house shoes and returned to the small kitchen to pour sweet tea, but the glasses were already on the table. They each took a seat as she asked, "Well, did you address those winos today? You said you'd handle that, or do…" Jake busted in and said, "I fought off a three-hundred-pound sow and her two fat boyfriends and all I got was a tin cup." He aimed at the shiny little cup sitting inconspicuously center of the table between the salt and pepper under the bright light. The fluted form was malahacked from its ramshackle life and the longer the two stared at it, the more it seemed to silently cry in desperation for a voice.

Its thick rim had held a thin chain which had scratched it over the years forming crisscross patterns. Tarnished and still not washed, it held the pristine time before the first Indian was ever slain by a colonist. Miss Lucy's blue eyes doubled as she asked, "May I?" as she reached for it and he obliged. She devoured it; delving inside, and fingering its rim and turned it upside down and bit her lip, "Is that a mark or dirt or what?"

"I wanted us to discover that together," he sweetly smiled, "I swear, it's identical to the one Bruce had: Just like it. I think this is it, Lucy."

She filled the sink with warm soapy water, and they agreed to let it soak while they ate because they didn't want to disturb its history any more than it already had been and Jake said, "Let's pray."

They swirled and twirled and slurped excitedly as Jake told the "pig-tale" and they laughed with their mouths full and wiped their chins. They hurriedly scraped plates and stacked them on the counter. "It's been out in the weather all its life," Jake mused, "and we're treating it like a kitten found in the rain."

"Well, it is raining," she gingerly pulled the cup from the water and rubbed it over and over with her bare hands and dunked it again and rubbed it more until Jake said, "Want me to do that?" "It's no bother," she rubbed it so hard her fingers bled white and Jake said, "Hey, I've got some chrome cleaner in the barn. Should we try that?"

"I don't know the answer to that. I guess it isn't going to hurt, if it is real silver."

Jake slipped on his raincoat and dashed out into the cold dark and his flashlight found the barn door ajar, "That Ken," he quipped and grabbed his cleaner from a box of car wash items on a shelf and secured the door with the heavy wooden plank.

Miss Lucy squirted a baby spoon-sized dollop of cleanser onto a dish cloth and rubbed it over the inside of the cup and when it shined up at her she held it out for Jake and he said, "Let me do that," and she handed it over. "I am so selfish. Sorry, Jake. I'm just as excited as you. I feel like an archeologist." "Me too," he rubbed the cleanser in fast swirls over the silver cup and in a few minutes, they beheld the lower case "a" thickly imprinted into its bottom. "We gotta look this up. Get your laptop, Lucy Mae!"

"Why don't you use your pc, Jake, not that it matters."

"I worry that it's bugged."

"You do?" flabbergasted, she hurriedly placed her laptop on the kitchen table, "You'd better get it checked."

"I'm going to take it to Raleigh and have someone there clean it up and check it out."

"That's a good idea. No one in Raleigh will know what you're doing, will they."

"I'm telling ya, Lucy, these Lumbees have infiltrated every single aspect of our lives here and they'll do anything to keep the Tuscarora down."

"It's just awful how they treat one another," she sat next to him, "They're so prejudice," and they searched another website with jewelry appraisers. She scrolled down and as the "a" appeared in line with the year 1558 [47] they shouted, "That's it!" "That's it!" "That's the exact time when this cup would have been present at the colonist's site, Jake," she cried, "We've got it! Oh, my Lord, I just don't believe it," she covered her mouth in wonder and Jake held up the cup to the light and said, "Believe it, Lucy. We have crowned the king here tonight and he is due reparations in the gazillions, brothers and sisters!"

Jake watched over the cup and searched the internet for any pertinent facts while Miss Lucy showered and when she returned in her nightclothes, Jake held up a label-less bottle of wine, "Tonight, we celebrate. We have done everything in our power and now it's up to the big guy and the powers that be. Have a drink with me? It's from Bruce's private collection. You might say we're including him by drinking his wine."

"That's lovely, Jake. I would love a glass, half a glass." Her blue satin pajamas were lined with silver buttons down the front and when she held the silver cup up close to her chest Jake's melancholy mood changed, "You are absolutely royal with that cup in your hand," he said as she held out the shiny silver cup and he poured the wine.

"You say this was just hanging off a branch in the yard?"

"It sure was. I don't think your winos have a clue what this is."

Miss Lucy's head fell to her chest and back up to Jake, "Fisk is pure genius, Jake. He is. I know because, because he's been in my life."

"Is he the man who you were in love with?"

Her eyes narrowed at the corners like a lost pup's as she explained, "I refused his proposal thirty-nine years ago next month. He was a biology teacher who loved archeology, still handsome, curly brown hair, shaved clean and white dress shirts and a big healthy smile." Her fingers danced under her chin in a tight clasp. "He came in regularly and checked out reference materials for his lessons. That's how it started. A year into our relationship, he told me about some sketchy ideas he had and showed me a few items and I think they could have been stolen."

"Why do you think they were stolen?"

"Because teachers are poor. He started drinking heavily and I could see there was nothing left to hope for."

"I'm sorry. I see this still gets you." Jake refilled his glass and daydreamed out the window.

"I believe Daniel Hawthorne Fisk knows the exact significance of this cup and put it in plain sight believing no one would think it was worth stealing if not hid like his other items."

"You might be right. I just can't wrap my head around Fisk being intelligent."

"Get over it," she rinsed the silver cup and they discussed where to hide it and wondered what else Fisk might have protected by his swine. "It's been so many years; I can't recall every single item that was in his closet. There was a safe and he made a big deal about it. It was the night he proposed." Sleep was deep and morning came refreshed and promising with their newfound hope as they parted to begin their Friday workday.

Ken had taken a three-day vacation from school right before Christmas crazies and called Jake at Zoskiroro's at ten o'clock. "Hey, can you come help me for a couple of hours? Say, get here at three?"

"Sure, I can. Whadaya need?"

"Hold a few boards while I screw 'em down. Dad's shoulder is worn out. Rotator cuff."

"Ooh, that's a mean one. Getting surgery?"

"Looks that way. See you at three then, right?"

"If not before. I'm in good with the owner."

They enjoyed a laugh and hung up as Cassie's orange bob passed by his door and he called out, "Good morning, Cassie dear," but she darted past and went to the front desk to blast the poor salesclerk instead.

Jake left at two and picked up a six pack of beer. As soon as he arrived home, he leapt out of his truck and held up the six-pack like a trophy kill, but Ken motioned for him to come to the big house, but Jake shook his head, "No."

"We've got fried chicken," Ken called out as he landed at the tailgate, "What gives?" "Scarecrow intercepted me on the way out. Was at the crossroads, think he's bugged my office phone too, but anyway, he had some news and I'm not sure what to make of it." Jake and Ken drank a beer on the tailgate as Jake's heavy heart unloaded and Ken agreed with Jake that he should tell David and Miss Sarah, because they knew all about the history of Robeson County.

They were welcomed into the kitchen as Ken poured Jake a glass of sweet tea and said, "Wanna tell Daddy about your new girl?" and Jake replied, "You say it," as he lumbered to the porch. Miss Sarah had prepared a fried chicken dinner and the leftovers rested in blue and white serving dishes. Jake took the binoculars hanging from the slanted nail and spied through the screened in porch's door, scanning from his house to the family cemetery. "Scarecrow and Lilly put wire on Miss Lucy's phone and checked her background. She's a old country gal like this town has never known." Ken placed a gentle hand on his dad's shoulder and bent over face to face. "You ever heard tale of a Prickenwrath from England?"

David worked his palms together and when he cocked his head down to the left his long
curly ear hairs twitched like the wisps of white covering his slick white head. He flipped out the napkin tucked in his overalls and wiped his hands clean of peach juice, "No, son."

"It's on the deeds," Jake cleared his throat, "Old land grants have Prickenwrath as owner all over the Southeast. Crow thinks she came here originally to do land research."

"Can't be," Ken planted his back against his chair, "The same Prickenwrath as ours?"

"The old land grants, you got 'em here?" Jake spread his open hand out toward the living areas. "Where's Luke and Miss Ginger? There's no tours till after one, right?"

"They're at your house by now. Well, in the Underground's office. Tomorrow there's a private tour. Some bigwig up in Raleigh and his special group. So, Luke is helping her clean up after the second graders. Popsicle sticks, gum, you name it. It's on the floor and since he's closest and will take a penny for each piece he got the job." Exilee lightheartedly laughed as Miss Sarah returned with a large clear plastic encased envelope.

"You know Miss Ginger isn't gonna stop to eat and risk him gettin' sleepy."

"Smart lady," Ken kissed at Exilee and she leaned over and gave him a nice one.

The hearty envelope was browned at the edges with exaggeratedly looped handwriting spelling out Colonial Land Office Patent, 1629. Further down in fine filigree was the verification, Lord Henry Prickenwrath. David tapped over the Prickenwrath name like he was smashing a spider. "We were the planters. He paid for us to come here and improve the settlement and he got the land. But before it was all done, he made some bad errors and was hung. That's how I heard it. His own people came over here and saw about it."

"How did we get this land?" Ken's bright blue eyes sharpened.

"Marriage. His daughter and one of my uncles. Have to look at those genie papers to tell ya 'xactly which." David chewed at the inside of his mouth and stirred up Jake. "Hey, she mention any a this?"

"No. All new."

Miss Sarah urged David to share Lord Prickenwrath's "errors" and when he waved her off, she hissed, "Don't try that with me."

"It'll just put more oil on the rag," he shook out his worn cloth napkin over the tabletop.

"The truth'll do that," Miss Sarah snatched his napkin and pushed it into her apron's smart pocket. Her apron was blue with little white checks and red birds like North Carolina's Cardinals flying from the hem upwards. Her sleek black hair is braided down her back and her Tuscarora cheeks were bright red with fury.

"Come on, Dad. We're all grown-ups here. Go ahead."

David peered down the pasture like something caught his eye and stayed there. "Lord Prickenwrath burned a house down. The English had sent their army people over to talk to him when word got to England that he'd taken up with Indians and had children and sent his white wife and children to the city. The English were gonna take his land if he didn't send his mixed children away and live proper with his white wife. Prickenwrath said he'd meet these soldiers at his house and give over his children." David's chin quivered. "They say the army men cried. It was horrible. The children were half out of the windows and he ran 'em back in with gunshot. They hung Prickenwrath right there." David pointed at the pasture down by MacGregor's Crest where they planned to dig the well. "Seems like history's a little ripple in the river. Just keeps on. Wind blows. Doesn't change. Water beats down the rocks. Doesn't change." He looked up at Jake and sniffled. "Maybe your book'll change it, Jake." As David grasped Jake's hand, he hugged the aged wise man like a teddy bear and David looked up at him with teary eyes, "I'm so tired of all this hating."

They wiped away tears. "We want to correct history and spur activism among our college students. That's where most grassroots movements begin and it's going to take years, if not generations," Jake stretched and Exilee said, "I wanna read that manuscript." Her back was cocked like a rifle. "Is it here?"

"Yeah, and a copy at the office."

"You are concerned," Miss Sarah took the peach bowl and asked if anyone wanted more and when no one responded she began clearing the dishes and said that she wanted to read it, too and to invite Miss Lucy for dinner. "We'll have a get-together. I need to see how Miss Ginger and her new man are doing together. Hope they don't have plans." From the kitchen she yelled, "Put down that chicken leg, David and no, you don't need a cookie."

"One of those kids got out, one of the boys or our Miss Lucy wouldn't be a Prickenwrath," Ken's haughty voice provoked Jake, "Only in name. Lucy is nothing like that man. Nothing."

"Probably the only Prickenwrath here," David popped another cookie into his mouth while Ken explained that the family sold out to housing developers, then the manufacturers and the chicken plant and that they didn't have attachments to land like they did.

David listed off several chores including a trip to town for Exilee and she said, "First, I wanna look at Jake's book. That okay?"

"I'll read it first," David told her, and she said, "Then I'll get to town and maybe I can read whatever your done with. How's that?"

"That's fine."

David Crowson read all afternoon. The first hour in the hard chair at the table on the
screened in porch. The second in the living room recliner. Then back to the screened in porch in the hard chair, but with a pillow on *Chapter 7, Pirate's Blood Then*:

"The party was held on the Crowson's big screened in porch overlooking the pastures that lead to the creek in the dark timberline. By seven-thirty, the summer sun had eased down behind the timberline and what was left of the bright Carolina blue day burned out in the thick treetops smeared in scarlet. Surreal, like a painting on the ceiling of one of those holy churches, Bruce breathed it in with a heavy dose of fresh farm air heavy with pony. Curious ponies twisted their heads out the fence boards to greet him from the nearby lot while those in stalls nickered and neighed, "Hello."

"Been a while since you've seen one of those, huh?" Jake startled him. "You've got a lot to look forward to. "Yep, no ponies in prison," Bruce smirked.

"In the morning we have coffee on the back porch and watch the horses run up to the barn. Ken's geldings do it every day like clockwork," Jake's melancholy grew, "There's two red-headed cockaded woodpeckers, a hawk and blue birds that get all stirred up when they leave the timber. Then the purple martins when the horses run in the barn." As Bruce stretched to see down into the timberline Jake shook his head. "Ken's geldings are in the barn by now. Put 'em up at night."

"Look, rabbits," Bruce's whites flashed like the floppy white tails as the two rabbits circled and leapt over one another.

"We've seen red pheasants strutting around doing mating rituals and turkeys leading their chicks, always lots a' rabbits, and foxes. Not at the same time. There's binoculars on the porch. You can have first debs on 'em in the morning. Never know what we'll spot."

"Love it. Need to overdose on this ta get rid of all the, all the other." Bruce's full lips pouted with the kind of sweetness a child has when a rabbit gets real close for the first time and discovers the innocence and wonderment of creation.

"You might wanna build your mansion next door to the Crowson's," Jake teased.

"He won't want me that close."

"Give these people a chance, Bruce."

"I am." Bruce scoffed. "Lums can be real charmers."

"They only enrolled because they couldn't get a new roof without their HUD or taking out a second mortgage and David's working days are done. All they've got is this land."

"I know all that. Still, makes it harder for the other Tuscs."

"Chill." Jake waved for Bruce to follow closer as they trekked across the field to the big house.

"Chill?" Bruce huffed as a bawling bull jerked him to a stop. "Gawd, he sounded like he was right behind me."

Jake busted a lung. "He's in your back pocket. Just passed his lot. He's on the other side of that shed."

"Is he sick?"

"Lovesick. We call him Two Tails." Jake caught up. "We'll feed him in the morning." A few steps from the screened in porch, a waft of Brunswick stew, cornbread and sweet pies lured them like a fisherman's jitterbug cast out across a still water teasing with its soft easy chatter.

"Two Tails, huh?"

Jake opened the screen door and Bruce stepped up. Already seated around the small table and leaning back in the rockers on the far side nearest the weeping willow out in the back yard, Miss Ginger, Exilee, Ken and both Magee boys with their parents. They exchanged quick hellos. The boys were eighteen and twenty something, sat tall and handsomely, too. The Magee family looked like kin of Sidney Poitier, that famous perty

Black and Native American Indian man who took on timely acting jobs pertaining to racial injustices during the nineteen fifties and sixties and won himself an Oscar, like he was born to do just that very thing. The Magee family is like that, too, descendants of the very Eber Magee whose foot is buried in the Underground Railroad.

They own the property on the other side of the timberline. The fifty acres was signed over to them by Mr. Crowson's great granddad when emancipation was declared some two hundred years ago. Every generation of Magee's been proud workers and successful entrepreneurs. Mr. Magee didn't get high school finished for working day and night, but his wife went back and taught school for twenty years and his oldest son got college in the Army and his youngest will be going to the community college. The boys had hardly had enough spare time to wash their cars much less see about keeping the legendary Magee recipe in circulation or fetch a dollar jar running for Bruce.

When a loud diesel truck rushed up and blasted its deep horn Exilee laughed, "Robin's back, y'all. We can eat now." Exilee nimbly lofted from her chair to greet Bruce and her curly black hair in a long thick braid down her back with a cute curly tip just above her lean waistline popped around her back like it had a life of its own. She wore tennis shoes, blue jean cutoff shorts with white cottony threads teasing her tight tanned thighs, and a baggy tee shirt that gripped the girls despite the extra fabric. "Hey," she hugged him hard and smacked his cheek with a surprising damp pucker. "Welcome to the farm, Bruce."

His cheeks bloomed as dark red as the plum jelly sitting on the table. "Glad to be here, real glad." Bruce nodded at everyone and the Magee boys twice before totally letting her loose. When Exilee raised her eyebrow up at him with a cocked jaw, he finally let go of her hand as well.

Exilee poured him a glass of sweet tea from the pitcher on the table and he finished half while everyone else on the porch welcomed him and Mrs. Crowson, a petite Native American Indian woman who barely looked forty came out of the kitchen with little four-year-old, Luke Crowson, her grandson, Ken and Exilee's boy. Luke was a pale child with orange cheeks. His build was square and solid and had soot black hair, straight, not curly like his mother's Indian-African hair and had his dad's English jaw, a strong wide one. He approached Bruce and lifted his open arms wide, "Hey, there. This your farm?"

"Yes. Are you gonna work the tractor with Papaw or help Jake and Mommy get my ponies walkin' the line?" Luke leaned back from Bruce's arms to check his expression.

"Whatever you tell me to do, Sir." They all laughed with Bruce. "What time does all this start anyway? I'm used to first light hittin' the floor runnin'."

"Hear that, Papaw? He's just like you!" Luke leaned into Bruce's chest and checked for Jake outside to discover him walking Robin inside.

"We have ta go get Jake up sometimes," Luke explained, "He goes city on us."

"City, huh? I'll fix that," Bruce chimed.

Luke squirmed down from Bruce and eagerly opened the door. Robin was wearing a white western tailored blouse, tight from the ribs down, tucked in deep, and unbuttoned so far the valley girls shone as her black satin hair swished across. Her hot pink jeans were tight and announced with a wide gold belt. "I got a chair for you, Robin, next to mine." When Luke beamed up at her she squatted her six-foot, five-inch frame down and kissed him. "Mmm-mm," she smacked his cheek and left a glossy red pucker.

"When are you gonna let me take him riding, Exilee?" Robin towered over Luke. He looked like a penguin wagging its tail with his dark hair, black jeans, yellow faux alligator boots and black tee shirt, other than the printing on the back: "Kiss me. I Rode a Pony over the only Authenticated Patch of Underground Railroad – and Survived." Robin's booted foot reverberated like a bouncing ball irritating Exilee until she threw her head like a mad mare.

"When I have time to go too. Just 'cause Luke can ride that pony in the round pen doesn't mean he's ready to go trail riding with you." Exilee fisted her hips. "You don't even stay on the trails."

"I ride with you on tours, Momma. I wanna ride with Robin." Luke rationalized.

Exasperated, Exilee led Luke from Robin and guided him to his papaw. "Robin's trail rides don't have prepped trails. You know how we drive the tractor over the paths and put down fresh sand clay and scoop the poop? Well, real trails don't have maintenance. They have limbs in the way and holes in the ground and yellow jackets. There's just so many things out there, honey. We'll go as a family sometime."

Luke armed one hand on his hip and the other on his papaw's leg. "What day?"

"We'll get it in next week, somehow. Okay?" Exilee promised as she tried to smooth Ken's grimace with a wink. Summer is a busy time for any farm, but for one giving tours it was hectic. Ken told Luke, "I'm gonna get you up early this week and we'll put you in the round pen with some obstacles. If you pass all the tests, we'll take you into the timberline on Still Pass Trail. A deal?"

"Deal."

Exilee pulled Robin into the kitchen. "Come here and help me in the kitchen, Miss Restaurant Lady and let Bruce get to know everybody," and Jake followed.

Luke told his papaw, "I don't ride a pony. I have a horse."

Mr. Crowson pulled him up onto his lap. "That's right. You sleepin' with me tonight or in Daddy's old room?"

"With you, Papaw." When Luke squeezed his papaw, Mr. Crowson told him that he was gettin' a grip like his and would soon be strong enough to change the three-point hitch on the tractor and it spurred Luke on to drill his papaw on when and if tomorrow was a good day and if not, could they do it the next.

Ken's bright blue eyes stood out against his dark farmer's tan as he greeted Bruce with an outstretched hand. Ken wore his dark brown hair in a crew cut and mirrored a primed drill sergeant or hellish jail guard, depending on the mindset, as he reached out for Bruce's hand.

"What's your schedule tomorrow?' Bruce promptly inquired, but Ken's humble smile and shrugged shoulders answered the real question. "The farm perty much tells me what to do. I look at the garden and know what to pick, or if it's time to till. The animals fuss if we don't see about 'em. We do a lot of mowing. Biggest thing going on right now is trying to figure out where to dig a well."

"I can help with that." Bruce was still shaking his hand when Ken gently pulled away.

"You wanna dig or carry rocks?" Ken's eyes danced.

"Shoot, I'll be glad to do both. I miss workin', getting dirty and sweaty. I even miss the smell of it. But I was really talkin' about witching the well with a divinity branch," Bruce explained. "Grew up witchin' for spring water."

"Yeah, that's right. I mean, well, everyone needs good water. You can show Dad." Ken's hands were flying. "You can show all of 'em. We'd all like ta see that."

"Y'all have water trouble?" Bruce asked Mr. Crowson and he gestured no.

"Nope." Ken's hands gently waved about. "We want a hand dug well for the tourists. We're gonna cover it with acrylic glass housing and hang a stainless-steel bucket over it for making wishes. Tourists can get a drink of water out of a fountain spigot next to it. Rock it up like our well to match. Wanted to the old timey thing and let folks drawl the water up with a wooden bucket. Insurance rep says not to."

Ken asked Bruce to take a seat. "We're going to cover it with a gazebo. Thinking about a post and beam or logs with dovetail joints and a wood shingle roof. It'll match the post and beam we put up over the passage. Run electric to it and have a recording from the Black Purse Papers. There's a lot of good stuff in there. I like the part where Onacona explains that the baby they're sending to freedom is being born again and will have a new life and new family on the other side. It always tears me up when Miss Ginger reads those parts." Ken leaned to the side and his scrumptious thick black eyelashes created a sexy shadow.

Miss Ginger, seemingly resting in the high back rocker, winked at Ken. "You could talk a squirrel into selling his nuts." She had slick short black hair, curled and set, her skin was dark polished copper, and she wore brown tennis shoes and a soft blue cotton pantsuit.

"That'll set the stage for old timey." Bruce peered up at Ken from the white wooden chair with his pale tired grays. "Sounds good, and you're gonna hand dig the well and place the rocks by hand. Use a corbel placement or they'll collapse into the well," Bruce said, and Mr. Crowson's blue eyes flashed. "You dug one, have ya?" His dark worn work jeans were thinned to light blue along the sides of his thighs, knees and the hemline. His plaid blue-and-brown short sleeve shirt was thinly worn, and one sleeve was ripped and stitched. He was wearing worn tennis shoes and his cowboy hat hung behind him on a hook next to binoculars while the smooth darkened areas on the arms of his once white chair claimed his grip.

Bruce wiped his sweaty palms down the sides of his jeans. "No, Sir. Six years of reading. I can make a lot of things," Bruce slightly cocked his head, "A solar water heater, house out of dung or straw. Wire a house to meet inspection. Read about raising goats for cheese and how to do it. You can ask me anything about making wine or dewberries in general. Can tell you about grapes, too. Got big plans for The Company." His words whisked out like they'd been whisked off a broom. "Already have an order list prepared for the equipment, storage, even the bottling procurement. First, I want to contact a metal building dealership, find the best deal." Bruce made firm eye contact with Mr. Crowson. "Can't say thank you enough for those vines, Mr. Crowson."

Mr. Crowson didn't push him further, but politely smiled. "You can call me David."

Ken slapped his hands together. Reached over to Bruce and held his shoulder. "You'll meet that steel building dealer in just a few. He's looking forward to meeting you, Bruce."

"Naw?" Bruce's lips rose. "He's coming over now?"

The two Magee boys smiled at him. The youngest, Thomas, gave him a flick of the hand, like the kind used in town to signal the store-church had a load to go, and Bruce caught the cue straight on, stepping back in time like it was just last week, and flicked his pointer finger up and down, the need-more-shine motion, and then pounced up from his chair with a "Good-gooboly-goo!" It was so loud and unexpected that everyone except Thomas and his brother were wide-eyed. Bruce and the Magee boys met in the middle of the porch to shake hands, but Bruce surprised them with bear hugs.

"You know you're famous, right?" Thomas asked Bruce and he replied, "Hope not," and grumbled with a wide smile, "Kid, you look great, both of ya. All cleaned up and spit-shined."

"You, too. Get cleaned up and all kinds of good things happen, huh?" Just like that, young Thomas set the dinosaur in the room a loose and it took up the entire screened in porch like a real horned triceratops.

"It's looking that way." Bruce gripped his jaw like a man pulling out that dinosaur's tooth, real stringent like. Then, as if huntin' season on triceratops opened that very second Bruce covered his eyes as headlights rushed him. Cars pulled in all over the place, parking every which a way. It was as if the fence lines were runway lights leading to a shindig held in one of those city coliseums where people pay to see famous folks.

Most of the arrivals were invited. The crowd from Sunday school meandered up the walk followed by staggered guests including the post-master and his seven boys who own small businesses, most of 'em in town. They all bustled in and wandered the cozy country home as they filled it with an abundance of homemade goodness. Biscuits and several pones of bread, pintos, tater salad, pies, cabbage with bacon, two big platters of middlin' meat, apple fritters, creamed corn, coleslaw, casseroles and cheese grits, fried chicken, barbeque chicken and roasted chicken and a ham slathered in pineapple juice passed and teased and filled the country home with the kind of goodness imagined in Heaven.

Bruce rubbed his hands together like he was trying to keep warm between greetings and handshakes. It dispelled the shake and he continued with a fine job of greeting, all cleaned up and respectable like, like he'd done that kind a thing all his live long life.

"Jake said it was just a few of his friends," Bruce told Ken, "Where we gonna put all these people?" and Ken's arm spread out across the field as the summer night's stars began to show themselves and the pond frogs chirped for mates.

"Ah, we got tables under the porch, here." Ken aimed at the willow tree down behind Miss Ginger and when he did, she hooked onto Bruce's arm and with her sweetest Southern drawl said that she had a date with him for breakfast and that she was gonna work up a mess of biscuits and gravy. Then she pulled him in closer, "Bes chicken bog in the fridge and I'll keep a cup of ellick hot for ya, chile, if you bes sleeping in." After her surprising vernacular warms him she let go and Bruce purred like a wildcat. "I swanny, I see right here youse gonna be my slam favorite Miss Ginger." When he winked at her she gently squeezed his hand as another group filled the screened in porch's doorway.

"Hope there's enough chairs," Ken told Bruce, "We'll have the lights on in a minute and you can see better. There's tables and chairs we got from the church fellowship hall out under that tree by the pond. Momma likes it out there."

Ken's former co-workers were hard to miss. The teachers flocked in like geese, honking and snarking and causing such ruckus they drowned out the bawling bull in the back lot, while researchers from up at the university had eased in quietly, and everyone was carrying covered dishes. Robin's parents,' Gili and Little John were loaded with Gili's take out boxes and casserole trays. Gili's salt and pepper bob bounced like her fast steps as her petite frame kept pace with her tall husband's long stride. She was pale as gardenia blooms with bright red lipstick and carried cake boxes. Little John was a giant dark- skinned Tuscarora - handsome in every way and walked like a buck, stealthily and assured even with his arms stacked with covered dishes. She stretched her neck out to yell, "Don't piddle, now." Little John lengthened out as he adjusted his long arms around the carefully stacked covered dishes threatening to tumble.

"Don't you dare drop those!" Gili screeched as she reached the steps and Ken eased her load and Gili locked onto Bruce and pinched his butt cheek. "You sweet little Lum, give me a kiss."

"You know how to treat a man, Miss Gili, but I'm a Tuscarora."

"Whatever, baby," she kissed his cheek.

"All those sweetnins gonna spoil my figure," he returned her kiss.

"Bones! Look at cho. You need one a these lime pies to keep for yourself. I'll put it up for you, baby."

Bruce thanked her and Ken steered Gili and Little John into the kitchen and hurried back to Bruce. "She's entertaining, huh," Ken chided, "Gili is a descendant of Custer, General Custer," he whispered, "the Indian killer." When Bruce didn't flinch, Ken went on, "Little John was ostracized from his tribe for marrying her. He's about as pure blood Tuscarora as you can get."

Bruce bit the tip of his tongue as his smile sizzled, "No wonder Robin's so hot, all that war pumping in her blood." Ken's exaggerated nods matched his goofy grin, "Put a bull in a head vice, I'll tell you that."

"Gili'll snap your hand off, boy," Little John excused himself to scout out around the pond and the screen door stuck open when the worn metal spring cinched up in the stretched out rusty spot. Ken told Bruce that there was always something to fix and went on to say that rust was common in high humid areas while Bruce stared up at the rust on the ceiling fan until he was diverted by more headlights.

The stunning bright lights spotlighted the rusty spring on the screen door. "Wouldn't take much for that ta snap in two,"

Bruce squinted. Ken agreed and then stepped out onto the steps with his arm up over his eyes as he inspected the curious mix of vehicles joltin' and slidin' into the farm. The seventy's chromed caddys and equally aged four doors to haggard sport trucks were marked in Bruce's memory like the dared cigarette burn scars on his forearms. He braced himself against the door jamb with his arms crossed over his chest and everyone on the porch stood straight up.

As vehicle doors were slammed the passengers united like soldier ants and charged the screened in porch in scattered formation. They were not carrying covered dishes, but toted pokes and jars. Jimmy Bean, a long lean handsome Indian with suntanned skin and gray eyes and mostly gray hair, reached the steps with a full smile, a jar dangling from one hand in a spider like grip over the lid and with his other, offered his poke. "Bes your favorite. Know'd you missed hit up in dat Beacon Hotel." His minty fresh breath eased Bruce's fears, but he was puzzled when he realized that the jar was empty. "Thank you, Snap. Mon, you are the best," Bruce said as Snap held the bag open. "You're favorite, orange pop in the bottle and salty nuts. Glad you're out, Buddyrow." He smiled as Bruce inverted the empty jar. "We all brought jars for ya. Minders we got debs on yer first batch a' wine."

Bruce pulled Snap and the jar close and they gripped one another like a chain holds a gate closed as Bruce quietly confided, "Can't wait to get started. The Crowson's even planted the vines for me. This is it, Snap. I'm gonna make it."

Bruce's rubbed over his head and Snap wiped away a fast tear as the anxious guests on the porch took their seats.

"Always knew you would, you stubborn cuss. Come fishing wid me after youse settled and no more cold biscuits and hot soda. I'm got a wife now cooks a spread that you'll set you for a two-hour nap, straight-on." Snap patted Bruce over and over and waved for his new wife who was busy talking to Edge. When his wife didn't pay him any mind, he told Bruce, "Runs that mouth like an outboard: leaves me in da wake." Bruce shared the laugh. "Sounds like a match made in Heaven. How does Edge like her new stepmom?" Snap smiled extra wide and told him that he should a' took up with her a long time ago. "Took kin so fast I didn't count for nothin' first year. Whadaya 'xpect? Edge was fetched up on the edge, ya know, those low downs. I took her in and did what I could. But she was longin' for a mother." Bruce agreed and commented on how things seem to work out for the best and asked Snap to take his orange pop to the kitchen and to hurry up and meet him back out on the lawn.

Bruce placed the jar alongside the wall and stepped out onto the thick summer Bermuda lawn and as he neared, his old pals sucked in heaps of honeysuckle and cantaloupe from the nearby melon patch and they contentedly settled on his lips like watermelon juice and sunshine, all nice and easy, like he was already pleasured up drunk.

Five more jar runners rushed to greet Bruce and joined in on the tail end of the conversation between Bruce and Snap.

Someone spat out that Snap hadn't caught a single fish since he'd married due to the racket he and his old lady made, and more excuses followed: "Like two politicians."

"Weren't that. Bes two crickets!"

"Bet they'd talk da hide off a beaver." His wife, only five feet away, was still busy filling Edge's ear and clung to the longing girl's bare arm as she stared after Bruce.

Edge held her chin down, head slanted, and boobs up or maybe they'd just grow'd up with the rest of her that way, perky as hot peppers. At twenty-two, she cleverly turned around and shifted her firm hips. Edge's short shorts had red bandana trim that matched her petite bandana blouse making her look like she was wrapped for something or another with the bright white bow tying back her curly light brown locks.

Edge toted a poke for Snap's new wife and Old Rodger Dodger who had lumbered before scurried to speak to Pig Pen and the two stepped off in private. Scarecrow's lanky frame was followed by the lovely Lilly. Bruce and Ken melted and drooled like Lilly was waltzing into their arms as Pig Pen and Dodger filled their mouths with chewing gum. Dodger discreetly emptied his half full jar by bending over and coughing as he flushed its contents into the tall grass by the fence post and Pig Pen kept watch.

Pig Pen was Cassie's oldest boy who was twenty at the time. Cassie was only fifteen when he was born, so they had perty much growd up together. His real name was Lassie

Ben Deere. But with all his name conjures up speaking it aloud was shut down, prohibited, outlawed, deregulated, and punishable by all sorts a' authority figures, when he was only in second grade, on account of fights. Pig Pen slung a rock with his juvember with such accuracy he'd knocked bulls out cold for as long as three seconds. From third grade on school records had plainly identified him as Ben Deere, but even at his high school graduation, when Pig Pen was called up to the stage, it was Lassie his classmates resorted to. They cheered, "Lassie, come home," and "Yea, Lassie," as Pig Pen had only one-and-one half arms, and with those same limbs he had saved the football team's beloved mascot, an aged ram named Horny.

The newspaper article had gone viral up and down the East Coast. Horny had climbed the stadium's outdoor bleachers and challenged an opposing team's audience member for their CD. CD's are those crispy fried versions of corn dogs made in North Carolina by Exilee's ex brother in law who had an affair with Jake which sent Exilee's sister, Glennie, totally raging mad to the extent of putting her in a mental ward. Anyway, Horny just loved those CD's, and when it wasn't offered, he butted the stingy man's chest. Well, the man stood up and proved himself to indeed be a large piece of a man, like a six-foot-niner with shoulders you could stack a record-breaking brick bat on.

He picked up Horny and dropped him down into the open area between seats where all the steel beams zig zag. Tragically, during the fall the ram's horns got stuck and he was suspended there like a goat on a rope.

Pig Pen was on the other side as all this went down with the binoculars he used when the cheerleaders squatted or bent over. Good thing it wasn't half time. Pen ran to help while the opposing team just jeered and cheered so loudly that Horny's wails were drowned out. It was just awful. In fact, that was the newspaper headline, "Awful Horny." Everybody read it.

Pen sprinted up the bleachers with his stump popping out of his shirt sleeve till he reached Horny. Horny had rubbed his horns back and forth over the metal till he'd worked one side slam off and was dangling by only one half of the set and was screaming just like a baby cries. Pen lunged down into the metal abyss catching on support beams with his legs and his one good arm as he descended, just like you'd see a monkey in the jungle swinging on vines. But Horny got all excited and broke himself loose just as Pen reached him and they fell to the ground together.

A crowd of concerned classmates and their parents had gathered. They witnessed the fall and good thing they did, or no one would a' believed it. Pen had got himself under the goat and cradled it, taking the brunt of the fall. That's the kind of kid Cassie fetched up.

Bruce grabbed Pig Pen's hand. "So glad you came. Read about you in the papers. Maybe you can help me with my goats. I plan to have a goat dairy with cheese on the winery's grounds. Say the word and you're my man."

"Horny," Pen snorted, sending bust-a-gut laughter over the group and the nearby ponies into blowing and nickering fits. It gradually settled and they caught up a little on Pen's life and his brothers' and Bruce learned that the economy was wearing 'em down like hard rain and no rain. Even with the butchering Cassie and her boys did it was not enough.

Tale was butchering was how Pig Pen had lost his forearm. Summer between his first year of seventh grade and second year of seventh grade there was a cow not prepared to be sacrificed under the guillotine they'd rigged up over the draining ditch. In fightin' the creature for its life he had lost one forearm. Pen had made do with one and one half arms, but it was not easy. They lived on a farm, rent free, in exchange for keeping the place mowed, and general maintenance, including anything with wheels, just outside city limits. They turned a dollar with outsiders' vehicle repairs, too. From feeding to mucking to hauling and killing and running down a yard chicken for supper, they took turns with all the chores.

They also took turns taking classes at the community college. Taking turns meant one took the class the first semester then the next in line so he could share notes and use the same book, when not updated with another, same with clothes and some girlfriends. The aura of mystique and rawness and that kind of plain dirt farmer charm that only comes from livin' it oozed from Robeson's Indians, the Tuscaroras. But this bate had even more than that. This bate had roots in jar runnin,' and that meant they'd all run from the law or been caught and jailed and some'd even been shot.

Bruce's toothy grin and busy arms embraced them in delight when not a single one smelled too much like likker, and sweeter still, their pokes were filled with store bought goodies they'd shared in by-gone days just like they'd gotten together and planned their purchases. But when overzealous Bruce grabbed a hold of Edge's waist to swing her around like he'd done since he was six and she was all of three, the chickens roosting on an overhead limb flew over, squawking and flapping and shedding feathers and fluff till she squirmed loose. A large Americana hen and her mess a' dibs chirped after the flying flock in a yellow streak and everyone around was wiping their heads, checking for chicken drop when one second later, the bull bawled and the ponies in the lot neighed and nickered.

The tracked wheels creaked as the big heavy barn doors opened and the orangey yellow light outlined Robin's curves. With one hand on her hip and the other waving, the chickens waddled inside. A minute later Robin called for Jake to help carry buckets. After he gathered two armfuls Jake yelled, "Got your chair, Bruce," as he held up a wee three and half pound stainless steel bucket, and they laughed when Bruce wagged his tiny tight tail.

As Snap proudly stood next to Edge, she confidently stepped up toe to toe with Bruce. "That how you gonna treat your employees? Swing 'em around and scare 'em half ta death? Everyone a' us needs a job and plan on being in on your winery,

Mr. Bruce Black. No one here's enrolled as a Lumbee, just like you told us not to do, and can't get hired around in this Lumbee county. We been with you on this recognition fight, Mister, and it's taking its toll."

"Mister, now, is it? Good thing I didn't get you too high off the ground. You're stacked up tighter than I thought." His red ears and lusty eyes were hard to see in the dark, but his mommucking up was real plain like. "You're all grown up, Elizabeth."

Edge leaned back a smidge. "Yes, and I'm serious 'bout a job too. Only reference I got is you. How's jar runner gonna look on my resume? You made me, so you're responsible."

Dodger hollered, "She's a-gotcha now."

"Well, I'm sure we can find a place for everybody, but you'll have to wait until I get this place underway," Bruce explained as he coyly hovered near Edge, "Can you read yet?" and she slapped his arm, "That's not lady like." Bruce cocked his jaw while he held her slim shoulder and scanned the bate a' them and hollered, "Bes be a great day, huh? To make revenue with the likes of us old likker head Indians, I swanny that'd be too good."

Edge fisted her hips. "I'm in my second year of college, who you calling likker head? I aim to be your bookkeeper. Didn't you read my letters?"

Scarecrow stepped backwards and coughed, turning his back in a not so non-obvious manner, as least for Bruce, and did his best to check out the wheels parked along the fence line and caught them with lightening flash clicks of his camera. Lilly called in plates on her cell phone and in one, two, five minutes slipped it back into her front pocket and smiled up at Bruce addressing his jar runners.

Bruce straightened up extra tall to pay both Scarecrow and Edge some serious mind when Ken stepped up to bat. Ken cleared his throat. "Bruce'll have plenty of positions available. I'm sure he'll be taking applications, soon as he gets a building up."

"Thanks, Buddyrow." Bruce ran a hand over the bank statement in his back pocket.

When Cassie pouted her plump lips extended past her gums. "Bes ritin' tests to work likker, just 'cause youse puttin' up a building? Dat's some jubious crap I'm ever heard. Brickhouse Bruce," she spat as her curly orange bangs bounced against her sun damaged forehead. "You know taint many of us who reads and writes." Even in the faint light her blue eyes pierced like tossed marbles across glass, threatening to shatter anything in their path.

Dodger belted out, "I don't want no reglar job. Bes a-bench warmer and batch taster, right chere. I'm da man for that and youse pay 'nugh my boy'll be done right. Gotdat, Jack!" His front partial loosened, but with his two first fingers dodged them back in his white bearded face. Disgraced and humbled, Bruce agreed, "Whadever he needs. It's covered."

Cassie got right in Bruce's face. "We all been praying for you. The Council's put word out to check for Lumbee cards and we've walked the Tusc walk all the way to scratch city. Our factory jobs closed, left town or the illegals took 'em. We's livin' off butchering scraps and whadever we get out a da ground. I won't take nuthin' from the state and kin only sell part a what we growd or we won't have nuthin' ta put up." She clamped down before slowly looking back up at him. "Can't come up with 'nuff for car insurance. We's all that way. Ridin' hot." Cassie's anguish deepened the lines in her weary face. "Tuscs been put out here in the pines to survive and now were all countin' on you." Her hot breath fumed up at him, "Bruce Black, say what you're gonna do for us, one time," she breathed the words like she'd prayed 'em over and over, "just one time, say it out loud."

Bruce clutched at his throat, "Swanny, Cassie Locklear, I bes real overwhelmed right now. I'm tired as hell. Don't think I've slept in two days, too excited, but I can tell you that as far as I'm concerned, you're family." Cassie looked about fifty, but was only thirty-four, with a passel of seven yurkers from several different men.

"You bes that for us, too," she drew in a deep breath and Bruce felt her passion, her strength, the need and hugged her and held her by the shoulder as he turned to his friends. "One thing I learned in prison, wherever there are two or more Tuscs, you are on the swamp." He scanned the faces of his brothers, made eye contact with Cassie and took the paper napkin she held up to him. "My vines need fertilizing. Need to do some tilling and mulching, too. Show up Monday, we'll get at it. Cash paid daily." He united them in Pow Wow fashion as "Yeeyee-yee-yee!" pierced the air.

When they calmed Ken said, "I'll haul a tractor over," and Bruce quietly accepted.

Cassie wiped away her fast tears and kissed Bruce as he flagged for the crowd to stop still. "Wait. Who needs car insurance? I'm not having illegals working at my place," and he pulled out a roll. Hands flew up to mouths, popped chests and waved over heads and within minutes his hands were empty. "Come on." Bruce waved, "They're gonna have my party without us." With cash in their pockets, socks and bras, they stood a bit straighter and walked a bit taller, and again like soldier ants, only this time, with a bust-r-go-broke Master of Ceremonies as their king, as they all headed up to the screened in porch.

Bruce held the door open and was handed the symbolic empty jars with gutsy grins and gratitude as he piled the tokens along the wall. When Cassie handed him her empty jar, she palmed his chest. "Bes yer mother's heart dere." She curiously shivered, but quickly reclaimed her stoic demeanor and toted her poke of saltines and chipped beef into the kitchen.

Bruce's chin was up in the air, struggling to keep it together, as he twisted around and smiled at Miss Ginger, still in the big rocker, "I'm waiting for a full jar myself. Helps with the joints of the morning, a hot tea with honey and whiskey'll do the job."

"I'll be selling wine, Miss Ginger. Oldest pain killer around."

"Well, I can take ta uppity spirits, too. Whatever does the job best, right chile'?"

Bruce beamed over at Miss Ginger like he used to do his momma while Scarecrow and Lilly held out to be the last guests through the opened door. "Add ten pounds and you'll be up to mixing crete with a shovel. Boy, yer skinny." Scarecrow pulled up Bruce's bicep and pinched it too hard. "Hey, easy now." Bruce rubbed down the spasm, "I'll be hiring that done. Looking for a contractor."

"That's how it is, huh? Well, start with your jar runners. Half of 'em been throwin' up buildings without licenses for years," he chided, but when Bruce's steel grays pierced under his angry slits, Scarecrow said, "Yank was on his way out and wanted ta claim a victory 'fore he went north. Or he'd a never took the word of Fisk. I lost my job, my whole career over this," Bruce still aimed, and Crow smirked, "All Yankees think they got something on us. Gawl dookie, their fat egos rub me wrong every time. I hate we didn't ship 'em out ta France when we's setting up the states. Some kinds just don't belong anywhere though." When Bruce was still rigid Scarecrow got quiet, "Been wantin' to tell you, but knew I couldn't say any names on visitation. Too much ta risk."

As Lilly circled around them with wide open arms, she exposed her pistol. "I'm so glad you're going legit, Bruce. You make us so proud to be your friend." She kissed his cheek and whispered, "We'll get Fisk."

After the trio disengaged Bruce led them outside. Five steps into the grass he faced Scarecrow. "What's with the camera?" But he eyed Lilly.

Scarecrow's big brown eyes doubled, and his lean pale face lengthened like he'd been stretched out on a pole. As his lips came back together, they strectched like a dog's over a half-chewed ham bone. "Fisk and Wart haven't been seen in months, but there's smoke coming out of their barn where they got that brickhouse of a still. Thing is all copper. Figure they're stockpiling, an outsider's running their jars, or they got a U.C."

Lilly checked around and stepped closer. "They bought that big copper still after stealing the last of your daddy's goods."

"I say they're gonna pay me back or that still is mine."

Like a crawling caterpillar, Scarecrow's thick black eyebrows met, "That'd be stealing."

"Repossession," Bruce calmly quipped.

Lilly flicked her long brown hair and her D cups perked. "We never had this conversation."

The gentlemen faced off fully loaded and neither backed, so Lilly detained Scarecrow by the arm down to the food filled tables.

After greetings with the kitchen ladies, the jar runners also tracked down to the tables under the weeping willow. It was lit up like a Holy Christmas tree with tiny white strings of twinkling lights braided down its long thin branches. Twinkling stars danced across the rims of platters, plates and bowls as the dangling strings ever so softly swayed, like little spirits blessing each morsel. The scents of warm comfort foods filled the cooled summer night's air as Mr. Crowson announced above the salivating crowd. "We need to bless this food before we get started." Frogs chirped, distant birds whistled, livestock's heavy steps slowly neared, and horses restlessly pawed and blew while ponies puffed. When a rooster crowed and chased his strayed cackling hens, a whippoorwill pierced above them all and silence swept like an ocean's wave.

"They're done, Papaw," Luke yelled, followed by the crowd's sweet hushed laughter.

"Heavenly Father, you've blessed us with another foundling, and we ask for wisdom and success as he makes a new life. Bruce is a smart man and we're blessed you chose us to get him off to a good start. May all his friends, new and old, join Bruce in his new life and know God's Grace and mercy is the only treasure we will know on earth to see us over to the other side." He raised his head and spread his arms across the crowd. "Hope to see every single one of ya in Heaven." After a short pause, he said, "Give us two stomachs and pig jaws. We've got a spread here that'd choke a crew a' hay balers. Pass me Momma's tater salad first. Amen."

As laughter and Amens made rounds, a lone slow-moving vehicle sounded alarm Rough metal scraping metal followed by a booming backfire set all eyes on the newcomers. One headlight was higher than the other. Jake fled from Robin's side to grab a hold of Bruce who was three yards away munching on a strip of cracklin' as he made fast tracks toward the rattletrap's ruckus. As a larking voice heralded from the opened door, "Mon, ain't you a-making tracks!" Jake and Bruce marched straight on, but their lips formed fat circles as Mark propped against the hood and posed real purty like he'd popped a slug in a prize-sized bobcat.

"Gotcha, huh?" Mark busted a gut till he spit on himself. "Knew I would. Delayed getting' here long as I could." He hissed, spit and hissed some more while Bruce and Jake awkwardly smiled. Bruce's beefy top lip curled as he asked his cousin, "What in the world made you buy that junked jalopy off a them? And how'd you ever talk your momma into riding in that thing? Good Gawd." He peered in, "You talked her husband into the back seat, you rascal." Bruce opened Thelma's door and she said it wasn't necessary but thanked him as he raised the seat up and helped her husband squeeze out. Other than the grunting and growling, he was polite and quiet about it.

Mark's slender arm reached up for the tennis ball slowly bobbing on the CB antenna welded onto the running board and whacked it. When it zinged back and forth on the hefty steel rod threatening to raise a bruise on his noggin he stepped back. "I'm making a float out of it for the parade. Got it cheap, well, with a trade."

"Trade for wooden nickels, I hope," Jake swung a hard left at Mark and the boy ducked.

"Hey, you got a haircut. Joshing about you looking like Jesus paid off, huh?" Mark popped Jake's shoulder and Jake told Bruce, "We're in the same class at church."

"That was the trade." With bright blue eyes, tawny skin with high cheekbones and chiseled features, his Tuscarora blood shone.

"Say what?" Bruce stood back.

"I grew my hair out while you were gone, grieving thing, I guess. Cut it off the day I heard you were getting out early. Fisk and Wart were up in town and heard about it. They came to the barbers and offered the car and everything. I went to their place and they had three junked out and building another. I think they're trying to build a battery-operated one or something 'cause they had a solar panel welded down across the hood of an old station wagon, the kind with the wood grain siding."

"No telling what they're gonna do with it." Bruce's brows met while his jaw hung in suspension. "How long did it get?"

"Long enough we couldn't tell if it was a he or a she," Jake teased and Themla slid her the side of her hand down to Mark's hip and Bruce huffed, "One braid for men. Grow it out again, Mark. Our hair is our way of showing the world we are proud Tuscarorians. We need to keep up our traditions for your sons and my sons."

"You growing yours out?" Mark asked and Bruce said, "All the way, brother."

Thelma admired Bruce's lean build and how his cheekbones were more astute. When she commented that he looked healthy Bruce explained that he went on a diet like his ancestors had after reading how it promotes longevity and it made him lean. His aunt said that it brought out his magnificent features.

After the covered dishes were ladled out and bellies were full, most guests left for home.

"Still got to feed up in the morning," Jake said as he set up the counter. He pulled out the likker jar he'd been saving especially for Bruce's homecoming from behind the surplus sauerkraut in the pantry of his little colonial home. He encircled the prize jar with thick glass jiggers he'd purchased at the dollar store and set a bowl of pretzels on the side. At eleven-thirty, Miss Ginger poured half a glass of buttermilk and sat back in her rocker and sipped as Mark eagerly poured the six jiggers of Old Man Black's finest.

Miss Ginger stopped rocking as they belted it down with gasps and fast hot ears. When nary a one a' them choked, she resumed rocking. Scarecrow, Ken, Jake and Bruce held their jiggers out for seconds. Mark and Robin set theirs on the counter. Robin got all the attention when she suddenly held down the girls like they were gonna bolt out of their stirrups and knock her in the chin. Then she threw her hands up over her head. "Hot damn! I'm ready to ride now!" She stomped her boot against the wooden floor and when she posed like she was going to rope a somebody, Jake calmed her down, "You'll get hurt out there in the dark."

Mark flipped his glass jigger upside down on the counter, and Robin squirmed away from Jake's tender grasp. "It's half-moon. There's plenty of light. Come on, y'all, let's have some real fun," Robin's long black hair shimmied across her long back and teased the crest of her firm seat. "You can ride, can't cha, Bruce? Exilee, we can put him on Choctaw." Robin pulled Mark up to her side and embarrassed him as she held him real close. His eyes were level with her valley. "I'm gonna let this boy ride pony style with me." Mark eagerly threw his arm up over her shoulder, "Okay!" and took in an eyeful.

Miss Ginger's hard-soled shoes tapped like a judge's gavel against the wooden floor. "Put that jar up for one of you breaks a leg. Why don't we do something we can all do?" "We?" Jake leaned like he was sloshed, "Anyone need to use the bathroom first?"

Lilly and Edge were pointed down the hall as Exilee said, "We can go to the big house and sleep. There're three empty rooms upstairs. Ginger's old bedroom is off to the left on its own. We won't bother you, Miss Ginger. I promise."

"Oh, no bothering about it. I'm with you." Miss Ginger stood a foot shorter than Exilee as she seized command with her crooked pointed finger. "See, I missed my youth, chile, busy raising you. I'm what you call, a retroactive senior." She mischievously grinned and proclaimed, "Read about it in a magazine, how women like me is called, dating and working. That's what I am, retroactive."

Exilee sucked in what had to be two full lungs of fresh oxygen before releasing. "All right, then. What do you want to do? But remember, this is Bruce's welcoming home party. Don't make us play bingo, pl-ease."

Jake and the boys, including Mark, had another jigger lined up at the kitchen counter. In sequence, they threw it down. Mark held himself steady against the counter and brazenly ogled over the ladies and attempted to discreetly undress Lilly.

"Like melted butter right down ta my toes," Ken's Southern drawl melted Exilee, but she told him not to have any more that she had some real butter for him later. The men poked and hammered Ken that maybe Luke needed a little brother.

"Oh, my word," Miss Ginger slapped her palms together and threw back her head. "Men ain't got enough blood for both heads." The guys hacked and laughed as Miss Ginger bullied between them, but when she hastily snatched up the lid and screwed the devil's loose lip juice closed, the boys ceased. Lilly and Edge cheered on Miss Ginger as they returned from the living room. Exilee shouted, "I can't believe she said that. She's not herself tonight, really."

"Oh, you don't know the half of it," Jake yelped. "Never know what she's gonna say."

"I'm in a dangerous state, old enough to know better and young enough to do it." They hysterically gawked at the prim little nanny in the blue pantsuit as Ken wrapped his arm around Exilee's shoulder and warmly whispered, "Any chance of getting a tour of the Underground Railroad tonight?" in his deepest bedroom voice, while he winked over at Miss Ginger and most everyone returned his goofy grin.

"No more likker for this boy. Over," Exilee shrugged away from under his sexual connotation and asked Miss Ginger, "Good idea, that's something we could all do, Miss Ginger," and smiles ignited. "You give the best tours."

"Something's not right," Mark squinted.

"Tours don't come wid sugar tits and baby wipes. You wanna see the Underground Railroad sober up 'n come on," Miss Ginger whisked out her palm sized flashlight from her polyester pants' pocket and plotted toward the laundry room. At the basement door she turned around. "I'm not carrying you babies down the stairs." She slipped out the key tied to her wrist and unlocked the heavy-duty lock from the sliding Dutch bolt on the basement door. As it scraped open, she clicked on her flashlight. "Jake, get a couple more." And she creaked down the stairs. Lilly was first in line as Jake took Robin by the hand and Edge stalked Bruce like a fox on a pheasant. Her red-tailed target was midway against the counter. Predictably, she followed Bruce as he followed Ken and Mark, but then Bruce managed to get between them. Like a chicken lost in a fox's den Mark clumsily followed Edge down the stairs while Exilee grabbed a flashlight from their bedroom.

Scarecrow had stepped outside to take a phone call and suddenly reappeared in the hall. "Geez. I didn't see you." Exilee braced the flashlight like she'd cock it against his jaw. "Sorry."

"No, I'm sorry, Exilee." Scarecrow lowered his arms. "I

should've let you know my whereabouts. Just making sure the home is clear. Gonna lock up?"

"No," she shrugged and hurried to catch up with the others who were already in the basement. "No one ever messes with anything around here. Come on."

"Bruce's door was the only one shut." Scarecrow didn't budge. "Shouldn't we at least close the entrance doors?" He insisted as she hurried down the steps.

"Go ahead. But you're gonna miss the best part. Ginger gives a dramatic introduction," Exilee projected from the stairwell.

Scarecrow took a mental picture of the cozy home; its horse and cowboy statue on the table next to the recliner, the red pillow on the worn orange and brown plaid couch, the sketch on the wall, the likker jar, the glass jiggers, and exactly how he'd set the bedroom door with a sock under it.

The basement's staging for the Underground Railroad was like a real movie set. Like it'd been professionally staged with life-sized fiberboard cutouts of slave families and farmers and Native American Indians with pieces of European clothing over their crafted animal skin shifts. Wall mounted oil lamps with electric bulbs replicated shadows on the stacked rock walls just like the runaways would have experienced.

But the door to the Underground Railroad was not to be seen. The room appeared to be a food cellar with jars of beans, tomatoes, corn and kraut. A wooden barrel with a tight fighting lid and piles of potatoes and hanging braids of onions. Exilee pointed above their heads to the Leather Britches. Hanging across the low ceiling in row after row, were dried green beans. She explained that Leather Britches were best cooked in a dab of bacon fat and water in an iron skillet and were delicious. The guests sought out the door again.

Miss Ginger held up a candle to the right of her jaw. "Tonight, you will be taking a tour of the Underground Railroad. It is the only authenticated passage in North Carolina. I will be your guide. I'll be quotin' from The Black Purse Papers as well as telling you things I know and left out, if you prove yourselves trustworthy. The papers have been studied and verified as the only written history of the Underground Railroad written in time as it was happening. Names, towns, rivers, 'long with facts on the true beginning of the Trail of Tears, facts on trading with the Tuscaroras and their light-skinned prisoners and the exact origins of Black Indians."

Jake and Bruce simultaneously reached out to tap one another's forearms and jumped. Jake whispered, but everyone heard. "Welcome back, Bruce." Jake and Miss Ginger exchanged sheepish smiles as Jake kept a firm grip on Bruce's arm. "This is your proof, Buddyrow."

His gap grew into a smile when Miss Ginger said, "Hope yer sober. This took some plannin'."

"Yes, ma'am. Thank you."

Edge pat Bruce's back, but when he didn't acknowledge her quit. Robin, on the other side of Jake smirked at her attempt while Mark glared at Robin's backside.

Miss Ginger examined faces like a schoolteacher. "Before folks and babies left here they prayed. All kinds of danger was ahead for 'em. Devil Masters, that be the slave owners, hired bounty hunters to bring back their property. Sometimes they'd be ordered to be kilt if they'd took a likin' to running away over slavin'. Bounty hunters were the worst and did whatever it took to track 'em down. They'd question any folks along the way, all peoples who did any trading, and especially slave owners who had been tolt on for being easy on their slaves. Not only did they question people, they tortured people to get word on where runaways were hiding.

One of the things many don't know is that Devil Masters even paid slaves to track their own people, like the soldiers made traitors of Indians. Many believe the enslavement of Negroes is when the derogatory slang, nigger, originated. Others believe it began as term for slave traitors." Miss Ginger placed the candle on the simple wooden podium holding a stack of leather string bound papers. She unfolded the mini reading lamp from under the podium, clicked it on, blew out her candle and the original Black Purse Papers radiated.

She kept eye contact with Bruce. "The Black Purse Papers were written in Onacona's time, in her language. The professors from the state college said it is called pidgin. I told them I call it half Tuscarora and broken English, 'cause that's 'xactly what it is, and they laughed up there for a minute at that fancy college but agreed with me one hundred percent. Over the course of two weeks, I read it to them and deciphered it. They had me on recording and everything. Now any student can go to their library and view the tape there at the media center. Imagine that? Been kept secret all these years and now the truth can't get out fast enough."

With spread eagle hands she hovered over the pages. "I spent my life studying it, every single word. If it meant four months findin' a ninety-year-old Tuscarora or spending an afternoon with a crodgedy black man, I fount out what each word meant in their time. My reading for tours is from the translations or you wouldn't understand it. And this one tonight is not my regular. It's for Mr. Bruce Black."

Her crooked rigid finger followed the line on the page. "This is what Onacona writes about the Underground Railroad passage we are standing in right chere: Pox saved our Negro babies. When pox came to nearby farms a plan was made with white women in nearby towns who wanted to help runaways. They got pregnant right off. When de mid wife came, who was commonly a Negro house slave, she gave her a small gourd with pokeberry juice. In the gourd's tiny opening was a cloth rag. The new mother was schooled on when to give her newborn pox with the stained rag. Then the mid wife would return for a doctor visit and claim to take the baby to the specialist who had been tolt ta clear up pox from other babies.

The specialist was a doctor who was also a big-time conductor. The law had fines and prison and even death for those who helped runaways. Slaves were valuable property and helping one was looked upon like helping thieves. The doctor risked his life, his wife's and their own childrens to save these babies. He'd have as many as five pox babies in his house for his poor wife and older chidrens to tend to. Course there weren't pox, but there was still bottles and butts 'round the clock for that poor wife a his. Dere'd be a few mothers who'd have to take on the pokeberry pox and put on suffering like with the babies at the specialist's house from time to time to ward off suspicions and to get some help for his poor wife. Cause no one else wanted to help with the quarantine sign hanging on the front door.

Now this plan started on 'count when a Negro slave had a baby the owner could decide whether or not he wanted to keep his property or sell it and that new mother had no say at all and the white mothers saw their pain. The Lord works this way still today. He gives us suffering so we will know why, when and how to help others. It's a terrible pain to lose a child, a pain that leaves a hole inside that can't ever be filt.

The slave mother was schooled on the pokeberry pox, and then often as quick as a few days after birth, she'd give her baby the pox. The master'd be told, and he'd come down to the slave house or send someone he trusted to check and decide if he wanted to let the baby take doctoring or just risk it dying on his property. This is where the biggest love you ever learnt comes in. Knowing she'd never see her baby again, the Negro slave mother let her baby go, to live in freedom and most likely never ever see again. She handed over her new baby to the mid wife who took that precious chile to a station where the Underground Railroad's Pox House started. That'd be right chere!

As the Negro baby traveled the Underground Railroad he went in many clever disguises. The baby'd be on wagon rides in barrels of grain resting on the bottom in a hidden compartment and in hat boxes and cloth bundles. They'd be in saddle bags strapped behind saddles on slow walking mules and Onacona writes that a baby in the mountains was delivered to freedom up North in a fine cherry dresser drawer. And they were all delivered to houses where babies with the pokeberry pox had been sent to white Doctors. The white mothers took those Negro babies onto their swollen breasts like they were der own. Doctors as far away as West Virginia and New York became specialists for sake of freedom. The specialist would fatten up those white babies with goat's milk and bread pudding and those big enough were fed creamed corn and mashed taters, and there was always a gourd hid for case a stranger checked in, but with the pox scare, there were hardly none. It was the plan of all plans. Everybody gained something.

But the Crowson's specialist was 'ventually fount out. A husband who didn't pacify like his wife turnt the specialist in when he came home unexpected and saw his wife caring for a Negro baby. There's no other words on that family.

When pox was wiped off babies with a wet rag the specialist was fined many thousands and imprisoned. Prison was wood floors, no air stirring in summer and no fire in the winter, pure de hell in the South, with the foul stink of a life rottin' chained to a wall. They didn't kill him. They tortured him. They gave him the slave pacifist's punishment, torturing him just like a slave. They whipped him out in the street, branded him, stretched him and cut off toes. They did all 'cept cut off his tongue because they wanted to know who was helping. His wife moved to Canada with their children where she schooled Negro children and he starved himself to death."

"Oh my God!" Exilee clasped her hands together, "This story is like how the Lumbee want to take the Tuscaroras and enslave them."

"The Lumbees weren't even named Lumbee then," Bruce rushed to correct her and Exilee said, "I mean, the Lumbee are planning to claim Tuscarora heritage in their next recognition hearing if they don't get it this time."

"Who said that? Know someone in NCCIA?" Bruce's raised voice echoed down the dark chamber, "C.I.A.?" Exilee ignored Miss Ginger's impatient smirk and answered, "You know how word gets out. One loose lip and it trickles down. That's why you're here, Bruce. We want to keep you out of their clutches. They'll do anything," she whispered, "any-thing."

"They're mafia, mon," Mark quipped, "They tried claiming Tuscarora before and were told to desist by the New York Tuscs."

"Save that talk for later," Miss Ginger said, and she continued, "The mid wife got sold to Mr.Crowson's farm, which was a slave working plantation," but Mark whispered, "I was at UNCP's library and saw what they're doing," and he took everyone's attention, "Got a whole cart of Tuscarora history upstairs in a office, just sitting there. Said they were going to digitize it. Checked two weeks ago. Still there." Jake held Mark's shoulder, "When did you first see it? Did you look through it?" "Yeah, history, documents, testimonies, all Tusc. Been there about seven months now."

"Do you people want to hear this or not?" Miss Ginger scolded and they apologized, "I'm not discounting what you're saying. But it's close to my bedtime," she gained their full attention and she stood taller, "After a couple of years when word had settled, they went on just like before. Gourds got passed around the nearby plantations and when a new momma wud 'cept the fact the only way her chile would ever know freedom and loved dere chile enough to let go, she gave her baby the pokeberry pox.

Only this time, the baby suffered. To keep the red pox marks from washing off on the checker's wet rag, hot wax was doted directly over the pokeberry pox mark. And not only did the pox stay red it welted up like a mosquito bite, so it looked like the baby'd been infected for several days. And everyone knew the pox was most contagious when the pox burst, and the puss run out. So, the baby was even a bigger threat than before. The master'd rush his slave baby off for doctoring here where slaves were watched over real good at the Crowson's." Miss Ginger flashed her showy smile. "It didn't take long for this very house to be made the Pox House and no bounty hunter dared enter for fear of pox." Miss Ginger swung her arm behind her to the primitive "Pox House" sign hanging beside the entrance doors. "I love that part, those smart blackies."

"Sometimes a master wud allow a mother to bring her baby to the doctoring mid wife herself. And there'd also be a few here with a case of pokeberry pox, daddy's too'd make it here, even a brother or sister, to keep down suspicions. Parents would go through with the sufferin' death of their innocent chile' and a funeral, of which were fake. They did it to for two reasons, to help themselves let go and to make their baby's death look real. Oh, they didn't put on for the good owners of the plantation here, but for bounty hunters laying in wait on the edges of the property. Their campfire smoke trailed in the skies like dark devil tails. That's what they call 'em here in these papers, too, devil tails. The Negroes were always in danger as long as there was white men owning slaves.

But the mothers' mourning was all too real. They'd be sick with grief. Onacona writes of songs sang to these merciful mothers, slave songs, as she combed out their knotty braids and greased them up again. Peoples on the Crowson farm ended up with one song in their heart. They'd be every which a way doing chores and any one of 'em could be heard singing as the sweet baby was sent to freedom from down here and an empty coffin was put in the ground up there. There's a cemetery, Bruce," she pointed, "between Ken's place and Jake's with near a count as possible of three hundred sixteen little coffins. Only a handful had a body."

Miss Ginger slipped her hand under the podium and pressed the recorder's button. Wind stirred the fields to sing as grains tapped and stems swooshed. The faint voices of playing children became clearer and clearer, until one distinctly said, "Momma." An ax split a log, cracking and falling to the ground. Chains rattled in the distance as a crow cawed. Reverberating claps beat against the walls, as if in rhythm with easy ocean waves and the welcoming home party gravely absorbed the Underground Railroad's true history.

A woman's mournful wail, then a man's angry moan, then the clapping again, and just as the hairs on the backs of their necks tingled, out poured the mournful yet proud voices of a complete robust choir.

"OH! Freedom, oh! Freedom,

Oh! Freedom, over me;

And before I'll be a slave

I'll be buried in my grave,

And go home to my God

And be free." [48]

The song reverberated off the stone walls from a loud eye-opening blare down to enjoyable to retrospectively low and then as faint background music.

Miss Ginger cleared her throat. "Now the mid wife had to keep a few babies back or the whities wudda come suspicious and not lowd her to doctor any. But over the course of her work and the work of seven other known counts of Pox Houses, there were thousands of Negro babies sent to freedom." She paused a good long while taking in their reactions, "That is love," her gaze landed on Bruce and he nodded.

Miss Ginger leaned over the podium toward Bruce who was front row center in the dark orangey basement. "There are five Onacona's. Onacona is a man's name. The first was a man. Onacona means White Owl to Iroquoian and it is like a title and a name. It was given to those who showed themselves as wise leaders or who were expected to be wise leaders. The second and fourth were also men. But the third and the one who wrote The Black Purse Papers was a woman, my great, great grandmother, rest her soul.

Yes, leaders were both man and woman in both Indian and African history. It is a white man's fault that women been put back." She sort a' growled and all the men leaned away.

"Tracing back with the State's professors her times were eighteen hundred twenty to eighteen hundred sixty. She died a terrible death. She got caught helping the runaways and got what was worst for women. One of those men carried that copulating sickness and it traveled to her mind. In prison she lay in sweat and puss sores for months before she died and then they took pictures of her in her coffin and put it in the paper. They did it to two more conductors working mid wifery and shot one dead after she let her wolf dog loose on a bounty hunter and it took his hand off. As punishment those bounty hunters axed off one hand of each of her four childrens. Their pictures were in the newspaper with warnings to slave pacifiers. The Pox Houses closed."

Miss Ginger heaved as the background chorus sang, "I'll be buried in my grave."

"But runaways kept coming." She grasped the podium. "They kept running. And they kept singing for Freedom, Oh, sweet Freedom." As Miss Ginger sang as tears ran down her neck and no one breathed.

"Runaways with gray eyes and blues with the cheekbones of Tuscarora warriors came and their words was adopted with the others. Man was called "mon." Measure was called "mension." Ask was called 'ax'. Knowledge was called "wit." House was called "hosen," and love was called "'ovend." Onacona did not know when she wrote these papers that the words were old Anglo-Saxon words from days of Sir Walter Raleigh and his mighty mistress, Queen Elizabeth. And Onacona did not know what she wrote then would solve a twentieth century people's crisis, a people who've wasted days upon days of trying to convince the world what blood runs in them, like it makes any difference."

Miss Ginger's crooked finger ran with the page's words and Bruce followed it like a mule on a plow line, heaving and urging. "This tribe's settlement was in a low woodland, a swampy region, what Tuscs called pocosin land. It was plenty in whortleberries and black berries. The Tuscaroras traded them and made berry wine which they drank mostly in feasting and marrying." She stretched her neck. "We all know the Tuscs lived in settlements on the Neuse River, on the waters of Black River, on the Cape Fear, Lumbee, what was then Drowning Creek, and be as far as the Santee in South Carolina. But the main one covered what we know as Robeson and Cumberland Counties, and Averysboro, and they shared trails with the Cherokee up to the mountains eastward. The three counties had trails that come together and became what we call Lowrie Road today.

Bruce Black, you and your kin and all da jar runners with a dab a Lum been runnin' the

same berry juices and runnin' the same trails from as far back as the sixteen hundreds. Whadyasay 'bout those apples?" When her eyebrows danced so did his.

He clasped the back of his head with an outstretched hand and heavily sighed, "Honestly, I'm about dizzy." Both Edge and Jake reached out for him. Edge kept a hold of his firm narrow waist while Jake held his bicep.

"Do you need to lie down?" Edge pleaded.

"No, really, I'll be okay. A big day. No alcohol in six years and it's whooping my ass. Don't stop for me."

"You have an angel guiding you, Bruce Black." Her honey smile melted them, "Bes too jubious not to be supernatural, boy. Not only do you have the blood right and the time right, you have proof for those vines."

"Vines?"

"Your People," she smacked.

Dogmatically, Bruce scorned Jake because he knew he'd told the secret but was instantly forgiven. Robin gnashed her tongue in her cheek and stepped back as if she couldn't bear to stare any longer, and when Mark nearly fell over trying to get out of Robin's way Exilee pulled him to her side, but Ken peeled him off.

"My great great great grandmother, Onacona, writes that our people received Lucretia dewberry vines as gifts from the Tuscarora of the West." Her crooked finger aimed. "I got this page copied for you 'long with da two on when they met and their Queen words. Onacona has every name of the people her people traded with and writes that they named one another from where they lived more than from who we show ourselves to be and sometimes who we are to become.

Come here. You will give this more honor than any glass case ever will." Miss Ginger pulled out a long turquoise beaded necklace and Bruce leaned down while she slipped it over his head. "You can wear this now. You are Master of Ceremonies." The glossy organic beads were about a fingertip wide. "The Tuscs were the greatest traders, and owned goods from all tribes and many lands," Miss Ginger stepped back, "You have big shoes to fill."

Bruce fondled the large palm sized effigy hanging from its center and held it up to the flickering bulb's orange glow. The well-worked stone shone even in the dark. "It's a bear." Jake aimed his light and agreed. The bear was about two inches by three, simple, but grand and made of a green turquoise with a golden-brown vein.

"Let me see." Edge stepped within an inch of brushing against him and examined the beads and effigy, shivering as Bruce breathed, "What's holding it on?" and as Miss Ginger answered, "Intestines," Edge backed. "Strong stuff, probably buffalo or big cat. They had black cats on the prairie. Onacona has charcoal sketches of all kinds of animals they dealt with. There's prints for sale in the office shed. Samples in the frames behind the register and the ones for sale rolled up in the basket. Miss Sarah and I have a few more we keep to ourselves. There's some gruesome things in those sketches. People being eaten by dogs. Slave families thin as floorboards squattin' over a single bowl of sweet taters. White men'd bet over mean dogs and one of those wild black cats hey had tied to chains. General public don't want mean things up on their walls.

Onacona seen a lot a hate in her times and a lot of love. There's birthing sketches and momma's nursing and daddy's gnashing their teeth at fake funerals. You can tell it's a fake due to the background fiddlers. They're all Negroes and to whites, fiddlers were for funnin' back then. To me, the pages are all priceless. But you can pick one of the copies for just five dollars, honey."

Exilee squirmed between Ken and Jake to get closer to Edge. "We're opening a gift shop next year. Working on sculpting babies for the shop and trying to figure out how to make 'em faster. My first weren't saleable. Miss Sarah loves them. But who's gonna pay forty bucks for a rock baby souvenir? And forty is cheap. That's paying myself four dollars an hour."

Jake and Scarecrow strained to see the turquoise bear as Bruce held it up. "I'll show it to you when we get done." He carefully gathered the strands and allowed the weight of the effigy to ease it down under his shirt. "Know what I'm gonna wear to the opening now." Bruce smiled and as he caught Robin smiling back.

Exilee gently pulled on Bruce's arm. "I put it on once and got a rush. Really, I felt something and had to take it off." Her dark pools of light permeated his grays as he agreed that the necklace must be attached to the spiritual world.

Jake poked him. "Hope you plan on pants, too, Naked Chief Tonka Wonka." They all giggled. "Or maybe you'll sell out if you're naked. Label a batch, Naked Chief Wine."

From out of the laughter, Scarecrow called out, "How about Looseleaf Chief?"

"Well, I'm not wearing a suit. They're for funerals." Bruce declared. "But for sure pants."

"And weddings," Robin casually added as Bruce and Jake locked grays and greens until Bruce disciplined himself away from striking up a fire with Robin's hot pink jeans smoldering like red hot coals under the dark orange light. Edge drew attention near the shelved fruit jars. "My daddy and I put up apples every year. They're best turned out with nutmeg in the sugar water." Her backside formed a nice blue heart trimmed in red right at her creases as she bent over the jars. Still under the influence, Mark goofily gazed and stepped closer. "You ever go out dancing, Edge?"

"Turned out?" Robin's hushed fuss silenced everyone as her shoulders swayed and Edge popped back up. "You're a Southern farm girl?" Robin's arched back and hipped hands hollered 'chick fight.' "I thought you were doing time in college now," like she was selling life insurance to shipwrecked bachelors, her cheesy smile and sweet tenor oozed.
"Girl, that bandana trim is perfect on you. Is that what you wear on campus?"

When Exilee jumped between them Lilly tapped Exilee's shoulder and she quickly turned to see who touched her. Lilly's calm repose instantly eased her. "What kind of medium are you using for your sculptures Exilee?" Robin and Edge did a bad job of acting interested while the guys looked down at their feet.

"Soapstone." Exilee answered Lilly while she told Robin to behave with a dash of her evil eyes. Robin rolled her tongue across her teeth and jutted her butt off to one side like she was cocking a loaded gun. So Exilee turned her back and blocked Robin's aim at Edge.

"Thought about making a mold?" Lilly suggested. "I took pottery class when I had some medical desk duty a few years back. Shot in the calf. Not serious. Get my hands in the clay every chance I get."

"I bet that is fun." Exilee's big brown eyes danced over to Ken. "But if I used a mold I couldn't sell the babies as hand carved."

"That's true."

Edge flagged Exilee. "They won't care, hon. As long as it looks like the real one and it's cheap. People just want a little souvenir. They'd sell."

Miss Ginger waved her flashlight across the overhead beams spotlighting Ken. "Get the door. We have a load for a friend of a friend."

"Huh?" asked Edge.

"Underground Railroad talk for sending a slave station to station." Miss Ginger explained.

"I love it. That's so clever. I can't believe this wasn't taught in school." Edge declared.

"It was," Robin huffed.

"Not like this," Edge swore.

Mark held up his hand and when Jake laughed at him, he put it down. "Habit. Anyway, the papers should be in the classroom. Some teachers do delve into the specifics on the Underground Railroad. But I never heard a lot of this, and you know how Lums talk."

"That's why I'm in their surrounding counties," Scarecrow mumbled. "Call me Scarecrow."

Mark boyishly grinned and tapped his fingertips together as he surmised the group. "In the ninth grade I wrote a sociology report on the Negro slave before and after emancipation. About your papers, Miss Ginger," he pointed, "in the research arena there are correlating dates and books, like, "The Croatan Indians of Sampson County, Their Origin and Racial Status" by George Butler. It was his summation for separate schools. Indians thought Negroes were dumb and dirty and they wouldn't go to school with them. On the sociology path, my report covered the ladder of status and how there's always been prejudice. There's also the newer work of Adolph Dial, "The Lumbee," and Karen Blu's, "The Lumbee Problem." Each of 'em perpetuate the Lumbee ideology instead of the true root – us Tuscs, the aboriginals. Later, it dominoed. English married natives and picked up on their traditions. When that mix married the emancipated slaves, they picked up a few of theirs, like their knowledge of natural medicine and religion. The language anomaly is as much of a barrier as any for us to make it into college much less a West Side housing division. That's why it sucks sometimes being Tuscarora. So many have lost their Indian heritage signing on as Lumbee for those HUD dollars."

Bruce clapped twice. "Give you another shot, and we'll learn how to create atoms with our bare hands, huh?" He ruffled his hair and Mark just grinned. "You always were a smart ass."

Robin wrapped her arm around Mark. "We don't care about bloodline. Okay?" She got right up in Mark's face barely missing his lips as she spoke but capturing Bruce's eyes straight on. "We love you just the way you are. Right, you guys?"

"Mixed mutts are the smartest anyway, right, Mark?" Exilee chimed.

"I guess so," Mark put too much thought into it while Edge declared she was a proud Tuscarora.

Lilly tapped Mark's shoulder. "So, in your report, what was the final decision on the psychology of the Indians?"

"The wave of history of the mixed race follows a self-existential crisis pattern as the people try to label themselves and can't find their box. They'd be better off on an island if they can't be happy just to be." Mark whitened every single smile in the dark orangey basement. "Humans want labels and add levels of importance to those labels. Just the way it is."

"Zoom. Zoom, aren't you on the ball?" Bruce proudly smiled. "Maybe you oughta be Master of Ceremonies," Bruce suggested to his cousin as he held his hand over the effigy tucked under his tee shirt.

"You haven't called me that in years," Mark sheepishly smiled.

"Zoom Zoom?" Jake asked.

"That's how he did everything when he was a kid." Bruce gripped Mark's shoulders like they were a steering wheel. "Zoom Zoom. Zoom Zoom." Mark revved up his pretend boyhood engine and when he backfired everyone guffawed.

"Thank ya, Zoom Zoom. You're very bright. If you boys are done now let's get on with with it." Miss Ginger aimed her light on the wall behind the shelves of fruit jars as Ken and Jake pushed back the primitive heart pine shelves. On rollers for ease of movement, but still heavy with jars, they strained over the cement floor. The floor was painted to look like packed clay and finally a curious small door appeared. The door was three slabs of thick heart pine with a slab across the top and one across the bottom. It was short, narrow and very old.

Miss Ginger curved her index finger into a black hole near the top left of the door. "This hole was kept plugged with a pine knot." When she pulled the door open it creaked as the cool damp air rushed out over them. She swept the entrance with her flashlight, first up then dowon and up again to dirt walls with wood ledges and thick overhead beams.

The pine was almost scarlet in places. "This is heart pine." She exemplified its density as she fisted the overhead beam and it barely made a sound. As particles sifted through the light beams she consoled them, "It's just dirt."

It was very apparent the measurements between the overhead beams were not in equal increments. "Use your indoor voice," she whispered. "Vibrations make the dirt fall and it ain't just dirt. It's soot, from lanterns and oil lamps." She bent over at the shoulders and tucked in. Her steady pace left them with the threat of being left behind to creep alone into the dark passage.

First thing they did was clamp their bare arms around their chests to ward off the chill as their hot breath steamed. Crouched over and cramped in slow steady steps, they crept deeper and deeper as their lights bobbed from wall to ceiling to floor. "Boo," Ginger unexpectedly blasted as she turned around with her light under her chin and held the bold enunciation on her lips, and they told her not to do that again.

"Effigies fill holes all 'long this underground passage. They were carved by parents of babies sent to freedom." Miss Ginger shined her light on a depression in the wall about six inches long and three inches wide into a shadow box with modern plexiglass protecting a primitive rock sculpture. "It's a man." The brown rock had been crudely chiseled into the cookie cutter shape of a man.

They studied it in wonder as they absorbed the underground. It smelled like pure dirt. Any area not marked by light was pitch black, and the passage was narrow while the ceiling was low, and the floor was not smooth. So, with dubious footing the newcomers either slid along or barely lifted their feet. But they were all stooped over and searching for whatever there was to see on full alert.

Edge traced the outline of a hole while Jake aimed the light. "Looks like the baby is sleeping. I wonder if it died before it could make the trip," as Miss Ginger moved ahead until her light was swallowed by the cold black path.

"Isn't she going to tell us about it?" Edge asked after Jake said something about it being a day past Ginger's bedtime. "Ginger has her ways." Ken's lighthearted tone lightened their dark moods. "She lets the passage do the talking for the most part. We'll catch up with her and you can ask her about effigies then. All right?"

"Here's two more." Jake aimed his light on the sculptures, a dog and a baby.

Edge had to touch the glass. "Babies and babies."

"Miss Ginger and I counted them. There's three hundred sixteen, just like Onacona wrote. It was a major wow factor for the professors. Course they took every rock and loose chunk of heart pine up to the college and tested 'em out with archeologists up there with lab equipment. It's all good." Exilee assured them.

"Archeologists exclusively? I'd love to read their papers and any anthropologists', too," Bruce told Exilee.

"Man," Jake huffed, "you did some reading, didn't cha?"

"Read and exercise," Bruce laughed. "Best thing ta do in there. All shut up. Habit now to read endings first. Know what I'm getting' into. Wish life was like that," and Jake whistled, "Say that again."

"I've got their numbers and one sent me a report. I read some of it, but after about the nineteenth hundred time of reading about the same rock and its iddy biddy centimeter gouge that surfaces like another rock hit it, I got bored and put it back in the envelope. There's close to a hundred pages on the effigies from just one professor." Exilee theatrically yawned. "Come on, you two," she told Lilly and Scarecrow. "You don't want to miss anything tonight."

"Got that right," Scarecrow projected, and it echoed repeatedly until it reverberated back, "God at light."

"Indoor voice," Exilee reminded. "We don't want to get covered in this stuff, y'all. You can't wipe it off. It just spreads. You'll have to shower."

Lilly and Scarecrow caught up with the others and then all three girls sighed over the baby effigies. Some were swaddled. Some were carved with caps indicating a boy. The uneven skull caps with rounded outcrops indicated hair and thusly, female. Some had open eyes. Some closed and all had at least one letter carved into their backside.

Jake pushed his flashlight into Bruce's hand. "Focus on the support beams."

"Why?"

"You count 'em to keep track of where you are."

With a half-smile Bruce faced him. "Like counting the cedars."

"That's right."

Robin gently elbowed Jake, "What's that about?"

Jake waited for Bruce to speak before answering and when he didn't Jake obliged.

"When we were kids, we worked a still in his daddy's woods and we'd count the cedars we planted to keep track of where we were. We were always moving it. Cedars lined up like graph lines."

"Oh, both of you were shiners? That's what you have in common." Robin jittered.

"We're like brothers. We grew up next door to each other, hon," with a gentle touch Jake rounded over her shoulders.

Bruce counted the beams aloud and on number seven stopped. "Yurkers in my momma's hair till she passed. Then we ate at his momma's all the time."

"That's right," Jake smacked. "Old Man Black never cooked, did he?"

"Oh, he cooked every night." Bruce chuckled, "But you can't feed a first grader shine and send him to school the next day. I ate with the Wilkes for eight years. They're like family." Their hushed conversation mimicked possums hissing and chewing in a cabbage patch.

"I can't hear the train. Y'all be quiet." Exilee's projected hushed voice was almost manly.

"There's no train around here," Scarecrow deduced.

"Not physically," Ken heightened their curiosity.

Bruce's and Exilee's lights shined on the plexiglass and new wooden support beams made to look primitive. It stood out against the ancient black passage. The passengers of the Underground Railroad huddled, fitting their bodies together like chicks around a hen, tucking limbs to fit as Bruce aimed on the plexiglass protected overhead beam adjoining the new ones.

"An inscription," Edge excitedly pointed. "That's old English." She told Bruce to aim his light at the beginning again.

"It's broken English," Robin hastily corrected.

"Same thing," Edge's head teetered as she leaned up closely against Bruce.

Ken kept his light on the inscription as he slipped on his teacher's hat. "Slaves weren't routinely taught to read and write. They were self-taught."

"Read that loud enough so everyone can hear," Jake said, and Bruce squeezed around till he and Jake were nose to nose. "You a teacher now, Buddyrow?"

"Just thought you'd like to read it." Jake shrugged. "It's your party. Do what you wanna do."

"Don't sing and I'll try to translate." Bruce licked his lips as his brows hunched. "It reads: Debl Massa tuk my Fut, selld my Son Den Debl Massa suld me ta Massa Crowson, Gud, gud sah. Lord hurd de cry an de fits en Pryres - Run Lady Run Git ares Son Sleep dey Run all de Nyht I see alhs de Chile's at de Lords Gate - Eber Magee." Bruce's deep quick breaths sliced at the light.

Robin offered her interpretation as she stepped next to Bruce's raised arm. "I've done this before." She wiggled in closer until she felt what she thought was Bruce's leg and let her hand slip from her own thigh. But Edge grunted. So, she just clamped her arms around the girls. "Devil Master took my foot, selled my son. Then Devil Master sold me to Master Crowson, Good, Good, Sir. Lord heard the cry and the fits in prayers. Run lady, run. Get our son. Sleep in the day. Run all of the night. I see all of the children at the Lord's gate. Eber Magee."

"That's real," Edge whispered.

"That's what they all say," Ken replied in his long drawn out way.

"Yea, it is." Exilee refrained.

Bruce aimed his light near Exilee. Found her face and then clipped her shoulder. "Magee like Thomas Magee?"

"That's right. David's people deeded the land over after emancipation." Exilee told Bruce.

"That's awesome, all this history under your feet every day. It's so inspiring." Lilly rubbed her arms, "This swampland holds the very beginnings of American history."

"Yes, it does," Bruce commanded.

"Bet your daddy has some ghost stories, huh?" Scarecrow widened some eyes and Ken gasped, "Ghosts? Heck, yea, but we're used to 'em. They're everywhere. Luke was three years-old and made his way into the cemetery after dinner one afternoon and Mom and Dad and Exilee and I were all watching him hop from rock to rock and stand on headstones. Didn't think anything about it. Dad asked him what he was doing, and he said he was playing keep away from the ghosts."

"That is so weird," Lilly enunciated with clear distaste.

"You ever seen one?" Scarecrow asked Ken.

"Yea. Don't keep count. They're everywhere." Ken nudged them forward. "Lead on, Bruce."

Bruce aimed from the ground then up the wall as the passage narrowed. Robin and Exilee could no longer squeeze next to one another. They all followed single file. Edge followed behind Bruce. Mark was right in front of Exilee. Ken was still last, and Miss Ginger was out ahead.

"I'm cold," Edge whined.

"Rub your hands together," Bruce suggested.

Robin hissed to Exilee, "If she'd pull her shorts out of her crack she'd get another two inches of coverage." Lilly giggled and when Exilee told her to hush Robin turned to Lilly, "You know she's not wearing any panties for them to crawl like that. She's a thong frog." Lilly gasped and clutched her mouth closed as Exilee pinched Robin's arm. "That hurt."

Mark turned around to the ladies like a little boy with a squirt gun and squeezed, "Underwear for women should be outlawed."

Jake and Bruce laughed as the echo traveled into an indistinguishable mumble as dirt and soot particles drifted down. Robin told Mark he should go tell Edge to pull her shorts out of her crack. "Just leave it alone," Exilee stomped and more soot dripped, and when that crazy Ken dared Mark to do it everyone hooted, and soot washed down till there were sneezes and complaints.

A few feet later when Lilly discreetly told Exilee, "You know, my UC work requires them," Exilee urged Lilly not to tell too much, that Jake had filled her in on the dancing details and that she was not being judgmental. Lilly huffed, "I can see what's going on."

At that, Scarecrow told the brood of biddies to stop pecking. Ten feet, then twenty passed. Then up to a thirty-four-support beam count they focused on warming their arms and keeping their footing in the cold damp earthen walls.

Exilee's flashlight made overhead circles as an updraft of air blasted toward them like a train running downhill with an 'ugg-gg-uggh-uggh' purr as their steps crunched against the gritty ground. Ken's footsteps went down flat, not heel to toe. Robin's steps were faint while Exilee's made a definite hard heel to soft toe. Jake's steps were that of an old man, contacting the ground with a flat force. His steps paused in cadence with Bruce's as the 'ugg-gg-uggh-uggh' purring equalized with a cool shaft of air level with their heads. Shoulders raised and chill bumps tingled as their temperatures shifted with the ice-cold breeze. Edge reached up for Bruce's shoulder and slid down onto his bicep, and the crouched group huddled closer like a clutch of biddies as they eased down the cold dark passage.

"Do you believe in ghosts?" Jake tried to whisper.

"Who're you asking?" Bruce whispered back.

"Robin. I know you do."

"I believe in spirits," Robin clarified.

"Then what's that?" Jake suddenly stopped.

"What?" Robin's startled whisper spooked Exilee as she grabbed onto the back of her shirt. Bruce aimed his light. A fluorescent yellow line was painted on recessed bricks on either side of the earthen floor. As Bruce's light shone on a wooden framed box recessed into the earthen wall Robin firmly squeezed Jake's arm. "Good try. Is this new?"

"It's been up a couple of months. Had to wait for the state to turn it back over. There was some quibble about burying it even after the Magees signed it over." Exilee explained.

Packed together at the new find they stretched as Bruce aimed his light on the metal plaque. "Eber Magee. 1836-1838, one of the babies." Then as his light hit the glass they gasped. "Oh man, a foot." Inside the shadowbox rested one adult size skeletal foot. Its brown and yellow bones were held together with steel pins."

"He buried his foot down here two years after it was cut off." Robin projected. Mark cleared his throat. "Gross, but common, I'm afraid."

"Yea, I remember that in class." Edge chewed on her finger.

Bruce turned to Exilee. "Any more surprises?" And she laughed, "Scared of ghosts, Mister Master of Ceremonies?"

"No. Just don't want anyone getting hurt." Bruce remarked.

"Uh-huh," Exilee tossed her ponytail. "Don't worry. No one will get hurt. The ghosts around here are like your Little People not like your big bad Totens." Intrigued, Bruce's on guard demeanor dropped. His chin tucked a bit as his eyes softened and he unconsciously outlined the bear effigy under his tee shirt. "Little People does not imply stature."

"I know. Your Little People help others, like our ghosts. But let's say you get someone to shout 'haunt' down here. Then we're gonna be on guard like you are for your Totens."

Exilee's Southern drawl charmed him. "Don't you know where the beliefs originally came from?"

"My mother was always talking about Little People, saying they moved things around the house, playing tricks on her. Once swore she saw a pair keeping the clothes on the line during a wind blast. Old Man's work shirts would've hit the mud hole, that kind of thing," Bruce took a step.

"Tokens is an Elizabethan word that means the same as toten does," Mark clarified. "An old Shakespeare play I read."

"Oh," Exilee studied him best she could in the dark.

Bruce leaned to her then suddenly jerked up his chin and tilted his head back like he was reverse parking. "Oh, is it the papers, too?"

"Some. Came across things researching. Like you and I are distant cousins." Exilee announced as she aimed her light in his face. "Oops."

"Can't be too related, you're a half and half."

"Who told you that?"

"Don't know when I learned it. You know how things get around."

"Well what are you?"

"Tuscarora Locklear, from the original aboriginals," Bruce shut her up.

Their quiet steps were met with the chilly breeze tunneling through. "In the late eighteen hundreds, that's in the Black Purse Papers, too, when a black Freedman married an Indian he usually got the rest of her family to help work the land. Same for Indian Freedman. It was a win-win."

"I got gypped," Ken yelled. and soot shook down over him till he had to spit it out. "All I got for marrying this squaw was a boney backed mare." Ken laughed and Jake nudged him on, begging, "Hey, I'll give you fifty bucks for the mare, but do I have to take the squaw?"

"They go together, mister, sorry," Ken snorted. "Got a triple C breast collar that goes with 'em, for plowing."

Robin and Exilee sarcastically laughed while Scarecrow and Lilly lingered at a baby rock sculpture in the passage wall.

"My dowry'll be so significant every educated Indian in the state'll be asking for me."
When Robin squeezed in behind Ken to follow behind Jake and Bruce, Ken pressed his backside against hers to aggravate her. "Your husband has a big butt."

"Me? Let's measure, right here. Right now. Who's got a boy scout survival knife? Why I do. And it has inches and centimeters right here on the handle. Whadoyabet she's a thirty incher? Is it legal to keep an Injun with butt that size or does she need to grow a little more?" Ken pulled her by the waist, and she whacked him so hard it echoed up and back down the passage while soot sifted down, and Ken shook off the burn. "Why can't you ever play along with me?"

"Cause your ideas are stupid, stupid."

"They always end up like this," Exilee huffed at Lilly who was right behind her. "Indoor voice, you two." She gritted her teeth as she wiped soot from her eyes.

Scarecrow's light zoomed. "Y'all expectin' company?" All the flashlights darted behind them. The creaking stopped and the door to the Underground Railroad closed.

The cool air grew cooler and their hyper aware heartbeats drummed in their ears. Their footsteps gritted as their breaths pitched from soft nose whistles to open-mouthed panting, and the purring chug of wind over their heads ceased as silence rang like a haunting ghost story. With Edge pressed up against him, Bruce tugged on Jake's arm to follow and he did, as he wrapped his full hand around Robin's and she jerked on Ken's as he held Exilee's shoulder and Mark, Lilly and Scarecrow followed the train ride out.

"The escape door is kept locked from inside the house now that it's public. Its purpose was to bring up a slave when its master sent someone to check up on his pox, like a bounty hunter. The parents went all the way to the opening at the base of the hill to let go of their children under the Freedom Train's sky but would come running if they heard the signal. It echoed down the whole passage. "Here, boy," followed by a whistle, just as if the family's beloved pet was being called home."

The group crept along taking the long way out to the opening at the base of the hill, a good twenty-acre pass from Eber Magee's skeletal foot's grave. A few feet from the opening Ken instructed them to turn off the flashlights. Near sober, they peered out from the cold black earthen embankment for the same eighteen hundred's view.

Tucked only a few feet behind ancient Longleaf pines and Father Oaks, the trickling creek splashed over rocks as mini waves crested. The trickling creek partnered with the summer foliage chanting a comforting blanket of, "S-Free, free, free," as it rode the soft wind up the hill like it was purposely blown to entice the timid. They stood completely enchanted as "S-Free, free, free," chimed over and over from the timberline seducing the entire group like they just might run away into the dark timberline.

Without a word, they looked up into the dark night sky at the steady North Star. They stretched and swallowed the past's nasty reality like bad medicine then scattered to roam and run the hillside checking for Miss Ginger even though Ken advised them to stay on the foot path. "Y'all need to be quiet. My parents have the windows open."

"They can't hear us," Edge sassed.

"Everything carries up to the screened in porch." Still in teacher mode, Ken directed with an outstretched arm. "See, no trees between here and there. The porch was the look out. Still is, some days." "Don't they have central heat and air?" Mark cocked his head.

"Nope. Attic fan and fresh air. And their phone's in the pantry." Ken grinned and Scarecrow agreed that was the way to live. Ken explained, "They visit people when they want to talk. Phone is for emergencies. Y'all be quiet now."

Scarecrow and Lilly talked amongst themselves and then Crow asked Ken, "Hey, was this area checked out, I mean the underground deal, back in 1973 when the FBI was searching for those stolen Indian records?"

"Gawd, I don't know. I wasn't even born," Ken squinted while he pulled his chin, "You'd have to ask Dad, but I can't say I ever heard him talk about it. How many records were stolen?"

"Over 700 thousand pounds of BIA files, and four thousand were found here in Maxton in a bus. FBI came out and they disappeared and found some later at Doc Henderson's farm, but there's still some around that've never popped up," [49] Crow and Lilly held hands as they walked away and chatted quietly before rejoining the group headed back toward Jake's house scattering like guineas once onto the open terrain and flocking together again, recounting the Underground Railroad party as the most educational party they'd ever attended, everyone, except Bruce.

At the top of the hill, Bruce lingered over the timberline view. He stretched out his arms as his dark shadow lengthened forming a long cross out from behind him, and with the crescent moon above Bruce wore a crown in the dark blue night sky.

As Ken led the men to Two Tails' lot and Mark said, "Yea, mon, I'm whiffed goanna many days. Gaumed up my sinuses," and Jake said, "You drunk little shit. You smell worse'n that cow. Look now, I skinned a stillborn calf to save this one, Two Tails. That's how he got his name."

"You skinned it?" Mark asked. "Did ya make a gambrel or just nail it up by the shin bones?"

"Neither. Had it all over the ground. Mostly held it between my legs. Really, I was a wreck. The newborn was born dead and Two Tails' cow had refused her. I called my vet and he said that the only thing he could recommend was an old cowhand's trick.

Tie the skin of her calf over the orphan calf. Well, she stopped bawling and now we have a big pet." Jake snapped his fingers and Two Tails cooed a soft moo.

"Regular cowhand, what this farm needed. But Two Tails is ruint. What are you going to do when it's trailer time?" Ken leaned against the rail, "Not long now, he's pushing two hundred."

"He's staying, Ken." Jake's greens pinched. "He does tricks," Jake told Mark. "He counts and he'll pull treats out of my back pocket with his tongue. Watch," Jake snatched a wad of grass and put it in his back pocket and climbed over.

"That's sort a' gross," Mark told him. "Doesn't your butt get all wet and slimy?" Scarecrow laughed as Two Tails looped his tongue around the grass and Jake checked his butt for a wet spot. "Trailer him over to Lumberton," Crow advised, "They know what to do. Hell, they eat anything, even butchering horses."

"Good Lord," Ken spat, "now that's perty low. Like eatin' a dog. Can't you put a stop to that?"

"When we catch 'em we will." Scarecrow begrudged. "Usually find the entrails and skeletal remains after the fact. Don't waste much. Make craft crap with the hides and hooves. Don't know what it's gonna take to end that mess." He sighed. "Well, till they all get sick. France issued a urgent call for the CDC to start horse meat inspections on account of deaths. Horse meat is full of toxic meds and parasites. Get Alzheimer, cancer, worms, just a mess what these ignorants are eatin'. If, and I mean a big f-ing if, horse slaughter is outlawed the Feds might send us some more UC funds. We can't be everywhere."

"That's just sick," Jake stomached.

"They steal 'em, too," Mark said. "Things are bad for the people right now. Illegals took their jobs. They're back to their old ways like they've got a real reservation, and gambling fetches big dollars and so much homegrown half the kids in elementary school been exposed to it and gang activity. Horse slaughter fits right in. No ethics. No honor."

"Gawled-dookey, there's no excuse for that gyarb. I got an education and fought my way out. I don't see why they can't." Scarecrow spit. "They keep it up and there won't be a swamp. They'll all be in jail and we'll only exist in a couple of history books." Mark's brows met as they each summed in agreement with tsks and quiet reflection.

Ginger was probably tucked in like a lamb, the girls surmised as Robin cantered up acting like she was roping a pretend calf which she named Edge. Her imaginary lasso slipped right over Edge's head when Jake bellowed out a wailing calf's moo.

Robin dug in her heels and ran straight on.

"You're a wild woman! And Black." Jake yelled.

Exilee shouted, "She's incorrigible."

Robin shouted that she didn't care that cowgirls take the dirt and Jake yelled, "Okay!

We cowboys like doing it in the dirt," real deep and coy like as he pulled her down to his impatient arms.

From his sanctuary on the hill, Bruce opened his eyes as the tree frogs chirped and a whippoorwill called. He mimicked the whippoorwill and in a few moments it called back.

He whistled for the Bob White. A Blue Jay's shriek. And the soft Bluebird chant, "Cheer, cheer, cheerful, charmer," the ones his momma had taught him. He repeated the delightful call, and on the third a mockingbird replied, "Cheer, cheerful, cheer." He laughed out loud and was in the middle of his Bluebird refrain when the moment was lost.

Ponies nickered at the chatty bunch of ladies as they neared Two Tails and the bull bawled like he was in pain when Jake passed his lot. Bruce jogged to join them and was halfway there when suddenly Miss Ginger ambushed them, "Stop right there."

Bruce's heart jumped as they all balked and gasped. "I've never had such a lollygagging group. What are y'all doing down there, making babies or what?"

"Good, gawd," Scarecrow chuckled. "Did she get into that jar?"

"Did you close the door on us?" Ken snapped and Miss Ginger laughed so hard she couldn't talk.

"You scared the daylights out a' us. Why'd you do that?" Exilee asked Miss Ginger.

"Thought it'd be fun. It was." Ginger wholeheartedly laughed and they joined. When their giddy fit wore off she told them, "Wait there. No. Turn around. To get the full effect we oughta be up here where we can look down over it all. I want y'all to experience what the real runaways did," and they obliged.

Miss Ginger's arm stretched out and the group followed till they had to turn around to see the timberline again. "The light was snuffed out as soon they felt the temperature change. The baby chile was kissed good-bye and the Freedom Train made its way into the timberline, hidden by the slope of the land from bounty hunters. Then slaves made their way to the cliff, the one that butts out over the creek, gathered supplies left for them and entered the cool creek with its spring fed tributaries. Sometimes, there was rafts or hand dug canoes to make their way to the next station. Mostly, they waded and swam in the deep places as the baby was rafted on makeshift tree trunks or bamboo rafts. It was scary and dark and the only way to be free."

"A storm's comin'." Miss Ginger stiffened as she checked the sky. "Listen. Must be way off, but it's comin." She was still questioning the numerous stars blinking back at her when distant beats pounded like drumming thunder lettin' loose for a summer downpour on the hot July night. It grew clearer. Louder. And faster. When the thunderous beats vibrated against their soles, they curiously looked about then Edge squealed, "What's that?"

Misun's white mane flashed in a light beam. "A pony's loose," Robin huffed as she marched toward the runaway's hoof beats but stopped as numerous distant eyes glowed. "Stampede! Get to the barn or get run over. Come on!"

Exilee broke away from the group hurrying to the barn and Jake was right with her.

"Misun?" he called out. "Misun, is that you?" In full throttle he turned to Exilee, "Well?"

Their eyelids ridged up against their disbelieving eyes when not one, but all three of Jake's dogs led by Misun rushed up in a barreling jog. They slowed to a pace then a fast walk and sought out the hands that taught them.

In sequence, they all obeyed, but anxiously spun their ears back from where they came.

"Exilee, whadaya thinks going on?" Jake asked as they panted.

The agitated pony backed away from Exilee and jerked his thick neck back and forth and when that didn't get any response, spun around and blew. "He's beautiful," Edge awed and Lilly agreed, "Look at his eyes."

With all the light beams his brilliant blue eyes sparkled out from under his long white forelock and his paint coat created a pleasing pattern of brown river rocks and black pebbles against his white coat. "Pretty is as pretty does," Miss Ginger quipped. "He's for sale," Ken called out as Exilee neared her Misun. When the pony trumpeted back a tingling squeal Exilee signaled for everyone to stand where they were as she got closer and he did it again. He reared with a mighty trumpet. "Quit! I got it," Exilee scolded.

Exilee aimed her light toward each of the houses and barns, the fence lines and white sandy road, and all their dark hidey holes, but when nothing stood out, she stroked his neck. As he jogged away Mark laughed and Exilee cussed. And again, she scoped out the perimeter's dark hidey holes.

"Don't think your pony knows German," Mark told Exilee as they noted the dogs on guard.

"He's trouble," Lilly pouted, "but he's gorgeous."

"This is going on video." Edge still had her cell phone's video recorder aimed at the dog and pony show as Exilee aimed her flashlight all around. "This is so funny."

"It's not funny," Jake reprimanded. "These dogs are priceless." Misun kicked up his heels toward the dogs and swung his neck for them to follow. "Crap," Exilee hurried.

"Sitz," Jake's deep voice pulled a smile from Robin. But Exilee grabbed Jake's shoulder, "Let em' track the trouble that started all this."

"Are you sure?"

"Yes! If they take someone down, it's their problem."

"Such! Such!" Jake's German commanded the dogs at a sprint with their snouts to the ground. Then down to a pace. Then a walk as they checked scents. Robin ran off in the direction of the flatbed trailers' barn where they had parked. "I'm getting my rope! Hold on, y'all."

"Bring your flashlights. Something's wrong." Exilee waved for Ken as the group cautiously followed Misun.

"No gyp is priceless," Bruce mumbled.

Ken tried to sneak up on Misun, but every time he would fart and dart. Exilee stomped toward her husband. "When are you gonna learn to listen to me? Just follow. Misun's fixin' to lead us right to it."

"To what?" Edge worried.

As Ken took heed and cautiously followed the pony with his flashlight the pony sniffed at the air and puff talked while the dogs sniffed. "Rabbits is all," Miss Ginger tried to remain calm. "There's enough folks out here. No one'll bother us, honey." Lilly pulled up her jean's pant leg and held out her once concealed handgun. Miss Ginger tapped Edge's shoulder and pointed. Edge zoomed in on it and then back to the animals' hind ends. "We'll, stay here," Miss Ginger told Lilly.

"No. Stay close to the group. Don't want to lose anyone." Lilly signaled Scarecrow as she went around to the screened in porch and he followed the dogs. His .357 shined silver when Miss Ginger's light ran over it and Edge zoomed in with her phone's camera. "This is gonna be so hot. It'll go viral."

The pony twisted his head at Scarecrow as he approached from the left and when the pony blew a wet hippo blast that startled a, "shit," out of the brave former UC, Edge zoomed.

"The sound on?" Mark whispered to Edge and she affirmed with a shiny white grin.

Exilee mumbled that she was tired of the hassle and approached Misun again. This time, she quietly cooed, "Oginalii, oginalii, do-i-s-di-hi-na?" Misun flung his head up and down and then mouthed Exilee's shirt tail like a foal does a teat. "Someone scared him," Exilee told Ken.

"Ssh," Ken flashed his palms as Scarecrow pointed out an odd figure and the dogs whined as they rushed. A dark shadow drug itself along the road. Jake yelled, "Such! Pass auf Wache!" The dogs bolted like feral badgers.

But Misun outdistanced the dogs, jumping fences and clearing ditches, before they even reached the pony barn as the shadowy figure lurched with arms out for support in a hop-jump-run. The light beams flashed over the dogs, neck in neck and in noses and hooves. While Ken, Jake and Scarecrow did their best as Mark disappeared behind the big barn. Ken sprinted down the sandy two-lane path, and then it was just Jake and Scarecrow against the pack ripping the stranger apart.

In a dead run, Exilee yelled, "No, Robin! No!" as her lariat hovered over Misun's ears. Robin hastily jerked back and fell as Misun farted and darted and spun around to blow contempt. The harried stranger sliced through the jet-black night with a shining machete. Jake signaled and the dogs backed up and surrounded the stranger with raised hackles, snarls and snaps.

Scarecrow commanded the stranger to drop to his knees with his gun at his back, but the stranger threatened with his machete. Crow jammed the barrel between the stranger's shoulders and the machete spiraled down in a silver sliver and barely missed Exilee as it twanged into the earth like an arrow, and the stranger raised his arms in defeat.

Instantly, Misun pinned his ears and joined the pack. "Pass auf Wache!" Jake commanded. Their necks swelled with heated threats, raised hackles and swollen necks as Misun pinned his ears flat and lowered his head. Pawed and snapped in a motion to charge as the dogs' fangs shone white against their dark coats and a chorus of trembling growls encased the stranger as Scarecrow holstered his gun and dove into the snarling pit.

Scarecrow prepared to pull the thick man to the ground when the stranger screamed,
"No-o-oo!" Misun snapped the thick man's thigh, and blood pulsed in long streams up over the pony's white writhing mane as the pony jerked the screaming man three feet off the ground.

Women screamed and the pony ran away dragging the thick man's upper body across the grass as the snarling German Shepherds' snapped at his head and flinging limbs. Onacona hung on by a mouthful of hair as the stranger reached for her ears. Jake and Exilee ran, commanding the pony in both English and German to drop it and for the dogs to guard it. The wailing man jerked on the dog's ear and she released only to snap his ear and he screamed again as he covered his bloody ear. "Help!"

From the edge of darkness, growling like a beast, Bruce charged at Misun as the dogs gained on him and the pony darted off with his prize. One dog lunged at Bruce's outstretched arm, but in mid-air Bruce stabbed it in the neck with his rock rigid bare hand and it retreated as Jake sprinted, shouting, "Hier!"

But the dog went back for more, with the pack. The dogs snapped at Bruce's flying legs as his pants ripped up the sides and fangs lunged for skin. Bruce kicked dogs straight in the snout. Elbowed another and whacked the pony across the neck. The dogs lunged again in fierce rage and were hurled to the ground as Bruce seized the floundering man from the pony's gapped jaws whipping the stranger's thick body against the dogs. Bruce pinned the man under his boot right over his gushing flesh.

"Arghh," he cried and Misun returned to sniff. "No!" The stranger threw a handful of sand in the pony's face, screaming, "Back, you son of a bitch!" and to Bruce, "Youse gonna be all the sorry in the world you little prince," he panted and squirmed, aghast that Bruce wore that same smirk he wore when he was a kid. "Be still." His hot whisper threatened, "I know what you're after."

"Pfui," Jake commanded the dogs not to touch the nasty man, and Bruce pressed down even more against the round man's severed femoral. Bruce pressed and the man screamed again and again. Finally pulling himself up over his severe gut with his mouth wide open like he was fixin' to bite and Crow served a swift kick to the jaw and the man fell unconscious.

Scarecrow blew, "Didn't think he'd ever shut up." He told Bruce to stay on the lookout while he searched his pants pockets and when he said he didn't find anything cussed. He scoped out the area. Told Bruce he'd call for EMT and was going to check out the house.

Robin took her time dusting off her butt and swooned like Edge while the two dreamily gazed at Bruce. Robin gazed through her lusty brown eyes. While Edge lusted through her camera lens at the brute of a man who in less than twenty-four hours had become a primal mystical powerhouse. Edge zoomed in on his thick honey lips. On that soot stained boyish face, then down to his tight hiney and his barren thighs scratched with fang lines and dripping dots of blood as his jeans' legs flapped open against the cooling night wind.

Edge zoomed out for a full view of his heroic stance over the pinned man then aimed back up at his mysterious gray eyes and zoomed back to other places and licked her lips over the primal heat he'd stirred as Robin finger combed her slick black hair up over her gracious bosom. Every flashlight was aimed on Bruce as his gray wolf eyes drawled the two ladies like doe in rut over the horned ornament. Bruce's chest heaved up and down, expanding over his small waist as he glared out into the darkness.

From discerning views, the rivaling ladies unabashedly curved their mid backs and sashayed over to the heroic scene where Misun blew and pawed near the unconscious man. Bruce told the pony to back off, but Misun continued. Exilee marched over and commanded, "Check his pockets. Take his pants off. He's got something," as she rubbed Misun's withers and he tucked his head up under her arm. When Bruce stated that Scarecrow already had a clean search, she stared him over and then pried open his mouth with a stick and checked his nasty snaggletooth mouth to no avail.

The dogs paraded like a pack on wait for a meal, whining and sniffing at the man, the air around him, and Bruce. "Onacona," Robin kissed at her dog, but it did not obey. "Lasses," Jake signaled his dogs to leave the men alone and then hand signaled them to be at rest and they restlessly circled around, one by one, and lay down in a loose huddle.

"Good Lord, you make a scene, don't cha, Buddyrow." Jake stared at the sight: Robin gawking over her hero and Bruce pressing harder and harder against the unconscious man's wound. "You don't have to keep pressing. He's not gonna struggle. He's passed out," Robin told him, but Bruce's locked jaw prevailed as he continued pressing.

"Is he dead?" Edge asked as Miss Ginger eyed the scene.

Jake dropped to his knees and checked the pinned man's carotid. Then took off his sooty tee shirt and told Bruce to get off so he could put on a tourniquet. Bruce took a breath and said, "I'll keep some pressure while you do it." Jake assessed the possibility, aiming a light all around the bloody wound site. "You're right," and Robin swooned. "You saved his life. I thought you were just being mean."

Edge kept the video running as Jake worked his wound-up tee shirt under the thick man's big upper thigh while Robin aimed a light. Jake's biceps pumped the hardy blue veins under his white shoulders as he strained to tighten the tourniquet. "Let off easy now and let's see if it stops the bleeding." Jake studied the tourniquet as Bruce eased off and blood pulsed over his shoulder. "Put it back." Jake grabbed Bruce's bloody boot.

"You're gonna have to keep it there."

Ken rushed back from the sandy two-lane road. Ten feet from the group he hollered for them to get their lights out of his eyes. "Just me. It's Ken. His ride just tore out a here. Looked like a girl, long hair, yellow sports car. Certain of that." Ken got closer. "Not a very good get-away car." Ken grimaced over the scarlet sight. "That pony. I'd a never believed it if I hadn't seen it." Ken looked up at Bruce. "Man, whadathey feed you in prison?"

"They're after Bruce's cash." Exilee rubbed her arms. "One of his friends probably went blabbermouthin' about how he gave out some cash tonight and they came after the rest of it. That's all." The bloody man's shiny white inverted pockets dulled as the tee shirt tourniquet failed. The stretchy knit fabric didn't hold and the blood slowly seeped. "Damn," Jake told Bruce to keep pressure and he boldly asked, "Jake, exactly where'd you put Momma's things?" He held his hand over the bear effigy under his dirty sweat-soaked tee.

"In the big barn." When Jake stretched out his arm all four dogs honed-in on the big barn. "On the flat-bed trailer with the busted axle. No one knows about that stuff. It's just toys and pictures, things from your momma's room, isn't it?" Jake told Robin, "Woman kept everything. Covers a twenty-foot flatbed," and Robin just shrugged.

Bruce breathed like he'd bust wide open any second. "Where's that rescue squad comin' from?" He spat. "Glad it's not one of us bleeding to death." His angst showed all the way down to his bare blood dotted throbbing thigh as he pressed into the wound even harder. "Turn that damn thing off."

"Okay. No prob, cuz," Edge flipped it closed as she mumbled to the others as Bruce directed Jake to hold his foot down on the wounded man, but Jake refused. "I need to get in my house and see what's missing." His arms cut through the dark night. "And we'd better wait for the medics and do this thing right. The Law's tricky. We don't want him suing us later."

"Yea, we better wait," Exilee calmly advised and the others agreed. "Call again and see how long they'll be," she instructed Robin.

"Who the hell is he?" Jake strained and Robin said, "He's a human being for Christ's sake," and Edge said, "But would he save one of us?"

Bruce told them to wipe the blood off his face and Jake took off his shirt and tried to remove the blood clot on the end of his nose and he jerked away. Jake wiped and wiped, but it only smeared as the dying man struggled and tried to bite, clenching the bloodied shirt in his snaggle-toothed jaws he madly growled with his eyes shut tight.

Jake stood back as the madman writhed and he faintly said, "Never seen him before in my life," panting and exhausted he threatened to faint and fell to the ground and raised his legs and Robin quickly went to him and told him to be still as she called 911 again demanding logistics and she was told they were enroute less than one mile from destination. Robin rubbed over Jake's head, fondling his hayseed hair as she lingered over Bruce, studying his muscular neck, back up to his mysterious grey eyes and back to Jake's jealous greens. When he winked at her she sheepishly winked back.

Unexpectedly, the pony nudged up against Exilee from behind and she jumped with aimed fists. But Misun puff talked like pony's do and she embraced the little charmer while breathing in his musky grass scents. "Do you have more cash here, Bruce?"

"Not worried about it," Bruce moaned. When he quickly cupped his package, the ladies looked away.

"Here they are." Edge's neck stretched out like a Thoroughbred's on guard. "Yep, that's them." The big white hood charged the corner. Passed the hay pastures and roared toward the houses with a cloud of spewing sand. The ambulance's blinding lights held them as Edge resumed recording. "Just this part, Bruce, I promise."

"Damn, this is gonna wake Sarah and Luke. Get prepared, y'all. David'll wanna know the whole shooting match," Exilee cracked her knuckles.

After a speedy assessment, a rushed EMT punched needles as another capped his face with an oxygen mask, securing over his wet bloodied head. Their bright spotlights shone into his eyes, but no one identified him. They called in stats as Robin spilled out the entire pony-dragging-karate-chopping -dog-whoppicodling heroic fight. "What happened to his ear?" asked the EMT checking his pupils again and reading his pulse.

"That was my dog," Robin proudly answered and all four EMTs dogmatically checked behind their backs. "Oh, they're on rest command," Robin assured. "Don't worry. They know a bad guy when they see one."

"Must be one bad dude," replied the EMT reading the blood pressure monitor as another guided the EMT with the tourniquet cuff to lock it down as he added, "Baddest man in the whole damn town. Geez." The EMT with the tourniquet monitor justified that it was locked down and directed Bruce to slowly ease his boot off from the toe to the heel in slow increments. When no blood seeped, they reflectively sighed.

Miss Ginger and the others cringed at the gooey red blood, the purple clots and thick caked blood covering the chunk of missing flesh from the man's thigh. Bruce scraped and rubbed his boot across the grass while the four EMT's lifted the man onto a stretcher. As they hopped into the ambulance the last one in told Bruce, "He could've easily had a heart attack from the shock alone. Knocking him out saved him from that. But your boot did the trick, preventing death by exsanguination, only takes four minutes."

"I don't know what happened." His statement took them aback. "Well, it went down so fast," he rationalized as he squeezed his palms together. Eyebrows danced. Doors closed and sand spun, and the tour group checked one another's soot covered bodies in the orangey red taillight.

"Barn wired for light?" Bruce asked Exilee and she explained where to find the switch. Edge offered to take a flashlight and Robin honed-in like a hawk. "Just what does Bruce have to do to prove he's a big boy now, scalp somebody?" She rolled her shoulders in conjunction with her hips leaving no doubt she was the princess on petty as Jake stroked the dog's ears nearest him.

Edge shined her light over Bruce as she recorded his stealth toward the big dark barn. When Exilee called out for them to tell Mark it was okay to come out now if he was still in there hiding Bruce sped up. "Wait for me," Edge urged and matter of factly announced into the mic, "Bruce Black in action again to find his cousin" and he laughed. "You haven't changed a bit, you little pest."

He wedged open the huge double doors. Felt for the switch and flicked it on. Suspended fluorescent bulbs flickered and dinged until darkness was snuffed and the edges of the loft glowed. At once, the disturbed yard chickens peacefully slumbering in their dark barn clucked and chattered. When Bruce and Edge sought out the middle aisle and didn't near the roosting chickens the chatter ceased as their footsteps gritted against the sandy dirt floor. From above, the occasional flutter of a purple martin's wings filled the big barn.

The middle of the big barn held two humongous tractors, mowing attachments of various sizes, hay baling equipment, and two rows of more farm equipment. Stacks of drying lumber posed in the loft. Up against the back wall were two flat-bed trailers. One was empty. The other held Bruce's beloved cardboard boxes. Mark popped up near a disheveled box sitting open on the earthen floor and gasped at his find. "Mom took this game when I was just a kid."

Bruce streamed down the aisle. As the item became clearer at ten feet away Bruce stated, "It's a war game." Mark's dry mouth choked him as he shook the shiny black laminated box. It was no larger than a shirt box but screamed as large as a tattle-telling teenage sister that Bruce's stepbrother was pilfering. With eyes as wide as a tot's over a daddy's belt, Mark squeaked, "Mom doesn't like violence." Two feet away, "What else did you find," Bruce cocked his head, "Buddyrow?"

"Nothin', I swear."

"You snuck in here soon as ya got the chance."

"No. It wasn't like that." Mark stammered. "I thought if somebody was in here I could
chase him out. That's all."

"You tell people about my things being stored in here, my old toys? They're worth something for a collector." Bruce breathed hot bull steam as he peered over Mark's shoulder at the rummaged boxes. Several on the front row were wide open. "Or are you lookin' for something more valuable?"

Mark sidestepped out of the way and told Bruce to look for himself. "Nothing else is missing. I swear."

"Don't run off."

Edge began another video. "Stay right there."

"Give me that." Bruce snatched at her phone, but she jerked it away and hopped backwards like a crow with a stolen trinket. "Okay, I'll turn it off." Edge slipped it into her short's back pocket. As Bruce inspected his boxes, she tucked it into her bra, tightly against the left cup. "You lookin' for anything particular? I can help." She flipped open a box and before he had a chance to answer was turning pages in a picture album.

Bruce rummaged through the open boxes. "Did you even think about closing 'em so barn dirt doesn't get in everything? It's all I've got left of my family." He swallowed the anger and heaved. "When are you gonna grow up?"

"I swear. I didn't open any. These were already open." Mark tapped at a box on the front row. "There's one in the back. Check it. It looks like it's been opened, too."

Bruce carefully stepped onto the flatbed trailer and eased boxes aside until he stood over the box with the flaps standing askew. He glanced back at Mark. "There's dirt all over it, 'cept where someone just opened it." He glared down at Mark. "Scarecrow will run a set of prints for me. All I got ta do is ask." Mark didn't flinch as Bruce laid back the flaps. Lifted his momma's old jewelry box and fought his burning eyes.

The dull finish had old nicks and alarming freshly cut grooves. Bruce freed the jammed crooked drawer sticking halfway out, and dime store earrings and tarnished silver costume jewelry fell out into the jammed open drawer beneath it. The drawers were as plain as the outside of the box. No velvety red lining, but the box had been well crafted with dovetail joints. He carefully scooped up the jewelry and placed it into the top drawer which held a simple gold chain.

"What'd you find?" Edge tried to see.

"My mother's jewelry box. It's broken." With it clutched to his chest he faced them.

"Damn," Mark winced. "I'd love to know who did that."

Bruce climbed down and sat on the edge of the trailer and his bare blood dotted legs shone under the florescent lights. When he gently manipulated the drawers closed a square chunk from the bottom fell and dusty barn dirt flew up as it landed. Bruce's weary red eyes welled up as he held the box up to his chest. One leg uncontrollably vibrated while the other twisted around his blood-stained booted ankle.

"Maybe we can fix it." Mark warily observed.

Edge picked up the wooden chunk. Dusted it off and placed it on Bruce's bare thigh and when she did, allowed her fingertips to linger long enough to feel his heat. Bruce inspected the piece and then tilted the box in varying angles as he inspected the damage underneath the box. He lifted it above his head toward the rafters and his eyes grew wide as a box peeked from between hay bales.

The dry dirt splashed up again. Bruce cradled the coveted box up to his chest. Held his breath and let out a resounding sigh over the sight of the fallen chunk. It sparkled like the Little People had lit a thousand tiny live fires.

"Oh my God, look at this." Mark held it up to the light. "It's beautiful." Edge reached up for it as Bruce sat spellbound and Edge aimed the light. Mark blew on the golden filigreed cross and the black stone's center blinked. "Wipe it off, Mark," she nearly whispered. Diamonds encircled it.

"It's the real thing." With eyes as wide as silver dollars Mark held it out by the edges. As Bruce beheld the unbelievable bejeweled cross Mark stood extra tall, "Royal, mon."

Bruce marveled at the cross with the same serendipity smile his momma had had and Mark wiped it with a clean spot on his sooty tee shirt, but it was still hard to determine what the other stones were, so Edge told him to spit on it and when he did the rubies shined outlining the Maltese Cross.

Bruce grabbed it as he sprung off the flatbed, "All those years ago, in that chair," Bruce softly palpated, "this is what she held." With both hands he held it up to the light as the serendipity smile quickly vanished after he jammed the cross down into his front pocket. "You two are in jeopardy now, like me."

Mark backed up as Bruce seized Edge by the arm. "The Society won't let this happen. Everything that's gone on tells me that." He panted and she winced. "No way, never, you can't tell a soul. Understand?" His fierce penetration frightened them both into silent agreement.

"The secret council, it's for real?" Mark's quickened hushed words spread chill bumps. She rubbed them down as her nostrils flared. "That's all rumor," she cried, "Some stupid teenagers started that junk at a Pow Wow. There's nothin' to it. It's in all the schools now. We're from the Lost Colony. Heirs to royalty, and we'll never get federal funds. It's so stupid. England is a million miles from here. Who cares about them?"

Bruce jerked Edge up by the shoulders and shook so hard the white ribbon holding back her long brown curls fell to the dirt. "You got it wrong, girl." She tried to jerk away but he jerked her back square into his glaring grays. Scared a squeal out of her and clasped his hand over her mouth. "This is the last time I'll tell you. Not another word. This never happened."

The chickens chattered as the trio left the barn to its dark and Bruce palmed the turquoise effigy hugging his swollen chest. "I'd say I'm lucky to be alive, but I believe there's more to it."

Mark secured the big barn doors and the trio walked in silence until they reached Jake's front steps. Edge said she didn't think she should drive home. That she was too tired. "I can sleep on the couch."

"That's where I'm sleeping," Mark informed her as he cautiously peered around the dark corners of the house. "Wonder if those dogs are put up?" Edge said the dogs wouldn't bother anyone unless they ran and that she can sleep on the floor on a pallet. But Bruce told her to drink a cup of coffee and that she'd be fine. "Just don't stop anywhere." He held the screen door open as he told Mark, "If anyone else was with that fool he's long gone."

Indoor voices merged into a dull roar and amplified toward the open door. "Get inside. Sounds like everyone else is." The trio stepped inside, and Edge went straight to the coffee pot. Bruce to the hallway and Mark squinted through the screen door. When Miss Ginger asked, "Who's out there?" Mark jumped and flashed a wild smile. "Oh, just telling the farm animals good night is all." Mark plopped down on the couch and leaned over the arm rest nearest her rocker. "Isn't that how y'all do it?" Onacona was curled up on the floor between them.

She raised her head and Mark reached down to finger her thick coat. Then firmly rubbed her eager neck.

Miss Ginger winked. "You stay all weekend, chile. We need to get you city boys straightened out. Okay?"

"Plannin' on it." Mark swung his legs over the couch cushions to recline. But in mid air Miss Ginger yelled, "Uh, uh, uh, pull them filthy boots off. Youse covered with soot. Get up." She threw him a blanket from beside her chair. "Wash a blanket lot easier than that couch." As Onacona sniffed his boots Mark tightened up all over. The large German Shepherd's ears flattened back, then one pointed toward the hallway.

"We need your office, Miss Ginger. Yurkers taint got no raisin' these days." Scarecrow stretched out behind Mark as he pulled off his boots. Crow ruffled the boy's hair and lowered his towering frame over the back of the couch and coyly cuffed Mark's ear. "Whadcha find out there, boy?"

"Nuthin." When Mark clamped his lips like he was fixin' to be spoon fed sulfur, Onacona whined at his knees, but Mark hatefully told the dog to go lay down and Scarecrow remarked, "Never send a boy for a man's job."

Lilly pressed her finger into the dented door jamb before she opened the passage door inside Jake's colonial home. "They succeeded. Russ, look at this." Scarecrow shook his head. "Claw marks." Lilly examined Scarecrow's growing fury. "Fisk and Wart," he seethed.

Jake's eyes whitened. "Those dents tell you that?"

"Hammer claws; their signature," Scarecrow blew. "Been closing the bars on 'em for years. You'd think they'd smartin' up and use something else."

Scarecrow led them back down the hall and, on the way, swept down over the couch and popped Mark's crossed arms a loose. "Thought Bruce might have a little trouble with some old jar runners or a shiner. And I was right. Someone went through Bruce's bag." Pillow fluff scattered as they inched through the mess in Jake's room and he picked up Bruce's clothes halfway folding them as he layered them across his arm and scornfully surveyed the ruined room. "They must've searched everything." They all pitched in and when Bruce simply asked for a trash bag the monumental tension threatening to scatter them separate ways was swished away and filtered out the little square frames in the front screen door."

Chapter 8

Agotsinnachen Now[50]

David Crowson sat the pages in his lap over the quilt his aunt had made for their fiftieth wedding anniversary and Miss Sarah asked, "Well, will this book help? If we get caught our lives are fish bait," and David cracked his knuckles, "This is only one chapter, eight, it says here on the first page. If the rest of it is like this, our people will relate to it and might leave the Lumbee roll and strike out to reestablish our Tuscarora Roots," he blew a long cleansing breath, "Our people have done been bled to death, Sarah. If there's a chance in fixing all this, and it means two old folks might end up in the state prison getting free medical and meals, I don't see a damn reason not to."

She kissed his forehead, "We've gone too far to back out now. Federal offenses, they say, are guaranteed time."

When he smiled up at his wife, their smiles faded, "We could run away."

"We couldn't."

"Why?" he asked.

"If the FBI is determined "to get their man" and we aren't here, they'll take our boy."

David rocked and Sarah piddled in the bedroom with her sewing, "This blouse is all wrong for me. I need a darker shade of blue." She pulled out the cardboard boxes from the wardrobe closet and fished through the colorful folded fabric piles atop the documents. "I wonder if Miss Lucy would like this one."

"Stay away from her now. You'll blab everything," his gruffness startled her. When he breathed normally, she turned on her affections, "David?" "Yes?" "She's going to be there too."

After supper, Miss Sarah read Chapter 7, and David read *Chapter 8, Agotsinnachen Then.*

The early morning summer dew rested on the wooden deck and Bruce all but dropped the two cups onto the railing to catch her as she began to slip. "Never know when the Lord is gonna call you up. Do we?" Miss Ginger was not smiling.

Bruce handed her her coffee cup as she sat on the top step and he slid past her to sit below, situating himself so he could lean back against a spindle.

"Spill it," he smiled. "Like you said, we never know." His coffee went down in one long gulp. "You didn't come over here this morning to hand over my morning ellick."

"No. It's all like it's supposed to be, I reckon. Presbyterians call it Providence." She took a sip then leaned into him. "Your ear is marked with the cross."

"That's a birthmark. A defect."

"The natives had odd ways about 'em." Her head stopped bobbing back and forth.

"When they took the whites, they marked 'em and each of their childrens so they'd know where they came from. They wanted the white blood because they knew they had powers too.

Settlements migrated and chiefs married the mixed breeds, they changed up to marking only the chief's children, the descendants of Governor John White's daughter. He was given the cross by Sir Walter Raleigh." She cocked her head down at Bruce's front jean pocket. "Queen Elizabeth took it straight off her bosom and gave it to him for finding the New Lands." She gasped up at the dark shadowy sky as the orange and blue gleamed its edges. "I don't know if they believed it had powers or not. But they knew for sure it didn't belong to them."

"Is that in your papers?"

"No, chile," she whispered, "It's too dangerous. Folks with power and money want to keep it, not hand it over to their victims when a judge declares reparations."

Bruce looked away out into the timberline where he'd handed Robin the yellow cactus bloom then back to Miss Ginger. "Are the Crowsons in danger?"

"Not right now, but you've got to claim your heritage so all this can stop, you hear?"

When the bluebirds sang their morning cheer a hunting hawk swept in and they dove into their hidey holes. The hawk, too low and too close to stop, landed on a split rail post. Stared right at Bruce. Opened his sharp bill and showed his tongue. Ejected upwards like a rocket on fire hurling fluffy little scrap feathers that slowly stilled on the dewy grass.

"The Society, are they the ones who killed my mother?"

"I don't believe that for one second." Miss Ginger quivered. "The Society wants the Tuscarora to fight for English blood rights, for honor and money in it too, millions and they want land, like millions of acres of the federal land preserves. This group is big time," her arms spread out, "across the oceans. They're not interested in piddly HUD funds or wanting to get set up like The Lumbee Council keeps hopin' on for the feds to do with Indian rights. Government says the Lums don't have enough red to have to pay 'em. I know. I talked to them face to face. I been in the beltline, boy. Take a switch ta me if I get that notion again. Snake pit of damnation! I never!" She jabbed at the air. "I was right there in Washington and spoke with representatives who'd been pissed off at one thing or another and was willing to give me a word. Most of 'em thought I was just a simple-minded old Negra woman." She guffawed then quickly focused back onto Bruce's eager eyes when he asked, "Why do you use that word instead of African American?"

"Honor," she spat, "no such thing as African American unless it's one going back and forth with a visa and lying to one country or the other on loyalty. Use "black" too 'cause it's got the same roots, like your society, the Tuscarora's Second Society: Hatterask Indians."

"You have great orenda, $_{51}$ for a black woman."

"Tuscarora; when I use my spirit gifts."

. "Yes, you see right through me and you're so invested in us."

"Oh, chile, I been all over, up and down the East Coast visiting retired congressmen, chiefs on their death beds and shriveled up Negroes who tell it like it is and like it was when it was all going down." She cautiously stopped when Two Tails bawled in the distance. "Someone's out. You said Mark was in the barn." "Yea, that kid," Bruce sighed and looked down into his empty cup. "He knows something's up. Maybe you oughta warn that boy 'fore to the wrong folks. This is serious now. The Lumbee Council is in Washington right now looking for more votes to get on board. They're not gonna let The Society get in their way, if they can help it." Miss Ginger backed off and pulled her lips together like she was fixin' to dare the truth out a' somebody.

"You believe that fool here last night was sent by The Society or The Council?"

"You don't really need to ask me that, do you?" When Bruce shook his head she added, "Bruce, you been protected for years by The Society as much as possible without giving away who you are. Lord knows they pulled some fast ones to keep you from gettin' kilt or beat to a pulp being in the middle of all that likker business all your life."

"Who told you that?" His grays begged.

Startled, Miss Ginger held her cup to her lips and studied him over the rim.

"Don't play games with me." Bruce's baby face implored, "I need to know everything. I gotcha on the Crowsons. So, they know and you, but who else? I can't stand not knowing who is in on this, who's a part of The Society, who to trust," he seethed, "I can't stand it."

"I know. But I don't have those answers. When The Society opens itself up to you, and they will, be open to the truth."

"The truth? I thought you just gave me that, Raleigh's jewel from the queen and the mark and the fight. God knows, what else is there?"

Miss Ginger grasped his forearm. "People been waiting a long time for you to be ready. I'm sure of that. And I got a strong feeling they know you're 'bout as powerful as a bull after last night. If not, they'll know by lunch time."

His quizzical expression begged. "Just tell me," he huffed. "What else is there? Powerful for what?"

"Easy," she sternly warned, and he took it well. "You just watch. This little town'll have every ear bent down to the Coast and back before noon over your welcome home visitor last night. They ain't stupid. Someone come in here like that knows you got some powerful medicine worth risking their life for."

"I took care of that last night," his nostrils flared, and her eyes darted.

"I moved my medicine where no one can find it," his words had rushed together and she noticed his bloodshot eyes and tired pink-rimmed eyelids and her empathy blossomed, "This thing is bigger than what all we seen. And chile, when the truth comes out, embrace it, no matter what. Your momma would 'a wanted it that way."

Before he could open his mouth, Mark hopped up the steps. "I knew it was you, early bird." He lightly swatted Bruce's big bare toes. "What time we meeting your building dealer?" He sniffed up at the open kitchen window. "Sausage? I thought we were meeting him for breakfast. You buying? I think we should go to a buffet."

Miss Ginger stretched and surveyed the little back yard up to the side of the house where the split rail guided the tourists. "Do I hear those dogs? Or something else out?"

"It's the dogs. They been out all night." Mark called for them. "Onacona started whining and when I opened the door to let her out these guys greeted me." He took turns playfully rubbing their necks. "They're so big. Glad they like me."

"Did they follow you into the barn?" Bruce asked and Mark's shoulders twisted like a child's twirly bird toy, "Naw."

Miss Ginger laughed as she headed back inside. "Exilee counts those birds with Luke every morning. His favorite is Chirper." From the doorway, she turned around to face Mark. "Luke's chicken only got one wing with feathers. He wore the others off. How he carries it around."

Mark scratched his neck and swatted at the no see-ums. "I didn't see where they messed with any chickens."

"Come on," Bruce stretched out like a slinky across several steps and when he stood stretched some more. "Let's eat."

Mark reached out to pop his cousin's concave abs, but Bruce was too quick. "You need a few pull ups over at Eacha Up's Pizza," Bruce released Mark's wrist, "and have the milkshakes." But when Bruce squinted like he'd suddenly got a headache and squeezed the railing Mark asked if he got into the likker jar after everyone went to bed. "No, kid, but I might today."

"All right," Mark played the railing like he was jamming drumsticks. "Knew I'd have a good time this weekend."

The old copper hinges creaked so loudly the dogs rushed up the steps and wind up at the kitchen window. "Bet she's hiding your fun right now," Bruce bantered.

The stealthy German Shepherds took turns circling to rest on the deck. Their dark brown eyes glimmered with the morning's gold sun. The brilliant ball of orange fire lighting up the dew-covered Bermuda lawns and the fescue and orchard grass pastures defined day from night as it highlighted the Alpha's golden undercoat. Onacona was the last to circle. As she surveyed her pack and rested her head on her front paws her rich dark sable coat parted in folds like shimmering golden silk.

As soon as they heard them, they ran with sharp squeals of delight as they greeted the young family. With soft strokes and Luke's tail teasing the dogs escorted them to Jake's front door. Exilee knocked once then told Luke to take off his dew-soaked boots and let them dry on the porch.

"Papaw doesn't put his on the front porch. He has a rack." Luke fisted his hips.

Ken signaled the dogs off the front porch while blocking them from knocking over Luke in their excitement. "Better put 'em on the rail or a dog might drag 'em off." Ken instructed as he hurried to take a seat at the kitchen table and Bruce asked, "Y'all this early every day?" When Ken's poster boy smile assured him that early rising taint never killed a soul Bruce let out a little whistle, "Can we catch a nap under a shade tree then?" Ken popped the kitchen table, "We do that all the time."

"When you're at Papaw's you can do it like him. When you're at someone else's house you do it like they do." Exilee firmly explained as she finally guided Luke through the open front door.

Jake sleepily stumbled into the living room. "Let's eat," and the dogs happily cried for their master.

"I thought you took 'em back to the kennel last night," Exilee asked Jake.

"Was going to, but Scarecrow told me to leave 'em out. Said they'd keep anyone else from comin' up. Least slow 'em down."

Miss Ginger filled the brown earthenware bowl with steamy scrambled eggs. "Better fill up, busy day comin." After she placed the bowl on the table gently squeezed Bruce's bare shoulders. "Put a shirt on." "Knew she was gonna getcha," Jake sported, "Hurry up."

Sausage with eggs and Miss Ginger's pan bread fried in the rendered seasonings with apple butter topped over it like icing set Bruce up for a nap. But he just yawned and threw back another ellick. Then left to help Ken and Jake make rounds and feed up. The dogs were fed and kenneled. The ponies were greeted and fed, then cows in the calving lot. Luke spread pieces of broken bread for the chicks and Miss Sarah tossed a pan of scraps. Water troughs were topped, and Jake promised they'd get the beans and tomatoes fertilized and weeded, soon. The heavy breakfast under July's humid sky in combination with the metabolizing likker, soaked their backs and underarms, so they changed shirts before piling into Jake's pick up. Jake fondled his gold luck charm wiggling from his keychain and smiled when Lilly's pearl button sparkled.

As they left to meet the steel building dealer, they waved bye to Luke standing on the furthest slate slab of Papaw's walk. The kenneled dogs wagged after Jake's truck when it passed and cried in vain as it turned onto the graveled county road and was enveloped by the pristine Longleaf Pines. "Y'all were gonna eat at Crossroad's, right?" Jake asked as he turned onto the pavement. "Yep. I'll talk him into a biscuit to go." Bruce opened his eyes and covered his yawn when the truck stopped and felt for the jeweled cross deep in his pocket. After Bruce went inside to greet the metal building dealer, Exilee wiggled out of Ken's lap out into the parking lot and stretched, and it quickly became apparent the restaurant's glass front made for good viewing. Exilee's signature blue jean cut off shorts were very popular with all the old timers and farm hands. Ken wisely waved her back into his lap as Bruce exited the restaurant followed by the salesman and Edge who waved like a child on parade wearing a fresh white blouse, but the same hot red bandana trimmed shorts.

"Think that's a coincidence?" Ken inferred and Exilee told him to be nice.

Forgotten in the bed of the truck, Mark suddenly slapped the roof of the truck. "I like short shorts," he burst into song, "Give me those short-shorts."

"Shut up," Jake yelled over his shoulder out the window while Ken and Exilee snickered.

"I'm gonna ride with him," Bruce called out and Edge rode with Bruce in the salesman's car.

As soon as they arrived at Bruce's land, Jake pulled up close and unlocked the steel gate's chain. The existing shed was a post and beam structure with heavy tin siding and rain-washed rust stains. Wildflowers and somewhat sad pear tree with long draping branches and squirrels feasting on its fallen fruits, humped over next to where the makeshift road ended. The dark pond reflected the tips of trees in the timberline and they waved hello when a crane launched from the bank where the pussy willows waded. The picturesque setting was so surreal with the flock of bluebirds dashing this away and that and charming little bunnies circling about the tender young vines that they all quietly absorbed it like it was an assignment to remember every little thing about Bruce's promising vineyard.

Jake shook hands with the salesman as Bruce counted rabbits. "I'm Jake Wilkes. Too busy last night to introduce myself."

"Mike Kendall, nice to meet you." He was a slender man, middle aged, with barber's eyes. He wore a light blue dress shirt, short sleeves and no tie and had on light weight navy dress pants and smart brown loafers.

Ken told him good morning as Exilee, and Edge ventured off to check on the dewberry vines. Mark introduced himself and went on to ask if Bruce had told him about the after party, but Bruce gave Mark the look and he smartly diverted the subject towards short shorts and Ken gave Mark the look. But not before Mark spoke up, "Isn't Edge wearing the same shorts she had on last night?" When no one acknowledged Mark, he asked for a bandana, a red one, and complained of being sticky, and Bruce finally gave him the tap, "Ouch," and the eye.

Bruce led the men to a hill overlooking the young vines encircling the large dark pond. "This is where I want the distillery. It needs to go up, pronto." A rabbit ran right between them and another threatened to follow. At the timberline a white and gray tail slipped into the thicket. Bruce grumbled about getting rabbit traps, even though Jake offered to bring a Bassett hound from one of the local rabbit hunting sheriff's deputies, and all the while a rabbit family played gleefully at the pond's edge.

He turned his attention back to Kendall and informed him that he wanted a cash price on his quote. "Gonna ship in grapes until mine are mature and get my recipes down. The grape vines will encircle the Zoskiroro's. An aerial view will look like a jewel," he paused and sternly smiled at Mark, "like a big brown pool jewel circled with diamonds. It'll be gorgeous." They agreed and talked on about who could take them for a plane ride to get an aerial photo and Kendall informed them that one of his brother's had a pilot's license. "Well, I know where to go if I need something. Your daddy knew what he was doin' to have all those children. Huh?"

"He's a smart man."

"With a smart son," Ken piped. "How many men you know with two jobs? That's smart. All you Kendalls are bright like that."

"Wonder if the girls need any help?" Mark jeered as he began to sprint off, but Bruce grabbed the back of his tee shirt and told him he'd better stick around. "What if something happened to me? Who's gonna carry on the Black legacy? Make fine wine and handle all my money?"

Mark's gums were thinned pink as he accepted the responsibility and Jake just tried to hold back his laughter. Bruce discreetly winked over at Jake and with his arm firmly around Mark told Kendall, "I'll add on to the steel structure, so when you price out grading go ahead and include the showroom area, too." He let go of Mark to walk out the dimensions and he swung open the imagined showroom's front doors. "Got it all drawn up just gotta get a blueprint run."

"I can handle that, if you like. Cost ya between four and six if the architect doesn't have ta make a lot of allowances." Kendall offered. "This is a great spot. You can see everything."

"Just to run a blueprint? I didn't make myself clear. Those drawings are designed by a professional engineer." Bruce caught Jake's questioning eyes. "Brother up for fraud. He spent twenty for it and lost his house, wife, kids, but the Lum who ratted him got it." Bruce read Kendall's embarrassment and held his shoulder. "Hey, I'm not him. I don't hold a grudge like that. In fact, I'm thankful for the time I spent. I don't have a grudge against any brother Lum or whitey or any others. I can tell you're a Christian, Kendall. I am too. What do you think of dropping that expensive claim to get federal funding?" Kendall didn't budge and Bruce had his full attention, so he went on. "We don't have enough Indian blood and I believe it's more important to be true to who we were originally destined to be anyway."

"Who's that?" Kendall's dry lips formed a circle.

"Tuscarora."

"Yeah, but Dad's on the Lumbee Council." Kendall stiffened.

"No problem. It doesn't matter. This is just business, right?"

"Right." His relieved smile plucked Mark.

"Kendall," Mark stepped up to him, "are you on the Lumbee Council?"

"No, not on it. Been to meetings. It's important to know what's going on, on the swamp."

Bruce surveyed his property again. "Spent a lot a days here, daydreaming about this," Bruce scoped the area like it was the first time and as he rounded the dewberries encircling the pond smiled over at Ken, then back to Kendall he said, "The showroom will be a two story deal with rustic cedar siding and old bubbled glass paned windows like you'd see a hundred years ago. It'll be wider than the steel structure. Don't want the manufacturing side visible from the entrance."

"So, do you want me to see about the drawings?" Kendall asked.

"Yea, I want to get this up pronto. Need to work on my recipes. Make sure I haven't lost my touch."

"I can start today. My wife can handle the barbering and beauty departments. No problem." Kendall checked his watch as he pulled out his electronic tablet from his waistband and activated the internet. Punched in the dealership and stated that they can handle it all online with a simple signature as he held up the vivid images sequencing across the screen.

"Technology grew overnight, didn't it?" Bruce observed the small three-by-five display screen. "First time I've seen one of these other than the in the tv room on the television."

Mark squeezed in shoulder to shoulder. "You can play games, too. Poker, Bingo, even watch a show. Know what I mean, a show-show."

Jake and Ken agreed that the tablet was going to save forests but hurt local pulp tree farmers. "Plymouth is laying off fifty workers. It was in the paper last week."

"I hate driving through those paper mills. Smells like septic," Mark frowned.

"Don't matter, Mark," Bruce said, "Won't be long pulpwood is history. We are the hemp gatherers and that's my next project, paper and textile.

"We can make it any way you want." Kendall held up the screen for Bruce. "Have kits ready to ship. Know which one you want? There's ridged steel and arched and slab, and colors."

"I have a vision," Bruce mumbled as he took in the sliding images. "There, that's just like it. It was in one of the brochures I ordered."

"You could mail yourself things in prison?" Mark asked. "Why didn't you order yourself a file?"

"Are you planning to work for me?" Bruce shot his grays as one eyebrow furrowed.

"Yea, at some point. I'm still in college."

Edge returned sniffing a tender limb in her grasp, "What's this? There's a city block of this stuff growing over there." Her thumb jutted out over her shoulder.

"That's sassafras," Exilee told her as she smelled its leaves. "It's an indigenous plant. Was there anything else there or just that?" Perspiration dotted her temples and purged the baby curls napping tenderly along her forehead. She wiped them down, following the length of her thick black braid, pulling it over her shoulder.

"Just this, like he's growing it," Edge puzzled over the limb and chewed the severed end.

"Tastes good, this for your wine?"

With a warm smile and grays darkened under the shadow of his hand held over his brows he assured the young trees were cultivated. "Add sassafras and chocolate and strawberries, all kinds of natural flavorings." Bruce plucked a leaf tangled from Edge's light brown curls.

"Where's the chocolate patch?" Edge's hips shifted as she batted up at Bruce. Mark pointed out past the pond. "Go look over there." His opossum eatin' grin announced his intentions. "Check if the seeds sprouted. You'll have to get up close. Just bend over. Don't get all dirty on your hands and knees, unless you don't mind that kind of thing."

"Pig." Edge pulled down on her short's red bandana trim and huffed.

When Bruce told Kendall to order the plans for the steel building image on the screen the ladies instantly became interested. "That's a church," Exilee exclaimed.

"I know," Bruce affirmed. "It'll be perfect, the rustic showroom and the shiny chapel where the grapes are crucified into wine." They all sighed. Bruce turned to Kendall,

"Can I get a dark purple roof, Zoskiroro's dewberry purple?"

"Yes, sir, just sign here." Kendall held up the tablet while Bruce looked for a pen. "You use your finger."

"Amazing," Bruce signed for the metal church structure with a deep purple roof and tapped his chest and when he did felt the bear effigy and clasped it. "Momma would a' loved this place."

"Now, what about equipment, Bruce? I researched wineries and found major satisfaction with this manufacturer." Kendall held up the tablet for Bruce as miscellaneous forms flowed past.

"Any tanks, bottles, and other distillery equipment we can get from Bavarian dealers in steel or copper."

"Got that all squared away, Kendall. My brothers will be commissioned to make most of it. Even got a glass blower in mind for the bottles. Thinkin' about settin' him up on the property." When Bruce's chin darted toward Jake his arms flew up to the top of his head as Bruce clarified. "Got my heart set on this big honkin' copper still from a set of Lums. You probably heard of 'em, Fisk and Wart."

Kendall's eyes 'bout popped out a' his head. "They lookin' to sell out?"

Bruce winked. "Think I should make an offer on Fisk's big copper momma? Or should we just reclaim it?"

No one moved. Ken's eyes were as big as white biscuits. "Heard it took up the whole baccar barn." It's like the bate of 'em were stuck. Their shoes were cemented into the shifty sand and legs locked down straight over 'em.

"I'm not helping you steal that thing. I'm not." Jake closed his eyes and turned his head.

"Who said steal? Did anyone hear me say steal?" Bruce confirmed with each of them and Edge especially when shook a negative. But Exilee serenely smiled and surprised Ken when she went on to say that they'd be glad to help. Why he couldn't even speak.

"Well," Kendall stepped off toward his car, "Looks like we're done for now. I'll be in touch."

Bruce brought Kendall back by the elbow and sincerely conveyed to the group the terrible injustice of Mr. Fisk and Wart stealing the pallets of likker from his daddy, who was then Preacher Black, after Bruce had worked so long and so hard, digging and hiding dirt piles and luggin' each jar on a separate day or night into his specially hidden pit to save a little piece of his family history and how that big copper momma was rightfully his. He explained there was no way those slime balls would own up to the theft. "Never in a pine tree stump turned ta lighter will they come up with the money they made off my daddy's likker and pay me back."

"Yeah," Mark cheered, "Just like the feds can't even come close to paying us back for taking our own country!"

"I'm in!" Yelled Exilee and Ken mouthed, "Guess we'll help too."

Bruce pulled Kendall up so closely he could've kissed him and whispered so lowly no one else could hear. But what was clear was that Bruce was enthralled with the dark insignia sewn onto Kendall's shirt. Bruce nearly ripped it off tugging on it. But Kendall held it down. "This is not The Society they had in mind."

In those few minutes, those few short zingin' minutes, Bruce convinced Kendall that he was not planning to steal anything, but repossess, and not only that. Bruce convinced every single one of them to help repossess the big copper momma and to do it in the light of day when he was sure Mr. Fisk and Wart would be sleeping off the night's drunk.

"You tie and I'll hold 'em," Bruce told Jake. "Know you'll want a front row center for this." Bruce's teeth shined like white blinds.

"Oh, no I don't," Jake spat. "I don't want any part of this. I'm going back to college. I'm gonna be a vet. And you just said they'd be sleeping, so you sneak in there yourself."

"They'll be asleep when we get there. But we don't want to take any chances. When those copper sheets start falling they'll be ringing like bells." Bruce tilted his head back and laughed like a crazy Zoskiroro Chief, barreling it out until he had to hold his knees before he was ever done with the laughing fit. With all the seriousness of a caped heroic cartoon guise, his gray eyes set in deep. "I can't wait to see their filthy faces."

Ken and Mark worked together hastily removing the boxes from the second flatbed trailer and hooked it up to the transfer truck brought over from Kendall's brother's garage while Bruce and Jake convinced Mr. and Mrs. Crowson that if there were any damages to the trailer, and swore that there wouldn't be, that Bruce had enough funds to cover it.

The borrowed truck had to be back before morning at ten when Kendall's brother returned from the men's retreat. (That time the Methodist men were learning 'Forgiveness in Families and Why it Matters Most.') Jake drove the borrowed truck because he had a license. He had attained a CDL for hauling hay with the Crowson's pristine thirty-year-old big rig. Bruce sat co-pilot and Kendall straddled the console. Ken, who was most familiar with his aged farm rig, drove it to haul the other flatbed to Bruce's old stompin' grounds, from where The Company was moved six years prior, and the entire time Mark questioned Ken on married life.

After being dropped off at Crossroad's Restaurant, where Edge had left her sporty red two-door, she spun out making a doughnut in the middle of the road. The jealous waitresses bitched out the window as smarty pants got all the attention and it took all of eight seconds for 'em to call the law. Edge zoomed out of sight. Turned around and made two more doughnuts, reveling in her position on the repossession team. She was performing well as those stunt drivers on television in those competitions making figure eights when the first red light whipped around, and Edge reined her "horse" to the center and spurred like the world was on fire. "Hot Damn!" She checked the rear view. "Harnett County, too. I love you Harnett County, boys. Those roads flat as your stupid heads. Come on." She did not give them the pleasure of reading "Kiss This" plastered on her bumper, but anyone could've read her flagged finger.

Exilee's position was to notify as many jar runners as possible. Bruce needed all hands to dissemble and haul in jet speed. First, she called Robin. People in the restaurant business get to know people, so Exilee was sure she'd know how to reach Bruce's people who had showed up with the empty jars.

Exilee told Robin, "Do not under any circumstances tell anyone." The entire time Robin was trying to concentrate on the phone her momma, Gili, was bellyaching about being short on help and Robin begged. "Exilee needs me today. Just today,

Momma. It's important." Gili gave in and said that whatever was so important had better make her some money because she was not getting paid for her time off gallivanting. Robin slipped the memo pad used for take-out orders into her pocketbook and with the names and numbers of customers, specifically jar runnin' customers who ordered their exclusive half-price specials, she fired up her diesel to meet Exilee.

The two ladies excitedly conveyed to the jar runners that they were to bring screwdrivers and crowbars, five-pound hammers, rope, blankets, duct tape, any available dollies and anything else that they believed may be needed, and Pig Pen was told specifically to bring a pig, a large hungry pig. There were few questions. No hesitations. And they were so excited to be included in the repossession not one asked for monetary compensation.

Mr. Fisk and Wart lived and operated only twenty or so minutes away right off a major four lane highway where the exit into the sleepy town of Prospect slopes off. In the newer rig, Jake, Bruce and Kendall passed two rip roaring Mounties as Jake casually obeyed the speed limit and casually pulled into Mr. Fisk's and Warts' unleveled sandy road. The tractor trailer's air brakes shooed and shooed as it slowed to a stop near the unassuming tobacco barn just before the little ramshackle once-white house.

The old baccar barn that housed the big copper momma radiated the kind of sweet yeasty scents a bakery emits only there was corn sprouting up all around the barn like something'd been crapping it. Bruce marched right through the erupting piles and with a crowbar pried off a board from the barn's back wall. The black fabricated insulation board was thin and light. Ken pried off one end of a six by twelve heart pine board and they all peeped like schoolboys ogling over a show-show.

Meanwhile, under Mark's guidance, Ken pulled onto the dirt road that ran behind Bruce's old home place that had been sold six years before. Mark strained out the windows checking for witnesses. "This orange giant is extra loud now, huh?"

"Yep. Double that." Ken prayed aloud that the ruts weren't deeper than they looked.

"Dad liked the bright color 'cause he drives as slow as Christmas Eve. But you're right. It does seem extra loud," Ken opened the door when they reached the road-block boulders and Mark waited anxiously in the transfer truck. "How long are we supposed to wait?"

"We're not. Get out and help me." Ken closed the door and studied the large boulders flanking the drop off at the end of the dirt road. "They don't look fake," he yelled.

"Well they are," Mark gripped the lip of the window with his chin just over the edge.

"Aren't you something," Ken barked. "Come help me before someone hears this truck."

"Not with alligators out there. Hurry up." Mark leaned out looking and Ken groaned as he rolled the water laden vermiculite boulders to the wayside and looked down the drop off. "Good Lord." He worked up a good sweat and climbed back inside.

"I still don't see how this is gonna be an alibi," Mark called out.

"The trailers are identical. Everyone knows this truck belongs to my dad, best man in town. Bruce and Jake are going by Kendall's brother's loggin' site to get logs. They'll stack 'em around the copper sheets. It's right down the road from Fisk's. Fisk uses same outfit for logs to cook with. We'll say we unloaded logs or switched out trucks 'cause this one gave us trouble. All we gotta do is confuse the law if one of us gets pulled. That shouldn't be too difficult." Ken winked. "But pray anyway they don't get caught in the act. Don't believe we could get out of that."

"Hmph," Mark pondered, "what about serial numbers?"

"Nope, Dad and I made 'em. Did all the welding, the floors. The axles were bought used. No serial numbers. Just tags and I don't have 'em. Jake's got 'em."

"Shit. And exactly what are we going to tell the law when they ask why it's here?" Mark sassed. "You know someone's gonna call this in." Mark was truly clueless to the exact details of their position in the plan as he had had to walk off into the woods and take care of business while the plans were doled out.

Ken told Mark, "Be still, Mary Lou. You worry too much," and parked parallel to the big dark pond. Rippled waves rolled the old john boat tied to the rinky dink pier. It was missing an oar and was heavily littered with leaves and pine straw.

Mark blew up like a teenager. "So, already, what do we say? One could show up, ya know?" Mark studied the tall grasses as Ken got out. This time he left the door open.

"You're gonna overheat. Better get out." But Mark yelled, "I'm not kidding you. There's gators out here. Totens and haunts and probably some skeletons, too." When he couldn't see Ken, he panicked. "I'm tellin' ya, Old Man Black put 'em here to keep away instigators. Hey, get it, alligator, instigator?"

"Koom! Ka-boom!" Ken's .357 echoed as the alligator hissed its last.

Simultaneously, back at the sight of the repossession, the July sky burned bright red stripes down their hairlines. By the time Snap, Dodger and Cassie with her seven boys showed up, the entire back side of the baccar barn was laid open. They smiled up at the big copper momma. "Fisk and Wart secured?" Snap asked.

Bruce sucked the salt from his beefy lips. "Well, they're tied up somewhere."

Cassie scowled, "Explain dat."

"They weren't here. Went inside. No sign of 'em." When Bruce didn't ease her concern, Cassie hunted about like a yurker with a fishin' pole going to snag the rumored granddaddy bass. Bruce asked her, "What are you so fired up for? If we see 'em are you running out on us?" and Cassie scowled, "Our guillotine's gone. Bolts, too. Fools set on dying." Cassie's youngins cussed like everyone else, while Bruce was stuck on "fuck."

"I'll help ya' look. But it probably isn't here," Bruce fumed. "They'd a takin' it to the scrap yard. Paying good on steel." Cassie agreed, but didn't stop searching.

After Bruce and a few others had searched the back Cassie went around front and came back around cussing. "Keep your eyes open and put the word out." Cassie tucked her chin and aimed. "Bes a mommucked up life take our token. Bes a family thing. Ain't gonna have a bit a peace till its back wid me. Gotdat, Jack!" Snap assured her they'd get
it back. "Lordy, we's not all de sorry in the world got thieves on the swamp take yer tools of trade. Bes a price, Cassie dear. Heads will roll." Everyone got the picture as Stink dropped a big rock from a dirt mound, and it rolled to his momma feet and she glared at it like she already had the thief's head. "No peace for any a-us." She stood tall and rigid as she caught each eye.

"Where's that pig, Pen?" Bruce adamantly asked Pen.

Without so much of a grunt, Pen jogged to his momma's pick up and pushed and pushed the wooden crate down the planks. He lifted the cage door and guided him. "Where you want him?"

"That's no pig." Jake exclaimed as he backed up into a tree. "That's a hawg!"

"Figure the snakes are by the fixin's. Y'all help herd him inside." Bruce directed as he warily followed. "Can't believe Scarecrow's late. He's never late."

Snap stepped inside the barn scoping the walls, the junk, the crates and all the nooks and crannies. "Crow won't answer his phone. Must be his day off. Laid up, ya' reckon?"

Bruce squinted. "Poor Lilly." They quietly giggled as the huge hog's gonads bounced in conjunction with his aggressive rooting. He rooted and dug until his snout was covered in orange-red clay and had dug a fine hole next to the fixin's barrel where a sheet of tin was secured with two large field stones. "Stay back. Won't take him long."

Some swallowed their spit while others spat at the hawg. Dodger caught his teeth after an especially aggressive kapooey splat on the voracious beast's butt. Someone got its ribs. Spit spun down its spine and someone else crouched down and whizzed a line straight at its gonads while its head jerked up the tin lid over the snake pit.

The slithering mix squirmed and hissed. And Pen warned Dodger not to mess with his hawg as the hungry beast blissfully chomped with crunching grunts. Slimy wiggling sections slowly stilled as nasty red snake blood streaked the earthen clay floor and the hawg. Several grown men held their mouths shut. Some leapt about the baccar barn as snakes escaped the hawg's lethal jowls. Brazen Cassie stood firm with her legs braced for stompin' and Kendall held a garden hoe up like a dagger.

"I'm gonna vomit," Cassie's youngest told his momma.

"Gyet," she pushed him out while Dodger argued that the hawg would clean it up.

Snap asked Pen if he wanted a picture. "Yea, get that. We can sell tee shirts, Mom. Whadayathink?" Pig Pen clapped for his snake eatin' hawg as Snap took pictures with his cell phone. "Looky, he's got two and there's one biting his belly. Get that, Snap."

Snap took the pictures and then ran at the hawg with an old baccar stick and batted the snake that was wrapped around its head, but its fangs were lodged like a fish-hook. "I can't get it off. That moccasin'll kill him."

"Not Snowball, Ma," Cassie's youngest scrambled toward the hawg as Pen snatched him up from the back of his jeans. His legs thrashed in the air. "Not my pig." His red afro shook like cheerleaders' pom poms.

"Get back, Snap. Move," Cassie commanded as the beast spun in rage at Snap who, from the pig's point of view, was a competitor for his snake dinner. As the hawg spread his jowls to bite Snap snake chunks fell from between his giant crusty canines while smaller chunks stuck. With one coiled snake atop his head with imbedded fangs and another still lodged to its belly it snorted twice before lunging. Snap sprung up the side of the baccar barn clinging onto an axe hewn log and shimmied up into the rafters like he still had a lot of yurker left in his fifty-year-old bones and the threatening hawg rooted up at Cassie. She voraciously clapped as it neared and the clapping spawned, diverting the hawg back to the pit for more snakes.

"Snakes don't kill pigs," Dodger plainly spoke up at Snap in the rafters. Then explained, "Bes fat ta take in da posin."

"Ohh," Snap climbed down.

Bruce checked out the cooking pit. A suspended black iron hanger held an old black iron cooking vessel. He heisted the lid. Dropped it and coughed like he'd hurl. "Snakes, snake stew." He stepped out back and was quickly freed of his heavy breakfast. Cassie was first to mention that there should be some concern over whether the humongous copper vat was full. She panged the side with her open palm and when she couldn't determine pulled a flathead screwdriver from her painter's jean's loop and gave it hard knock. The big copper momma sloshed. The smile on her face grew until she looked like the kid on the snack cake packages, full of sugar and spice and freckled and nice. Only she had a wicked little laugh.

"Should I mension hit?" Pen wandered about the vessel with his finger up like he's bound to find an inscription with increments. "Snowball's probably thirsty now. But not that thirsty." Cassie's other sons scrounged up several Styrofoam cups and chipped bowls and hurriedly rinsed 'em with the hosen off the other side of the baccar barn.

When the youngest one held up a pitcher without a handle to Pen, he discreetly told him not to let Ma see, but she was already on to 'em and hurried around to the hosen. The various vessels cleared the boys' heads as she flung them into the woods and Pen shoved the pitcher into a mess of jars with his boot.

Kendall chuckled as he used his electronic tablet to calculate figures as he paced off the vat's circumference, "one hundred two," then guesstimated height, "one hundred fifty ish."

The big copper momma moaned. Kendall anxiously looked for Bruce and he told him to hold on, that it was too late. The zealous helpers had already unscrewed bolts from the highest areas they could reach without a ladder as Kendall announced that the big copper momma will hold five thousand gallons.

The gaping hole screeched like a hawk before a kill as snakes spewed out of the pit when the yeasty half-brewed likker gushed from the four by eight and growing hole. Big fat brown ones with hexagonal designs on their backs, yellow bellied, those perty red, black and yellow ones that are poisonous and the same colored ones that weren't, washed up onto the clay floor and went crawling up anything and anyone. Poor Pen's pig was full as a hawg and he grunted and groaned as Pen pushed his bulging balking ass back toward the snakes.

Pen screamed like his butt was on fire, as he grabbed his left cheek but the snake bit deeper. He slapped at his hawg chasing after the snake on his butt as the hawg proved how fast he could run. Cassie told him to turn around and hit him in the snout as she chased after them. While the men in the barn fought off snakes with rakes, shovels and baccar sticks, stabbing the wet snakes crawling all over like they were in a tizzy. They dumped the dead snakes at the edge of the woods where there was a mess of metal and engine parts, pure tee junk and a few good grocery carts. The snakes hung over and on in every which a way and Snap took their picture. They became seriously determined and knocked some snakes off some tall metal parts in the pile and hauled them into the baccar barn to stand on while they dissembled the big copper momma.

Back at the alligator hidey hole, Ken showed off his handgun in a most threatening manner and Mark whined but pinched his nose and obeyed. The dead alligator had released a belly full of the nastiest, rottenest, most sulfuric and almost silent gas imaginable. The two hurried past the stink and Mark lunged into the John boat.

"Oh, my gawd. Oh, my gawd." He jumped in with both feet making the boat jar from side to side as Ken struggled to untie the seasoned rope's knot.

"What are we doing out here?" Mark cried as he sat down on the small plank seat and the little boat shimmied. Ken kicked the boat from the pier, and it rattled off uneasily as he took up the only oar and explained the most pertinent part of the plan Mark happened to miss out on. "You're gonna pull up a prize and load it on the flatbed."

With the oar in one hand and gun in the other Ken exaggeratedly grinned from the rinky dink pier.

"You're freakin' crazy. You're trying to kill me off. You know all about Bruce being the one, don't cha? You know I'm next in line, don't cha?" Mark ranted, "And I don't believe Bruce told you to do this. Did he?" Mark attempted to stand in the small craft and it dangerously tipped. "You'll get caught. My momma'll search the ends of the earth for her boy. She'll never stop, I tell ya. We're royal blood, Ken Crowson. The Society'll come for you, too, and your boy. They'll want an eye for an eye. That's how they are. We're cut-throat." Mark took in a deep breath and Ken finally blinked just as Mark became determined and paddled with his hands. "Keep your hands out of the water," Ken warned as the rolling black waters propelled the little boat. Mark grabbed a hold of his seat. Stiffened and tried his best not to breathw, just in case an alligator sensed his heartbeat drumming acid rock through his nervous ass.

They both gawked as the lumpy back surfaced. Ken nervously aimed and Ally got pissed. With its giant white snout snared open it rushed the bank toward Ken. "Koom! Ka-Boom!" the .357 did not echo further for the bullet lodged deep in the abyss.

Ally's middle suddenly blew up like a balloon with the echoing charge and deflated just as suddenly. The alligator closed its mouth and slowly rolled and sunk. One big bubble later several little bubbles spawned and what seemed like hundreds of little baby alligators swarmed from the banks into the water as Ken squealed to the end of the rinky dink pier with both the gun and the oar.

As the gentle undertow of the water lured the john boat to the dam and within reach of reeds, Mark prepared. "Do you see a chain? There's supposed to be a chain over there. Look for it. You gotta pull it up before you get out. Bruce said you'll never reach it from the bank. That's the way his old man did it." Ken yelled the instructions as he kept watch.

"I see something." Mark took off his tennis shoe and gently paddled.

"Just let the boat wander over on its own. It'll go straight to it, according to Bruce." Ken
blew and Mark fumed, "Well fuck you. He also said only one gator was left." The water calmed as the trees held their bird songs like cork lined walls and their heartbeats drummed like the firing squad's death march to the boat's hypnotic rhythm.

"Must be the water inlet." Mark looked over his shoulder to Ken. "What am I going to pull up? I have a right ta know."

Ken studied the perimeter. "Look for a jar inside another jar."

"A jar? That's it! Bruce can do this shit himself. He's always Tom Sawyering some idiot into doing his mess. But it won't be me. Not this time." Mark reached for the reeds on the bank and was about to step out when Ken fired a shot. "You didn't!" Mark trembled.

"I don't know why I care or what all this is about, but my dear wife thinks she's gonna save the world if we can help. Now pull that damn chain up right now!"

"You stupid hayseed. We'll both end up in jail over this. Stealin', or attempted stealing
anyway. Crap. They can book us on killing endangered species, too." Mark hit the boat's rim with clenched fists. "How did you ever become a teacher? You can't teach shit. I don't see anything."

Ken did his best not to impede the insipid punk or shoot a hole in the John boat by keeping aimed at the ground in case of an accidental reflex. "Boy, we tell the law we're waitin' on

Kendall's driver to deliver with his loggin' equipment. We got yellow tape to string around the loblollies and any oak under three feet around. That's one alibi. And we can kill any alligator that threatens our lives while we're doing business. It's legal. Got it?" he paused. "Now get the damn chain so we can get back in the truck."

When the logger's diesel engine putts and purrs down the rutted gravel road Ken shrugged and headed back to his truck and Mark cried like a little girl. "Get back here with that gun. You better watch over me." But Ken kept walking. "You better not let anything happen to me," Mark cried as Ken waved for Kendall's brother to come on down to the grassy path. "I mean it," Mark yelled. "Okay, I'm pulling up this stupid ass chain!"

It didn't take long for the swarm of young alligators to feast on the freshly killed mature Ally, considering they hadn't had any fish to eat and all the frogs were et and there's nothing left except extremely thirsty birds and occasional squirrels, feral dogs and occasional strangers. Not long at all.

Mark noticed their beady red eyes blinking up at him as he nervously grasped the slimy jar and quickly unclasped the steel clasp from the chain and made quick notice of the steel guideline attached to the water inlet and John boat and went starboard to work his way back to the pier and the jar rolled against a sharp shim and it broke open exposing the clear jar within containing a hand-written paper.

Back at the snake ranch, the jokes were told on Mr. Fisk and Wart and the jar runners began to tease Bruce for acting like he cared for their wellbeing. "Can't afford chicken. They use every dime on raw product," He walked around back, "Looks like they gave up on the pig business again. They'll be tore up about those snakes."

"Snakes, soldiers, whatever," Pig Pen crushed a Styrofoam cup as Cassie neared and cussed, "This is good medicine. Feels good." His stubbed arm raised with his whole arm, "Knows it now. Killing off the cheatin' whites and taking back what was already ours to begin with," his arms clasped one over the other and the rattletrap truck sputtered down the sandy drive, "Good," he smirked, "medicine.

Bruce pushed his screwdriver into the back of his jeans and marched straight-on as the long-haired driver checked out all the vehicles and the transfer truck. One by one, the jar runners peered from the baccar barn as Bruce and Cassie faced off and a passenger slowly emerged from the rear window. With a floppy sage-green turban wrapped around his head, Wart purged from the backseat window like a sloth as his signature wart at the end of his nose hit the light of day. He wiped his eyes as he took in the bate of 'em and cried as he rolled up the window.

"I know that hair." Cassie's boy with the lisp whistled for Bruce. "That's your cuz's hair." Bruce gapped, "Mark's?" and the yurker declared, "He sold it. I was there." Cassie looked back at her boy like she's fixin' to whopicoddle his yurker tail, but instead just gave him the hush signal.

Bruce practically danced, "Mr. Fisk, you've changed," he said as he jerked off the badly made homemade wig and Fisk spat a wad of black nasty and it streamed down his chin. "Swanny, you'se a jubious sight on my side a' da swamp." Fisk flicked his wrist over at his barn as his face grew good and hot. "Think I don't know what yer runners are up to?" He spat out a yellowish-brown drizzle daringly aimed at Bruce.

"I'm taking my copper vat and all its parts, *and* its finely engineered improvements, you did good by the way, as payment for the pallets of shine you stole." Bruce stepped closer while Snap took pictures and Kendall took video with his tablet.

"You think I won't steal it back?" When Fisk grinned like he's got the game by the tail his mostly toothless gap sucked in air making him whistle. Wart mumbled from his seat somewhat safe in the yellow car that Bruce had something in his pants and Fisk licked across his toothless top lip and panted. "Too hot for this today, Buddyrow. Let's make a deal."

"No deals."

"Bes dat bear charm on yer a-neck? That'd make it even." Mr. Fisk's thin eyebrows danced.

"Shit," Bruce growled and pulled down his neckline and Fisk's face faded white as his once white house. "Only way you'd know about that is if you had eyes on me last night. Is your grunt gonna make it? He lost a lot of blood."

"Bes a tuff un," Fisk growled back. His beady eyes all but disappeared under his swollen lids. "That Indian trinket da only charm you wearin' dese days?" Fisk trembled.

When Jake sprinted toward the porch and told Fisk to stay out of Bruce's business Dodger told him to stay out of it, and with a stern squint, so did Bruce. Wart rolled down his window and Bruce's chest heaved up like it had done the night before, "You gonna die today?" and Wart rolled up the window.

Fisk lowered his head like he was gonna pray and his bald spot shined up at 'em from between the two un kept piles of gray curls at his ears, and he pushed his glasses up and took a deep breath. "Thoust may have it." His humped back lowered in a slight bow as his outstretched palms shone up and he mockingly mumbled, "Your Highness."

Bruce leaned close, "Whad you say?"

Fisk slyly straightened as best he could with his hump. "Get it out a here 'fore I change my mind."

Cassie's youngest yelled, "Hineys. That weirdo called Bruce a hiney, Ma," as his red afro cheered. "Git over here." Cassie pointed down to her side like she possessed a telekinetic ray and slid the yurker in and held him by the scalp.

"You need that still, Mr. Fisk." Bruce rubbed his backside, "You can't just give it to me…without a fight," Bruce focused on Mr. Fisk's beguiling smile and was paralyzed like he'd been snake bit by a mighty moccasin.

With a sweeping hand, Fisk dismissed him. "Get it out a here. Still's got a Toten on it. Taint made a good batch in her yet. Just get it out a' here." Mr. Fisk's back humped over like he was plum tuckered out as Wart slithered out from the car limping and went around the front balancing on the hood. Safely at the once white house's rickety front porch they woke a fat old coon hound with a booted nudge so they could open the front door. The dog managed two steps and threw itself back down when suddenly Pen's hawg jogged past. "Ya got my snakes?" "What about dinner?" Wart cried.

"Jus be," Mr. Fisk patted his old friend's shoulder. "We bes all right." He whipped around to Bruce. "Throw out my snake stew?"

"Didn't touch it."

Fisk curled his top lip up at Bruce. "We'll get a bog together," Fisk comforted Wart. "Come on, now. A few ellicks and I'll hit the creek up for a nice moccasin or two and raise another mess. I'll let you stomp 'em this time and I'll hold the sack. Would you like that?"

"Oh, Fisks," Wart's lisp begged, "My leg," he stopped and began again, "Bes all de sorry in the world you bes bit by a posnis un. I holds de sack. I dos it. Okay?" Fisk agreed as he held the door and Wart wobbled inside.

"You haven't fooled anybody here, but yourselves," Bruce challenged, "We know you two ran up on us and then spent the night at the hospital and don't have a damn thing to show for it."

"I swanny, boy," Mr. Fisk flanked the front porch like he was fixin' to declare war. "Thoust more trouble now you got all brickhouse. Mess easier when you was no more'n us'ns." He let the door slam and the coon hound stirred to stand taking notice of all the trespassers and wagged his tail before tucking in for another nap.

Snap took a picture of the sleeping hound with Bruce in the foreground and turned to the runners and took a shot of them as they threw their hands up in disbelief. Even Bruce. "Well, you heard him. Let's get 'er done. Don't rush too hard, now." He trailed off in thought as he whistled a light-hearted tune.

"Yes!" Jake's joy sent him practically skipping back to the baccar barn like a yurker after sweetnins. "Hey," Bruce pulled on Jake's arm, "Get your phone and try Edge before Snap breaks my legs. Lord, I hope she wasn't pulled."

"I bet you do." Jake asked Bruce for her number and realized that his friend wouldn't know it either. "Should I make Snap think I want a date with Edge, or what?" "I don't care. Yea, say it's a date."

Snaps' callused hands were thick and burly like he'd been turning wrenches or turning tractors inside out. He snapped out one bolt after the other in the time it took Jake to unscrew one. "Hey," Jake casually called to him down from the ladder, "can I have Edge's phone number?"

"Naw." Snap climbed higher and snapped out another and it barely missed Jake's head, "Edge is at home. Busted out a' folly's ditch."

"Oh, no, she wrecked?"

Cassie sashayed over and patted Jake on the back. "She got away." Cassie winked. "Bes brothers on the swamp. Nuttin' goes down we don't know." She gently palmed his scarred cheek and boldly reached down into his front jean's pocket and pulled out his keys, "Thoust pearl token, for instance." Cassie dangled it over his head.

Chapter 9

Stolen Treasures Now

A year and a half since Jake's first speech, an officer shifted into the corner and his badge flashed like the prim lady's silver slippers. Miss Lucy shuffled her feet and signaled the genealogical society's meeting to commence. "Welcome, Mr. Jake Wilkes," said the president, with one arm cocked off his side like a Cardinal's flapping wing, he motioned their guest to the podium. The club's president pushed up his thick black-rimmed glasses with the tip of his trimmed fingernail, "We can't stop talking about this," He coyly looked down and over the rim of his glasses to the prim lady seated near the podium before sliding onto a seat behind a small desk alongside the wall where his bright red pants jutted out.

The desk was stacked with three rows of Jake's controversial articles and his new business cards. Over the desk was a new black and white banner: "Coming soon! Tuscarorians' 21st Century War," the title of Jake's book co-authored by H. Prickenwrath. As the officer in the corner shifted his rifle, so did the officer on the podium's far right, while Guilford County's Chief of Police motioned to his man out in the parking lot sharing donuts with the UC Feds to get into position.

"Out of North Carolina's sixty-five thousand registered Lumbee's we could only make room here tonight for one hundred and still maintain fire code. Thank you for squeezing in. I am Jake Wilkes, rumored as the 21st century *sidekick* of Bruce Black, your famous Tuscarora hero, like your Henry Berry Lowery of the 19th century. Bruce and I grew up together here in Robeson County where I operate his business with twenty-three full time employees, Zoskiroro's and we are branching out to the Bertie County area with another winery and plan to reclaim the East Coast in the name of the friendly Indians, Blount's Tuscaroras. This, my friends," Jake's zeal snapped, "is the power of the blood! So powerful, that even in his absence, his work continues." He waved a deep purple scarf flagging the Tusc's colors and draped it over the podium.

"I have learned so much about the Tuscaroras now and want you to know that it is not easy to find credible resources. False narratives based on erroneous or biased data, and authors working to set agendas fill library shelves and continually label the Peoples of Robeson County as Lumbee and there's a ton of it *written by* "Lumbees." For instance, scholars know perfectly well to use concise language and when they do not, it is seen as an intentional tactic to draw the reader away from the facts to set agendas. For example, when a scholar writes that "Croatan chiefs" did this or that, instead of "Tuscarora chiefs," the inference is that "Lumbee chiefs" did this or that. Because the Lumbee were once named Croatan.

But Croatan is the name of an island where Tuscarora traded and lived, and the name Croatan became an official name of the People of Robeson County who are now named Lumbee.

Croatan Island is Hatteras Island, home of the Mighty Tuscarora. See, how that false narrative pushes the Lumbee agenda? It erases the Tuscarora history.

Another example is population errors. A study in 1997 records the total population of Tuscarora in 1712 of the Roanoke, Tar, and Contentnea Creek settlements was close to 8,000 individuals and that they've been here since 800 AD. [52] That was before the war and they took a 20% loss, so the population would be about 6000 to 5000 Tuscarora remaining in the area after about 250 went to New York. But the book, *Indians of North Carolina*, rounds them up at only 6000 before the war. [53] A 2000 difference may seem like a piddly argument, but when we discuss how a family grows, that 2000 difference is very significant.

I'm a gonna tell you why.

On page 16 in the 1988 *Lumber River Scenic & Wild River Report* states that there were **thousands** of Natives in Robeson County living along the river. [54] Not a few hundred survivors of the Tuscarora War and oppressive 1714 law, but thousands of people who made thousands more, etcetera, etcetera. The Hatteras Tuscarora had found a new swamp among the pines to call home. And you are still here.

I am confident when I say Tuscarora, because of all of the strong lineage testimony," Jake held up his notecards, "straight from their mouths, have said they are Tuscarora, like Henry Berry Lowrey. Tuscarora lineage is proven from the time of whites writing history: Sarah Kearsey, William Locklear,

Ishmael Chavers, Cannon Cumbo, Aaron Brooks, Malina Chavis Brayboy, Allen Lowry, [55] and there's more on the 1790 Robeson County Census.

Historical documents need to be brought to light and the so-called scholarly works of those pushing false narratives need to be burned!" Jake's palms flashed, "I say this because false narratives can fool even lifelong scholars," he cocked a smile, "Don't burn any books. I just got carried away in the moment. Now, there's a history professor who has honors up and down and had not discovered the research I found when he wrote his report that there were only a *few hundred* Tuscarora here in Robeson County after the war. [56] This was based on the same research that all the Lumbee scholars and powerhouses use to say that there is no way all the Peoples are Tuscarora, rationalizing that there must've been other tribes. The difference of setting agendas with false narrative is motive. The history professor was working to assist the Tuscarora and I happen to know he was rushed in preparing it, and that he used research he'd gathered which was known to be credible.

But there were not hundreds, there were thousands of Tuscarorians living in your swamps and if there were other tribes, they were absorbed by the Mighty Tuscarora. It is the nature of their People. They only denied Tusc heritage to survive because of the 1714 trade laws, the threats and oppression.

Now that report was sent to the state in a recognition package that was denied. Granted, it wasn't denied based on this report, but the numbers matter because we are talking about how many Tuscarora were here and not how many "others," like the Lumbee claim. It is the "others" that steal the Tuscarora history and their futures."

"You will find a copy of this ground-breaking map on the second page of your flyer, and here it is living large," his vivid smile outshined the bright screen.

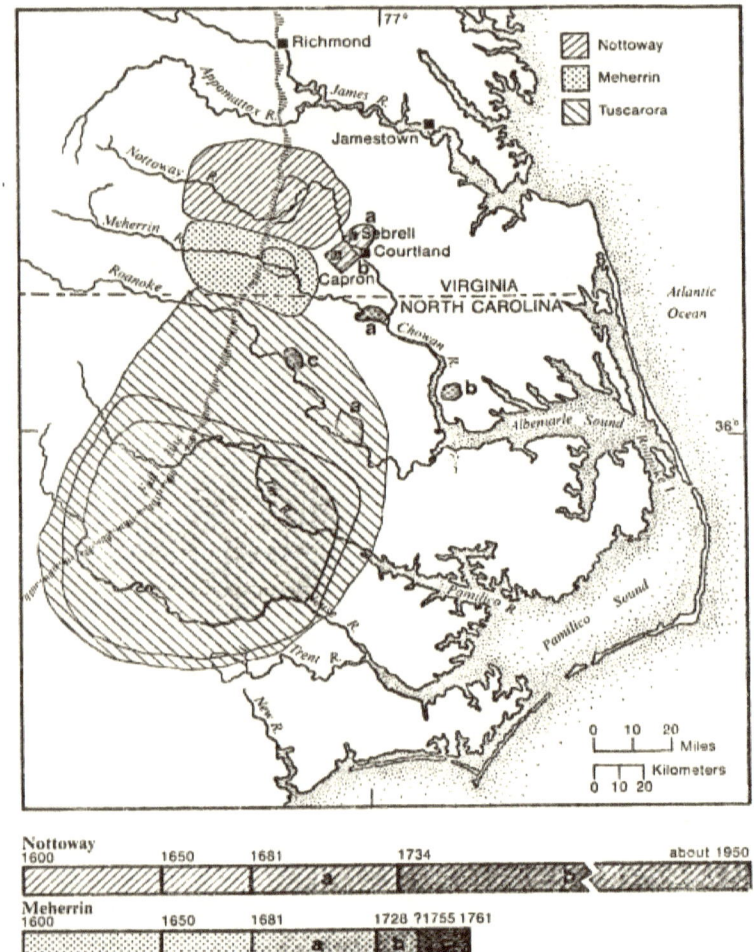

Fig. 1. Territory of the Tuscarora, Meherrin, and Nottoway in Va. and N.C.

Source: Handbook of the North American Indians, volume 15, Northeast, Bruce G. Trigger, ed. (Washington, D.C.: Smithsonian Institution, 1978), p. 282.

"Tuscarora's were the hardiest of Indians and traded with sailors from foreign continents and other tribes. It is in their blood to be independent, to overcome and proliferate, to become legends, like our Bruce Black and Henry Berry Lowery."

Honking and angry shouts continued from the roadway, filtering into the conference room as red and white lights periodically swept through the transom windows, illuminating the standing audience and the television crew. Lumbee picketers chanted on the sidewalk, pounding their signs echoing through membrane strands until it played a chorus of warring drumbeats and indiscernible words as if the indoor audience was being serenaded by people who spoke a different tongue.

Ladies smiled up at Jake with raised shoulders and cocked smiles. Even if Jake didn't have his dusty albeit respectable light gray cowboy hat resting in his chair and scuffed cowboy boots and the kind of jeans loose only in the tail where you can tell a man is used ta' struggling with heavy equipment like tractors and wrestling cows and such, any woman would've said that he's a hardcore cowboy. His neck and forearms, all tanned and muscular, had veins like heavy duty power cords pokin' up each time he tapped the podium to still the applause. The prim lady stared up at his bright green eyes and layered blonde hair, silky as a show pony's mane, as she twirled a pencil in her grown out salt and pepper page until the eraser pulled strands into a knot and she awkwardly chirped as she yanked it out.

Jake took up the microphone and walked to the front center aisle, "You're here tonight because you want to know why "Lumbees" are disenrolling from the tribe. You want to know the facts about your heritage and you want someone to put on a new roof on your granny's house and a bowl of chicken bog on every table," his dimples dug as pleasant laughter spilled across the rows of cushioned folding chairs. "Why would people expect their blood brothers and sisters to "do" for them? Tribal belief systems? Yes, and retribution," he bent at the waist and squinted down the aisles, "The American Federal Government has taken the Peoples land, heritage, language, their entire identity and now the People are oppressed economically, logistically and educationally, by the same group.

Why are the People reaching out to the same group who stole everything from them when there is a larger group, an older group, a group with ties so deep in this land, that your People carry their names?

The settlers stole their lands and wouldn't let the People hunt and fish in the plentiful forests. This is when the People got mad enough to kill and this is when their People were sold into slavery when captured alive. Pennsylvania bought so many native slaves from North Carolina that they didn't know what to do with them all, and on top of that, the Five Nations threatened war, so the whites passed a law in 1705 not to sell anymore, but they did. There's proof. In 1710, the Mighty Tuscarora sent a petition of their own to stop the enslavement of their women and children. All this, and the 1714 trade law drove the Peoples to try to fit in as best they could to trade and survive amongst their conquerors. The same people who enslaved their Peoples and raped their women and forced them to breed with white slave owners and black slaves to produce more slaves."

He scanned their faces, "Forget the Lumbee Tribe now, it's not their fault for anything going on in your life unless you are dependent on them for your existence. You get that? A Tuscarora carries the blood of aboriginals, independent People. There are two sets. One is in New York and they don't want anything to do with North Carolina's Tuscaroras unless it means taking up on old deeds like in Bertie County."

Click. The screen's text flashed. "Let's read this," Jake said, "It's from a letter to his majesty requesting permission to help save King Blount from his own People. Remind you of the situation here with the Lumbee claiming the Tuscarora as a "splinter tribe"?"

Ordered That a patent Issue as prayed for Tom Blount, Chief man of the Tuscarora Indians having represented to this Board that he has certain Intelligence of several of the Northern Indians that design to make him a Visit this fall with an Intent to seduce the young men of his nation from him in order to Comit mischief on him and on the white people begging the assistance of this Governmt That some Englishmen may be sent to his Town to lay them out a ffort to prevent the Dangers threatened from the sd Northern Indians which this Board taking into their serious consideration and finding upon the

like Complaint during the administracon of the late Governor assistance was sent to him being agreeable to the treaty with him and his People Do therefore Order that Mr William Charlton have power to procure Six able body'd young men for the service aforesaid and that he forthwith see them at Rasewtokee there to assist the said Indians in laying out and making them a ffort and that the sd William Charlton continue with them as Interpreter for which service the Honoble the Presit is disired to give each of the men so Imployed a Certificate for the time they

are upon the said service on the publick for their wages
and to Mr Charleton as Interpreter the Secty indorsing
upon the order the names of the persons so Imployed [57]

Jake held up a loose-leaf binder, "This is the lineage of
Blount's Tuscarora who have lived on the swamp since they
were starved out of their Indian Woods in 1700's by the
oppressive 1714 trade law created by their conquerors.[58] The
ancestors of these Tuscarora are the Native Americans of
Robeson County, North Carolina.

Now. Are you going to let the Lumbee control your
existence? Are you going to enroll for that little card that
identifies you as a member of the so-called tribe so you will fit
in, so you will get a job? I know the discrimination around here.
Lumbees hire Lumbees, just the way it is. Unless you have the
blood. The blood of an aboriginal Tuscarorian."

"Bruce Black had the blood. Bruce sat in prison for six
years and read every book pertaining to the history of Tuscarora
and books on law and how to write professionally and he wrote
and wrote and wrote. Bruce wrote to the mother of his sister's
people. When I say his sister's people, I am addressing the
origins of the gray eyes. The Mighty Tuscaroras took in the Lost
Colony's survivors and they worked their copper and their blood
united. Get over it. Acknowledge it. Embrace it. Your destiny is
larger than you ever imagined and as soon as we have the
support of a majority of Tuscaroras we will proceed to reveal
documents that will change the course of your history. There is
safety in numbers and the threats have been recorded and

continue to be recorded. The disenrollment will empower the Tuscarora to build their own "El Dorado."

Jake aimed at the projector screen and an English royal is quoted, "In colonization, we won the battle but lost the war for those who had signed treaties in peace with us in the 1700's. We vow to work with your country to make reparations."

Silence lingered as their eager shoulders reclined and Jake flipped through his note cards before he solemnly continued. "Before I ever got out of the truck, I prayed y'all would be open to this. I'm asking a lot. I realize that, for you to risk your most cherished treasures, for our Lumbee guests here, the very core of their self-existential beliefs. My best friend, my Buddyrow, died in my arms. It made headlines. I'm doing this for him. It's all he ever talked about." Jake sipped water from his favorite cup and when he sat it down on the small serving tray it sang, "T-t-tink," from its fine silver fluted form.

As the lights dimmed, a single shaft of light filtered up through the suspended royal blue carpet fibers to the overhead projector's screen. Click. The screen lit up with bold text:

In 1609, a Native informant called Machumps told a writer named Strachey who was working on the history of the colony how the colonists had survived. Machumps said that "the People have houses built with stone walls, and one story above another, so taught them by those English who escaped the slaughter at Roanoak." The copper mines of Ritanoc where the Tuscarora worked the seven surviving English colonists; four men, two boys, and a young maid, is in our

backyard: Randolph County. This is paramount evidence because, number one, it places the Tuscarora here in the 1600's.

And number two, it provides explanation: The English's work ethics saved them. Machumps said the lost colonists lived peaceably for "20 and odd" years with Natives until attacked by Chief Powhatan's warriors. This chief was also known as Wahunsonacock. [59]

"All these details of the precious ones," Jake tucked his chin and deepened his voice, "The royal English knew," his eerie words vibrated, "Other native tribes knew. Everyone who counted knew where the lost colonists were and with whom. You, my friends, have been fed a sack of sassafras and pay to see it again and again at their plays. People just love some sweet mystery crap all decorated with killing and royals." He spun on his heels and turned back with a loaded hand, "Look-y here: When the English were taught how to grow tobacco and saw how the Native Peoples were addicted, they had already found their "El Dorado" gold and those colonists were nothing more than dust in the wind," his voice softened, "Those English never came back seeking their lost ones again. You have been used and abused. Sue the U.K. for abandonment. You'd get funds and still have your freedom."

"The Croatans were defined *by the whites* as the South's mix of Native Peoples, meaning they had Native, white, and black blood." When Jake directed them to the woman on the screen the audience grinned up at the bare breasted lady with dark wavy hair and light eyes like they'd just won an Island vacation. "This could be the image of any woman born in Robeson County. Tuscaroras who absorbed the colonists were named Croatans *by the whites* in 1885; a group of white men who made up the rules. Really? Do you think the Mighty Tuscarora forgot who they were? Most couldn't read to vote and those who could were bamboozled by their own preachers who told them that by signing on with the state as Croatans, their people would get education, and they did, a couple of years later. But it was too late for the indigenous natives – the Mighty Tuscarora. Their name had already been changed, and the only reason the name was changed was to erase their heritage.

These whites knew who the Mighty Tuscs were and they knew their people from the second colonization attempt were captured by these mighty warriors and did not want to be held responsible for *not attempting* to "save them" and by erasing their heritage, erased their responsibility to pay reparations. The white government could have just as easily funded an educational system for this rural area leaving the heritage intact. But no, hate got in the way of that too."

Jake took a deep breath and grasped the podium, "Do you hear me? The whites purposefully erased your heritage so they would not be required to pay reparations."

"So much of the foundation of the white's written history is all wrong. They believed the lost colonists blended with Algonquins when it was the Mighty Tuscarora who seized them and benefited greatly from their coppersmith skills and building techniques. We got that covered already." Click. The screen read:

Washington's Indian Office did not know of the existence of Croatan Indians until 1889 when 54 of these Indians sent a petition for financial aid listing themselves as descendants of White's Lost Colony.

The Ethnological response: No trace of the colonists was found except the word Croatan carved upon a tree. Lawson (surveyor who tricked Natives and sold their lands and was set afire to burn to death) however, 100 years later found the colonists had blended with the Hatteras – the Hatteras Tuscarorians. [60]

"Lawson's account is arrogant, but it is logical." Click. The screen read:

A farther Confirmation of this we have from the Hatteras Indians, who either then lived on Ronoak-Island, or much frequented it. These tell us, that several of their Ancestors were white People, and could talk in a Book [read], as we do; this Truth of which is confirmed by gray eyes being found frequently amongst these Indians, and no others. They value themselves extremely for their Affinity to the English, and are ready to do them all friendly Offices. It is probable, that this Settlement miscarry'd for want of timely Supplies from England' or thro' the Treachery of the Natives for we may reasonably suppose that the English were forced to cohabit with them for Relief and Conversation and that in process of Time, they conform'd

themselves to the Manners of their Indian Relations. And thus we see, how Human Nature is to degenerate. [6]

"John Lawson thought highly of himself to add that last line," Jake shook his head. "Anyway, the Hatteras Tuscarora are written in official Washington records as the aboriginals who blended with America's first Christians, the lost colonists," his hayseed bangs tapped above his greens flashing "go!" "Since 1889, Washington has *officially recognized* who these people are, has had the records, and continually denied reparations because they owe them everything. Millions and millions in funds and lands. They know people," his testosterone rose as his warrior blood pumped, "They know," he marched back and forth across the podium, stopping at the podium, and thrusting it forward before blowing a cleansing breath.

"Each one of you has a handout listing the documented facts of the Tuscarora Peoples. Every single word is documented in Washington, DC. They know who you are." Jake tapped at the screen and an archeological dig uncovered bones from an ancient burial ground. "The Tuscarora of New York do not care about the remains of their people held at the university here, ECU, or they would collect them, wouldn't they? Anyone here *not* disturbed by the idea of digging up their people?"

When no one raised their hand, Jake stomped his boot and the podium echoed, "If the Tuscarora of North Carolina are not recognized and given sovereignty, more ancient grounds in Bertie county are up for digging if the People do not get recognized somehow, be it federal, or creating their own village with a trust under a corporation. There was a previous dig a few years ago. Now, lost colony theorists have their eyes on a second site. This group of theorists is largely anthropologists, history professors and lawyers. People with funds and political ties. I interviewed them and was told that all it takes is money.

Now ask yourselves, "How did the act for the Lumbee to add the Tuscarora as a "splinter group" go down so quickly?"

Jake viciously clapped, "Reality check! Other federally recognized tribes and Americans make fun at our Peoples because they are an *obviously* blended people. The swamp was an ideal place for anyone who needed to escape persecution. People were drawn to one another then, just like they are now, and races continually mix." Click. The screen's text read: **Graffenried's manuscript relaying his experience with colonization in volume 1 of NC Colonial Records, page 981. I also noticed among the Indians...rites that come nearer to christian divine worship...In the midst of this heathenish chapel...Facing the rising sun, was planted in the ground a wooden post, with a carved head, painted half red and half white. In front of it stood a big stick with a small crown at its end, wrapped up in red and white; on the other side, which looks towards the setting sun, was another image, with a horrid face painted black and red. By the first, they mean some god and by the other the Demon, which they know far better.**

This last statement, "which they know far better," is Graffenried's opinion, not an observation of their worship. Based on this, Graffenried was biased. [62]

"Graffenried wrote this in the 1700's and his bias has bled straight-on to 2020. Scholars quote his material, infected with the same Graffenried hate this man had when he came to The New World and traded the Tuscarora out of a chunk of land for his 400 Swiss and German friends, and bleeds out the Tuscarora truths. Which is, they wanted peace and fairness just like they do today. Not hate.

I've interviewed lots of families here and when a proud Lumbee woman said, "There's no nigger in my blood," their friends' children hid behind their parents. I must of looked like I was in shock because I was then told, "That's how it is in Robeson County," and I wanted to say, "All y'all need to get over it! Prejudice keeps your people down and it must stop, or you will never ever overcome the self-existential crisis that plagues all of you," but I was far outnumbered and real close to the swamp. Know what I mean?" Grunts and bobbing heads fell like dominoes.

"Another tie to an outside race is traced to pre-Columbian voyages in the fourteenth century when English Protestants were under persecution. Portuguese were leaders among seaman. They made the craft, the sails and the seas their own and were hired to explore The New World under Columbus. The Portuguese seamen were a rough and tumble lot, hardy as the life aboard ship claimed them, and their language reflected such.

And Portuguese settlements were within Tuscarora range. As we know, language is a strong origin indicator. Scholars point out the Portuguese vowel usage, such as 'oy' in the so-called Lumbee language. The use of present tense such as 'I am' instead of 'I did,' 'I be' instead of 'I have' or 'I will,' and dropping the 'g's' from plurals. An example of common Robeson County vernacular is 'I'm bes fixin' to whoop up a mess a' chicken bog." [63] Audience members varied from giggles to dropped jaws and furrowed brows. "So, let's add Portuguese to that Lumbee language definition that all y'all Tuscs speak when you're on the swamp."

"Bullshit."

The officer cleared his throat and Jake testified, "The four-thousand proud Tuscarora of Robeson County are working on restoring their native Iroquoian language and no longer promote the local vernacular. They are promoting their traditional culture as they have practiced for centuries. But all y'all get on the swamp when you're with friends. It's your community's language. Just happens that the Lumbee claim to own it."

"God knows why the Lumbee Tribe has its childrens' program learning the Tuscarora language. Seems like identity theft to me, but what do I know; I'm white."

Click. The screen shadowed over them as a dazzling dark-skinned 1500's soldier threatened while Jake read from his note cards.

"I wanna show you how history gets twisted, how ancient hate speech poisons us now. It is fact that in 1500, Natives were being exterminated during Spanish colonization in The New World and replaced with Africans. It is also fact, as documented by Hodge's *Handbook of North American Indians North of Mexico*, that intermarriage practices grew – especially fast in *South* America." [64] Jake made a squishy face, "Y'all are in North America. If this fast-paced intermarriage thing was quoted without clarifying it was recorded in South America, the truth would be jeopardized. That is one way to get twisted history, leaving out logistics.

Now, if someone said or wrote that Tuscarora *"worshipped"* a black deity, citing Graffenried's hate speech from that *Colonial Records of North Carolina* handbook, the one who thought the Tuscarora "knew the demon well," then Graffenried's hate speech needs to be revealed in the same statement or the truth is covered up. If someone said or wrote that Tuscarora were afraid of the black deity, that could be true, based on that *Handbook of American Indians North of Mexico*, volume 2, pages 51 through 52, starts out with *"Indians of Massachusetts in 1633*, coming across a negro in the top of a tree, were *frightened,* surmising that he was Abamacho the devil. [65] But, this *Handbook* reference of Massachusetts is not even in the same region. On top of that, that reference was about how Negro slaves were bred with Indian slaves to increase their usefulness. Look it up. It's on the back of the flyer. Got all the references on this speech tonight there for ya."

A feminine, "Hey," broke the heat, "Is it the one for Tuscarora religion with the handbook or the one under it on being afraid of red heads?"

"The first one you said," Jake's long arm sprung out toward her and she mouthed, "Thank you."

Jake propped his elbow on the podium, tapped his cheek and bit his lip, "Let's see," he squinted, "The Tuscarora red and white "god" had a crown and faced the sunrise." He grabbed the podium and said, "The Tuscarora black and red "demon" had a horrid face and faced the darkness. Universally, light is good, and dark is bad in the spirit world.

Lawson's summary of Carolina Indian beliefs is a primary source because it was written by a witness to the events as they occurred. Lawson observed the death rites and interpreted that they believe a good and hard-working dead person goes to the Country of Souls where the sun visits. This is where the red and white sun god is kind of understood. When a lazy and thieving bad person dies, he goes to a dark place." Click. Instantly, the screen surprised them:

… for these Indians that are lazy, thievish amongst themselves, bad Hunters, and no Warrious, nor of much Use to the Nation, to such they allot, in the next World, Hunger, Cold, Troubles, old ugly Women for their Companions, with Snakes & all sorts of nasty Victuals to feed on. There is marked out their Heaven and Hell. After all this Harangue, he (the Conjurer) allows others to speak in turns telling the deceased's life story. [66]

"How about an elder Tuscarora being interviewed to learn their beliefs?" Jake rested his head while the audience whispered elders' names. "Interviews with authorities are also primary sources."

"It is fact that the Tuscarora accepted Africans into their tribes and into their families. Another fact is the racial tension between Africans and Natives during the times of emancipation when Natives were labeled as "Colored" by the one-drop rule, which is common knowledge around these parts. Another reason there's so many haters today.

When we keep reading it and hearing and learning it, hate just grows and grows like somebody might be wanting it to grow. Huh?"

"Look at this little ditty. Were the Tuscarora were frightened of red and blonde-headed people?" The screen held text titled: **Tales of the Tuscarora by Mrs. Coombs, 1968.** [67]

One day he showed us where Geroux had died and told us some of the stories about him. He, Labeer, had never had any trouble with Geroux, although the latter would never be considered a desirable neighbor. I suspect they had but one thing in common, Tuscarora blood. This all transpired well before World War One. Geroux had said his Tuscarora ancestors had been late comers, having waited for many years before they followed the others. There were a number of late comers and by the time they reached Niagara, the earlier ones had almost disappeared and the late comers language was different from all of the others.

Geroux had been exposed to some Jesuit education and had heard about the Tower of Babel. He thought what had happened to the Tuscaroras was something of the sort in a minor way—a punishment for a crime—what he didn't know other than it involved a big boat and a little boat.

A white man had told them that the big boat was the mother of the little boat and had thunder in it and spit fire. This they saw and heard. The mother boat went away and the Tuscaroras found the little boat filled with people they did not like, so they took the ones they wanted and the ones they did not kill. They put four in the little boat and pushed it out into the waters. The four were strange and they feared to harm them, for their hair was not like that of the Indians but was yellow like the friendly sun, and one was red, like the angry sun.

The Indians had been told that if they harmed the little boat, the mother boat would make thunder and spit fire at them, so they did not harm it but put four who might belong to the sun in it and allowed them all to be taken care of by the god, as he willed.

Where was this supposed to have taken place? Down south where they comed from. He said, "Any fool would know what they should have done".

Someone suggested—"Not harm the people?"

"No", Geroux replied. "Kill ALL of them, sink the little boat and they wouldn't have had to stay away from the water." Geroux was practical. He was also a bully and liked to argue and to win. He was an expert with a knife and a heavy drinker. In addition, he was believed to be running a sort of sanctuary for fugitives from justice who, being in a vulnerable position, would be careful to allow him to win.

He lost an argument with some beavers, and in a way it kill it...

"This excerpt is from a non-scholarly source. It is legend and what is called hearsay. There are some truths here, mixed in with legends, but that does not make it scholarly. So, this source can't be cited as a primary in a scholarly work. Is it true that the Tuscarora gave up the reds and blondes to the Croatan who formed the Lumbees? We're going to answer that here shortly.

I believe what facts tell me. I ask myself, "Does this information match up with any other primary sources?"

Look, I don't have an apple in this pie. I'm white. That's why I am less biased. I believe that the Croatan are the Tuscarora, for three reasons.

One. Look at any of Dr. Wood's maps in the appendix of his "Tuscarora Roots" and you'll see Tuscarora were all over the southeast and monopolized trade and then match that up with the 1590 John White map. See the pink one on The Lost Colonist's site and look at their *Croatan Land*. Smack dab where these Croatan are concentrated on that map is the area known as *Territory of the Tuscarora.*" [68]

Two. Tuscarora weren't afraid of anything. If they believed the color of red and blonde hair held great powers, they would a' married them to increase their Peoples' strength.

Three. The word Croatan was a strategic political move to forsake reparations to the Hatteras Tuscarora, the Natives who absorbed the colonists. Croatan is Tuscarora.

In my research, I have found that older texts are less bias in general. The reason it's important to share this is so you will understand how Tuscarora history is being erased. Do your research people, before you're completely bled out.

Jake's pearly whites flashed the man who'd grumbled earlier, "Crazy as it is, there's another "Lost Colony" out there from the 1500's when about 300 South American Indians and 100 negro slaves went unaccounted for at Roanoke. Were they released from duty as a reward for their assistance in raiding and pillaging Spanish settlements along the Caribbean to Sir Francis Drake when the raiding scoundrel was fleeing the continent from threats of attack by our coastal Natives? Did they drown? Did they stay in Roanoke and intermarry, creating maroon Natives? [69]

How convenient. History tells us that the Tuscarora did not kill all their invaders – just enough to intimidate the survivors into submission. Tuscarora, the chief traders, used their resources at hand as new slaves for their fellow Natives, and to make more fruitful trades.

You know what those Tusc's were thinking, don't cha? Humans have skills and provide labor and well, don't you know those dark soldiers looked like warriors, their favorite kind of folks," Jake's sly grin spread.

"Surnames mark the Tuscarora who stayed in North Carolina," he jabbed at the audience, "while history marks that *prejudice* over intermarriage may have tipped the scales over who stayed and who went to New York. The whites believed the mixed Natives were nicer, so they were allowed to stay in the Carolinas. *The Handbook of North American Indians North of*

Mexico reads that the "so-called Croatans," our Hatteras Tuscarora, were red, black and white and the Canadian Tuscarora pureblood." [70]

"Bes a gaumed up talk on gettin' recognition. You see me!" harped the graying dark-haired man in the back row, but Jake closed his eyes and turned away.

Click. An image of a pale and so very young queen adorned with a double strand of pearls from which a fanciful cross hung, coldly filled the screen's white palette. Her fire red hair, slicked under a pearl coif, claimed her heart shaped face. "Another honorable tie is the result of Queen Elizabeth I, known for always wanting more wealth and land. Sir Walter Raleigh, a privateer pioneer, sought glory and gold and both of them wanted freedom from the Catholic rule. Raleigh founded a secret society, "The School of Night," which was attended by highly prominent Elizabethans. Beliefs were discussed and it is closely related to the mysterious Rosicrucian movement which is tied to the disbanded Knights Templar and to our present-day Freemasons." He pulled up his silver cup, rushed down a mouthful of water, winked and took another.

"Truth be known, Queen Elizabeth I was as much on fire as Raleigh on religious freedom and condemned the persecution of Christians in her later years. She was nothin' like her half-sister," Jake's arms swept across the room, "Queen Bloody Mary, who partied over the ordered massacre of Christians. Staked, burned, and beheaded them." Jake sucked in air and sent a guillotine's whistling strike into the microphone as he chopped down across the podium. "When Mary died, the citizens loaded tables into the streets and burned bon fires for days to celebrate. She was a monster." Jake's blonde layers shivered as the prim lady pursed her lips so tightly, her top lip formed a hook over the bottom like a bird's beak.

"Queen Elizabeth I was a Christian pacifier. She never married. A king would have put his interests first and she wouldn't put her people in jeopardy." As Jake's wide palm stretched out to the queen's portrait, he flicked the screen creating the illusion of her majesty walking into the room. "There were many suitors, especially from Spain. And it was no secret she sought out the friendship of her childhood friend she had assigned to royal duties, but she did not fulfill her heart's desire. Instead, she directed her passion into aiding the Protestants like she was on a mission from God. The combined forces of the queen and the pioneer, Raleigh, set in motion America's biggest ongoing mystery, The Lost Colony, which we have solved!"

Click. Governor John White's watercolor of the original Virginia coastline with an elaborate compass and royal crests, and ships with their bellowing sails plunged starboard over the front of the room. A gentleman taking notes on the front row leaned up as he raised his hand. "I've read several books on the Lumbee and The Lost Colony connection. I don't recall a link to the Portuguese in any of 'em."

"The Lumbee agenda has infected thousands of scholars who've written false narratives, Sir. When y'all first saw that

Portuguese lady in the first clip did you think she was a Native American?" Jake scanned their faces and so did the gentleman taking notes, while several admitted to the native theory. "Raise your hands if you first thought she was a Native." Three quarters of the room filled with raised hands, but the back rows still had a slew of tucked chins.

"Did everyone notice the queen's necklace? Bet it's worth every drop a' moonshine and copper from North Carolina on up to Kentucky, huh?" While he wryly grinned across the audience, keeping his eyes on the back rows, he took notice of those who shared his enthusiasm. But his grin quickly faded when the umpire glared up at him. The back rows huddled into a fast roar looking put out and fired up.

Click. The screen displayed a large golden filigree cross with a white rose at its center surrounded by rubies. Jake read the Rosicrucian statement, "What think you, loving people, and how seem you affected, seeing that you now understand and know, that we acknowledge ourselves truly and sincerely to profess Christ, condemn the Pope, addict ourselves to the true Philosophy, lead a Christian life, and daily call, entreat and invite many more unto our Fraternity, unto whom the same Light of God likewise appeareth?"

The next image was an English pilgrim in one of John White's sketches. The white man was reading the Bible to a Native, "These, my friends, were America's first Christians."

"One God knows all, like dis bes a-catawampus," a nearly masculine voice from the back row announced.

Jake held up the next note card. "This is an excerpt from "A Role for Sassafras in the Search for the Lost Colony," by Philip S. McMullan Jr. On March 25, 1584, Sir Walter Raleigh received a letters-patent from Queen Elizabeth "for the discovering and planting of new lands not possessed by any Christian Prince nor inhabited by Christian People, to continue for the space of 6 yeeres and no more."

"Raleigh's first expedition was a short reconnaissance voyage between April and September 1584, by Amadas and Barlowe. Two Indians, a Croatan called Manteo and a Roanoke called Wanchese, came back to England with them. Croatan is Tuscarora. Our first representatives were Tuscarora."

Jake cast his arms behind and bowed, "We are in the presence of royalty," and rose with outstretched arms, "We are in the presence of descendants of America's First Christians."

The medieval image that followed sat the audience members deep into their seats as Jake leaned so far across the podium it tilted. "Put yourself in Sir Walter Raleigh's shoes. He was an intelligent industrious man, a Christian man. Okay, we have to be factual, so let's add that he made some bad choices along the way, such as an illegitimate child and the killing of innocent Natives to plunder their wealth." He jabbed at the audience, "I want you to think about what drove him to do what he did. Okay? This is the psychological drive.

That's what we are exploring, why people do what they did and how it can prove historical theories based on basic human behavior. In 1572, Raleigh witnessed the St. Bartholomew's

Day massacre where French Protestants were massacred by French Catholics in Paris." The screen's medieval image held an ancient oil painting of naked Christians writhing in the streets as sleek dogs devour the bodies and lamenting wounded. "The slaughter of Protestants, Raleigh's fellow Christians, spread throughout Paris. It lasted several weeks. Modern estimates for the total dead vary from 5,000 to 30,000. So, it was only logical for Raleigh to charm the queen in order to be the chosen one to find a "New Found Land."

The ancient Church of Egypt, one of the Oldest in Christianity, St Bartholomew's martyrdom, bloody as it is, is commemorated on the 1st day of the Coptic Calendar, which currently falls on September 11." Jake's rigid finger pointed at the screen as it clicked to a daunting image of The Twin Towers as the second plane strikes, fires erupt and the structure collapsed. "Let me tell you something. The Knights Templar have always been crusaders against Islam. That's why they were organized in the first place. In America, September 11, 2001, will live on in epiphany." His zealous passion spread across the room like seeds in a wind gust. "Christians must bring the truth out into the light. Stop being the meek politically correct puppets our liberal media conditions people to be and help end this Holy War. Let it begin by claiming your rightful heritage and remove your English name from the Lumbee roll!"

When the members hastened against the chairs their intentions took flight, and Jake somberly added, "How many times does the Bible mention bravery?"

"A lot. It's a shame that in the land of the free and the brave so many have become afraid to speak up. I understand it though. So, if any of you have something, they want to share, any little thing, your daddy's daddy told a story about a group of leaders who had a secret meeting, or your aunt told your momma about a heirloom that was handed down through the generations, something that proved they met up with the Iroquoians or better yet, the Lost Colony, their journey to the swamp, anything," Jake aimed behind him toward the desk, "take one of my cards and call me." The genealogical society's president sitting as his desk offered up a card.

"Make the call, a heroic act of valor. You could be the one to save our Tuscaroras from exsanguination."

Jake twirled the cup as he scanned over his strewn note cards and suddenly stopped twirling as he thrust up a card. "I almost forgot, Portuguese seaman worked aboard Raleigh's commissioned trips, but weren't listed on the ships' registers. That's why their DNA isn't included in the studies currently being conducted, but their surnames, like Chavis, are." The man taking notes who had raised his hand indicating that the Portuguese woman's image resembled a Native smiled. "It's only logical. Drop off a group of gentle Europeans in the wilderness and a group of hearty Portuguese seaman. Which group'll have more survivors?"

The man taking notes raised his hand.

"Yes?"

"John White's watercolors are in museums and reference books as chronological markers for Early Americana. I've studied them and there's not a single Portuguese." He tapped his pen on his notepad.

"The curly haired Natives in White's paintings are a clue that the Portuguese "mingled." These people manned ships and helped build the colonists' settlement, but they wouldn't have stayed on. They were set free or worse. The Europeans are notorious for beheading those who offend them. And the lot of seaman, as needed as they were, were rough and mean and just as soon cut a man as back down from a fight."

Click. Moses, as portrayed in a rich oil painting on Mount Sanai with the stone tablets inscribed with the Ten Commandments roared down to the people on the big screen. "In the Holy Bible, Exodus 34:4, it states that the Ten Commandments were written on stone tablets from Mount Sanai. A section of tablet with thirteen symbols was discovered in England near a holy well where a medieval chapel once stood. It is believed to be a section of the Ten Commandments. The tablet is made from the same arenite sandstone as Jabal Musa, near Mount Catherine which is traced back to the time of Helena of Constantinople. Saint Helena, (ca. 246/50 – 18 August 330) found relics of the True Cross while building The Church of the Holy Sepulcher in Jerusalem."

Click. A larger than life image of the Dome of the Rotunda of the Church of the Holy Sepulcher, in Jerusalem penetrated the audience like a Holy presence had just set foot in the library's conference room. "The site where Jesus was crucified."

With his fingertips cupping the edge of the screen, Jake gave them time to digest the Dome's splendor. Its holy light curiously refracted into the room as if they'd transcended space and time.

"St. Helena built several churches on Holy Land and recovered many Christian relics. She ordered the Temple of Jupiter demolished to build one of those churches, The Church of St. Cyrus and St. John, on the Holy Land of Jerusalem, Temple Mount."

Click. A stone fortress smack dab in the middle of an arid desert city made up of smaller stone structures glared down at them from the screen. Inside the fortress was a large hexagonal stone structure with a golden globe finial. Under the picture was the description, which Jake read aloud, "The Dome of the Rock is the structure in the middle. It's in the location where the Bible declares the Holy Temple should be rebuilt. In the early 1100's crusaders were knighted to form unions against Muslims trying to invade Holy Land. For nearly seventy-five years the Knights Templar, Christian Crusaders, protected Temple Mount."

Click. An image of a medieval knight in his tunic, with a sword and bearing the cross interested the members and they whispered amongst themselves calling names of Freemasons in the audience. Several men adjusted their seating positions as Jake continued. "The Knights Templar are believed to have been given many Christian relics to protect over the years, including St. Helena's discoveries. One of those relics is from the Passion of Christ, the tip of the lance that pierced his side to prove he was dead. It's documented that it was taken to St. Helena of Constantinople and she hid it in the church of St. Sophia. Later, it was enshrined with the Crown of Thorns in the Sainte Chapelle and in the French Revolution, moved to the Bibliotheque Nationale. The Crown is preserved. But the lance's tip is long gone.

Considering the mysterious healing powers associated with pieces of the True Cross, and considering human behavior, the tip was most likely stolen. I suggest it is in the hands of a group known for miraculous healing, a branch of crusaders named Knights of Hospitallers or it might be in the possession of a local healer. A conjurer may find it useful too. Sending demons back to where they came from takes a lot of power."

Gruff huffs and shuffling shoes sparked from the middle rows as squeaky little old ladies whispered like gossiping Sunday school girls.

"You see, the Knights Templar were not only warriors. In fact, most weren't warriors, but were philosophers, engineers, healers and bankers and formed branches to assign these talents. The Knights Templar had begun as poor Christians and became wealthy as Christians supported them. Soon Kings were borrowing from them and this led to their virtual demise. The rulers couldn't pay back their debts so erroneous charges were made against their threatening dear crusaders.

What would have changed in history if the crusaders had overtaken the Royal Kings' positions? Would Christians have complete rule over the majority countries? Would Christians have maintained the Temple Mount? Or is our history as it should be, according to the Holy Bible?"

The image of a modest church on a country hillside appeared above an illuminating tunnel featuring keystone bricked arches lengthened over the screen like a slithering snake. "The Knights Templar is credited with building many churches and tunnels and caves with scripted messages on the walls during their openly active years from 1109 to 1312. One such cave is the Rosyton Cave." Click. The screen's primitive drawings on the chalky cave walls depicts urgency. "The drawings are medieval and depict Jesus' crucifixion and the two tail stars of the Big Dipper called Benetnash and Mizar. These stars depict the same guardian angels on the lid of the Ark. The Ark of the Covenant is said to contain the tablets of stone Moses wrote the Ten Commandments on. These drawings reappear in church murals and a famed Kirkwall Scroll in the possession of the one and only Knights." Jake's raised arms jolted up and down over the podium. "The movement and behavior clearly convey the Knights Templar were consumed with knowledge of the Christian treasures and they had an urgency to relay this information, but only to other crusaders, like the baptized Tuscarora."

Jake asked for lights and as the recessed lighting filled the room, he took a folded chair and stood front center of the middle aisle. "Who can tell me how the Tuscarora are linked to the Knights Templar? Sit right here." He unfolded the chair. "And I'll give a Franklin to the one who tells us which Christian relic the knights protect now." He patted his wallet and walked around the chair like it was a pit he struggled not to fall into spreadin' out his arms for balance. Several guesses are thrown into the air. A few sound ones.

But Jake sat after a grave man stated that the knights are sworn to secrecy and then asked, "Where'd your water cup get to?" Jake lightheartedly smirked up over his shoulder, "Miss Prickenwrath, I'm not done yet. Don't pack up everything"

He leaned toward them and in a secretive kind a' way shared, "There were over twenty thousand of these crusaders, from England, France, Jerusalem, Tripoli, Hungary, Antioch, Croatia, and Portugal. There it is again, that Portugal denominator. Common sense, human nature and the honor these crusaders upheld is enough for me to believe they did not dissolve but went underground. Some joined military orders, taking their treasures with them, groups like the Order of Hospitallers," Jake practically danced along with his roping hand like he'd snagged a calf by the hind legs. Made a quick check on the back rows. Turned his back to them and returned to the podium. "Some were pensioned and allowed to live out their days as commoners.

A lot of 'em went to Portugal, because of the Christian persecution in the rest of Europe, just like the Tuscarora were persecuted by the 1700's law forbidding trade. They migrated to the swamps of what was then Bladen County. Persecution is one explanation of the Templars in Portugal. Was another place the New Found Land, our old Virginy?"

A hand rose from the mid-section. "One of the leading temples is in Portugal. The knights are real proud of that." The middle-aged man in a sport jacket and dress pants offered.

"Yes, sir, thank you for sharing that. And I'd like to elaborate. The knights built a full-fledged fortress and called it the Castle of Tomar for the first king of Portugal. Most folks don't help others without wanting something in return. Right?" Jake grinned. "When the King of Portugal, a fairly new country still under attacks, invited the knights it was because he needed their protection. Later, when the Pope disbanded the Knights Templar an intervention was made so Portugal could keep the knight's treasures they had brought with them, by forming the Order of Christ Church. That was a swift one, huh? No one knows 'xactly what those treasures were."

"What is known is that the Turks, as in Islamic, waged war on the Christian Greek city of Constantinople and just as the prophecies said, the city fell and the Antichrist showed up with the face of a 20-year-old and a disturbing name: Mehmed. Constantinople is where Jesus Christ was preached to the slaves. It was a very Holy place.

After a long bloody war, four thousand were dead and Mehmed II rode his white horse into the Church of Holy Wisdom, also known as St. Sophia's, full of arrogance and darkness to fulfill the Antichrist prophecy with plans to control the entire world. City by city fell and the prophecies were fulfilled. The power of title-hood and deeds and arms became his, but he needed more. He needed the supernatural powers of the church's Holy relics.

The Holy relics missing after the fall of Constantinople included that spear tip that stabbed the side of Christ when he was on the Cross. There is a lost emerald with the image of Christ, and a leg bone and skull of St. John the Baptist, and the fingers of St. Thomas. That Mehmed II even pretended to be a Christian to try to win over the popes for control of their lands, but the Knights were defenders of the "true religion" and fought him off in several wars from 1469-1480. Yet, the Antichrist Mehmed conquered more Christian civilizations until Europeans believed the only safe place for Christians was "The New World."

"Knowing what drives your conquerors is as important as knowing the facts of your own blood. Thank you for being patient and being so interested or seeming to be. I just want you to know that most Christians here in America now realize what horrible wrongs happened to your people and we are sorry and want to help. I also want you to realize that history has a way of repeating itself and you may learn a way to conquer Washington's control over your destiny by knowing what happened in the past."

Jake smiled and took a seat in the chair, and began in a firm whisper, "Some believe the Templars possessed a fleet of ships at La Rochelle in France, even though there is no proof." Jake clapped his hands and the front row jumped. "Is anyone seeing a cycle of secrecy here? The Templars didn't wanna leave proof. They had too much ta risk. They took off to the New World on old Viking routes, making one of the pre-Columbian voyages. And like we were just talkin' on Portugal, the Knights Templar did not really disband. They just changed their name to Knights of Christ. Just like the temple they built was renamed to the Order of Christ. In 1492, this group from Portugal provided the navigators for Christopher Columbus' journey, and the Order's cross was on the sails of his ships, however there is no actual evidence. Of course not." [7]□ His face reddened, "There's too much at risk." He shook with each defiant syllable. "Just like there is no such thing as a Lumbee Indian, and they won't set their only verified link to aboriginals free – the Mighty Tuscarora!"

With a fistful of purple scarves, Jake ferociously waved, "Sail on up here and claim your heritage. Sail to freedom! Make your own world! We've got your colors for all those who sign a Lumbee disenrollment form and reclaim their Tuscarora heritage!"

Metal chairs clanked as Jake rose above the complaints while the front rows broke away and the remaining guests vanished in a purple haze.

Chapter 10

In the Wind Now

Jake and Miss Lucy thanked their host and drove home drunk with hope and exhaustion, as usual after their presentations, to their separate homes. Miss Lucy retired quickly with a cup of cocoa and her latest edit of Jake's book, *Chapter 9, Stolen Treasures Then.*

The never-ending ocean wind sent a lonesome longing with its sharp rhythmic whirls, like a lovelorn whippoorwill's call singing its refrain. Bruce's curly blonde locks whipped about his tawny orange cheeks while he scouted for the odd new delights, spoots, scattered in outcrops, like his new family, roaming the black sandy shore. With his bucket half-full he called out, "How many do we need?"

"O best get a bucket full. Games bring da players. Thy'll have drinks and eats at it all along. Summer dim 'ere. No dark ta speak of. Be dancing, too. Frances bes calling on tha ladies. Dark hair's comin." The old man's stocky frame pushed along against the wind becoming a darker version of himself until outcast beyond definition.

Other men were strewn about like crabs, each on their own quest, as men do when competing for food, or charmers, or loot. Changing hands when their buckets wore heavy and cleverly counterbalancing wind gusts without falling, as shirttails flapped like wings. In their thick leather soled boots, they walked backwards across the sands at low tide sporting knives and buckets and bellies happy with dark brew. Upon meeting, they each checked the other's buckets looking over their shoulders and stealing peeks as they kneeled to free the razor clams from their black sandy beds. With brimmed buckets, each man found his way back to the courtyard and rinsed his load at the well. "Take mine to the cooks, would ya, Pops? I'm gonna walk on the beach."

"Walk, eh? Keep tha boots on or we'll be packing razor cuts fer sure now. Our Orkney undertow haint fer sissy boys. Takes a man's last chance 'ere."

Past the soft sand, he pulled off his shirt and dashed toward the crashing waves. Summer in Orkney is a high of 54 Fahrenheit. But with the cold wind it felt more like 35 on bare skin, so the invigoration exceeded to exhilaration as the cold wind washed his tears to his ears and he braved the frigid forty-degree splashes. "Good goo-oo!" He doggedly waded up to his hips until the force pulled and tugged and begged, like a lover from the other side of the world. His muscles strained and stung, but he held and buried his heavy boots into the sand like posts into clay. The cold ocean slapped his chin and splashed over his curls, soaking him senseless and numb as a hapless little baitfish. As a vicious white wave promised to turn him catawampus or drown 'm dead, he jerked free and dove toward the crashing shore.

He laid face down on a pillowy sand bed, thrashed and pecked free of spoots and its kind by the various fowl. Hot tears wet his forearms as his heaves purged suicide's lure and the ocean's greedy laps licked over his legs and forcing his hips to sway. The cool sand and stinging wind numbed his pain and he turned onto his side to admire the shoreline.

Rocky passes with lush green blades whistled over and up to the hardy wildflowers much like the daisy aster outcrops in his pinelands. Busy gulls screeched high in the sky and on the shore, while puffins chirped and purred only feet away. With the only true human footprints being the shingle rooftops, the threat of seclusion in exile screamed until his throat burned and his leather boots tightened like irons. When gulls circled overhead and dove closer at his teasing goldilocks, he stood and shook off what sand he could.

All pink and sticky and polka dot black with shiny sand, he picked up his shirt and jogged to the stone wall encircling the courtyard and on the other side, pulled off his strict boots and wading trousers and tossed them onto the weather-beaten work bench where fish were cleaned and lies primed. Protected from the cool ocean wind, he gazed past the courtyard's open gateway to the mighty ocean and off to his right, spied the sign. The magnificent aurora borealis waltzed across the clear summer dim sky into the open abyss claiming his only thought of happiness, a second chance at love, and warmed him enough that the chill bumps blistered red calmed to a tawny pink.

In his soaked tighty-whities he bounced through the courtyard to the largest stone house. The island claimed forty people when they were not on the water fishing. Half lived in the five stone structures making up the men's quarters. Half of those were smilin' wide at Bruce's buck n' hide as he whistled back and catcalled again, "Hey, mama's boys, anyone up for a swim?" He politely mooned them, politely being that he didn't bend over, and his numb butt shined like bright red rouge on a white whore. He spun back around to his riled mates and pulled at his waistband. "All natural if you can get the dark hair over? Whadayasay, Pops?" Instantly, all catcalls ceased.

Pops cracked the broom handle against the stone floor and thrust the bristled end against Bruce's backside as he passed in the open foyer. "She's me sweet niece. You'll not be showin' 'er dat sport or you'll be danglin' yer dillywhopper fer bait off me rig." Laughter rounded out the parade. "Gotdat, Jack?"

"Yes, Sir, boss man." Bruce hurried to the kitchen where the sweet meat was purged from the shells and the roasting orgasmic aromas clenched around the sweet tender spoots like lips.

"Gawl dookie, youse folks can cook. Must be in heaven's kitchen. Love it! Love it! Love it!" He opened the half door's base and the ocean wind trapped it open, hurling in a gust of salty sea air as Bruce spattered salty black dots across the smooth stone floor where the men cracked spoots open and boasted on their loaded buckets. The large kitchen was steamy with the large dome brick oven's live fire. Hearty garlic cloves roasted with onions mingled with the sweet rosemary as the scents permeated his pores while he warmed up with a whiskey and turned like a rotisserie toasting near the hot dome oven where his manhood grew.

Two men cracking spoots held up their pinky finger-sized spoots and asked if there was a girl on the island who needed a wee man. "Let us know. We'll take two." One claimed it is not size but the action and pushed his tongue in and out of his beer bottle and another followed with a spoot mating his beer bottle. The cook announced that if there was a woman who needed to see a real man to come see him. "I'm be da only one among ya' that's cause fer a fight," he hung over the words as he realized the true dilemma. Bruce was half erect and half drunk and didn't feel his engorged endearment.

"Newby, lad," the cook waved his potato peeling knife, "be a help and get that pickle out o' yer pants. Silly me," he chuckled at Bruce, "Get the pickles from the pantry."

Bruce poured his glass half full again and asked where the pantry was as he opened cabinets. When he leaned over the large kettle with the creamy sauce he pushed his finger in and sucked it clean and the young man chopping parsley and thyme told him not to and that he'd better get dressed before the girls came or no one else would get to dance. "Ya, yer peely-wally now n' needing ta lay down. Git n' an hour and youse bes the man tonight!" called out the garlic peeling man with the wild-haired arms thick as fence posts.

Bruce made his way down the stone hallway, half drunk and melancholy admiring the décor. Portraits in dark walnut hand-hewn oil rubbed frames hung in the wide-open hall like the oven hot Orkney spoots smothering in the creamy garlic sauce: Overwhelmingly attractive. He rubbed down the fresh scar tissue tightening between his ribs as the promising sting of the spoots' saltwater bitters and sweet meat formed drool pools in his cheeks. The scent was so fresh he couldn't help himself but to lick his forearm when he was sure the hallway was clear. And the act purged more memories. More angst. More thirst. Thirst the afternoon's drink could never quench, like the motherly woman in the portrait gazing at him. Her piercing blue eyes followed him while her dark curly hair swept across his bare shoulders like the surge of windswept memories he'd attempted to drown, and he went airborne down the stone hallway and shut the door.

He dressed in quiet reflection sure his life was in purgatory and nestled into the comfy covered chair. "I can still kiver up and pretend I'm all the fine in the world." The rattling windowpanes hypnotized him into a sweet swampy dream when there was a knock at the door.

Pops winked and handed him a package. "Mail from Carolina. They've cherished the photos round n' round and wish to see the films after dinner. What do ya want me to say?" The stone wall held the tall windows while a walnut paneled wall held aged tapestry scrolls, and Pops asking Bruce for permissions held Bruce's tongue as he rose.

"Well? What'll it be, lad?"

"Why here?" When his forlorn gaze and angry jaw made their demands, Pops closed the door behind him and motioned for him to sit back down and when Bruce obliged, with a keen eye he witnessed the transformation. Pops held his palms up to the scrolls and proclaimed, "We got it safe 'ere. Thar's one fer tourists at the manor." He looked over his shoulder at Bruce, "Don' be touchin' it. Yer oils'll take what life's left in 'er, eh?" As Pops drawled the sailcloth's thick braided cord and unveiled the ancient text with hand-painted maps and symbols, his tunic shifted and the upper third of a red cross tattooed on his lower hip flashed. "The Kirwkwall Scrolls."

Bruce followed the maps and intricate details.

"They traveled to Portugal and helped fight off tha dark Islamics and built mighty fortresses and came 'ere to Scotland fer tha same. Story of tha first times. Fine historians, theologians, philosophers and warriors. K'ept records of everything. Templar Knights. Ships passin' in tha night on thar separate ways to live and build new worlds, Christian worlds. We protect our own and other Christians, lad. We Knights have a duty. You have a duty." Bruce studied the cloth's odd symbols and Pops warned, "It comes wid a price. We pray you'll come aroun ta believing we can work together and understand God sees all faiths."

"Why Kirk?"

"How no? Kirk bes tha church, tha Word, laddie," with his steely hand gripping Bruce's shoulder and his stinging icicle blues alarmingly close, Pops confided, "There's not time fer bargainin' and you're da best choice, ya hard-headed lug. I'm thought you'd drown out dar wid yer curls soaking in da white foams. Had me prayers smokin.' Bout ta dive in fer help if ya hadn't turn' about."

"I didn't see you."

"Don' be fooled. I'm over me youth. Proud eighty-two and a Knight till I'm under. I'm tellin' ya now. We all are here."

"And the dark hair, your niece? Are the women knights?"

"O, most wicked, lad. Tha bonnies'll kiss and take yer heart an' life an' no back to it till it's out from under ya. Now get together. You've got ta make an impression. Every man here's asked fer me niece."

"And?"

"N, she's been waiting fer a man who'll take da wakes with 'er."

Bruce banged his chest like an ape and twirled around to find him opening the door and halfway out when Pops said, "Rest yer flippers and clean yer ears. Kate's o lot o' woman fer any man, even a prince."

Bruce sunk into the chair and scowled, "Prince? How does that shit fit in with my Tuscarora ascendancy?"

"A corner stone, you're marked from the blood of us, the northeast corner stone, and the blood of the mightiest of your country, the Tuscarora." He pulled a book from the shelf on the far wall and handed it to Bruce and he read the title, "*The Symbolism of Freemasonry: Illustrating and Explaining Its*

Science and Philosophy, Its Legends, Myths, and Symbols. This explains why my People have been marked, huh? What about my Native spirit? Do you expect me to bleed it out and separate the bloods? How the hell do you expect me to jump into this? Are you telling me this is what I'm expected to do to survive?"

"Thoust be our prince, learn and *appreciate* all your ancestors and reprations'll come further, Bruce White." He held Bruce's full attention, "Europe's sins bled yer peoples out. Sure, dars Irish masons' sins, blast Neales cheatin' the Hatteras out a dar Indian Town. [72] That was then," his chest grew wide, "Now we's got our freemasons contracted and we're together on reprations. All yer boxes r here, Bruce. Crowsons shipped 'm just like dey said. We'll be studying dose tomorrow best." Pops lamented as he held the door, and agreed without hesitation to delay dinner, so Bruce could dive into his precious gift. The films on his Peoples were chosen for after dinner, promising to share the Henry Berry Lowrey film first.

"Where are the papers?"

"In yer boxes."

"Know what they are?"

"Yer BIA docs. We're all 'round, Bruce," Pops closed the door and the musty old book in Bruce's palm opened itself up in the middle at page 160. Under the *Corner-Stone* heading it read, "As, for instance, in Psalm cxviii. 22, "The stone which the builders refused is become the head-stone of the corner," which, Clarke says, "seems to have been originally spoken of David, who was at first rejected by the Jewish rulers, but was afterwards chosen by the Lord to be the great ruler of his people in Israel;" and in Isaiah xxviii. 16, "Behold, I lay in Zion, for a foundation, a stone, a tried stone, a precious corner-stone, a sure foundation," which clearly refers to the promised Messiah." [73]

When Bruce returned it to the shelf a copy of *The Croatan Indians of Sampson County, North Carolina. Their Origin and Racial Status. A Pleas for Separate Schools* by George E. Butler protected in clear plastic, among several other American works on his People lined up next to a hand-beaten copper sculpture of a Native's bust atop a heart pine wedge. Bruce admired the sculpture as he removed the aged book from the protective cover. He hurried through the pages mumbling about Washington's "so-called Special Agent" who wrote false narrative to erase the Tuscarora ascendancy and cussed over page 12 when his People were intentionally mislabeled as Algonquin. "We absorbed those pansies and the rest ran when we stood our ground." Pages 15 – 16 carried McMillan's list of Lost Colonists' and held him in silence as he read over the italicized "Indian" names and smiled. He laughed at page 17, "Found? 200 years ago. We introduced ourselves to Spanish invaders in the early 1500's and no telling who else before that." Bruce nodded over the reference to Robeson County and Henry Berry Lowrey and winced at the description of his People's friendliness. [74]

"Yeah, and that greedy man in with the anthropologists at the coast couldn't stress hard enough he believed only the Algonquians were friendly. Tuscs were friendly when they first met those invaders so they could see what all they had to trade. Those early explorers didn't know the difference between tribes. We all looked the same and they were just guessing. He probably believes that we didn't know any Algonquian words either, but we traded those, like everything else. Wampumpeag is wompum for our belts and it was from an Algonquian word and we made it into an Iroquoian word. [75] That's what we did. We took what we wanted and made it ours, like the swamp. Only thing those greedy goats want is to dig up our ancestor's remains. He's gonna be surprised … Hatteras Tuscarora, that's who I am."

Bruce enjoyed the front cover of Jake's book with its bare-chested shadowy form enveloped by two continents coming together with her in the "V" as a symbol of the tribe. Bruce flipped through the chapters, sunk into the deep chair, and covered up with the quilt and began *Chapter 1, In the Wind Then.*

The gravel's lime dust swirled and settled as jar runners backed up to Eacha Up Pizza, Maxton's best. They jumped out with cash burning holes in their pockets and placed bets on passing motorists having out of town plates. Dodger and Snap placed one-dollar bets and when stakes were raised, walked. Cassie's older boys were loving South Carolina. They bet between themselves while the two youngest played hide-and-seek around the restaurant until the six-year-old chunked a rock and the four-year-old to fell flat in a muddy rut. The red headed brat swore like their older brothers as he tried in vain to wipe off the mud. "Run!" their older brothers yelled as Shorty hollered, "Here comes Ma!"

Cassie gave two fast slaps to the yurkers' tails and swung them up into the truck bed and held down the older and secured him with a bungee cord. She pulled out a sack of tee shirts from behind the driver's seat and sorted through for one without big holes as the youngest jerked back the bungee cord. "Damn it!" sounded the sting and the bright orangey red afro bounced away in a frenzied escape. When Cassie spun around the crying boy's eyes doubled, "Get Stink away from me, Ma! He's got a stick!"

Pen snickered and asked Snap, "You got a cell phone?"

He flipped it open. "Gambler's anonymous?"

"Very funny. Call Bruce." Pen's arms were held out rigidly crossed against his chest.

"Easy, he'll be here. Probably helped feed up or something like that."

Snap rested back against the hood of his adored late 1960's pale green boy toy, "How's the bite?"

"I'll have a big dimple where the flesh rots out." Pen wore loose dress pants, but the butt bandage's outline was still there. "Momma's seeing 'bout it."

"Thought she got you to the doctor?"

"Yea, I got a venom shot and antibiotics. Three refills."

"More hits on you than a ball bat." Snap admired the young man's strong muscular frame and veins like rigid pythons choked up 'round his pit bull biceps. "Bet you'd be a tough'n ta take down." Snap's tee shirt matched both his car and his banded straw cowboy hat. His strong angular facial bones were tanned extra dark while his long rectangular hollow cheeks were lighter. His full lips bled red while his gray eyes darkened under the shade of his brim. With his jeans tucked inside his fanciest alligator skin boots he was a double for a hottie on the rodeo circuit.

Dodger peered into Snap's nice ride. "Honeymoon over?" and Snap half grinned. "She's resting. Woman works hard. Said to bring her a take-out."

"Oh, she's already got you trained." Rodger Dodger slapped his leg. "Eacha Up has a large cheese pizza on special tonight. Let her dress it up way she likes."

"Good idea, Dodge."

"Is Edge staying home, too?" Pen casually asked.

"She's already here. Got a early ride in." Snap smiled. "Go tell her "hi." His big gray eyes flashed from under the brim of his straw cowboy hat.

"Oh, I can wait."

"Go talk to her. You kin get a beer inside."

Cassie rolled her eyes at Snap and smiled at her son, "Not yet, Lassie." Pen was rather handsome that summer's eve with his stubble shaved. Even with the oversized dressed pants Cassie had rushed in and bought at the dollar store so he could be comfortable with the thick wound dressing, Pen charmed the eyes. With his red curls buzzed into a smart crew cut he was every bit a soldier fresh from the heat of battle with his half arm's fleshy scar tissue sunburned scarlet to deep purple.

After Cassie draped a clean tee shirt over Stink, she batted her bright blue eyes up at a shadowing cloud. As it stagnated over them in a welcoming respite from July's stifling heat in the dusty parking lot, it dulled the bright orange in her curls to an appealing red. She wore it pulled back in a short tight ponytail with baby nap curls around her freckled ears adorned with tiny jade buttons. She wore a button-down white shirt, clean blue jeans and nearly white tennis shoes. Cassie was very becoming, even with the red-headed afro tot wiping boogers on her jean's leg in his mud stained tennis shoes and adult-sized tee shirt. Onto his mischief, she plopped him into the back of the truck and checked for sticks, threatened him and joined Snap.

As the cloud covered the sun in its slow descent, she checked across the street for oncoming traffic. At six o'clock on a Saturday night there was little traffic and as the locals passed she called them by name. "Bet Williford is having fish tonight."

"Saturday nights they're trying to use up everything before it times out. Get more that way." Dodger checked Cassie over as she tied her loose tennis-shoe strings. When she rose from her squat he asked if she was going out afterwards. "You kidding, Dodge?" She spat. "Aint you beat? I'm tuckin' in early. Bes a lot to clean 'fore the next round. Gotta sharpen all the damn hand axes and knives."

"We's on ta a name with who stole our guillotine."

"Who?"

"Same idgit took our Book got our blade."

"You sure?" Cassie's cheeks filled.

"Fraid not. Or we'd a-stole it back already. Reckon?"

"We got our Bible back, Dodge." Toe to toe she swore. "And we'll get our blade back and we're gonna keep it fer good. Hear?" Her lips curled. "Do you like lamb?"

"Too greasy. Why? Plannin' on a-thinnin' out the field?" Dodger nervously looked around. "Dear, we're talking about letting go, right?" And Cassie half grinned as Dodger flicked off a chunk of nail along with the black line of filth with his trusty hawkbill. Cassie told him to go wash. "Same overalls you wore this afternoon?" She fisted her hips as Dodger lumbered into the restaurant with a hitch in his giddy up. "Damn, youse a' bossy woman." Snap hollered, "Whadya do to yer self? Real work get cha' today?"

"He's not young anymore, Snap. That still job was hard on all a us, can't cha be nice?" Cassie winked.

As the Magee boys pulled up the jar runners tightened up and bowed up. But the Magee boys walked straight on to Cassie's boys and offered their stash on the game as a blinding white luxury car passed. "There's no one around here with that much money. That thing's fresh from Detroit, man." When Thomas Magee held up a five, it waved like a dropped flag.

"Thomas's can. They own the whole town. Or the McKeithan's." The wiry and pale, gray-eyed middle boy with blonde bouncy curls, Alice, snatched Thomas's five. He held it up to his cherry red lips and kissed it. "Thank you, gentlemen."

"Check it good," Cordy yelled to his younger brother, Shorty, as he strained through the binoculars right next to the highway. "Don't you drop those, Shorty," Pen warned his brother.

Joe Ray flipped the bills in his brother's hand and asked, "How much we got, Alice? Give ya a' pinch for a five." Joe Ray jerked up his gut of snuff and when Alice tried to snatch it he pushed it back into his pocket. Alice bowed up and pushed his brother's chest. "I'll tell Ma if ya don't give me some after dinner."

Thomas Magee nudged his big brother and when he didn't jump on the feminine name, young Thomas did. "Alice? What's that about, man? You the mom when Cassie's out or what?"

Pen's chest increased two-fold as he eavesdropped on the forthcoming punches, and so did Cassie's. With her magic finger she drew the circling wand of peace and the boys laughed it off like it was the best joke of the day. With a big smile Cordy informed Thomas that it was a family name and that he'd better call him Al.

"Sure," Thomas's tongue ran his teeth like a motor cross warm up. Like he'd learned right along that a dry mouth was much more likely to get a broke tooth 'cause a fist just don't slide as well, "Alice."

"Shit." Pen rushed as Shorty gave his brothers the thumbs down from the highway and ran for the fun. "Put dat wad in yer pocket, Cordy. Don't lose it!" Shorty slid in and yanked Thomas down by the ankles. Down in the gravel, he took a mou'ful, but it was the kick in the face that cut his lip. Thomas' big brother held back two by the necks in a bear claw as Cassie folded her arms one over the other and whistled a shrill ear-splitting yurker call so loud that the curtains in the restaurant spread wide open. "Bes an index to pizza and all else in two seconds you don't listen up, boys," her red face threatened.

After the boys shook off the fury and most of the dust, they had to divvy up the wad over their momma's command and shake hands. Shorty smiled so politely it was sickening,

"Good doin' business wid cha." While Cordy waited for his momma to go check on the young boys in the back of the pick-up and when he was sure, asked young Thomas, "Where's yer daddy?"

"You know where he is."

"Afraid ta say, boy?"

Big brother Magee was finally ruffled, "Your family doesn't want recognition because it knows it won't help any more than it does now. So, what's the difference?" His spicy aftershave mixed with their stale breath. "After all, universities want English speaking students."

"We's all going to the community college and paying our own way." Shorty snubbed.

"Bes pride in keeping the swamp. Our teacher says long as we can, whad she call that word, Cord?"

"Convey."

"Long as we convey the message cross it don't matter." Shorty's nose pert ner flattened out. "Your daddy's a traitor to real Indians. Tuscaroras don't want nuthin' from whites. No special nothin' and no federal anything." Shorty bowed up, "Us'ns got pride." His fourteen-year-old chest puffed out like the bona fide sixteen-year-old on his driver's license.

"Man, you don't get it. You pay attention tonight and you'll figure out a thing or two. Like, we want to help, Shorty. I like you guys." Thomas scanned their faces. "We go back, all those years of runnin' for Bruce. Man, we grew up together."

"We're keepin' our roots." Shorty strutted like a rooster about to go into the ring for a master Lum's cock fight. "Look at cho, chocolate Tuscy. Only injun in ya is that ma a yours. If she is your real ma."

Cordy reared up as his dartin' fingers stabbed at the Magee brothers' chests. "You two got all the easy runs."

"No," the elder Magee boy's testosterone drummed. "We got the ones your ma said was too dangerous for her boys. We handled all the coloreds for your own good. There was no favoritism. Bruce isn't that way. And our father is in Washington. Without men like him they'd have the county bulldozed." The elder boy's nose flared as it drew in the heat and his jaw tightened 'till the thick muscle pulsed. "Those people don't get small town ways. My dad does and he cares. Got it?"

But young Thomas Magee's jaw was loose as an idiot clown's jumping out a' barrels in a mad bull's ring. He stepped up real close to Cordy. "Now, can you say, "Who's your daddy?"

Snap sprinted over to the heated group. "We're here for Bruce. Let's go inside and get a sweet tea now. Come on."

Stink popped off the tailgate, ran inside and as the door closed, struggled to lock his brothers out while his tongue writhed about like a wet snake over his jaw. He jumped up and hit at the latch over and over until Edge pulled him away.

Shorty walked in record speed to be in front of Thomas and asked Alice, "Who invited them?" Snap whipped at Shorty's shoulder. "Bruce did. He invited all his friends." As Pen's juvember's thick rubber band worked up from his loose dress pants' waistband, Thomas told Snap, "They were lookin' for trouble," and Pen pushed the juvember back down.

When the older Magee replied, "Some things never change," Pen squared up, "We have to change first." When they gave him the eye, added, "It has to start with us. Right?" and shoulders relaxed. Heads bowed. And Snap looked to the sky.

Cassie freed her rock-chunking son from the back of the pickup, and he ran into the restaurant, found Stink and yanked his ears. Stink's face matched his hair until he became one little hot ball of fire. The two scrapped like hog littermates grunting and biting and kicking. The staff, owner and patrons watched in disbelief as a pitcher of sweet tea wobbled when the pair rolled under a table.

Dodger rose from his straight back chair and it fell to the tile with a fat clack as he yelled, "Bes all de sorry in de world yer ma sees dat. Help me, Edge." On all fours, she jerked Stink by the leg and drug them both out. Stink stayed on top with a mouthful of nose as his brother pulled his ears. Dodge cracked both against their thick heads and they winced and grabbed their fast whelps. Stink stood ready to kick Dodger, but he held him back with a fist full of red afro while Edge shook his shoulders. "You gonna end up in the broom closet, hungry! That what you want?"

Cassie was a firecracker, "What are you doing ta him?" She yanked Edge's arms off her baby boy. She didn't even have to touch Dodge. He let go of Stink and the six-year-old tattooed with bright red teeth indentions across the bridge of his nose confessed, "We weren't fightin, Ma. I swear."

"Shut up and sit down."

Stink didn't pay his momma much mind for lookin' over Edge like she's an unwrapped candy bar as he licked his lips. "I'm thirsty." Stink clasped onto the red bandana trim on her short shorts as she sashayed over to a table by the window. Stink was on the verge of spanking a cheek when Edge pulled out a chair for him and he climbed up.

But the owner came out from behind the counter and directed them all to a large secluded area in the back. The cinderblock walls had no windows and dark purple drapes hung open at either side of the adjoining wall. "We gonna see a movie, too, ma?" Cordy asked.

Miss Ginger had ridden over with the Crowsons, and they had picked up her fiancé on the way. Bruce had said he wanted to get to know him if he's gonna be sparking his new best friend. Ken, Exilee and Luke drove their own truck because farm life put the child up at daylight or before and that meant Luke could get fussy and they'd probably have to leave early. That left Jake, Bruce and Robin to ride together. Robin sat in the middle wearing a scent of musky waitress; roasted peppers, beef du jour, and sweet lime sorbet in her turquoise tee shirt and yellow jeans. When she loosened her long black silk from the red band, a wave of gardenia blooms threatened to hypnotize the twitterpated friends into proposals.

Robin sang those crazy for lovin' you classic lines with the radio in her deep sultry manner and when she aimed Bruce's way, he told her, "I'm making time to get my license first thing tomorrow. Break ground and get 'er done. Won't take long. I'll be a millionaire, Robin." Jake turned down the radio so low there was only a faint glimmer of classic country love crap in the stuffy cab and Robin stopped singing. Jake placed his hand on her tight yellow thigh. "Did Gili find someone to cover your days off for our trip?"

"I did. Exilee's gonna do it. She knows how important this horse is to you," and Robin told Bruce, "It's his first. Well, the first he's shopped for."

"That's ri-ight." Bruce leaned up gave Jake his best smile, "Let me know if you need any help."

Jake's tongue dug a hole behind his front teeth. "You read about horses, too? All that extra time on your hands, huh?"

Bruce adjusted his jaw and with an arrogant brow studied the parking lot as they pulled in. "The Belgium can be traced back to Medieval Knights when wars were fought on horseback. Writers called them the Great Horses."

"I didn't know that," Robin exclaimed. "You must have tons of information. You wanna come with us to South Carolina? You could help us decide. Ya know what? You might want one, too. I can see you now, riding your horse across the vineyard." Her hands waved like she was playing horse puppet across the dashboard. "Didn't he say there was another one, Jake? Two geldings, one was seven, the other a little older?" She swiveled to Bruce. "I know you have the money. Do you feel any different now that you're so rich? You had it so hard growing up. You must be walking on clouds."

"I'll be walking on cloud nine tomorrow when I go to the bank and we get it all put in my name." Bruce slyly held his hand over her leg, about an inch away from her heat. "Feel me and tell me. Am I different good or bad?" One side of his mouth grinned while his tongue damned back the extra saliva before it streamed down his chiny chin chin. But with an elevated shoulder and shameful smile she pushed his hand away and Jake rolled his eyes. "Hon, we can pick out a horse for Bruce, if he wants us to. He'll be too busy next week. He's got a business to set up. Okay?"

"You're right," Robin arched up after the men got out and slid out Bruce's open door.

"You trust us to pick out a good mount, right?"

"Course, I do." Bruce closed the door as Jake hastily paced to open the restaurant's door. And Bruce slowly escorted Robin inside, pausing to coyly adjust her pocketbook's strap over her shoulder as it pulled on her blouse and exposed her bra strap. With a cracked smile, "There you go." Toe to toe, Bruce's nose was just above hers, "Let me know if you need anything else adjusted," and Robin stared straight on at Jake by the open door, "Don't make her mad or I'll make you ride home in the back. Gotdat Jack?"

"Might ride back there anyway," Bruce jested as Robin marched off huffing behind the heavy purple drapes and Bruce detained Jake by the arm, "Sorry. And for what it's worth, I'm glad she has you. She couldn't have found a better man." They quietly merged passed the black velvet painting toward the back room lit with wall-mounted decorative lanterns and candles on the table. Bruce curiously gestured to one of the tapestries, "Don't remember this, you?" The long narrow black and white forms and geometric patterns suggested a story being told, much like the creation story at the top of the fabric. Their hot ears cooled as they studied the curious old textile.

The middle depicted a regime or city and then movement. Beside the long tapestry was a coat of arms much like the design on the tapestry: An alter was flanked by a female and a male winged angel with horse legs. A five-pointed star and all-seeing eye in a sea of clouds were above them. The coat of arms was painted on old tongue and groove boards, unframed and lacking all luster, in simple azure blue lines.

They lingered over the two wall hangings as drink orders were taken, getting the waitress's attention by clicking as if to urge a pony to giddyup. "Sweet tea." Jake told Bruce, "Never seen this artsy fartsy stuff before." And Bruce bit the tip of his tongue.

Once drink orders were served and pizza preferences made Bruce told the waitress to keep bringin' 'em. "Wonder what's keeping Scarecrow and Lilly?" Jake asked Bruce. "Think they called it a day?"

"I doubt it." Bruce and Jake sat across from one another at the far end of the table. Robin sat at the end of the table, like a queen fitted between them. Exilee tried to get her to sit next to Luke and her, but she declined, obviously, because Edge was next to Exilee. An empty straight back chair divided the Magee boys from Cassie's boys and on the opposite side an empty chair protected Miss Sarah from Stink. When word got around the table, which was six rectangle tables butted together, that there was no imminent danger of the law becoming involved in the big copper momma's repossessing, they relaxed and joked about their day's bizarre accomplishment.

Mark defiantly stood, "It's not that funny." He explained the litter of squealing alligators eating the monster alligator that'd been shot, and the gun and the boat attached to the steel lead line, and laughter roared into the hot kitchen. Stink asked why Mark didn't think it was funny and Luke asked when he could go see the alligators.

Mark said, "Never," as he pulled out the mystery letter. "Why'd you wait till now? Why didn't you do it yourself a long time ago?" Mark sat back down. "Sometimes I think you're just tryin' ta get rid of me."

"Geez. I didn't even know it existed until last night. Scarecrow told me." Bruce stared as the letter was passed down. Comments declared its age, fragility and earthy scent. Bruce trembled as he breathlessly unfolded the tight creases. He held it close to his face as Scarecrow and Lilly, dressed in matching blue tee shirts and khakis finally arrived and stood directly behind him. Bruce stoically and carefully unfolded the letter and placed it in his shirt pocket.

"Can't believe not one a you sorry Lums called to check on me. I could a been dead in a ditch." Scarecrow shook Bruce's chair. Lilly quietly took a seat between Stink and Miss Sarah while Scarecrow looked about the room as if he was considering sitting in one of the chairs up against the wall as he made his way to the chair between Thomas and Pen. Cassie sat at the head of the table where she could keep an eye on all her boys. Lilly faced the dimly lit path from the kitchen to the dining area while Scarecrow faced a set of double doors with an emergency exit sign.

The big copper momma and alligator stories were highlighted, hyped and spread as thickly as the cheese on the hand tossed pizza. The stories were told over and over until everyone was full of happy, pepperonis and salads. Cassie's boys rubbed their bellies and burped into their hands as Dodger's heavy eyelids closed when he leaned against his straight back chair. He had guzzled one beer while waiting in the front room and two more with his dinner.

Miss Ginger woke him when she twanged her fork against her heavy ceramic dinnerware plate to introduce her fiancé, Mr. Warren Croom, as a professor of history from North Carolina State University. Mr. Croom stood and welcomed Bruce and stated that he'd waited a long time to meet Bruce Black.

"You have?" Bruce's grays filled out like silver dollars.

"Don't worry, Mr. Black, I won't query about anything contrary." Mr. Croom spoke seriously, alarming the waitress and she turned around without serving the pineapple and apple pie desert pizzas.

"So, what *are* you going to ask?" Bruce nonchalantly quipped as he studied the tall lean professor in his dress shirt and slacks.

"Mr. Black, does this mean anything to you?" Mr. Croom drew out a paper from his coat jacket and displayed it for all to see.

When Bruce didn't answer Cassie's boy, Cordy did, "Isn't she the Queen of England, the old one?"

"Very good. Precisely, Queen Elizabeth I, as she contracted Sir Walter Raleigh." He handed the picture to Bruce. "Is there anything in this picture that stands out to you? Anything?" Mr. Crooms was the only one politely smiling.

Stoic Bruce coyly passed it to Robin. She passed it to Jake, then to the Crowsons. Dear Miss Ginger bit her lips and passed it to Edge. Edge stared at the queen and then down to Cassie and then Edge stared at her silverware as Lilly took it from her. Lilly's eyebrows twitched, but she casually passed it on. When

Cordy commented on the queen lookin' like his momma Cassie told him that he was a silly boy. But Mr. Croom locked down on her and then to each of her boys until he hit on Bruce again.

When Scarecrow stared at the page, he licked his lips and breathed a bit faster. "I have something on paper, too. Might be nothin'. Came across it when we were, uh, talking to Mr. Fisk earlier." Scarecrow stood and handed the sketch to Mr. Croom and he tapped the tabletop. "Let us in on this. It's interesting to say the least. Who is Mr. Fisk?" After noting the sketch Mr. Croom handed it to Bruce.

"He's a Lum with a still operation. I do some work for the county concerning that business and had the opportunity to attain this from him." Scarecrow's cheeks sucked in just the slightest.

"When?" Mr. Croom innocently inquired, "He offered it, or you discovered it?"

"Can't say exactly."

"We were there all day and didn't see no law," Shorty affirmed and Stink grinned. "Only pig there was eatin' snakes."

"Shh," Cassie warned as the boys giggled.

Lilly held her palms up to Scarecrow, "The gig is up," and Scarecrow agreed with a tumbling sigh as she explained, "Scarecrow tracked down the yellow get-away car last night and took the two men to a safe place for interrogation. We were up at your barn, Cassie. We walked 'em in by gun point letting 'em think it was over if they didn't tell us something. They know pigs'll get rid of a body overnight."

"Oh, my gawd," Robin huffed as whispers and hushed tones spread.

Mr. Croom's eyes loosened from their aged draped lids as he took his seat.

"It was the only way," Scarecrow said. "This sketch was drawn by The Lumbee Council for Mr. Fisk and Wart's mission. They were to find the jeweled cross in that sketch and take it to them. It's proof of The Lost Colony's contact with the Tuscarora. It's the deal breaker, boys."

The Magee boys gasped, then the elder addressed Mr. Croom, first with his piercing stare, "Are we in danger? What about us? Is there any proof of when Black blood mixed with the Croatans? Is the council after that, too?" Young Thomas' worry propelled him up from his seat, "Do you know my dad?"

"Yes, I know your dad," Mr. Croom calmly held their attention. "He contacted me after a thesis was published and that was over thirty years ago. We've talked on Congress' floor together. We've traveled extensively," then anxiously to Scarecrow, "Are we in imminent danger?"

"Until we press charges, yes." Scarecrow scanned the private room again.

"What's stopping you?" Jake ignited.

"In a court of law, you'll have to have the proof of the cross." Exilee cocked her chin at Bruce. "This is a win-win, ya know. You'll make history. The newspapers and your business will grow so fast you won't believe it. That's what happened when we went public with the Black Purse Papers."

Edge scooted the two pizza crusts around on her plate and then cut them into little itsy bitsy pieces with the side of her fork. Luke whined to get down and explore the room, and as he did was joined by Cassie's two youngest boys. On all fours, they played hide-and-seek as pretend puppies, yipping at one another from under the double row of chairs stacked against the far wall.

The waitress's squeaking rubber soles announced her along with the intoxicating sweet pizzas as she entered the private dining room. She asked each guest's preference, peach or chocolate, and served the slices, lingering over Bruce's shoulder and commenting on the turquoise beads peeking from the collar of his tee shirt.

"They're ancient, from a good trade on the Tuscarora's trading path." As his grays shined up at her, so did Robin's scorn. Brightly smiling, the warned waitress moved on to play with the three young pups. She whistled for them, "Good boy," she cooed. "Sit and I'll give you a prize." After the sweet pizzas were served, she asked if they'd like a cherry pizza as well, but it was declined.

As soon as her footsteps faded Jake and Bruce stared one another down and just as they were on the verge of leaving their seats Mark brazenly cleared his throat. "Read that note now."

"You already read it, huh?" Bruce rubbed over his jaw as he contemplated, while Mark blankly stared.

Ken placed both his hands on the tabletop. "Me, too, Bruce. It's important. Read it."

"My mother wrote it," Bruce's voice cracked, "Scarecrow just told me about it."

As Bruce spread the letter open his jawline softened.

My dearest Bruce,

Every prayer from my lips is for your survival. I love you and at this last minute realize I need to tell you a few more things. I pray you get this. It is in your special place with your dried frog and bug collection. There is only one other person at this time who knows of this letter and its dangers. She will do everything possible to ensure you get it before it is too late.

The many years of ridicule and torment we survived at your father's hands while secretly meeting to keep our heritage by learning it from the elders, learning proper English and having to speak the Robeson vernacular is, in retrospect, the easiest part of our charade. You see, the reason your father denied me calling you "my prince" is because you are.

You are the Prince of the Queen's Second Society, meaning the Queen of England. Governor John White was given the assignment to establish The Society in her behalf on the New Found Lands. For this task White was presented a treasured cross. It was to be presented to any new explorers in their settlement to verify their royal assignment.

The safety of the new society upon arrival in the New Found Lands was ensured when they met the Portuguese Knights. Some of these knights had blended with African explorers who had forts along the same waterways as the

Tuscaroras. To the queen's pilgrims, searching for land not claimed by other Christians for a period of six years or more, this was a blessing. Because according to the queen's proclamation they had the authority to claim any land not inhabited by Christians for a period of six months or more. And the closed-minded pilgrims could not conceive the natives as Christian.

This is your heritage, the child of warriors, the child of protectors, the child of royalty and blessed by God. If you are indeed reading this, you are in danger. Should the Tuscarora grow and establish a safe pathway to federal recognition, you may return, until then, you are safely banished to live the rest of your days with your other family.

Behind your ear is the mark of the cross. All of John White's daughter's ancestors were marked with that cross at birth. It is our duty to preserve the colonists' honor by simply aspiring to educate ourselves and protect our heritage from demise. That means, Prince Bruce Black, should you be asked to present the cross in your lifetime to America's Federal Government, do it. We are to honor Christianity. Mark your children with the cross and tell no one. As I told my husband and surely ruined your childhood as he hated you for who you really are from that day on. I am so sorry. I pray one day you will forgive me.

I love you so much,

Your Mother

Lizzie Black, married name

Gladys Elizabeth White, birth name

Bruce stealthily approached Cassie at the head of the table on the far side. Bent over her shoulder and down to her ear politely asked, "What all do you know about this?" Instantly, she panted. He spun her straight back chair around on one leg as she clasped her seat. Tears welled. Her freckled face reddened, and her ears stung scarlet. She mouthed, "no," but Bruce motioned for her to stand. Her boys were frozen in their seats as she sullenly followed Bruce. As soon as he hurled her chair into the middle of the room, she sat. He paced back and forth behind her as Cassie gripped the seat.

"You were the one who cleaned the blood. Her bloody fingers ran down the walls. It wasn't an accident. Was it?" The purple veins in his neck rippled up and shined like writhing snakes. "Was it, Cassie?" Bruce checked behind her right ear. Leaned his head back. Sighed. And closed his eyes. Then behind her left.

When she jerked in deep wails her boys gapped open in awe. Pen's leg vibrated like a revved three-fifty engine against the table until the sweet teas threatened to tumble.

"No, don't make me do this." She sunk to the floor on her knees and begged. But he wouldn't look at her. When she pitifully cried over her shoulder at her boys, Stink threw his chocolate pizza to the floor and hurried over.

Bruce quickly lifted Stink into her lap then pulled back his ears as Cassie quietly sobbed into his unruly red locks. Bruce directed each of her boys to come. Cassie's rock chunkin' son was second.

Exilee called for Luke and Ken met him halfway. Scooped him up and took him back to the table. His grandpa wrapped his long arm around them like a thick roadblock and Miss Sarah cooed kind words about his puppy belly being round and full. But Luke asked if he was next and was sad that he wasn't.

One by one Bruce checked behind their ears. He wore the poker face of champions, the one ingrained from a psychohistorical Tuscarora tradition of trading and gaming. The same one Kings have worn through the ages when dictating, "Off with his head." The same one Negro slaves have worn when facing horrific masters and swore on the Holy book that they don't know nuthin' 'bout no underground railroad. Bruce wore it so well that when he was done and walked the line of seven boys lined up straight against the back wall that they all flinched when he summoned Edge.

Mark piped up and asked, "You want me, too?" Bruce told him to come on first. He checked and then aimed over at the line and Mark joined them while Stink got a napkin from the table for his ma to blow her nose and climbed back into her lap.

Exilee assured Edge that she'll be okay, that Bruce was only revealing facts and that the truth was the most powerful tool in the world. But Edge molded down into her chair.

Snap smiled at his daughter and told her, "It's your turn," and she stoically waltzed up to Bruce and turned her back to him.

He checked behind her ears and twirled her around. Face to face, he traced her hairline and the curve of her brows. The way her left ear turned out just a smidge and the dimple in her chin. Then, in one brief moment, as her bifurcated tongue jet between her teeth it was as if they were the only two in the room. He held her face in his hands. "I think," and his smile returned. "Uh, I think you're my sister or a very close cousin." She excitedly examined Bruce as he exclaimed, "Jimmy Bean, tell me something here." Edge checked behind Bruce's ears. "It's the mark, just like in the letter," she hummed.

Snap mumbled, "She's your sister," and looked down at his peach pizza.

"We didn't hear that," Bruce roared. "Move your hands so we can hear you." His sudden intense rage frightened Edge and she hurried backwards.

Snap slowly raised his reddened eyes. "Edge is your sister, Bruce."

"That would make my mother a slut."

"No. Not on my life. Never. Lizzie needed a little kindness." His hands shook out before him. "But it got out a' hand like those things can do. Can't you imagine what it was like for her?"

"My mother cheated on Old Man Black," a crooked smile broke and Bruce guffawed,

"She got one over on him. Amen, brothers and sisters!" He wildly clapped.

Snap sat up taller. "It was the year he was up for cutting that UC in Raeford. You were just three, probably can't remember. Lizzie went up to Western Carolina and worked a casino job for the Cherokee last four months of her pregnancy."

Edge's void expression claimed her. "You been lying to me. My momma weren't no drunk. She loved me, didn't she?"

Snap defensively stood, but Miss Ginger and Miss Sarah begged him to sit back down and explain it all out to her and to give her a minute to take it in. Snap took a drink of sweet tea and cleared his throat. "*I am* your real daddy, Elizabeth."

"Oh, God, I love you. I'm sorry," she cried.

"There's nothing to be sorry 'bout. Come here."

Instead, Edge stood straighter than she ever thought she could, and it made her so tall and gave her such presence that Bruce rightfully asked her, "What are we gonna do with Cassie?" Edge scowled over her pitiful bent frame like a queen over a thief, "Get the truth out of her, any way we got to, brother."

Cassie attempted to rise, but Bruce quickly bore down on her shoulder. "What did you do to our mother, Cassie? You with the Lumbee Council? Huh?" His grays penetrated like totens' souls were sparking out. "Speak, while you can." The slap startled her. And Edge said she'd do it again.

Cassie took the assault like a logger. Adjusted her jaw and seethed as she aimed her darkening blues. "No," Cassie kicked as she fought Bruce's hold. "It's not me. That's not it. I swear it."

"The council is behind this. I've figured out that much. But what I don't get is those marks on your boys." Bruce echoed as a customer peeped in through the dark purple curtains but was shooed away with Scarecrow's long swing.

"She altered their marks," Dodger glared at Cassie as he leaned into Scarecrow's shoulder. "She won't let him go. I tell ya."

At first, the footsteps signaled the waitress, but when they were too hard and tapped like leather, Bruce braced. He stood at ease when it was just Eacha Up's owner. His arms flew up as he smacked his lips, "Nadie amor el repartidor de pizza." And the ignorant group politely smiled. His greasy apron streaked with yellow butter and red sauce covered his signature red pants and white button-down shirt. His thick black rimmed glasses increased the size of his big brown eyes and rested on his thin humped nose.

When he removed his apron and hung it on the coat peg, flour flaked off like snow. "Ready or not, this meeting needs the moderator. I am Allen Bishop, owner of Eacha Up Pizza, elder at Beaver Bridge Baptist Church, and member of The Second Society – a Mighty Tuscarora. Presently, I act as secretary, but I'm going to step beyond my assigned duties tonight and make the administrative decision to enlighten you before we're interrupted."

"I know who you are, about this place. I'm remembering it. My momma was right here." Bruce pointed down at Cassie and squeezed her sunken shoulder. "Do you know what this woman has to do with my mother's death? 'Cause that's what I wanna know and I'm not leaving until she tells me." His heavy hand squeezed her thin frame and with a refrained grunt she sunk even lower.

In the most relaxed manner imaginable Allen requested Scarecrow and Lilly secure the doors. Scarecrow drew back the heavy drapes and the front dining hall was void of patrons. Half empty glasses and pizzas littered tables. Crumbs trailed across the tile. And the sign on the front door read "Closed" to outsiders. He pulled on the metal bar and verified the door was locked. Flipped off the front room's lights and returned as Lilly returned from the kitchen followed by another man with red pants.

Allen welcomed him with an open arm. "This is Frank Sheffield, known by most of you as Principal Sheffield. And to Exilee, Dad. He is our President."

"Whoa," Exilee whispered.

"Thank you, Allen." Frank quickly paired up with Bruce. "Exilee's mother was a descendant of the original colony, the Moor family. Out of honor for her I accepted this position."

"How long have you been doing this?" Exilee's words buzzed out like drunk drone bees.

"Since I married your mother. She educated me and I've been determined," Frank took a deep breath, "to stop them."

Bruce roared and the room gasped. Allen pleaded for Bruce to hold on, but he just grimaced and pulled Cassie up by the neck. "Tell me. Tell me right now. What happened to my mother?" Cassie's boys bowed out from the wall ready to fight, but Scarecrow pulled back the strap on his holster and secured their steps. "Bruce, easy now. Your mother wouldn't want you to do this."

With Cassie by the neck, Bruce demanded Edge to come. "They can have Cassie and then they'll want you." He wrenched Cassie's neck until her pleas were chicken-bone garble.

But Pen was loud and clear. "Let her go."

Lilly and Scarecrow both stood armed at the exits and with a clear shot Lilly drew. But Scarecrow signaled no. "Stay out of this," Bruce spat.

"My son had the mark," Allen pleaded. "He died in an auto accident. It's been 18 years now."

"Well no one's tried to kill me!" Bruce screamed. "I don't believe it. You people are fools!"

"Oh yes they have, over and over, but you outsmarted them. And you've been protected," Allen adamantly explained. "And you have Scarecrow," his arms stretched out across the room, "and all your friends here and the ones you don't think are your friends." His bared hands banged like a diamond hoe. "It is no coincidence for a single one of us to be here. We have saturated the state. The country. We are worldwide, Bruce. With a powerful rein all the way from England, to this very day. For this very moment." As he calmed, he clasped his hot hands into prayer. "We want you to go to Washington, Bruce. You. They all say you're the prime candidate and the timing is crucial." But Bruce shivered and stammered and reared back with Cassie like a rag doll as he drew her to his chest like a shield.

David's chair strained as he rose, and Miss Sarah clung to his hand until he had stepped out of reach. "Bruce, you are a smart man. Surely you know what we are giving you tonight."

"Giving me? Fuck you!" His passion pulsed around Cassie's cinched neck until her dry gasps and purple lips pleased him, and she fell limp down to his hips. With a snarled smile Bruce jerked the jeweled cross from his pocket and slung it across the slick floor. "I have my own plans." As Edge bent to pick it up, Pen clamped his juvember in his scarlet stump, loaded a small steel sliver in the band and whizzzzz, Lilly aimed too. "Boom, Ka-Boom!" Screams echoed as they ducked and huddled, and a stream of blood declared the hit.

Bruce held the sharp gapping flesh between his ribs as Cassie gasped and heaved deep breaths. On her knees she squirmed to her boys and Allen rushed to her side, "Cassandra Elizabeth, tell me you're all right, dear."

As Bruce smeared the fresh blood in long denying swipes across his chest, his dear forsaken Cassie still reached out for him. Still, in anguish and disbelief until her sons fully encircled her and she crumbled.

Grappling her dear Lassie's legs, she cried, "Oh, thoust precious, child, what have I done? My prince, my dear, they will try to take you too." Pen stooped down and cradled her while his brothers stood paralyzed, even Stink, until the dense smoke from kitchen bellowed into the room. "Ma! Fire, Ma!"

The extinguisher gushed. Clanged up against the block wall, and the waitress exclaimed, "Find the rear exit!" as she rang two pizza tins like tambourines. "Follow me!" Smoke, foam and frenzy filled the private room as Allen leapt over flames into dark smoke and disappeared and reappeared with two more extinguishers. "Help me." Ken snatched one and they sprayed floor to ceiling and the smoke slowed to gray puffs. But the fire crackled on from the kitchen like a waiting lion. "We're gonna need help." Allen yelled and Ken yelled, "Wet the drapes!" Wind swept in through the open exit door, feeding the flames.

Robin wailed when Jake pushed her out the exit door and told her, "Call the fire department," as he lunged back in for Bruce and was enveloped in the gaseous haze.

Smoke swirls eked from the ceiling like iridescent snakes licking at Cassie's head as she stealthily approached Jake. She slicked down her unruly red curls behind her ears and along the way jerked the jeweled cross from Edge.

Jake called out, "Bruce! Has anyone seen Bruce? Gawd! Answer me." And Cassie stroked Jake's scared cheek with one hand and with the cross in her other held her fist like an anchor at his chest. "Lizzie was a tower for her dear Prince. Always. And she taught me everything. She taught me how to protect my own. But I took it one step further." She almost smiled. "After The Society sent their laymen to mark my newborns I waited and altered them with a red coal, except for Lassie. He was too old by the time I had full knowledge." Jake cried out for Bruce again and Cassie gently covered his mouth and nervously panted, "I helped Lizzie write the letter. I'm the one who fought Old Man Black." She held his forearm and forcibly shook him. "He wouldn't let her go. He was too big. You must believe me. He pulled a knife on her. I did all I could possibly do."

Pen escaped the smoke and heaved, "Jake, be on your way. Forget about us or you'll never have peace. I'm telling you." He panted as Cassie patted his chest and Pen aimed at the exit. "Out or in? And you've seen in, Jake. So, don't claim you weren't warned." Pen's flagged. "Things aren't always what they seem," he soldiered up, "on the swamp."

"But Bruce," Jake cried as turquoise flashed through fumes on the other side of the secluded room and he started for the telling color but stopped when Stink neared and dangled it up over his head and proudly slipped it on. "Bruce vanished," Stink's severity held Jake as he continued searching for Bruce in the pillowing smoke, "Come on, Jake," Stink pulled at his shirt, "He's gone in the wind."

Cassie waved for Edge and when she cautiously neared, pulled her in close. Placing Pen's hand over Elizabeth's while pushing the jeweled cross into Elizabeth's other hand. "I, Cassandra Elizabeth White do ask you to marry and keep yourselves pure for our mother society in Christian martyrdom and for our Second Society here, for all Tuscaroras to come. I ask you to mark your children. School them. And if it's not too late, choose one. One like Bruce Black and present the truth, when we are prepared." Her lull quaked and warranted.

"I ask this of you, as Queen."

Bruce woke from his nap from a knock at the door, "Come in," he called out from the comfy chair where he rested under the quilt. The light footsteps slowly approached, and he rose to meet her. The quilt landed on the cold stone floor as his grays landed on the long-lost lady from the portrait in the hall. "You. Are you?"

"Yes, my prince."

Annotation List

1. Peter H. Wood. (2019). *Testimony of Prof. Peter H. Wood, Duke University, on Behalf of the Tuscarora Nation of North Carolina, for Their Meeting with the NCCIA: April 30, 2019,* Raleigh, NC. Para.

2. Parramore, T. (1982). *The Tuscarora Ascendancy.* The North Carolina Historical Review, 59(4), 310-311.

3. Ibid.

4. David Beers Quinn. (1985). *Set Fair for Roanoke: Voyages and Colonies, 1584-1606.* University of North Carolina Press. 371-376. The Lost Colonists were Tuscarora's coppersmiths- see also: R.H. Major. (2017). The Historie of Travaile into Virginia Britannia: Expressing the Cosmographie and Comodities of the Country, together with the Manners and Customes of the People. Gathered and observed as well by those who went first thither as collected by William Strachey, Gent., the first Secretary of the Colony. In *The Historie of Travaile into Virginia Britannia.* Routledge. https://doi.org/10.4324/9781315557236 Page 26.

5. Marino, Ruggero. (2007) *Christopher Columbus: The Last Templar.* Rochester, VT: Destiny Books. 1, 68, 87, 117, 147. See also: Cumming, William Patterson, and De Vorsey, Louis. *The Southeast in Early Maps* 3rd ed. / rev. and enl. by Louis De Vorsey, Jr. Chapel Hill: University of North Carolina Press, 1998. Plate 36. [Map 68]. See also: Lederer, John.,

Cumming, William Patterson, and Winthrop, John. *The Discoveries of John Lederer, with Unpublished Letters* by and About Lederer to Governor John Winthrop, Jr., and an *Essay on the Indians of Lederer's Discoveries* by Douglas L. Rights and William P. Cumming. Charlottesville: University of Virginia Press, 1958. From Lederer's book: page 2: "Three ways they supply their want of Letters: first by Counters, secondly by Emblemes or Hieroglyphicks, third|ly Tradition delivered in long Tales from father to son, which being children they are made to learn by rote."

6. Robeson County, *NC Crime Rate 2017* http://crimereporting.ncsbi.gov/Reports.aspx. See also: towncharts.com/North-Carolina/Demographics/Robeson-County-NC-Demographics-data.html

7. Bennett-Begaye, J. & Kickingwoman, K. (6 Dec. 2019.) *Lumbee Recognition Act: Why are we here?* Indian Country Today. Para. 8.

8. Pearce, H. (1938). *New Light on the Roanoke Colony: A Preliminary Examination of a Stone Found in Chowan County, North Carolina.* Journal of Southern History, 4(2), 156-58.

9. Marino, Ruggero. (2007) *Christopher Columbus: The Last Templar.* 1, 147

10. David Beers Quinn. (1985). *Set Fair for Roanoke: Voyages and Colonies, 1584-1606.* University of North Carolina Press. www.uncpress.org Pp. 375-76. See also: Cumming, William Patterson, and De Vorsey, Louis. *The Southeast in Early Maps 3rd ed. / rev. and enl. by Louis De Vorsey, Jr.*

Chapel Hill: University of North Carolina Press, 1998. Plate 36. [Map 68]

11. Pearce, H. (1938). *New Light on the Roanoke Colony: A Preliminary Examination of a Stone Found in Chowan County, North Carolina*. Journal of Southern History, 4(2), 157.

12. *U.S. Congress, Report of the Joint Select Committee to Inquire into the Condition of Affairs in the Late Insurrectionary States, Testimony of Giles Leitch, July 31, 1871, Civil War Era NC. History* digitized by NC State University.

13. Jeans, Peter D (1998). *Ship to Shore*. Oxford, England: ABC-Clio. Term is used to identify ships by jib sail shapes and used interchangeably to identify people.

14. Stephanie Sellers. (2019). The Buzz about BAGS – The "new" B.S. Agricultural Science Degree. *The Pine Needle.*

15. Lederer, John., Cumming, William Patterson, and Winthrop, John. *The Discoveries of John Lederer, with Unpublished Letters* by and About Lederer to Governor John Winthrop, Jr., and an Essay on the Indians of Lederer's Discoveries by Douglas L. Rights and William P. Cumming. Charlottesville: University of Virginia Press, 1958. Pp. 19-20.

16. *Tuscarora Petition for Federal Recognition, 1980.* pp. 436-37.

17. Cumming, William Patterson, and De Vorsey, Louis. *The Southeast in Early Maps* 3rd ed. / rev. and enl. by Louis De Vorsey, Jr. Chapel Hill: University of North Carolina Press, 1998. Plate 36. [Map 68]. See also, Lederer, John.,

Cumming, William Patterson, and Winthrop, John. *The Discoveries of John Lederer, with Unpublished Letters* by and About Lederer to Governor John Winthrop, Jr., and an Essay on the Indians of Lederer's Discoveries by Douglas L. Rights and William P. Cumming. Charlottesville: University of Virginia Press, 1958. From Lederer's book: page 2: "Three ways they supply their want of Letters: first by Counters, secondly by Emblemes or Hieroglyphicks, third|ly Tradition delivered in long Tales from father to son, which being children they are made to learn by rote."

18. Douglas W. Boyce. (1940) *Iroquoian Tribes of the Virginia-North Carolina Coastal Plain. Handbook of North American Indians*, volume 15, Northeast, Bruce G. Trigger, ed. (Washington, D.C.: Smithsonian Institution, 1978), p. 282. See also: Lawson, John, and Lefler, Hugh Talmage. *A New Voyage to Carolina*. Chapel Hill, NC: University of North Carolina Press, 1967. Pp. 68-9.

19. University of Duke Professor of History, Dr. Peter H. Wood, Deborah Montgomerie and Susan Yarnell. (1992). *Tuscarora Roots: An Historical Report Regarding the Relation of the Hatteras Tuscarora Tribe of Robeson County, North Carolina, to the Original Tuscarora Indian Tribe*. Descendants Chart, Pp. 1-5, and Pedigree Chart, Pp. 1-5.

20. Hudson, M. (2013). *Searching for Virginia Dare on the trail of the lost colony of Roanoke Island* (2nd ed.). Lewisville, NC: Press 53. See Chapter 9

21. Michael Futch. (Oct. 20, 2017. Updated 21 Oct. 2017). *Legend has it Virginia Dare buried in Robeson County*. The Fayetteville Observer. See interview with Adolph Dial: "The late Adolph Dial, a Lumbee Indian who headed up the Department of American Indian Studies at University of North Carolina at Pembroke and served in the N.C. House of Representatives, was convinced that the lost colonists were the ancestors of the Lumbees. He believed that he himself was a descendant of Virginia Dare."

22. *The North Carolina Booklet.* (1906). VI,I. Published by The North Carolina Society, Daughters of the Revolution. Pp. 5-6. See: metaphors and a nose-cutting. Original at NC State Library, Raleigh.

23[a], 23[b], 23[c]. University of Duke Professor of History, Dr. Peter H. Wood, Deborah Montgomerie and Susan Yarnell. (1992). *Tuscarora Roots: An Historical Report Regarding the Relation of the Hatteras Tuscarora Tribe of Robeson County, North Carolina, to the Original Tuscarora Indian Tribe*. Pp. 74-75. Descendants Chart A, P. 1. See Also: Harper's Weekly, *The North Carolina Bandits*, Harper's Weekly, March 30, 1872, Civil War Era NC, accessed December 25, 2019, cwnc.omeka.chass.ncsu.edu/items/show/170. See Also: A.W. McLean. (1915) *Indians of North Carolina*. U.S. Sentate, 63rd Congress, 3rd Session, Doc. No. 677, Washington, D.C. Pp 123-125. See also: *Interview with Cecil Hunt and Elisha Locklear* (Feb. 2004). Interview refers to "Lock-a-leer" pronunciation. drive.google.com/file/d/10NaPiR_XUU4-

Vo1jJpvK7CtiF06g6eeu/view "Those people were semi-literate. When they wrote their names down Bennett gave his name as "Lockalar"
[Locklear], typical Prospect, Long Swamp, so I knew immediately just reading his name
on the Revolutionary War roles where he did actually live because of the way he sounded
his name for the man to spell it out. So, he was Tuscarora, had already moved in here with the earlier migrations, had settled down, and had established himself before he went into the war of revolution. So, Bennett is a direct link to Tuscarora in Bertie County for the people here because he was actually called by the whites a Tuscarora Indian."

24. *Interview with Adolf Dial.* (1994). Barbara Ritter. UNC Charlotte. Retrieved from nsv.uncc.edu/interview/nadi0020.html.

25. Biography. Angus W. McLean. N.D. UNC Library. exhibits.lib.unc.edu/exhibits/show/evolution/biographies/mclean

26. United States. (1972). *Seizure of Bureau of Indian Affairs Headquarters Hearings before the Subcommittee on Indian Affairs of the Committee on Interior and Insular Affairs, House of Representatives, Ninety-Second Congress, Second Session.* Washington, U.S. Govt. Print. Off. Pp. 3-11.

27. Podcast: DG Martin talks to Malinda Maynor Lowery about her book, Lumbee Indians In The Jim Crow South on UNC-TV's "North Carolina Bookwatch." unctv.org/ncbookwatch

28. United States. (1972). *Seizure of Bureau of Indian Affairs Headquarters Hearings before the Subcommittee on Indian Affairs of the Committee on Interior and Insular Affairs, House of Representatives, Ninety-Second Congress, Second Session.* Washington, U.S. Govt. Print. Off. Pp. 3-11

29. Ibdo

30. Ibdo. See also: Muckrock Report. Emma Best. Ed. JPat Brown. (2019) *The Journalists and the Case of the Stolen BIA Documents: FBI investigation into Jack Anderson and Les Whitten reveals Whitten's role as a confidential informant.* muckrock.com/news/archives/2019/jan/07/fbi-bia-stolen/?fbclid=IwAR2g7cZGxBTaxBbEWyLNNkN7se2M90zO wAooI9eFIInH0sM7liWsuRAQhVs Pp. 108-133 Interview with arrested reporters.

31. Glenn Ellen Star Stilling. (2012). *The Lumbee Indians: An Annotated Bibliography. McLaurin, C. E. McLaurin, Old Main, Grocery Destroyed as Robeson Fire Continues.* Robesonian 19 March 1973: 1. See also: Glenn Ellen Star Stilling. (2012). *The Lumbee Indians: An Annotated Bibliography.* See also: *Deputy Tells of Finding Missing BIA Papers.* News and Observer 14 Dec. 1973: 35. NC Appalachian State University

32. Jessiekratz,, Posted In – Great Depression. (2015). *Indian New Deal. U.S. National Archives: Pieces of History.*

33. University of Duke Professor of History, Dr. Peter H. Wood, Deborah Montgomerie and Susan Yarnell. (1992). *Tuscarora Roots: An Historical Report Regarding the Relation*

of the Hatteras Tuscarora Tribe of Robeson County, North Carolina, to the Original Tuscarora Indian Tribe. Pp. 66-72.

34. NORTH CAROLINA COMMISSION OF INDIAN AFFAIRS 2 RECOGNITION COMMITTEE FINAL RECOMMENDATION ON 3 PETITION FOR TRIBAL RECOGNITION 4 SUBMITTED BY 5 "THE TUSCARORA NATION OF NORTH CAROLINA" 6 7 Part A. Summary of Preliminary Findings and Deficiencies 8 9 On January 26, 2018, the North Carolina Commission of Indian Affairs ("NCCIA"), Recognition 10 Committee sent to Petitioner Tuscarora Nation of North Carolina ("TNNC") a Preliminary 11 Finding and Deficiencies report ("Preliminary Findings"). This report reveals the ideology of the government erasing previous treaties made with the Tuscarora to benefit the government and the Lumbee.

35. Muckrock Report. Emma Best. Ed. JPat Brown. (2019) *The Journalists and the Case of the Stolen BIA Documents: FBI investigation into Jack Anderson and Les Whitten reveals Whitten's role as a confidential informant.* www.muckrock.com/news/archives/2019/jan/07/fbi-biastolen/?fbclid=IwAR2g7cZGxBTaxBbEWyLNNkN7se2M90 zOwAooI9eFIInH0sM7liWsuRAQhVs Pp. 108-133 Interview with arrested reporters. Pp. 65-91. P. 74, Item number d. 30-page report entitled "Trail of Broken Treaties - Chronology of Events."

36. Ibid.

37. Dr. Dean Chavers. (2011). Tom Oxendine: First Lumbee Pilot. *Indian Country Today.*

38. Kotlowski, D. (2003). *Alcatraz, Wounded Knee, and Beyond: The Nixon and Ford Administrations Respond to Native American Protest.* Pacific Historical Review, 72(2), 201-227. doi:10.1525/phr.2003.72.2.20. Pp. 201-202.

39. Ibid. P. 204.

40. Alison Owings. (2011). *Indian Voices: Listening to Native Americans.* P. 37-43

41. Malinda Maynor Lowery. (2018). *The Lumbee Indians: An American Struggle.* Copyright © 1985 by the University of North Carolina Press. Pp. 16-19.

42. University of Duke Professor of History, Dr. Peter H. Wood, Deborah Montgomerie and Susan Yarnell. (1992). *Tuscarora Roots: An Historical Report Regarding the Relation of the Hatteras Tuscarora Tribe of Robeson County, North Carolina, to the Original Tuscarora Indian Tribe.* Pp. 24- 47. See also. Lumbee recognition: hearing before the Committee on Indian Affairs, United States Senate, One Hundred Eighth Congress, first session, on S. 420, to provide for the acknowledgment of the Lumbee Tribe of North Carolina, September 17, 2003, Washington, DC.

43a, 43b, 43c. Virginia. General Assembly. House of Burgesses. *Journals of the House of Burgesses of Virginia, 1712-1714, 1715, 1718, 1720-1722, 1723-1726* Paperback-January 1 1912. P. 20. See also: The North Carolina Booklet. (1906). VI, I. Published by The North Carolina Society, Daughters of the Revolution. Pp. 5-6, 20-22. Original at NC State Library, Raleigh. See also: *Letter from Christopher Gale*

to [his sibling], including a memorial concerning attacks by
Native Americans, Gale, Christopher, ca. 1679-1735. November
02, 1711. Volume 01, Pages 825-829. Colonial and State
Records of North Carolina: *Documenting the American South.*
docsouth.unc.edu/csr/index.php/document/csr01-0441

44. Heather Cox Richardson. (2010). *Wounded Knee Party*
Politics and the Road to an American Massacre. New York:
Basic Books.

45. Walter Clark. (1902). V. 2/3. *Indian Massacre and*
Tuscarora War 1711-13. The North Carolina Society of
Daughters of the Revolution. Pp. 3-16.
http://digital.ncdcr.gov/cdm/ref/collection/p249901coll37/id/141
65. See also: *Letter from Christopher Gale to (his sibling),*
including a memorial concerning attacks by Native Americans.
(1711). V. 1, Pp 825.829. See also: J.D. Lewis (2007) *The*
Tuscarora Indians. Carolina- The Native Americans. [Lists
Tuscarora towns]
www.carolana.com/Carolina/Native_Americans/native_america
ns_tuscarora.html

See also: *Letter from Christoph von Graffenried to Edward*
Hyde [Extract] (17110. Pp. 990-992.

46. Walter Clark. (1902). V. 2/3. *Indian Massacre and*
Tuscarora War 1711-13. The North Carolina Society of
Daughters of the Revolution. Pp. 11-13.

47. Giorgio. B. *English, Scottish and Irish Sliver*
Hallmarks, London Silver Date Letters and Symbols, The Guide
to Marks of British Silver – London.

silvercollection.it/englishsilverhallmarks.html. Accessed Jan. 1, 2020.

48. Upton Sinclair, ed. (1878-1968). *Oh, Freedom* printed in The Cry for Justice: An Anthology of the Literature of Social Protest, 1915.

49. The News & Observer. (Dec. 14, 1973). Raleigh, NC. *Deputy Tells of Finding Missing BIA Papers.* P. 35.

50. Frederick Webb Hodge. (1907-10). *Handbook of American Indians North of Mexico*, ed. Vol. 2. Washington, Govt. University of California Libraries Digitization. (2006). Pp. 178-79. "agotsinnachen (by both Hurons and Iroquois), the first signifying One who examines another by seeing," liter-ally, 'one customarily looks at another.' But beyond this occult, knowledge of hidden things, they professed the fur- ther ability to perform still other won- ders by means of certain ..."

51. Frederick Webb Hodge. (1907-10*). Handbook of American Indians North of Mexico*, ed. Vol. 2. Washington, Govt. University of California Libraries Digitization. (2006). Pp. 178-79.

52. John E. Byrd. (1977). *Tuscarora Subsistence Practices in the Late Woodland Period: The Zooarchaeology of the Jordan's Landing Site*. N.C. Archaeology Council, Publication No. 27. Pp. 2-3.

53. A.W. McLean. (1915) *Indians of North Carolina.* U.S. Sentate, 63rd Congress, 3rd Session, Doc. No. 677, Washington, D.C. P. 177.

54. United States Department of the Interior NATIONAL PARK SERVICE. Southeast Region. (1988). *Lumber River 2(a) ii. Wild & Scenic River Study Report.* P. 16.

55. University of Duke Professor of History, Dr. Peter H. Wood, Deborah Montgomerie and Susan Yarnell. (1992). *Tuscarora Roots: An Historical Report Regarding the Relation of the Hatteras Tuscarora Tribe of Robeson County, North Carolina, to the Original Tuscarora Indian Tribe.* Descendants Charts. Pp. 1-24.

56. Peter H. Wood. (2019). *Testimony of Prof. Peter H. Wood, Duke University, on Behalf of the Tuscarora Nation of North Carolina, for Their Meeting with the NCCIA; April 30, 2019, Raleigh, NC.* P. 5.

57. Minutes of the N.C. Governor's Council. (Aug. 1723). *N.C. Colonial Records.* V. 2. P 496.

58. H.R. McIlwaine. Virginia General Assembly. House of Burgesses: Virginia State Library. *Journals of the House of burgesses of Virginia: 1712-1714, 1715, 1718, 1720-1722, 1723-1726.* Richmond, VA: The Colonial press. E. Waddey co. (1912). P. xx

The other two laws paſſed—the one for raiſing a public levy and the one for permitting the ſale of certain entailed land—need no ſpecial attention, but there were two bills offered—both of them in the Council and the only two originating in that body—that are of more than uſual intereſt. They were ſent to the Houſe by the Council the ſame day, *Saturday, November* 15, and on *Monday* both were promptly rejected. Their titles were "An act declaring what ſhall be accounted a ſufficient ſeating and planting of lands hereafter to be taken up and patented" and "An act to prohibit all trade with the *Tuſcarora* and other Indians concerned in the late maſſacre in *North Carolina* and for the better regulating the Indian trade." Of the firſt of theſe *Spotſwood* was himſelf the author, as is ſeen from his letter to the Board of Trade, and it is probable that he was alſo author of the latter. The eighty-fourth art'cle of *Spotſwood*'s inſtructions as governor had to do in general terms with the conditions of granting land, and he had been told to have the ſubſtance of the inſtruction paſſed by the General Aſſembly as a law. He had made a ſtep in this direction in ſecuring the land law of 1710 and was now endeavoring to take a ſecond ſtep. His bill was probably the ſame one which actually paſſed at the following ſeſſion, but as yet the Houſe of Burgeſſes was unprepared for it. The "Act to prohibit all trade with the *Tuſcarora* and other Indians concerned in the late maſſacre in *North Carolina* and for the better regulating the Indian trade" was one to which the Houſe of Burgeſſes could not poſſibly have had objections ſo far as the firſt part of it—that in relation to the Indians engaged in the *North Carolina* maſſacre—was concerned, and it is therefore probable that the regulation of all Indian trade was the feature for which they were as yet unprepared. *Spotſwood* wiſhed the Indian trade conducted by a chartered company which ſhould have a monoply. The bill this ſeſſion thrown out by the Houſe probably embraced this feature, and either the majority of the members of the Houſe of Burgeſſes at this time oppoſed the principle or certain of the proviſions of the bill were diſagreeable. In 1714 a law embodying *Spotſwood*'s ideas was finally enacted.

19 Hening, IV, 32–36.

59. Haywood J. Pearce. (1938). New Light on the Roanoke Colony: A Preliminary Examination of a Stone Found in Chowan County, North Carolina. *The Journal of Southern History* 4, no. 2, pp. 148-163.

60. George E. Butler, E. Emanuel, and C.D. Brewington. (1916). *The Croatan Indians of Sampson County, North Carolina: Their Origin and Racial Status: A Plea for Separate Schools*. North Carolina: s.n.

61. Ibid.

62. William L. Saunders, ed. (1886-1890). *The Colonial Records of N.C.* v. 1. Raleigh, N.C. Pp. 905, 981.

63. Dannenberg, Clare J. *Sociolinguistic constructs of ethnic identity: the syntactic delineation of Lumbee English.* Diss. Chapel Hill: U of North Carolina at Chapel Hill, 1999.

64. Frederick Webb Hodge. (1864-1956). *The Handbook of North American Indians North of Mexico.* Part 2. Pp. 50-1. See also: Richard Price. (1973). *Maroon Societies: Rebel Slave Communities in the Americas.* [1st ed.]. Garden City, N.Y: Anchor Press. P. 149.

65. Ibid.

See also: William L. Saunders, ed. (1886-1890). *The Colonial Records of N.C.* v. 1. Narrative by Christoph von Graffenried concerning his voyage to North Carolina and

f. Religious worship of the Carolinian Savages.

I also noticed among the Indians who dwell at the place where I settled and started the building of New-Bern, another kind of rites which come nearer to the christian divine worship. They had there a kind of altar, cunningly interwoven with small sticks, and vaulted like a dome. In one place was an opening, like a small door or wicket, through which they put their offerings. In the midst of this heathenish chapel was a concavity where they sacrificed beans, corals, and also Wampons. Facing the rising sun, was planted in the ground a wooden post, with a carved head, painted half red and half white. In front of it stood a big stick with a small crown at its end, wrapped up in red and white; on the other side, which looks towards the setting sun, was another image, with a horrid face painted in black and red. By the first, they mean some god, and by the other the Demon, which they know far better.

I cannot but relate here, to amuse the reader, what happened to one of my tenants, a tall, strong, well-built fellow: passing near by these idols, he examined them, and knew at once the difference between the good god, and the one which represented the devil. The latter being painted in red and black, which happen precisely to be the colours of the Bernese flag and arms,[24] he became so angry about it, that he split in two, with his axe, the Devil's statue. When he came home, he boasted about it, as if it had been an heroic feat, saying that he had split the devil in two with one stroke. Though I could not help smiling, I could not approve his action. Soon after, the Indian King came, exasperated at this sacrilege, and complained loudly. I first told him, in a jocose way, that it was only the wicked Idol, that there was not much harm done, but that if he had cut the good Idol to pieces, I should have rigorously chastised him, and that, in the future, orders would be given in order that no such thing could happen any more.

Although the Indian King saw well that I spoke of the all thing as a joke, he did not like it much, but looked very serious. I accordingly told him, quite as seriously, that that man's action did not please me at all,—and that, if he could show me the one who had committed such a scandalous offence, he should be rigorously punished. To appease a little those Indians, I treated the King and his retinue to some rum, a liquor distillated from sugar-dregs, and a very healthy beverage, when taken moderately.

the founding of New Bern [Translation] Graffenried,

Christoph von, Baron, 1661-1743-1708. Raleigh, NC. p. 981.

66. Lawson, John, and Lefler, Hugh Talmage. *A New Voyage to Carolina*. Chapel Hill, NC: University of North Carolina Press, 1967. Pp. 185-188.

67. Llewellyn Forrester Coombs. (1968) *Tales of the Tuscarora*. Pdf.

file:///E:/Coombs%20Manuscript%201586%20-1717(15).pdf

68. University of Duke Professor of History, Dr. Peter H. Wood, Deborah Montgomerie and Susan Yarnell. (1992). *Tuscarora Roots: An Historical Report Regarding the Relation of the Hatteras Tuscarora Tribe of Robeson County, North Carolina, to the Original Tuscarora Indian Tribe.* Appendix One: Historical Maps 1-4. See Also: The Lost Colony Center for Science and Research. *Maps, Images and Photographs Gallery*. White-deBry Map, 1590; annotated. (Is pink.) Last updated 2014. lost-colony.com/galleryside.html

69. Richard Price. (1973). *Maroon Societies: Rebel Slave Communities in the Americas.* [1st ed.]. Garden City, N.Y: Anchor Press. P. 149. See also: David Beers Quinn. (Transferred to digital 2010). *The Roanoke Voyages, 1584-1590. Volume 1.* Surrey, England: Ashgate. p. 254.

70. Frederick Webb Hodge. (1864-1956*). The Handbook of North American Indians North of Mexico*. Part 2. P. 52.

71. [This "summary" annotation begins with the first mention of "America's first Christians" within this text.] Ruggero Marino. (1940). *Christopher Columbus, The Last Templar*, Translated by Ariel Godwin, (2005). Rochester, VT: Destiny. Chapters 1-3. See also: Charles G. Addison. (1842). *The History of The Knights Templars, The Temple Church, and The Temple*. London: Longman, Brown, Green, and Longmans, Paternoster Row. Ebook (2012). Accessed at Gutenberg.org. Pp. 1-3, 177, & 289.

72. Mel Covey. (2018). *Croatoan's Old Indian Town Revealed: William Elks and the Rest of the Hatteras Indians' 1759 Land Patent & Interpreted Survey*. Pp. 18-21. https://issuu.com/melcovey/docs/croatoan_s_old_indian_tow n_revealed [P. 16 reads that the Hatteras Tuscarora are all dead. This inaccuracy is due to the H.T. moving to inland swamps to survive.]

73. Albert G. Mackey. (1869). *The Symbolism of Freemasonry: Illustrating and Explaining Its Science and Philosophy, Its Legends, Myths, and Symbols*. New York: Clay and Maynard. *P. 160.*

74. George E. Butler. (1868-1941). *The Croatan Indians of Sampson County, North Carolina. Their Origin and Racial Status. A Plea for Separate Schools*: Electronic Edition. Pp. 1-24. See also: Richard Price. (1973). *Maroon Societies: Rebel Slave Communities in the Americas.* [1st ed.]. Garden City, N.Y: Anchor Press. P. 149.

75. Barbara Graymont. (2005). *The Iroquois: Indians of North America*, (Revised). Broomall: Chelsea House. Image E. Also: Interview with Dr. Noleen McIlvenna. (Jan. 21, 2020). "Oppression is an ancient issue," as Dr. Noleen McIlvenna explained concerning her historic reference book, *A Very Mutinous People: The Struggle for North Carolina, 1660-1713,* "poor people of every color were left out of the telling of history." "We cannot completely depend on anything written by early explorers. Yet it is true that they came to understand quite quickly that many groups considered themselves "different" from each other and often rivals or even enemies." Different refers to Algonquian or Iroquoian. Also: Interview with Dr. Arwin Smallwood. (Jan. 27, 2020). How did early Europeans, (1500's) "know" the difference between Algonquian and Iroquoian Natives? Is their written labeling of the Algonquian and Iroquoian 99.9% correct? **Smallwood, "They didn't. The earliest explores were learning on the job. As you or anyone would doing something for the first time. Yes, they made mistakes. Also, many Native American did not trust Europeans and either gave them misleading information or withheld information from them. The Tuscarora were known to be a very secretive people and at first contact did not trust the English.** University of NC at Pembroke's, The Pine Needle newspaper, March 4, 2020, UNCP Makes Moves to Recognize Tuscarora by Stephanie Sellers.

Map(s)

Page 253, Map Title: *Territory of the Tuscarora, Meherrin, and Nottoway in VA. And N.C.* Douglas W. Boyce. (1940) *Iroquoian Tribes of the Virginia-North Carolina Coastal Plain. Handbook of North American Indians*, volume 15, Northeast, Bruce G. Trigger, ed. (Washington, D.C.: Smithsonian Institution, 1978), p. 282.

Photos

A part-white Tuscarora holds a war club. Taken during 1960's in Bertie County, NC's Indian Woods. Photo from the F. Roy Johnson Collection. Digital. NC State Archives, Raleigh, NC. Call no. PC 367. Mars ID 877.

A part-black Tuscarora holds a stone ax with carving on it on the front porch of his home in Bertie County, NC's Indian Woods in the 1960's. Photo from the F. Roy Johnson Collection. Digital. NC State Archives, Raleigh, NC. Call no. PC 367. Mars ID 877.

Other sources:

http://dna-explained.com/category/lost-colony/

grahamphillips.net/ark/ark7.html Sir Walter Raleigh

http://www.lost-colony.com/Beechland.html

http://www.she-philosopher.com/gallery/powhatan-map.html

http://digitalcommons.unl.edu/cgi/viewcontent.cgi?article=1020&context=etas

http://www.elizabethan-era.org.uk/sir-walter-raleigh.htm

http://historical-melungeons.com/portuguese.html

http://sciway3.net/clark/freemoors/lumbee.html

http://en.wikipedia.org/wiki/Convento_de_Cristo

http://www.robertlomas.com/Orkney/scroll.html

http://www.econ.ohio-state.edu/jhm/arch/kens/kens.htm

http://www.blueridgeinstitute.org/moonshine/common_blue
_ridge_moonshining_ter

ms.html

http://en.wikipedia.org/wiki/Perceval,_the_Story_of_the_G
rail

http://www.water.ncsu.edu/capefear.html

http://en.wikipedia.org/wiki/Rosy_Cross

http://en.wikipedia.org/wiki/Order_of_Christ_%28Portugal
%29

http://mkharrison.com/Html/Lumbee_Indians.htm

http://www.grahamphillips.net/Ark/Ark_7.htm

http://www.washingtonwatch.com/bills/show/111_SN_173
5.html

http://people.ds.cam.ac.uk/bv230/langvar/wolfram%201999
%20dialect%20identity%20in%20tri-
ethnic%20context%20-
%20lumbee.pdf

http://ashevilleoralhistoryproject.wordpress.com/2012/11/2
7/a-full-and-true-orphan/

http://www.lost-colony.com/surnames.html

www.huxford.com/genetics_lumbee_results.htm

www.huxford.com/genetics_lumbee_results.htm

http://www.ncga.state.nc.us/EnactedLegislation/Statutes/PDF/BySection/Chapter_71A/

GS_71A-1.pdf

Marino, Ruggero. (2007) *Christopher Columbus: The Last Templar.*

http://en.wikipedia.org/wiki/Cherokee_freedmen_controversy

The American Garden Vol. XI by L. H. Bailey. Also available from Amazon: *American Horticultural Society A to Z Encyclopedia of Garden Plants.*

Guide to Robeson County, NC's Vernacular

This vernacular is an endangered language. A-prefixing is no longer common. Example: He was a-looking for the cooter. A-prefixing is more common with older Lumbees as well as the pronunciation of 'i' to 'oy' such as, high sounding hoy, which is a Portuguese language tradition. To hear the elders talk is to hear their history sung.

Dropping 'g's from plurals is a Portuguese tradition.

Mon means man and is used at beginning of greetings and is from Elizabethan era.

Juvember means sling shot or forked stick and is from Portugal. Is Elizabethan era.

Mommuck means wild mess or treat something badly and is from the Elizabethan era.

Toten means omen and is sign of death. Can be smelled or heard and is from Elizabethan era when token was interchanged with toten.

Meddlin' means interfering.

Crone means push down.

Ellick means a cup of coffee with sugar.

Lum means belonging to the Lumbee community.

Crotched up means caught up.

Dib means a baby chicken.

Nary means not any.

No'rs means nowheres.

Malahack means mess up.

Thou or Thoust means you and is from Elizabethan era.

Kin means family or treated as such.

Index means to stop.

Hope m' die means hope m' clare.

Gut of snuff refers to quantity of snuff contained in animal intestine. Whether or not the snuff is in plastic or tin the term is still common.

Gyp means a female dog.

Haint means a ghost.

On the swamp means being with other Lums or in the neighborhood.

Baccar means tobacco.

I'm means I have and is from Elizabethan era.

Weren't means wasn't.

Jubious means strange.

Yurker means mischievous child.

Gyarb means a mess.

Across the river means on the other side of the tracks.

Headiness means very bad.

Pleasure it means enjoy it.

Listen at means listen to.

Bes means is and is from the Scotts.

Breath it means to tell.

Cam means calm.

Colic means illness and is from early English.

Catawampus means not square.

Swanny means swear.

Brickhouse means upper status.

Liketa means nearly.

Buddyrow means friend.

Bate means lot.

Kiver means cover and is from Elizabethan era.

Liable to means likely to.

Kyarn is something nasty or rotten.

Sorry in the world means sad.

Chicken bog means chicken and rice.

Chunk means to throw.

Conjure means to invoke spirits like a magic charm.

Put a root on means to cast a spell on someone.

Cracklins is a crisply fried slice of hog skin like fatback.

Fetched up means raised up.

Fine in the world means doing well.

Gambrel is a carcass stretcher.

Gaum is a mess and is from Elizabethan era.

Goanna is fertilizer.

Chauld means embarrassed or disgraced.

Cooter means large swamp turtle.

Cuz is greeting for fellow Lumbee.

Damn Skippy means right! Is an affirmative to a speaker.

Gallanipper means a large mosquito-like insect and mosquitoes.

In the pines means snobby or uppity.

Orta notta means should not have.

Pappy sack is male child endearment.

Pearly means a small dainty piece.

Pocosin means big swamp.

Pone means a loaf of bread.

Pow wow means a Native celebration.

Pure means certainly.

Purty means ridiculous-looking.

Pumpkin seed refers to a bream family fish.

Pyert means lively.

Slam means very.

Smash means to press.

Sow cat means endearment toward a child.

Sweetnins means cakes and pastries.

Mension means measurement and is from Elizabethan era.

Hit means it.

Hosen means hose.

Housen means house.

You see me means you just ask me about it.

Wit means knowledge.

Epilogue

This work is for anyone who has ever been oppressed by a larger group and seeks social justice. The ending was most difficult because as an outsider, I cannot fully comprehend, even with my deep empathy, what it must feel like to be suppressed from the time when history was first written to the present while it is suppressed by your community and leaders.

So, the only alternative was a totally outlandish ending which carries the symbolisms and allegories of colonialism and the fact that the Natives had blended with Scotts, another mighty people.

This ending represents the underlying truth that many North Carolina Tuscaroras are descendants of Europeans and Iroquoian Natives and both groups want to be happy.

Most everyone that I have interviewed agree that their Creator is the one in control.

Sometimes, the best we can do is live well in the moment and good books with historical facts make for good living.

I pray the historical annotations being conveniently located in one work, lead to a greater knowledge base of the true history.

Thank you, NC Tuscarora Donnie Red Hawk McDowell, 2015 UNCP NAIS graduate, for your insight and guidance as you prepare to be a voice for your People.

www.ingramcontent.com/pod-product-compliance
Lightning Source LLC
Chambersburg PA
CBHW051532250626
47157CB00001B/16